Also available from Rhenna Morgan and Carina Press

Men of Haven series

Rough & Tumble
Wild & Sweet
Claim & Protect
Tempted & Taken
Down & Dirty

Ancient Ink series

Guardian's Bond
Healer's Need

Coming soon from Rhenna Morgan and Carina Press

NOLA Knights series

His to Defend
Hers to Tame
Mine to Keep

Also available from Rhenna Morgan

Unexpected Eden
Healing Eden
Waking Eden
Eden's Deliverance

To Joe Crivelli—my best friend, my champion, my partner, my heart. For all the strong, insightful and caring heroes I've ever imagined or written, you surpass them all. Every second of the wait to find you was worth it.

DOWN & DIRTY

———

RHENNA MORGAN

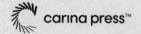
carina press™

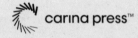
carina press™

PLEASE RECYCLE
THIS PRODUCT IS RECYCLABLE

Recycling programs
for this product may
not exist in your area.

ISBN-13: 978-1-335-14545-1

Down & Dirty

Copyright © 2019 by Rhenna Morgan

www.CarinaPress.com

Printed in U.S.A.

DOWN & DIRTY

Chapter One

Ringing ears, a raw throat and throbbing feet. Every pleasure had its price. A consequence to be paid after the indulgence was over. But for Lizzy, that cost was not only worth it, but necessary. Especially since the bulk of paying her bills came from abandoning herself to the thing she loved most.

Nothing beat sharing her music with a live crowd. Absolutely nothing. There was a connection behind it. A raw energy fueled by the emotions of those around her that flooded her insides and smothered all the day-to-day minutia. All that was left in its wake was pure bliss. An indescribable aliveness akin to fantastic sex—only without the vulnerability and risk of heartbreak.

Hopped up and fresh off the stage from her last set, she strode into the dingy ten-by-twenty storage room that doubled as the bar's staging area, her bandmates hard on her heels.

"Lizzy, baby! That was fucking *awesome*!" Tony's praise ricocheted off the once-white walls now stained with too many years of nicotine. At six-two with long-ish dirty blond hair, dreamy blue eyes and a wicked smile, he attracted female music lovers with little more than a crook of his finger. How the guy could pound the massive drum kit he set up for every show and still have this much energy five hours later, she'd never know, but it'd take him a good two more hours to come down.

She snagged her guitar case off the crude wooden shelf, laid it out along the third- or fourth-hand leather couch and flipped open the lid. "The place might be a dive, but they draw a hell of a crowd."

"Ain't the bar that draws the crowd," Skeet said, following suit with Lizzy and stowing his Telecaster. His vibe was the polar opposite of Tony's. More of a biker meets cowboy combination with the Marlboro raspy voice to go with it. He paused just before sliding the black-and-white beauty into its plush-lined case and eyeballed her over one shoulder. "It's you."

"Man, you keep that shit up, she's gonna clam up on us again." Ever the pragmatist, Dewayne—or Phat D as a recent reviewer had dubbed him—propped his Rickenbacker bass on the stand he'd left in the corner and dropped into the oversized black chair in the corner with a sigh. "She knows what she's capable of. When she's ready to make a move, she'll make a move."

"No shit, Skeet," Tony said. "Don't kill our buzz."

"Not killin' our buzz. Just drivin' home my point."

Said point being that it was time to start working their way into some of Dallas' better gigs. Of course, to get those gigs you had to have connections and public relations wasn't exactly her strong suit.

Actually, people in general weren't her strong suit. "No point to drive home. I'm not sticking to dive bars on purpose. As soon as I can get a foot in the door at the better places, I'll make a move."

"You've had three promoters hit you up in as many

weeks," Skeet fired back. "You want a foot in the door, you're gonna need to actually talk to them."

"And I told you—Rex and I can handle it."

"Rex is a good guy and a helluva friend, but he ain't a promoter or a manager. He's a welder and an artist."

"He's also trustworthy and doesn't fuck us around."

"Skeet." D wasn't the most charismatic of the group, but when he pulled that low grumbly voice, people shut up and paid attention. "Give it a rest."

"Buzz. Kill," Tony added.

Lizzy grinned and dug her phone out of her purse. For all Skeet's hounding, she knew he meant well and wanted the same things she did. Hell, she wanted it about thirty times worse. While the rest of the guys had trade jobs to help pay their bills, ringing up groceries at the local Aldi didn't exactly set her inspiration on fire. "It's gonna take a lot more than Skeet pushing me for better gigs to kill tonight's buzz."

She glanced at her phone and the unread text message plastered on her home screen.

Rex: Stuck doing overtime. I'll try to make it, but if I don't, you're gonna have to deal with Vic the Dick.

Now, *that* was a buzz kill.

She thumbed through her passcode and flipped directly to her text app.

Nope. Still the same shitty message.

"What?" Still gripping his sticks, Tony sidled closer and craned his head for a look at her phone.

Lizzy killed the screen, turned her back and tossed her phone back in her purse before he had a chance to read it. The only thing worse than Lizzy dealing with

Vic the Dick—AKA the bar owner—was sending Skeet, Tony or D to collect their cash. God knew, they'd tried that approach a time or two and still couldn't manage to book any return gigs as a result. "Nothing. Just gotta take care of some business." She schooled her expression the best she could and faced them. "I'm going to go settle up with Vic."

D snickered, stretched his long legs out in front of him and crossed his boot-shod feet at the ankles. "Guess that explains the look."

"What look?" She looked to Tony, then to Skeet. "I don't have a look."

"Yeah, you do," Tony said. "Kind of like you've held a fart in too long and are gonna throat punch the next person who keeps you from getting somewhere private so you can let it out."

"You got a shitty poker face, doll." Skeet fired up a cigarette he wasn't supposed to have lit in the building and exhaled a healthy amount of smoke on a chuckle. "You startin' to see why someone with interpersonal skills might come in handy for us?"

"I'm starting to think the person I'm going to throat punch tonight is you." She tried to make it come out like the badass she pretended to be on stage, but one corner of her mouth curled up in a smile she couldn't hold back. Strolling past him, she punched him in the shoulder with an equally lame delivery. "If I'm not back in fifteen minutes, come see if I'm being hauled off in a cop car for attempted murder."

All of three steps past the doorway, their laughter was swallowed up by the chaos of the lingering crowd and the requisite end-of-the-night strains of "Sweet Home Alabama." As bars went, The Crow wasn't the worst Lizzy had played. The single-story was a free-standing structure and big enough to hold a decent crowd—a necessity when a good chunk of your pay came from a cut of the door. That said, it was also the kind of place where the bouncers didn't intervene unless more than two sets of fists were involved, and you definitely didn't want to see the place with the house lights on. The scarred tables and floor stains highlighted by the neon beer signs showed plenty as it was, thank you very much.

Lizzy sidestepped a three-woman posse that'd circled a lone man left unprotected by his wing man—and almost tripped in her four-inch-heel boots.

Standing with his feet braced in a casual yet confident stance behind one of the many black pub tables was a man who turned the rest of the room's predictability on its head. Dressed in tailored tan pants and a crisp white button-down with sleeves rolled up to show corded forearms, he looked like he'd just escaped long negotiations in a board room, and as tall and built as he was in the shoulders, every thread on him was probably custom-made. But where his clothes were the refined flip side to the rest of the room's occupants, his long auburn hair and beard completely bucked the businessman stereotype, and his sharp features spoke of life experience learned the hardest way possible.

A powerful man. One who commanded attention with nothing more than a look.

And every ounce of his attention was locked on her.

A whole different buzz fired beneath her skin, and her steps slowed, a sexual awareness she hadn't felt in years fueling the sway in her hips as she worked her way through the people between her and the bar.

"The crowd's light tonight." Vic's gruff yet petulant

voice ripped her attention from the stranger just in time to keep her from slamming into a table directly in her path. It took her a second to tag him behind the bar, half hidden in the shadows of one corner and counting out twenties. "Didn't help you were late starting up the last set. We lost five big tables waiting on you and your guys to get back to work."

Light crowd her ass. Every single table had been full right up through their last song, and the waitresses had been hustling nonstop since Lizzy first fired up her amp. Then again, Vic was a sour fucker of the first order and always acted like the whole damned world was lined up and eager to screw him when, in fact, it was him plotting to screw everyone else.

She pushed the insanely hot guy out of her mind and closed what was left of the distance to the bar in what she hoped looked like a laid-back stride. "The only thing you lost tonight was about a hundred bucks worth of Fireballs."

Vic paused in his counting and eyeballed her with one eyebrow cocked high.

For a second, Lizzy considered sliding onto a barstool in that ready-for-conversation way Rex always used, then remembered Skeet's comment about her shitty poker face and ditched the idea. "Oh, come on. You slid any woman who talked to you for more than five minutes tonight a free one."

One thing about Vic and his fragile ego—watching him puff up his chest like a disgruntled baboon while he huffed and puffed and grappled for a witty comeback was mighty entertaining. "Keeping women here is good for business. When my band can't hold a crowd, I do what I've got to do."

"Man, you can say a lot about tonight, but us holding a crowd isn't one of 'em. Every table was full until after we walked off stage."

Vic grunted and tossed a messy stack of twenties in front of her on the bar. "There's your base."

The too-thin pile of crumpled bills practically mocked her from the black Formica countertop. "The deal's base plus thirty percent of the door."

"Thirty percent of the door for a full house. Full house means the people stay. Not get up and leave before the night's over. If I have to resort to Fireballs to hang on to what you and your band can't, the cut's null and void."

See? This was why she didn't deal with Vic the Dick. Or humans. Rex would've known better than to prod his delicate male ego. Hell, the little girl that lived with the single mom in the apartment next to Lizzy's would have known better. "That's bullshit, and you know it. We've never had a clause like that in our bookings and, even if we did, the crowd *stayed*."

"Now you're calling me a slime *and* a liar?"

Fuck.

Lizzy forced herself not to fidget and ground her teeth together to bite back a good old-fashioned directive to tell the asshole where he could stick his accusations. In hindsight, maybe Skeet would've been a better person to pick up the cash because right now she was thinking a throat punch would be highly enjoyable even if she'd never shown an act of violence her whole life.

With no clue how to dig herself out of a hole and not end up one more bar short of places to play, she opened her mouth to start on damage control—but froze at the prickling awareness that swept down her spine.

"At a quarter to one, your man on the door was still

tracking headcount coming in and out." The deep masculine voice tinged with the barest Scottish accent registered all of a second before the ruggedly *GQ* man she'd ogled on her trek across the room moved in beside her. He clinked his empty tumbler onto the countertop. While he aimed an affable smile at Vic and his posture was outwardly relaxed, there was a heightened edge to his presence. A lethal dare barely masked by his easygoing facade. When he spoke again, his tone was just as poised and calm as before, but there was no mistaking the warning behind his words. "No reason to track counts unless you're worried about being over occupancy, now is there?"

"Who the fuck are you?" Typical Vicente. Clueless and classless.

Though, considering the mystery guy had all but waltzed up and firmly inserted himself in the middle of her business without so much as a hi-how-are-ya, she couldn't say she hadn't thought the same thing.

Before she could say as much, the stranger slid his tumbler a little closer to Vic, pulled out a wad of cash from one pocket and flipped it open. He thumbed through the bills and peeled off a few hundreds. "I'm the man keeping you honest to the deal you booked. A standard base of $500 plus thirty percent of the door."

This time it was Lizzy who almost interjected with a whole lot of *What the hell?*, but before she could draw a big enough breath to voice the question, her mysterious and seriously badass helper turned his head and gave her a look that made the question fizzle on her tongue.

Not a bad look, exactly. Yeah, it had a mother lode of a command behind it, but it was also comforting, too. An unspoken promise of protection and reward in exchange for the trust given.

And damned if the apprehensive knot that'd kept a stranglehold on her insides didn't loosen enough to let her draw a liberating breath for the first time since she'd read Rex's text.

The stranger's mouth softened, hinting at the promise of a smile. A subtle acknowledgment of her response and an approval all rolled up into one. And wow—didn't that just make her want to strut and preen even bigger than when she was on stage?

It was whacked. Absolutely, insanely *whacked*. Which kinda made her want to tell him where to get off on principle alone.

But before she could, he refocused on Vic and tossed his cash down on the table. "That's to settle up my tab." He nodded to the waitress quickstepping it after a pair of men who were likely trying to skip on their own tab. "She knows which one it is." He paused just long enough to cock his head a fraction. "Now, are you gonna do the right thing and settle up with Elizabeth? Or do you want to screw yourself out of booking them again and the crowd they've delivered every time they've played here?"

What. The ever-lovin'. *Fuck.*

Who was this guy, and how did he know how well they'd performed here? Not to mention, no one called her Elizabeth. Not even her parents, and they'd been the one to pick the damned name, which just proved how poorly it fit her. She cleared her throat and straightened as tall as she could, well past ready to reestablish who was in control. At five-foot-eight and rocking four-inch thigh-high boots, most people backed down on height discomfort alone.

But this guy? He still had two or three more inches on her and only eased a little closer. As if her shift in stance was due to discomfort and he was ready to step between her and Vic. "Pay the lady. No point in dragging this out when you know it's the right move. You don't and you'll not only cut yourself short a solid band, but other bands will find out what you did and think twice about playing here."

Vic's face turned a bright red not even the dim lighting could hide, and he huffed out one of those uncomfortable sounds only a bully backed in a corner could make. He pinned his gaze on Lizzy. "A word of advice. Your new guy's got the common sense of a thug. You want to keep booking gigs you'll go back to Rex for a middle man. No one's gonna want to deal with this dick." He punched open the register, snagged a stack of pre-counted bills and tossed it next to the first stack she still hadn't touched. "Eleven hundred. Your cut of the door." His attention volleyed to the man beside her then back to Lizzy. "You let me know what your plans are for this asshole and I'll let you know if your spot in July's still good."

With that, he slammed the register drawer shut and stalked away.

Lizzy watched.

And waited.

And tried like hell to keep the cocktail of rage, praise and outright fear mushrooming up in her chest from spewing all over the seemingly unfazed man next to her. She made it until Vic and his flat ass disappeared into the back office. By some miracle, her first words came out surprisingly restrained. "Tell me you're a friend of Rex's and not some stranger who not only just squarely stuck his nose right in the middle of my business, but knows enough details of my bookings to make me seriously uneasy."

There was no hint to the smile he shot her this time, the sheer devilment behind the curve of his full lips potent enough to make the most hardened woman giggle like a little girl. "Don't know anyone named Rex, lass, so we're gonna have to go with door number two. Though, I wouldn't let the fact that I knew how much you'd booked the gig for tweak you too much. Vic's not the most creative guy. Every band that's worth a damned gets the same deal."

"And you know about bands and their going rates because…"

"Because I know music and I know bar owners." He faced her fully and held out his hand. "Axel McKee."

Damn, but the man's voice was a weapon. Rich, deep, and made all the more intoxicating with the accent. But that was nothing compared to his presence. To the raw, masculine energy emanating off him and the startling focus behind his brilliant green eyes.

He kept his hand steady. Patiently waiting for her to take what he offered.

A crossroad moment.

How she knew it, she couldn't say, but she felt it in her bones. Intuited the gravity of the situation the way prey recognized a predator had marked them as a target.

And yet, rather than run, she lifted her hand and pressed her palm against his.

Oh. Holy. Hell.

A shiver she didn't have a prayer of containing moved through her and her breath hitched with all the subtlety of a woman who'd just felt a man's lips on the back of her neck for the first time.

His fingers tightened around hers. A tangible testament that he'd felt and witnessed her response, which in itself should have mortified her. Instead the deepened connection resonated through her like a tether in the middle of straight-line wind.

"Lizzy Hemming." The quaver in her response and the sexual rasp that went with it slapped her well-honed sense of self-preservation back into place, and she tugged her hand free with an awkward abruptness. "Though, you appear to already know that."

"Everyone in this bar knows your name."

"True, but not one of them saw fit to saunter over here and put my band's income at risk."

His smile really was a killer. Quick and loaded with mischief. "Vic's an idiot, but he's not that stupid. You covered a week's worth of hourly wages for half of his staff on his cut of the door alone, and the way he's trained his bartenders to short people on most of the drinks, you put him squarely in the black for the rest of the month. The last thing that's gonna happen is you losing a booking." He cocked his head the same way he had with Vic, only without the dangerous vibe behind his eyes. "Now, if you're ready to stop playing gigs like this, that's a whole different conversation."

Every DEFCON alarm hardwired from past experience went off at once, blaring with enough decibels to nearly make her outwardly wince. As lead-ins went, it was a smooth one, but she'd learned the hard way what trusting smooth talkers earned you. Especially the hot ones. "How exactly is it you know Vic, but he doesn't know you? And what do you mean, *I know music*?"

"I know Vic because—bad business man or not—he books good bands, and I make it my business to keep an eye out for good music in and around Texas. I know music because I love it. Have my whole life."

"You make it your business why?"

His expression shifted. Narrowed with a shrewdness that made her feel as though he'd easily peeled away all her armor and studied the raw woman underneath. "You're a guarded woman, Elizabeth. Why is that?"

"No one calls me Elizabeth. It doesn't fit. Never has."

One look. Ruthless determination behind his eyes and an uncompromising firmness to his lips. "It fits you perfectly. You're just afraid to wear it." He held her gaze a second longer as if to make sure his words sank in, then kept going. "Vic's known for the move he tried to make with you. When I overheard him trying it tonight and heard the frustration in your voice, I moved in because bullies piss me off."

"I would've handled it."

"Sure, you would've. But you hate doing it. I knew it the second you stopped looking at me and shifted your attention to him. Plus, you handling it would've robbed me of the chance to hand him his ass."

He slid one hand in his pocket and pulled out a slim case made of a fine camel-colored leather. He slid a business card free. "I'm a businessman. I've got fingers in more industries than even I can sometimes keep track of, but the one that interests me most is music because it's what I love. I've watched you and your band for a while, and I think you've got tremendous talent. The trick to making the most of it is maximizing the things you do well and surrounding yourself with people who can better handle the things you can't." He handed over the card, his stare so potent the mere act of breathing seemed impossible. "Think about it. If you decide you're willing to lower the drawbridge enough to talk, this is how to reach me."

With a grin bordering on smug, he dipped his chin and ambled toward the exit with the same confident air he'd exuded from the second she'd laid eyes on him.

What just happened?

The single thought whipped round and round in her head, propelled by a frustrating mix of want, appreciation and fury that made absolutely no sense. She'd have probably stood there forever if the sound of footsteps coming from behind her and Rex's smoker-raspy voice didn't prod her out of her trance. "Hey, kiddo. Who was that?"

She faced her near-lifelong friend, not bothering to hide what was likely a dumbfounded expression. With his gray hair well past his chin, faded Nirvana tee and even more faded jeans, Rex was the antithesis of the man who'd just walked away. More rugged than *GQ*. But just laying eyes on his tired mug helped her surface in reality and draw a decent breath. She glanced at the card pinched tightly between her fingers then back at the door. "I have no idea. But you can bet your ass I'm going to find out."

Chapter Two

Only two days into June and the heat was already stout enough to cause a visual shimmer off the busy four-lane that ran in front of Crossroads. Not exactly a surprising turn of events for Dallas, Texas. What was surprising was Axel spending a sizable chunk of his Saturday afternoon staring out the window and noticing those kind of bullshit details. Brooding wasn't his style, but for the last week he'd been stuck in a hell of a rut, trying to figure out if it was time to dig in deeper, or cut bait.

Swiveling his mammoth leather desk chair back to his desk, he refocused on the employee schedules he still had to knock out for the rest of June. Being this far behind on logistics of any kind wasn't his modus operandi either, and the fact that he'd let things ride this long just proved how much his first encounter with Lizzy Hemming had fucked with his head.

Footfalls sounded in the long conference room that joined his and Jace's offices on Crossroads' third floor, their weight and determined strides muted only by the room's plush black carpet. Jace showed in the doorway all of two seconds later. "You sure you're good to handle tonight?"

The inclination to growl in lieu of a civil answer was

mighty damned tempting, and with anyone else, would've been a foregone conclusion in his present mood, but considering Jace had put up with his shite since they were both five, he reined it in.

Or at least tried to.

"Why the fuck wouldn't I be?"

Jace braced his forearm on the doorjamb and grinned like Axel had just launched some ridiculously clever joke. "I'm guessing that big window next to your desk doesn't cast much of a reflection, 'cause if it did, you'd see the same red-headed ogre all the rest of us have been putting up with." He paused long enough to give the toothpick anchored at one corner of his mouth a spin with his tongue. "You ever gonna talk about what's up your ass, or are we gonna keep ignoring the pissed off elephant in the room?"

"I don't meddle in your shite, brother. Don't meddle in mine."

"Don't meddle, my ass. You get up in everyone else's business faster than both of our busybody mothers combined when it suits your purpose." He pushed off the jamb and ambled toward one of the two black leather guest chairs angled in front of his desk like he hadn't just thrown a prime gauntlet down. Unlike a good portion of the crowd that would pour through their front doors tonight, Jace didn't give a damn about dressing to impress or what anyone thought of him. Faded tees, jeans and boots fit his mood 99.9 percent of the time, and today was no exception. The fact that his dark hair was pulled back in a low ponytail for the first time in weeks was more a testament to the gusty winds outside than anything to do with style.

Jace dropped down in one of the chairs, knees wide

and elbows braced on either side of him in a let's-cut-the-shit pose. "You said you were out scouting last weekend."

"Yeah. So?"

Jace studied him a beat, one of those cautious evaluations that usually meant he was about to go for the jugular. "So, I happened to see Lizzy Hemming was playing at The Crow. Your shitty mood tanked all of three days later."

Hell, he wished it'd tanked three days later. The truth was, he'd been pissed as hell before he'd so much as made it to his Shelby in the parking lot. He'd just managed to keep the fury contained until he'd gone a full seventy-two hours without getting a call from Lizzy before reality started sinking in. "You been watching Dr. Phil again?"

Typical Jace. Rather than bite and start trading good-natured insults the way the rest of their brothers would, he just grinned and counted the non-answer as a bull's-eye. "So, you did go see her."

"Yeah, I saw her."

"And?"

And he'd plowed through the whole damned thing fifty kinds of wrong. Another in the growing list of behaviors outside the norm for him. Musicians normally loved him. Men, women—it didn't matter. Inside thirty seconds, he could usually strike a decent chord with any of them and have them lined up and ready to play in any one of his and Jace's venues shortly after. He also couldn't remember the last time he'd gone off so half-cocked. "You know that bullshit no-full-house-no-cut maneuver Vicente's been known to pull with some of the bands he's booked?"

Jace eyes widened. "He's still pulling that shit?"

Axel dipped his chin. "Tried it with Lizzy and the place was at full capacity."

The same knee-jerk anger Axel had processed last weekend must have moved through Jace, because a whole lot of pissed off settled into his expression. "I take it you intervened?"

"Not gonna let that fucker bend a stranger over the proverbial barrel, let alone a talent I've been watching for months. Of course, I stepped in."

"And?"

And he'd miscalculated. Had gotten so wrapped up in the need to shove Vic's dick down his throat, he'd forgotten to factor in how Lizzy might feel about such an action. "She got the cut she earned, but it cost me getting off on the right foot. I gave her my number and haven't heard a damned thing since."

The lack of an immediate response from Jace was about as uncomfortable as the prospect of his nuts getting crunched in a vise. When he finally rallied, the whole ball-crunching discomfort jumped to a new level. "Why are you watching this girl?"

Girl?

Axel might not know the nitty-gritty on Elizabeth Hemming's history, but he had a hunch *girl* was the least fitting word to describe her. *Female*, yes. *Woman*, definitely. But, *girl*?

No way.

If anything, he figured she'd come out of the womb with the presence and attitude of an Amazon. God knew, she'd grown into the physical equivalent and it turned him way the fuck on.

He shoved the response that always tried to force its way free with thoughts of Lizzy into someplace he hoped

Jace couldn't see and stuck with the basics. "She's got a great voice. Pure velvet on her lower range and a power-house at the top. Her songwriting skills are off the chart, and her presence on stage is electric. A rock star just wait-ing to happen. The crowd eats her up."

Jace grinned like Axel had all but shown his ass. "I didn't ask about her skills, brother. I asked why you're watching her."

"And I told you. She's gifted."

This time Jace huffed out a chuckle, hung his head and shook it. "I think you're missing the point."

"Then fucking make it already."

Jace lifted his head and lowered his voice. "You don't *watch* anyone. When you see a band you want to book, you book 'em. When you see a business you want to build, you build it. Our whole damned life you've zeroed in on what you want and made the magic happen." He leaned forward so his elbows were braced on his knees and pinned Axel with a hard stare. "What you don't do is watch and do nothing. So, I'll put it a different way. You want this woman. You can say it's on a professional basis all you want, but that's bullshit and we both know it. So, she hasn't called. Stop fucking around and do what you do best. Make the magic happen."

He wanted to. Badly. More so than he dared to admit even to Jace. Failure wasn't something he'd ever been afraid of at any other step in his life, but somehow fail-ing with Lizzy on either a personal or professional level left him stone-cold terrified. "She's got a past. No clue what, but she's got as much armor stacked around her as the rest of our brothers put together." He paused all of a heartbeat and forced out the rest. "Not sure I've got the ammunition to get past it."

The sound that came out of Jace's mouth as he pushed upright and reclined against the seat back was part scoff, part amusement. "You're overthinking it. You said a few weeks ago she didn't have a manager, and you forget I've seen a few pics of this girl. Looking like she does with no one to back her up? Hard to know who to trust and who not to. Especially with men like Vic. She's gotta keep her guard up."

"Not sure about the manager thing anymore. Vic mentioned some guy named Rex when our head-to-head was going on, so maybe I was wrong."

"Jesus, you're the poster child for gloom and doom." Jace sighed. "Who gives a damn who this Rex guy is? You've got some of the best venues in Texas to book. That alone's a solid reason to push competition out of the way." His eyes narrowed. "I take it you didn't tell her what kind of gig you were looking to book."

"You know how people act when they find out I'm the one booking The Green and Crossroads."

"Yeah, they sit up a whole lot taller and ask where to sign."

And therein lay the root of the problem. "If she's gonna work with me, I don't want it to be just because I can fill her calendar."

"Why? What else would you do?"

Axel's chest got tight, memories, hopes and dreams quashed years ago battering behind his sternum. Just saying the words out loud was a challenge. "When I say this woman's got talent, I mean she's *gifted*. The whole package."

"Yeah. I get it." Jace paused all of a beat, then threw down a familiar taunt. "So were you."

He had been, once upon a time. But dreams changed

and with change came new ideas. New risks. "That ship sailed a long time ago, and we both know it."

He met Jace's stare. To this point, he'd kept his plans to himself, too cautious about breathing life into his ideas too soon. But this was Jace. His brother in every way that counted. He took a deep breath and went for it. "That said, the ship hasn't sailed for her."

Jace stayed stock still. Not so much as a muscle or a twitch to telegraph what he was thinking. "What's that mean?"

Axel shrugged and hoped it downplayed the significance of what he was out to do. "It means I might be too old to chase a dream, but I've sure as shit learned the ropes. If I can't have what I wanted growing up, I figure the next best thing is to make it happen for someone else."

Apparently, his efforts at downplaying missed by a mile because a whole lot of comprehension rearranged Jace's passive expression to one of genuine shock in seconds. "You want to launch her."

Launch seemed a little lacking. Maybe a fitting word eight days ago, but now that he'd met her—now that he'd felt the guardedness in her and seen the pain behind her striking blue eyes—he wanted to hand her the world on a silver platter. Which made absolutely no sense given the fact she didn't seem interested in even talking. "Why not? I've got the means, the knowledge and the connections to do it."

Jace held up his hands in mock surrender. "Hey, I'm not knocking it. If we can't get your ass back in front of a crowd, then we might as well have your protégée."

"Yeah, well… I gotta find out who this Rex guy is first."

"Ask Knox. Hell, for that matter, ask Darya. She'd be tickled as shit to help you land a woman."

Axel glared at him. "Don't go there. That's not what this is. And even if it was, it'd be way too soon to get family involved."

Jace chuckled and hit him with that chicken-shit smug grin again. "Right. Just a run-of-the-mill business deal. I get it." He stood and started back toward the conference room. "You keep tellin' yourself that one. Let me know how it works out for ya."

The jibe triggered a memory. The words weren't exact, but the message was almost the same as the one he'd aimed at Jace just under four years ago. A damned fine idea for crossing the breech he'd created with Lizzy sauntered in right behind it. "Hold up."

Jace paused in the entry and twisted enough to look at Axel over one shoulder.

"I said it was too soon for the rest of the family to get involved," Axel said. "I didn't say anything about not dragging your pompous ass into the mix."

Cocking an eyebrow in that imperious angle he used to intimidate everyone, Jace waited without saying a word.

"You remember that ruse you made me run to get an in with Vivienne when you two first met?"

Jace faced him fully, a little wariness creeping into his expression. "Yeah, what about it?"

This time it was Axel who grinned. "It's payback time, brother."

Chapter Three

In the Dallas/Ft. Worth realm of live music, Crossroads
was just one click away from the big time. Not huge
arena big-time, but a stone's throw from the casino venues so many of the newer or old-school label favorites
frequented. It was also swanky as hell and catered to
every crowd under the sun.

Holding fast to her pre-show ritual, Lizzy meandered
through the colorful main entrance and soaked it all in.
Cobalt blue neon rods shooting up from mammoth rect-
angle planters as tall as her thighs. Red and gold leather
couches that looked fit for a contemporary king. Crystal waterfall chandeliers and thick ebony marble pillars.

And that was just the starting point. From there, the
place branched out into other rooms that offered something for everyone. To her right lay a techno/eclectic
space for the hipsters and geeks, and on the left, a darker
pub area for those in search of something casual and
close. But dead ahead was the mecca. A huge hall that
served double time as hopping dance club and high-end
live music venue.

In a nutshell, it was awesome.

Or as Tony had said the second they'd walked through
the front doors this afternoon—this place was *the shit*.

The question was how the hell she'd ended up with a last-minute gig to play here.

No. That wasn't the question. Not really. Axel McKee was the *how*. She'd researched every public piece of information she could find on him and knew he was part owner in Crossroads long before she'd ever gotten the request to play. The real question was why it'd been Jace Kennedy on the other end of the phone when the call came in instead of the handsome Scot. Not a single article she'd found on Axel implied he was anything more than a club owner and avid music lover, but the way he'd postured himself at The Crow, she'd been sure he was a promoter. Or—as she'd come to consider them—scourge of the Earth.

"I'd ask if you're lookin' for someone, but my bet is you're just out for pre-set recon." Even with the crowd around her and the music pumping through the dance club speakers ahead, she'd have no more mistaken Jace's voice than she would a Harley rolling in behind her.

She faced him. "Was I that obvious?"

He flashed her a big smile and kept ambling toward her. "Been doin' this awhile. I know the look of a musician out to learn their crowd." He stopped just an arm's length away. "Your guys settled in and ready to go?"

Settled in was putting it mildly. More like ready to move in and put down roots. "Are you kidding? I'm gonna have to force them out of the staging room when the night's over. They're used to dark and dingy. That place is closer to a spa reception area minus the sleepy-time lighting."

Jace nodded and swept the entrance with a calculating eye. "Got a good crowd for you. You think of anything you need, just flag one of the girls down and tell 'em to find me."

Oh, she needed something. Answers in particular.

Or did she?

Sometimes answers shed too much light on a situation. Forced a person to face things better left untouched. Or in this instance, drew people better kept at a distance into orbit.

Her thoughts must have shown through her expression, because Jace's gaze sharpened. "Something wrong?"

Ask?

Or don't ask?

Walk away, or dig in?

Common sense told her to stuff it and get her ass back with the guys for the first set, but stupidity won. "You own this place with Axel McKee."

Yep. There it was. Even if he tried to deny it, the confirmation was right there in the quick guardedness that slipped over his features. "That a problem?"

"No. Not a problem. He introduced himself to me at The Crow about a week before you called and offered us the opening this weekend."

"And?" There was an edge to the single word. A dare and a warning all rolled up into one.

She could shrug it off. Act like it was no big deal and head back to the guys in their pre-show paradise.

Or she could take a chance.

You gonna hide in the past your whole life? Call the man, already! Seize the day! Storm the world!

It'd been a nonstop mantra from Rex since the day he'd watched Axel walking out of The Crow. Now, standing here—feeling the energy around her and buzzing from the challenge in Jace's expression—she couldn't help wondering if Rex was right.

She shifted her attention to a cluster of women dressed to the nines and hoped the whole people-watching appearance covered how much the question mattered. "Just curious why you called me instead of him."

Silence.

So much of it she couldn't have kept her attention from swinging back to Jace's face even if someone else had forbidden it with a gun muzzle to her temple.

Even once she'd locked stares with him, he still held his tongue for two painful heartbeats. "And what would have happened if my brother had been the one to make the call?"

"Your brother?" The retort came out with a whole lot of no-freaking-way, but come on—there was absolutely *no freaking way*. Yeah, they both had a hardness to them that pointed to life experience beyond the norm, but that was where the similarities ended.

"By choice for more years than I bother to count anymore. Had my back since I was five and no better man on the planet." He cocked his head. "So, I'll ask it again. If he'd have called, would you have taken the gig?"

"Probably not." Much as it pained her to admit it, it was the truth. And the fact that Axel had known that going in scared her all the more. "He butted into my business without knowing anything about me, or the situation I was in."

"And yet, he worked in your best interest." He paused and lifted his chin toward the stream of people still filtering through the main entrance. "Twice."

His candor hit her with all the subtlety of a right hook, but she refused to back down. "You're going to tell me you'd have welcomed a stranger intervening in your business without knowing a thing about them? Wouldn't have been gun-shy after the fact?" She motioned to the room around her. "You can't tell me you have this place and all the others you own and haven't learned to be careful about who you trust and who you don't."

He pursed his mouth, scrutinized her a beat, then dipped his chin. "I'll give you that. But I've also learned there are some decent people in this world who genuinely give a shit about good people and want to give them a leg up. Axel wanted that for you." He paused, the intensity behind his stare ramping so high it was hard to draw a decent breath. "The question for you is if you're gonna be brave enough to take it."

Not waiting for an answer, his gaze cut to the big hall beyond then back to Lizzy. "Gettin' close to showtime. Like I said, if you need me, just flag someone down and I'll be there." He grinned and winked. "Just for the record, Axel's keepin' a low profile, but he's here, too. You know…in case you decide to wade into the good life."

With that he sauntered off with the confidence of a man who knew he'd not only laid the bait, but left the prey hungry as well. The whole cocky demeanor would have pissed her off if he hadn't absolutely earned the attitude.

But he'd been right. There were good people in the world. She might not have a ton of them in her life—Rex and her band being the only real people she considered close—but they were gold. Steady anchors and reliable friends in a world where she tried to keep most people at a distance.

Far away where they couldn't use or hurt her.

The thoughts spun and spun. Prodded and poked her so proficiently she made the trek back to the staging room without really registering the people around her. Gearing up, tuning her guitar and strolling with the guys to the stage was no different, her actions peppered only with the necessary quips to keep her bandmates unaware of the roiling ideas in her head.

The darkness surrounded her. Cloaked her and her band from those too busy on the dance floor to take notice. Almost zero wires surrounded them, the state-of-the-art setup that Crossroads offered making the wide and uncluttered expanse ideal for moving around and working the crowd.

The weight of her guitar strapped across her body and the smooth press of the neck against her palm was a comfort. A familiar friend that had kept her pain at bay for years and years.

Had my back since I was five and no better man on the planet.

She understood Jace's sentiment. Rex had been that for her since she was little, and she'd get more than a little bent out of shape if someone ever called into question his intentions.

You gonna hide in the past your whole life? Call the man, already! Seize the day! Storm the world!

There are some decent people in this world who genuinely give a shit about good people and want to give them a leg up. Axel wanted that for you.

Could she be brave enough? Just because things had gotten deeply personal last time, didn't mean this time would be the same. She could control it. Make sure things stayed firmly neutral.

The lights in the hall dimmed further and the DJ's voice rang out across the crowd. The standard banter intended to rile the people gathered and strike the right mood. The crowd ate it up. Clapped and cheered at all the right times until the moment was right.

The DJ took it. "Are you ready?"

The crowd roared.

"I said, *Are you ready?*"

Louder this time, the room filled with a potent energy.

"Then give it up for Lizzy Hemming and Falcon Black."

Tony clicked out the count.

The stage lights flared, and their heat washed across her skin, the vibrations from the first note bringing her to life.

She went with it. Poured everything she had into the moment and let the music flow.

Hell, yeah, she was going to take this chance. First with the gig—and then with Axel.

Chapter Four

She'd been looking for something all night. What that something was, Axel didn't have a clue, but he'd watched Lizzy on stage enough times to know there'd been more to her eye contact with the crowd than normal. A sharpened search between songs or when the stage lights flashed enough to bring the hall into greater focus.

Then again, it might just be his imagination. God knew, he'd entertained a host of outcomes for tonight in the two weeks it'd taken him and Jace to wrangle getting her here.

Leaning one shoulder against the windowsill that gave him a one-way, bird's-eye view of the stage below, he nursed his Scotch and welcomed the comforting burn that rolled down the back of his throat. The security door that blocked all but those with the highest permission from breaching their private offices on the third floor chunked open and closed. Given the tread coming up the stairway, it had to be Jace. The rest of his brothers were all tied up with their women or work—or in many cases, both.

"I'll give you one thing," Jace said strolling into Axel's office without so much as a knock. "Your woman's stellar on stage."

His woman.

It shouldn't resonate as good as it did. Hell, he barely knew the woman, but he'd been fascinated with her for months. Drawn to her in a way that defied logic or reason. It was instinct. The same whisper to act that had guided him in business for years and had helped him and Jace escape the hard life they'd been born into. "I'm never wrong with the talent we book here." He glanced at Jace as he moseyed up to the wide window beside him. "And can it with the *my woman* shite. I've got enough hurdles to clear with this one as it is. Don't need you adding height to the challenge."

"Oh, I don't know about that. Sometimes once you clear the first one, the rest even out, or disappear altogether." He reached into his back pocket, pulled out a folded white napkin and handed it over. "Candy's been trying to find you since the band's last break." He smirked. "Guess she's not used to her hands-on boss hiding in his office."

"I'm not hiding. Just givin' Lizzy a little space." Axel snatched the napkin and opened it. Blue ink in sharp lines shone up at him.

I hear you're here tonight. I'd like to thank you for the opportunity to play in person if you have time after the last set.

An elegant, but dramatic L marked the end of it. Fitting for the woman who'd thoroughly commanded the stage below him all night. And damned if knowing she'd taken a step and reached out to him didn't snare his focus like the rest of the throng below. "How does she know I'm here?"

"She'd done her homework. Knew we owned the place together and asked me point blank why I called instead of you."

So, she'd at least been curious enough to find out who he was and what kind of opportunities might be available if she picked up the phone and dared to call. Then again, she may have done that after Jace had called with the possible booking. "Yeah? How'd that go?"

"Well, you definitely yanked her chain going toe-to-toe with Vic without her knowing who you were, but I'd say she's figured out maybe you're not in the same class as Vic and knows a peace offering when she sees it."

God, he wished he could say tonight was a peace offering. The truth was, he'd moved the band they had booked here to another venue and made a hole for Lizzy for purely mercenary reasons. Like giving her a glimpse of what he could offer her if she'd let her guard down enough to trust him.

And man, watching her when her guard was down was a thing to behold. Thanks to the cameras piped into every nook and cranny of Crossroads, he'd watched his fill of the woman without her armor in place while they'd set up this afternoon. How easygoing she'd been with her bandmates and quick to laugh while trading lighthearted barbs with them. On stage, she was magnetic. A force to be reckoned with. But in person, without that mask she kept in place, she was a whole different person. Big smiles. A rich, throaty laugh. Languid movements that spoke of comfort rather than anything crafted to draw attention and sky-blue eyes that sparked as if she held a thousand secrets.

He wanted those eyes aimed at him. To be welcomed not just into the circle of those she trusted, but closer. To reach the secrets behind those eyes. To touch the soul that fueled the lyrics she wrote. To pry that fucking armor off her and guard her so she didn't need it anymore.

Serious thoughts. Disturbing thoughts for a man who'd been perfectly comfortable with only casual relationships. Especially when he'd barely traded more than ten sentences with Lizzy and pricked her temper in the process. He folded the note and tucked it in his pocket, but kept his fingers closed around it. "What's your read on her?"

Beside him, Jace stared down at the stage, his focus on Lizzy as she strutted from one side of the stage to the other with her guitar slung across her body. She might be dressed to wow in high-heeled boots, a skin-tight black dress and flashy rock star jewelry, but Jace had a knack for seeing much deeper. "I think you're right. She's got a past. My guess, one where the world's chewed her up and spit her out more than anything she caused directly." He shifted his gaze to Axel. "You've been watchin' her a long time. You done any digging?"

"Not much to dig through. Born and raised in Tampa, Florida. I found some live clips and publicity for her as far back as 2011. Mostly small venues. A few openers for mid-list or re-surging '80s bands, but nothing before that." Axel dipped his head toward the stage below. "Didn't have the same image then either. She still commanded a crowd, but all her stuff was softer. More broad-spectrum alternative than rock. Had a manager by the name of Joffrey Reynolds behind her."

"I thought Vic mentioned some guy named Rex?"

"Rex Niland." Axel shook his head. "I think he's a friend. Been in social media shots with Lizzy for as long as her accounts have been around."

"A friend, or something more?"

"They're cozy in the pics, but I'd bet money it's platonic."

"Then what happened to Joffrey?"

"He got a gig with Miramar Records around 2012. Lizzy fell off the radar and relocated here in 2014. She and Rex have separate apartments in the same complex. She didn't start playing anywhere here until early 2016. That's when the whole badass rocker vibe came out."

"New image for a new town," Jace said.

"Maybe."

Jace's gaze sharpened on Axel. "You got another theory?"

Frankly, he didn't know what to think. Ever since he'd first seen Lizzy perform he'd felt like he was fighting back a rising tide with nothing but a toy bucket to bail water. Meeting her and setting in motion all the things he'd tried to ignore had only brought the water level up to his neck. "When you go to war, you suit up. Cover yourself in Kevlar so you're bulletproof." He dipped his head in Lizzy's direction. "Or you turn yourself into a badass. Works great for the crowd and keeps people at a distance."

Jace grinned. "You gonna get her out of that Kevlar?"

That was the million-dollar question. The one he still wasn't sure he had the answer to. "Only if I can do it without one of us getting shot."

In a second, Jace sobered, even the muted thrum of the bass from the hall below dimming beneath his steady stare. "Nothing's guaranteed. You know that. Hell, our lives have been one huge fucking chance after another and we've done pretty damned well."

They had. Two boys who'd grown up in a trailer park with mothers who sold themselves to pay the bills, and now they had enough money they could sit on their asses until they dropped dead and keep their whole family comfortable along the way.

"So, how are we playing this?" Jace said. "Am I paying Lizzy tonight, or are you gonna grab ahold of those balls of yours and man up?"

Fucking Jace. Thirty-three years they'd been trading insults and throwing down dares, and the guy had to go with the least creative one in the book. "That's the best you can come up with?"

Rather than banter back, Jace lowered his voice. "You're a good man. You've got family who has your back in anything you do and damned near everything you've ever wanted. Everything except a dream you left behind to take care of the people you love, and a woman who's got you mooney-eyed for the first time in your life. You take this shot, you won't do it alone. Every one of us will be there."

Oh, they'd be there. Whether he wanted them to or not and likely with more interference than was good for his patience. "Why'd ya think I've been keepin' all this to my bloody self?"

Jace chuckled, but held his stare. "How are we doin' this? You goin' down to her, or you want me to bring her up here so you can talk business?"

His gaze slid to Lizzy and that same subtle nudge prodded his insides. He'd never ignored that feeling before, and Jace was right. Nothing in this world was guaranteed. Nothing except losing if you didn't dare to try. "Bring her up. The business angle worked for you. Maybe it'll be a good play for me, too."

Chapter Five

Hallways lighted like a movie theater and thick steel doors that required a hand scan to get through and could probably withstand a grenade didn't exactly cast a warm welcome. Then again, Lizzy had gotten pretty good at gauging how a night was going by the number of bartenders on duty and the flow of drinks they sent out to the masses, and Crossroads definitely made bank on alcohol. They probably had to have the main offices set up like Fort Knox just to keep the cash their patrons forked over safe and sound until they could laugh themselves to the bank.

The upside? It'd been a packed house that had kept those bartenders hopping, and Jace had offered her an unprecedented forty-percent cut of the door. The downside? It looked like Jace was going to be the one handling payout instead of Axel.

The reality shouldn't have upset her as much as it did. Heck, if anything she should be relieved Axel hadn't responded to her note. Better to mark tonight down as an amazing memory and hope it gave her the leg up for more bookings just like it. Onward and upward and all that jazz.

Jace opened another door and waved her ahead of

him up a flight of stairs. "First door you come to. Ignore the grumbling, though. His growl's worse than his bite."

Lizzy stopped mid-stride and braced the door open wide. "Whose growl?"

Even in the muted lighting, Jace's grin reeked of an ornery schoolboy up to mischievous pranks. "Axel's a stubborn fucker and as proud as they come, but he's not gonna ignore a pretty lady who can sing and work a stage like you do." He motioned to the stairs with a jerk of his head. "Go on. Settle up and say what you've got to say. Maybe even listen a little while you're there."

With that, he winked and left her to it, disappearing back down the shadowed hallway he'd led her through.

Well, hells bells. Wasn't that just the twist to jingle her insides?

The door at the end of hallway chunked shut leaving only the faint sound of a TV or some other similar background noise coming from the floor above. Where her arm had been pretty solid bracing the heavy door open twenty seconds ago, now it shook like she'd bench pressed four times her weight, and for the first time since she'd first put on heels, she felt as unsteady as a newborn foal.

She let out a slow breath and eased the door shut behind her. It was just settling up on money. Being polite and trading business talk.

A piece of cake, right?

The stairs were steeper than your average flight and the industrial carpet that covered them too thin to completely mask her footsteps. She'd just reached the top and planned to pause at least a few seconds to collect herself when Axel's deep voice drifted through the open doorway. "Ye take too much longer gettin' here, lass, and I'll have time to invest this stack of money you earned and draw interest to boot."

It was the first time she'd heard his accent so prevalent. Combined with the playful undertone he'd paired with the statement, it unwound a good chunk of the tension knotting her stomach and forced the breath she'd been holding free on a chuckle. She stepped into his office. "Well, you have to admit. Your digs are a little intimidating."

She'd meant it for the lighting and high-end contemporary décor, but the second he shifted his gaze from the massive mahogany desk, there was no question he was the most formidable feature in the room. Unlike the night he'd approached her at The Crow, his hair was up in a messy knot she'd never be able to recreate with her own hair, but the arms of his blue button-down were rolled up as they had been that first night, displaying tanned skin and a faint dusting of hair along his forearms.

He stood and motioned to one of the two black leather chairs angled in front of his desk. "Intimidation's the last thing on my mind. Impressive was more the angle I was shooting for."

"Everything under this roof's impressive. You even managed to make the condom dispensers in the bathrooms look classy."

He chuckled and prowled out from behind his desk. "Well, you know what they say about when opportunity knocks. Never let it be said we don't arm our customers up with the tools to answer."

Man, he was big. She'd registered the impressive span of his shoulders the first time she'd met him, but somehow her mind had downplayed the memory since then. Probably a survival tactic to keep her from dialing him up before he'd so much as pulled out of The Crow's parking lot.

Settling in the chair next to her, he crossed one leg over the other and rested his elbows on the low armrests with all the elegance of a well-groomed socialite. Which was totally weird considering how the man underneath the clothes seemed more suited to motorcycles and barbecues. His gaze swept the length of her then back up again, a languid, unapologetic maneuver that left a comfortable heat in its wake. "I'm glad you took the gig."

Power.

It practically pulsed behind his shrewd forest green eyes and demanded something she had no clue how to give.

Too flustered by the thought to hold his stare, she focused on her armrest and traced the leather piping along the edge with her finger. Her bracelets sparkled off the soft lighting overhead and jingled in the silence while she searched for an answer. "Yeah, I need to thank you for that."

Silence blossomed in the wake of her words, thick and supercharged to the point her skin fairly tingled with its potency. For five years she'd forced herself to be harder. More direct and fearless in her interactions. But around him, it was like the persona that had not only kept her safe, but had pulled her out of the ashes, refused to play. Completely balked at the idea of going toe-to-toe with this man. So, she kept her head down and tried to keep her breaths slow and even.

"Elizabeth." Low and as magnificent as approaching thunder. She'd replayed the sound of her name on his lips hundreds of times since she'd last seen him. Marveled at how he'd taken a name that had felt foreign to her her whole life and turned it into something special. Something precious. "Look at me, lass."

Odd. He hadn't spoken the directive any louder than any other word that had crossed his lips. If anything, it was softer. A velvet stroke against her senses. But it bristled with command. A gentle firmness that lifted her chin as effectively as physical touch.

He waited until her gaze locked with his. "We got off on the wrong foot the first time around. Mostly because I couldn't stand the thought of Vic pulling his shite if I could stop it. But this time we're doing it right and that means shooting straight from the start." He paused and studied her face as though gauging the wisdom of sharing what he'd yet to say. "I didn't book you here tonight to make up for stomping into business that wasn't mine to meddle in, and I didn't do it just to be nice."

There it was. The lead in to ask all the questions she'd juggled in the last three weeks. A door left ajar.

So, did she walk through?

Or ignore the bait, settle up and move on?

Curiosity and some other foreign instinct that seemed to take over in his presence answered for her. "Then why do it?"

"Temptation. Pure and simple." His gaze slid to the top of his desk all of a second before he leaned forward and snatched a thick, sealed white envelope off the top of it. He reclined against his seat back and handed it to her. "Capacity at Crossroads is two thousand. We weren't quite there, but we also didn't have enough time to promote you and half the people who showed probably thought they were getting the previous band we had booked. Those who showed stayed. At ten a head on cover, your cut's eight large."

Eight. Thousand. Dollars.

She'd expected a decent haul compared to the gigs she normally played, but not over four times the usual amount. "It'd be eight at capacity."

"And we'd have hit capacity if we'd had the time to promote you being here. Not gonna penalize you for another band's lack of drawing power, or the fact that we couldn't maneuver fast enough to promote your show. You'll make it up to us the next time."

"The next time?"

He grinned, the roguish slant to it only emphasized by his russet beard. "Take the money, Elizabeth. Not good to plan new business until you finish the business at hand."

Easy for him to say. The last time she'd held eight thousand dollars in her hands, she'd cleared out her bank account in Florida and had promptly dropped every penny of it on the Toyota she was still driving today.

Her hand was surprisingly steady for the tremor moving beneath her skin, and yeah, feeling that much cash between her fingers was enough of a high she was a little surprised she didn't just levitate right up to the ceiling.

Tearing the flap open and ogling the cash inside was mighty enticing. Instead, she laid it on her lap, folded her hands over the top and pretended handling a big payday was the norm instead of a cause for celebration. "Okay. Old business is done. There's no way you guys don't have bands booked here for at least three months out, if not longer. The band that was slated to play here five days ago played at another club you own in Ft. Worth tonight, so I know the opening wasn't because of a last-minute cancellation. Why jump through all the hoops?"

"I told you. Temptation."

"Why?"

His gaze turned thoughtful for a second, then slid to the wide window that lined most of the interior wall. He stood and held out his hand. "I want you to look at something."

He might dress like a model, but his hands matched the rugged man underneath the clothes. Big. Strong.

Rock freaking steady.

Like the first night they met, an overpowering sense of foreboding moved through her. Only this time there was peace behind it. As if at some point in the night, she'd not only chosen to step into whatever opportunity lay ahead, but had accepted the outcome that came with it. She placed her hand in his, fully expecting it to be nothing more than a courteous gesture, but low and behold—he genuinely pulled her upright. He motioned to the window and waited for her to pass in front of him.

At nearly straight up 2 AM, the crowd below had thinned significantly, and the VIP sections that jutted out in a U shape around the second floor were totally empty, but it didn't diminish how impressive the place looked. Blue and red lighting accented brushed steel pillars, and four massive bars with mirrored back walls, soft white light and every liquor imaginable stood ready to serve with both class and efficiency. At the front of it all was the wide stage where she and her guys had spent over four hours working their tails off. Hands down, it had been one of the best nights of her life.

Axel moved in tight behind her, not quite touching but close enough his heat registered against her skin. His voice rumbled just behind one ear and was even warmer than his body. Like the comforting burn of good whiskey as it settled in your belly and equally intoxicating. "I've watched hundreds of bands from this spot, Elizabeth. Not one of them captured and worked the crowd like you did tonight."

She couldn't move. Hell, she could barely breathe with him this close, let alone process whatever he was trying to say. So, she focused on the stage instead and let herself go back to the time she'd spent on it tonight. "That's where I feel the best. Where I can be any person I want to be."

"You can be any person you want to be on or off that stage. In time you'll figure that out. At least you will if I have anything to say about it. But when you're there—when the lights are on you and the music's around you—everything that's in you comes out and touches the crowd. It's the same with the songs you write. Your heart's in every word and it resonates with the people listening. That's why you're so good at what you do."

Not a line.

Not a pitch designed to leverage her talents in someone else's best interest.

It was genuine. A heartfelt statement shared freely.

But it was still a jumping off point. An introduction into something yet unspoken. And until she knew what she was dealing with, she'd be twenty kinds of stupid if she didn't stay focused and firmly grounded in reality.

She clenched the envelope tighter and forced herself to take one step away. Then another. Only when the room's chilled air washed away his heat did she turn and meet his steady stare. "I appreciate the compliment, but you're still not telling me what all this is about."

It was hard to tell if the glint behind his eyes and his quick smile were based on appreciation for her candor, or the joy of an unspoken challenge readily accepted. "You belong on stages like that one. Better ones. Bigger ones. And I want to help you do it."

Three weeks ago, she'd expected to hear him say something just like that, but hearing the message now whacked her like a surprise two-by-four across the cheek. "You're not a promoter. You book a lot of bands at your clubs, but you don't represent any specific acts."

His smile deepened. "Been doing your homework?"

The sound that came out of her mouth was somewhere between a chuckle and a snort and was better suited to shooting the bull with her band than a professional conversation. "You live this life long enough, you learn to research everyone, or risk being worked over every which way. Promoters and managers are the worst. So, yeah. I researched you."

"And when you figured out my interest in music centered only in the venues I own, you figured it was safe to move forward when Jace called."

Okay, so it sounded a little paranoid and mercenary when he put it that way, but far be it from her to dance around the truth. "Something like that."

He nodded, sidled closer to the window so they stood side by side and slid his hands into his pockets. She bet he spent a ton of nights just like this, staring down at what he'd created and all the people that came to be a part of it. "I take it your experiences with managers haven't been the best."

"I've only had one, but yeah—I'm a little gun-shy where they're concerned."

"Care to share why?"

God, where would she start? The lies? All that had been stolen from her? The utter lack of any moral compass compounded by physical and emotional abuse? Every time her mind so much as peeked at the things she'd allowed herself to fall prey to she wanted to rip herself a new asshole. "Not really."

Either the blunt remark or her dry tone, yanked his attention squarely back to her. With his calculated measure fixated on her, she halfway expected him to pry anyway, but instead he dipped his chin as though he understood. "Fair enough. And you're right. I'm not a manager or a promoter. Not in the purest sense where bands are related. For my clubs, absolutely, but not talent." He paused only a second. Just enough to give what he still had to say added weight. "But where you're concerned, I want to be."

"Why?" It seemed a logical question. One most people with business in mind always had a ready answer for.

But not Axel. "I've got my reasons." Before she could glean any further clues behind his vague response, his gaze swept the space below then locked onto movement on the stage. The house lights weren't up yet, but there was no mistaking Jace, and he was surrounded by Rex, Tony, D and Skeet. Axel tipped his head in their direction. "I take it that's Rex?"

She was already nodding to confirm his assumption when the fact that he'd never met Rex reengaged a good chunk of her defenses. "How do you know Rex?"

"I don't. But Vic mentioned someone named Rex at The Crow, and I clocked that guy headed toward the bar as I was headed out." His lips twitched, not quite successfully holding back a grin. "I've got my faults, but lack of observation isn't one of them."

Well, that made sense—albeit in a slightly discomforting way. If he'd picked up on something that subtle, it scared the hell out of her to think how obvious her physical response to him had been. She lowered her head and clasped the thick envelope between both hands at her waist, grateful she at least had some kind of prop to help cover the awkward moment. "Right."

"Tell me about him."

Her head snapped up, the focused question and the subject matter like a softball slow pitch compared to the rest of the night. "Rex?" Even this far away, it was easy to see that her best friend was the one leading the conversation. He was good that way. Always found a way to keep things flowing and made people feel genuinely comfortable, no matter the situation. "I've known him since I was five."

"Friend of the family?"

Hardly. More like the only man in Tampa her mom didn't sleep with—though, not for lack of effort. A fact that had made her father hate Rex as much as her mom wanted to tag him. She shook her head. "Next door neighbor. Gave me my first guitar when I was sixteen and hasn't stopped supporting my music since."

"Well, then. I'd say he's made a lot of people happy getting you where you are today. Me included."

And...cue the awkward rebound to the topic at hand. She cleared her throat, studied the tips of her boots, then realized what she was doing and forced her chin back up. "Listen, I know my people skills suck, and the guys have told me a million times I'd be stupid not to let someone who knows what they're doing help us all out, but I meant it when I said the whole manager thing wasn't a good experience." Her throat swelled so thick it was hard to breathe let alone speak. "Even if I agreed to hook up with another one, I'm not so sure I wouldn't drive them bat-shit crazy inside two days. I'm opinionated as hell and stubborn to the point a lot of people hate working with me. Plus, trusting's not my strong suit, if you haven't noticed already."

"Ah, but you've got no problems stating what's on your mind and that's half the battle to makin' any relationship work." A funny look swept across his face. One of those startled yet curious expressions that hinted at surprising ideas or unexpected revelations. He glanced back at his desk, then shifted for another look at Jace. He ran his thumb along his jaw, his gaze pensive. When he spoke, his voice was still distracted. "Do you have plans for tomorrow?"

"It'll be four in the morning before I unwind enough to actually sleep and my shift at my day job starts at seven in the morning on Monday, so I hope the bulk of it's spent sleeping."

The sass pulled him out of whatever thoughts gripped him and he blasted her with a sly smile. "Aye, but you'll have to eat at some point." He meandered to his desk, pilfered a piece of paper from a side drawer and went to work scribbling something on it. With anyone else, she'd have been more interested in what was going on the paper than the person writing it, but the way he braced one hand on the desk and the fine cut of his shirt, his shoulders were twice as impressive. An ancient warrior trapped in the wrong time, but utterly comfortable wielding a pen instead of a sword.

He straightened, tossed the pen to the desk and made his way back to her with a casual sophistication that belied the predator beneath the immaculate clothes. He handed the folded note to her. "Sunday barbecue. We usually fire up the grill around four, but the food rarely stops until after seven. Bring Rex and the rest of the band with you."

His handwriting matched his bold personality, heavily slanted to the right with a masculine artistry to each letter. "Who's *we*?"

"My family."

Yeah. And here she'd thought she'd already hit her quota for surprises for the night. "Your family?"

"You think you're opinionated and stubborn?" He motioned to the paper pinched between her fingers. "You've got nothing on them. And while I'm fifty kinds of crazy for letting them have a chance at getting their hands on you, it'll prove beyond the shadow of a doubt, your brand of difficult won't phase me."

Say no.

Better yet, say you'll think about it and then run and hide for a week. Or a year.

A softer thought drifted through right behind the first two. Tentative, but twice as powerful.

Say yes.

She wanted to. Badly. If for nothing else than simply to meet the people close to such an enigmatic man. She folded the note and pressed it flush against the envelope. "I can't promise anything, but I'll talk to the guys."

"Good." He stepped out of her path and held one hand toward the door. "Come on. After that show, you've got to be tired. I'll walk you down."

"No." She winced and squeezed her eyes shut. "Sorry. I didn't mean it as bad as it sounded. It's just…" Sighing, she opened her eyes and straightened her shoulders. "I'd like to talk to the guys first. Alone." Or more to the point, to get a word in edgewise about her thoughts on Axel and managers as a whole before Axel could work his magic on them.

She might not have said as much out loud, but his grin

said he'd intuited the thought all the same. "All right. Alone it is." He guided her to the door with a hand at the small of her back, and damned if the simple touch didn't make her feel more like a princess than an uneducated nobody from the back streets of Tampa.

At the top of the stairs, he held back and watched her walk down alone, silent until she opened the door at the bottom. "Elizabeth."

At least ten feet separated them, but his low voice still danced along her skin like a soft caress. She paused with one hand braced against the door and sucked in a shaky breath before she looked back at him.

"Be brave for me. One afternoon. A simple barbecue. If you can trust me in this, you'll see you've got nothing to be afraid of. Not from me."

"I don't even know you."

"Not yet. But you will." He dipped his head. "Sleep well, lass. I'll see you tomorrow."

And with that, he was gone. Leaving her alone in the shadows…and the first ray of hope she'd felt in a very long time.

Chapter Six

One thing about Axel's family—they knew how to adapt and turn on a dime. With their *family only* policy for Haven—the ranch he shared with Jace and his mothers on the outskirts of Allen, Texas—he'd had no choice but to call first thing this morning and ask the whole damned clan to relocate their Sunday barbecue to their estate in the city. But, if things worked the way he hoped they would, the fire drill would be worth it.

With the trunk to his Shelby Cobra unpacked, he hefted two armfuls of the grocery bags his mom had packed at Haven, snagged the handle of a third and wound through the cars and motorcycles lining the massive circle drive to the double front doors. Affectionately called the Compound because it had enough rooms that all eight men he called brother could bunk down at once, the house was smack dab in the middle of one of Dallas's most elite neighborhoods and had an Italian villa vibe that belied the gritty men who paid for and used it.

He kicked the front door closed and hustled through the grand entry toward the kitchen at the back half of the house. Per usual, his mom, Sylvie, and Jace's mom, Ninette, were ruling the roost, directing anyone within shouting distance in varied prep activities. Half of his brothers were MIA, likely in the backyard prepping for the day, while Beckett, Jace and Trevor wisely stayed quiet and out of the way at the kitchen table. Their women were moving this way and that with a practiced cadence that would've astounded a covert mastermind. He set the bags on the kitchen island. "This is the last of 'em."

Sylvie finished putting something into the fridge, spun to the island and peeked in each of the bags. "Jesus, Mary and Joseph, it's not here."

"What's not here?"

"The sugar." Ninette shot a wry smirk over her shoulder from the sink. "You hurried us out of the house so fast, she forgot it and you know how your mother feels about a meal without dessert."

"It's a goddamn crime," Jace snickered from the kitchen table.

Gabe giggled like a little girl, which considering how shy and reserved she'd been when Zeke first met her was an absolute joy to hear. She'd come a long way in the three years since they'd met—due in no small part to his family's support. "It *is* a goddamn crime. She promised me homemade chocolate chip cookies today."

Vivienne shut the pantry, spun around and eyeballed Axel. "And what kind of house doesn't have basic sugar stocked in it?"

"The kind that's more focused on liquor and beer than cookies," Beckett quipped from beside Jace.

Gia moved in next to him, sat a stack of paper plates and Solo cups in the center of the table and whacked him on the shoulder without missing a beat. "Don't be an asshole. Go get some sugar."

"Why me?"

Her smile was sugar sweet, but the sass behind her answer was killer hot. "Because I like chocolate chip cookies, too, and you love it when I'm in a friendly mood."

One second and what had been a relaxed moment between them went super-charged.

Fucking newlyweds.

"I'll get the sugar," Axel grumbled and turned back for the entry.

"Oh, no you don't." Ninette might have couched her words with playfulness, but there was an edge underneath them that stopped him cold before he'd gotten a third step in. "If you think you're skippin' out without explaining why we ended up in a situation that made us forget sugar in the first place, you're sadly mistaken." He turned in time to see her wave Beckett toward the front of the house. "Beckett, you go. And make sure Knox, Danny and Ivan didn't get sidetracked playing with Mary and Levi instead of setting up the grills."

Beckett might have been six-foot-four and able to obliterate physical threats in hand-to-hand, but when Ninette Kennedy gave an order, even a man like him got his ass in gear and did what he was told. He frowned at Axel and pushed back from the table. "Yes, ma'am."

Ninette turned her resolute attention back to Axel.

Sylvie did the same, the mirrored action so uncannily timed, it was like they'd practiced in advance. "So? Who's the guest that's got you pulling strings you never grab onto."

"I'm not pulling any strings. Just making the most of an afternoon and doing some business while I'm at it."

"Brother, I can count on one hand the number of times you've intervened in family plans and still have five fingers left over," Trevor said. "What gives?"

Beckett paused in the doorway, clearly more interested in the answer than making a last-minute run to the store.

Damned busybodies. He'd known his family staying the hell out of his business was a long shot, but he hadn't realized they'd dig in this early. He shifted his focus to Jace, more comfortable with his best friend's stare than all the others that had him in their crosshairs.

Jace huffed out a low chuckled. "I'll give you one thing. When you go, you go big."

Ninette volleyed her attention between the two of them the same way she used to when she was trying to figure out which one of them had been up to no good when they were little. She ended on Jace. "You know what's going on and didn't say anything on the ride over?"

Jace cocked an eyebrow at Axel. One of those *You gonna pull your head out of your ass, or dig the hole deeper* looks.

Natalie peeked up from the cutting board. "Mmmm. The plot thickens."

"There's no bloody plot." Axel swept them all with one of the grumpy looks that always made his bartenders and waitresses keep their distance and started unpacking the grocery bags. Better that than stand stock still and let the lot of them psychoanalyze things. "I told you, it's business. Got a new venture I want to focus on and the lass is a wee bit gun-shy."

Darya's head whipped up, the lettuce she was working on prepping for the hamburgers forgotten in a second. "The lass?"

Vivienne sidled up next to Darya and slid a plastic bag full of tomatoes and onions in front of her. Her words were coy, but the knowing look she aimed at him beneath her lashes said Jace had already clued her into more details than Axel was comfortable with her knowing. "And serious enough he needs family for reinforcements. How interesting."

His mother lost all interest in anything to do with the goings-on in the kitchen and just stared at him. A deep, penetrating look that left him feeling like he was two years old all over again.

Gia wasn't inclined to stay nearly as silent. "And this business venture…does she have a name?"

"It's Lizzy Hemming." He zeroed in on his mother who still seemed shocked speechless. "And it's really a business venture, so don't go surfing online for wedding cake recipes or ordering baby booties."

"Yet," Trevor chimed in with a knowing look.

"Yer all aff yer bloody heids." Axel zeroed in on Jace. "Fuckin' tell 'em what the hell's goin' on."

As evil smiles went, Jace's was about as wicked as they got. On the bright side, he didn't leave Axel's ass hanging out in the wind. "He's telling you the truth. She and her band played at Crossroads last night. Totally killed it."

"That's nothing new," Beckett said, still loitering for the real lowdown behind him. "You book gigs all the time."

"Yeah, but this one he's takin' an interest in more than regular bookings," Jace said.

Ninette's drawl was somewhere between mischief and pure surprise. "Reeeally? How far *beyond* are we talking?"

Vivienne and Jace both watched him. Waiting.

He didn't dare look at his mother when he shared the rest, but chose instead to answer Ninette directly. "I told her I want to manage her. See if I can't use my connections and get a little deeper into the music business."

Silence settled on the room in a second.

The easier path would've probably been to leave things where they stood and let his family fill in the blanks with whatever they wanted, but the easy path was usually for shit. His best chance for showing Lizzy what kind of man he was to introduce her to the people he surrounded himself with, and the best way to make sure they showed her their *real* selves was to come clean. Or mostly clean. "She's gifted. The whole package. With the right support, she could have the music industry by the balls, but she's been chewed up and spit out once already. Doesn't know who to trust." He shrugged. "I figured the best way to show her what trust looks like was to bring her here."

More quiet. Enough of the stuff he thought he'd choke on it.

"Well, then." Shocked or not, Sylvie McKee wasn't one to leave her boy hanging in an awkward moment. She smoothed out the apron she'd likely donned all of two seconds after hitting the kitchen and hustled to the pantry. "If my boy wants to take on something or someone new, then he'll do it with me behind him. Beckett, get me that sugar."

"Yes, ma'am." Beckett grinned at Axel. "Think I'll stop outside and check on the rest of the guys before I go, though. If we're on a mission, gotta make sure all the troops are geared up."

The doorbell rang.

The women all looked from one to the other with near giddy expressions.

Trevor snickered. "Better hurry. Looks like it's showtime."

A glance at his watch showed 4:05 PM. A whole lot earlier than he'd thought she'd show given how skittish she'd been last night. Either she'd had a serious revelation overnight, or her band had worked her over and convinced her to at least listen to what he had to say. Then again, it could just be a neighborhood kid selling something, too.

"Bloody hell." Admonishing the lot of them wouldn't do any good, so he turned for the entry and tried to ignore the swell of conversation that kicked in the second he cleared the room. His family meant well. Down to his bones, he knew that was the truth, and in every other situation that had incorporated family, he'd trusted them without doubt. But something about Lizzy and his clan converging was tantamount to bungee jumping off a mile-high bridge—either it was gonna be a thrill ride to top all other experiences, or he was gonna end up roadkill.

He jerked the door open a little harder than he'd meant to—and shot from irritated and jumpy, to tongue-tied and greedy inside a second. The band was there. That Rex guy, too. But none of them mattered. Not with Lizzy standing front and center in a pair of cutoff jeans so old they were probably soft as cotton and a vintage Stone Temple Pilots concert tank. Her killer body on prime display wasn't a shock—not with the outfits she wore on stage. But seeing her in something so soft and casual threw him for a helluva loop. And fucking A—seeing her in a pair of delicate tan sandals with bubble gum pink toenails instead of stilettos or high-heeled boots? Sexiest. Fucking. Thing. Ever.

"When you said *barbecue*," Lizzy said, "I expected grills and music in a somewhat regular neighborhood.

Not mansions on prime Dallas real estate." She jerked her head toward the muscle cars, trucks and motorcycles lining the circle drive. "If I hadn't seen all of those out front, I'd have thought we were in the wrong place."

The man he'd come to recognize from research and pictures stepped forward and offered his hand. "Only reason we're at the front door instead of circling back to change clothes is Lizzy didn't drive. I'm Rex."

Ignoring the whole bunch and indulging in only Lizzy was tempting as hell, but it probably wouldn't do much to further his trustworthy image. He shook Rex's hand. "Axel McKee." From there he made the rounds and traded handshakes with the rest of the men. "Glad you guys could make it. We've got a lot of food and a whole afternoon to enjoy it."

He was just finishing up the welcome when the slap of bare feet against the living room's wood floors and Levi's excited voice echoed off the high ceilings. "Are they here?"

Mary's sweet giggle followed right behind it.

Axel moved out of the doorway and waved his guests through the front door just as the two little hooligans rounded into the entry and ground to a halt right in front of Lizzy, both of them breathing hard from their sprint indoors.

"Hey!" Levi said, thrusting his hand out. "I'm Levi. Dad says you're a rock singer and Uncle Axel's gonna make you famous."

Lizzy's eyes got wide as dinner plates and the men behind her all chuckled, but she went with the flow and shook the hand Levi offered. "I'm Lizzy. And yeah, I'm a singer, but I'm not sure about the famous part."

Trevor, Knox and Ivan moseyed into the entry, all

three of them sporting shit-eating grins, which meant the family grapevine hadn't just been activated, but a plan to win Lizzy over hatched in the time it'd taken him to answer the front door.

Axel shot the three of them a warning look then zeroed in on Levi. "Lad, we're gonna have to talk about your timing and execution. You can't just bowl a woman over the second you meet her. You also didn't introduce Mary."

Never one to take correction in a bad way, Levi smiled huge, squared his shoulders and wrapped an arm around Mary's shoulders. At ten and six years old respectively, their height difference was barely more than a foot, but the way Mary leaned into Levi spoke volumes as to how tightly they'd bonded in the last two years. "Right, this is my cousin, Mary. She's a pretty singer, too, but she doesn't play guitar like I do."

The odd introduction made Mary frown up at Levi, and the shyness that had kept her quiet so far got pushed out in the wake of blossoming female challenge. "Not yet, but I will. Uncle Axel said he'd teach me, too, when my hands get bigger."

Lizzy's head whipped to Axel, shock and a little awe marking her face. "You play?"

Before he could answer, Levi kicked in. "Plays *and* sings. But he won't do it outside family. Dad says it's 'cause he's stubborn."

Trevor chuckled and dipped his chin. "Son, one of these days we're gonna have to talk about filters."

The inevitable *why* was poised on Levi's lips, but Axel intervened before the lad could voice it. "Everyone, these are my brothers Trevor, Ivan and Knox." He faced the men gathered around Lizzy and finished off the introductions. "Lizzy you've already figured out, but this is her friend Rex, her bass player, Dewayne, guitar player, Jacob—or Skeet, if you don't go by formalities—and drummer, Tony."

The hi-how-are-yas and obligatory handshakes got the band out from the semicircle they'd kept around Lizzy and gave him the chance to move in closer. Fortunately, his brothers knew a thing or two about strategic maneuvers and Knox engaged to dissipate the crowd a little further. He waved Levi and Mary toward the back of the house. "How about you two help us give the guys a tour of the backyard? Maybe earn that twenty bucks you talked me into giving you by taking drink orders."

Levi frowned and back-and-forthed a look between Knox and Lizzy. "But I wanna talk about guitars with Lizzy."

"Polite first," Trevor said, cocking one expectant eyebrow in a way that would make his own father proud, "questions later." He glanced up at Axel. "Besides, we wanna give your uncle a minute to talk business with Lizzy."

Clearly on board with that idea, Skeet stepped up and focused on Levi. "You know, I'm no slouch in the guitar department. You help me figure out where the beer's stocked and I'll talk shop all afternoon long."

Rex, Dewayne and Tony agreed with a mix of head nods and yeses.

Levi capitulated in a heartbeat with a whole new level of enthusiasm. "Deal!" He grabbed Mary's hand, took off toward the living room and motioned everyone to follow him. "Come on. The backyard's this way. My uncles are picky, so they've got all kinds of beer, but if you want stuff like Uncle Axel drinks, someone else will have to get it. Mom doesn't like me gettin' in the hooch."

Laughter swelled in the wake of their retreat and swallowed up whatever Levi said next.

"They're cute kids." As soon as Lizzy's words died off, she seemed to realize it was only her left in the entry and standing well within biting distance of the big bad wolf. She rubbed her palms on her hips and took a hesitant step away. "Unless you've got a wildly interesting family tree, I take it they're brothers by choice like Jace?"

Not snatching her wrist and tugging her right back where she'd been took every ounce of self-control he had. "That's a pretty specific way to put it. Either you're perceptive as hell, or Jace got awfully talkative with you yesterday."

A sheepish smile crooked one side of her mouth. "He might have used the word *brother* in relation to you and piqued my curiosity. Though, in his defense, I'm prone to asking lots of questions."

Questions were good. It marked at least a modicum of interest, even if it was simple curiosity. God knew he'd had enough questions of his own circling his head for the last six months, most of them still left unanswered. "Lass, you can ask me or any of my brothers anything you want if it means you're talking."

"Yeah?" Her grin turned mischievous. "How about we start with the fact that you're a musician?"

"What about it?"

Her smile slipped just a fraction, but the sincerity behind her gaze deepened. "You said you love music. If you can make it, why get other people on stage when you could be there?"

"You're assuming I've got talent. Levi said I played, not that I played well."

"He said you sing, too."

The all too familiar stab that came with thoughts of music and the passion he'd set aside years ago pressed hard behind his sternum. He held himself still to mask the pain, but his voice still came out a shade lower. "Aye, that, too."

"So why back other bands when you could promote yourself?"

"I don't want to back other bands, Elizabeth. I want to back *you*." He inched a step closer, to which she held surprisingly still. "And again, you've not heard a note out of me. For all you know, I can strum three chords and sing like a cat stuck in a lake."

"I somehow doubt that." She cocked her head, her gaze scanning his face like she could see right past all the bullshit excuses he'd cemented into place through the years. "I look at you and I doubt there's anything in this world you don't achieve once you've set a mind to do it."

She was right on that score. And damned if her unintentional vote of confidence hadn't just served up the perfect opportunity to let her know exactly where his head was at. He pushed his luck and pressed a little closer, the distance between them just a hair's breath beyond what most would consider uncomfortable. Without the heels to put them at a closer height, she had to tilt her head back to hold his gaze, and with the brilliant sun beaming through the entry's windows, her blue eyes matched the skies outside.

He kept his hands to himself, though it was difficult as hell with her creamy skin exposed by the tank and so much toned muscle underneath. "It's good you see that in me, Elizabeth, because I've got a mind to make things happen for you. And for us."

Chapter Seven

Us.

Such a tiny word. But spoken in Axel's low, whiskey-warm voice, it coiled around Lizzy with all the warmth and heat of a velvet rope. A promise and a claim that wriggled tiny fissures through all the warnings and lectures she'd fortified her resolve with since last night.

Lean in.

Just a little.

See what he feels like.

It would be so easy. A simple shift of her weight to encourage him. To bring her close enough to feel his heat like she had last night. Maybe this time feel his broad chest against hers and see if his strong arms felt as good around her as her imagination painted.

Don't screw this up, Lizzy.

You know how you are. How you twist things up and let people in you shouldn't.

Keep your shit in check.

She focused on his sternum. On the navy blue tee and the muscles displayed underneath. It was the most casual she'd ever seen him, the jeans he'd paired with them faded enough to imply he wore them all the time, but somehow, he still made the combination look like a designer had put them together. "Business and personal don't mix."

Approaching footsteps sounded from somewhere behind her, their weight lighter and unhurried. A feminine voice drifted in along with them, a much thicker brogue weighting each word. "Axel McKee, don't tell me you've cornered the lass before ye've even had the decency to introduce her to everyone."

Axel grinned and lowered his voice. "They do mix, Elizabeth. And I've got a host of examples in the backyard to prove it. But for now, I suggest you brace yourself and get ready for a wild ride."

The comment made zero sense, but before she could dig in and get any clarification, he splayed one hand at the small of her back and turned her toward a woman approaching from the massive living room beyond. At no more than five-two or five-three, she was petite compared to Lizzy, but the spunky way she carried herself said her personality was bigger than life. Her hair barely reached her shoulders and was styled in a way that matched her overall vibe—an edgy bob with a color that made her think of dark cherries.

"So!" The woman finished drying her hands on a kitchen towel and slung it over one shoulder as she stopped in front of them. The accent might have been her first clue to a relationship to Axel, but the smile she aimed up at Lizzy made the blood connection indisputable. "I hear we've got a celebrity joinin' us today." She held out her hand. "I'm Axel's mother, Sylvie McKee."

His mother?

No freakin' way. The woman standing in front of her couldn't be old enough to have a man Axel's age for a son. And holy crap—talk about your awkward situations. Had she seen Lizzy ogling Axel on the way in?

"I think your son and his clubs are a bigger thing than I am." Lizzy shook the hand offered. "I'm Lizzy Hemming."

"Elizabeth," Axel corrected, smoothing his hand up the length of her spine until it rested at the back of her neck. "And the celebrity status is just a matter of time. Ma knows I've got good taste."

Not releasing Lizzy's hand, Sylvie noted Axel's familiar touch at the back of Lizzy's neck, then his position beside her. The open curiosity on her beautiful features softened and a tender, knowing smile curved her lips. "Aye. My boy's got exceptional taste." She hesitated all of a second as if taking in the moment and storing it away some place sacred, then tugged Lizzy forward so she could take Axel's place. "Well, come on, then. Let's get you introduced to the saner half of the bunch."

"Saner's debatable," Axel said following behind them. While his accent hadn't been overly prominent in most of their conversations, it seemed to thicken with his mother's presence. "Though, I will give ye you're the better looking half."

"Better looking, smarter and saner," Sylvie said not missing a beat.

The banter kept up between them, a playful cadence that spoke of respect and love the likes most people weren't lucky enough to have. The kind she had with her band and Rex, only at a much deeper level.

She soaked it up. Let the flow of it unplug all the tension that had gripped her since she'd opened her eyes this morning and simply took in her surroundings. Like the entry, the living room they meandered through had crazy high ceilings, those fancy wood floors that looked like they'd been hand carved and an overall Italian villa décor that screamed of money.

But the kitchen.

Wow.

Lots of granite, stainless-steel everything, platters loaded up with snacks and condiments, bowls mounded high with chips and enough room for a team of five-star chefs to work. Or in this case, a team of seven women, every one of which claimed a unique beauty—and had their focus squarely aimed on Lizzy.

The temptation to spin and hightail it right back out the way she'd come in nearly knocked her over. Put her in front of a huge crowd with a guitar and a microphone and she was good to go. But a room full of women with no known commonalities to talk about? Yeah, that was pure torture.

Before she could come up with some excuse to escape to the backyard with the guys, Sylvie pulled her right into the thick of it, aiming first for a woman who was nearly as tall as Lizzy and had a waterfall of silvery gray hair well past her shoulders. Shutting off the kitchen sink, the woman faced Lizzy and smiled. While she clearly had a few years on the other women in the room, her classic features and startling blue eyes could have landed her on the cover of any magazine.

"Ninnie," Sylvie said, "this is Axel's Elizabeth."

Axel's Elizabeth? Lizzy scanned the room and found Axel with one shoulder leaned against the arched kitchen entrance, his arms crossed and an ornery grin on his face.

He winked.

Lizzy scowled back at him then forced her attention back to the gorgeous woman. "Actually, I go by Lizzy."

The woman smiled like she was thoroughly enjoying the undercurrents zinging between Lizzy and Axel. "I'm Ninette, Jace's mom." She flanked Lizzy's free side and motioned to three other women who seemed equally entertained by the unspoken byplay—one with long brown hair with enough curls to make most women jealous, a dirty blonde who rocked the Abercrombie look and a glamorous brunette. All three of them had a variety of beverages in front of them and appeared to be settled in for the long haul. "That's Vivienne, Jace's wife, Gabe, who's married to Zeke, and Gia, who just tied the knot with Beckett."

"Zeke pushes the Gabrielle thing with Gabe, too." Sylvie pried the lid off a plasticware container and uncovered what Lizzy would bet last night's income were homemade lemon bars. "If you ask me, it's adorable."

Gabe chuckled and snagged a chip out of a nearly overflowing bowl of Doritos in front of her. "Adorable unless he's trying to wiggle out of something."

Another brunette at the kitchen island snickered and stirred something in a huge metal bowl. "Wiggle you out of your panties, most likely." She punctuated the statement with a sharp tap of her spoon on the side of the bowl, sat it on the granite countertop and held out her hand to Lizzy. "I'm Natalie. It sounded like you already met my son, Levi, and my husband, Trevor." As soon as Lizzy released her hand she motioned to the drop-dead beautiful woman with long blonde hair as pale as moonlight beside her. "This is Knox's wife, Darya."

"It's a pleasure to meet you," Darya said. Perched on the edge of a stool with a wine glass casually cupped in her palm, she seemed perfectly suited for a photo shoot. Her Russian accent only added to her amazing looks.

She dipped her head toward the wide window overlooking the backyard and the cluster of men milling poolside. "Those are the men in your band?"

Axel watched her, a keenness settling behind his gaze that made it hard to focus and not fidget. "Yeah, mostly."

"Mostly?" Natalie asked.

"Well, Rex isn't in the band. He's more like family."

Gia shifted in her chair enough to get a better look. "Which one is he?"

"The tall one with the gray hair."

"Mmmm," Ninette hummed beside her. "The Sam Elliott lookalike."

"Who's Sam Elliott?" Vivienne asked.

"An actor," Darya answered. "Knox and I watched him in *Roadhouse* a few weeks ago."

"Oh, I loved him in that movie." Sylvie leaned one hip on the island, cocked her head and studied Rex the way a woman would study a tempting outfit. "He does have that look about him."

"Easy, killer." Axel pushed off his place in the doorway and sidled farther into the room. "The goal's to let Elizabeth see what kind of people we are. Not give you more boy toys to chase."

"Oh, Sylvie's not getting that one," Ninette drawled, still zeroed in on Rex. "I call dibs." She frowned and shifted her attention to Axel. "And why are you still here?" She shooed him toward the back door. "Go. Mingle with the men, beat your chest and make sure Jace doesn't burn the hamburgers while you're at it."

Vivienne toyed with the stem of her wine glass. "Um, hate to break it to you, but Jace isn't working the grill."

"Yeah, Beckett isn't either," Gia added, but shot a knowing look at Darya.

"Ah, shite," Axel said, clearly picking up on whatever unspoken message had been delivered and striding toward the sliding backdoor. "Knox'll have us all gnawin' on beef jerky." The second the glass slid open, the soft strains of alternative music and low masculine voices swept into the room. He paused halfway out and volleyed a semi-stern look between Sylvie and Ninette. "You two, play nice."

"We always play nice," Ninette said.

"She'll be safe as a babe in her mother's arms," Sylvie added.

Axel grunted, but there was a pleased glint behind his eyes to go with it. His gaze shifted to Lizzy. "Tell me what you want to drink, lass, and I'll see you get it."

A shot of tequila would be good.

Or better yet a bottle of it, because from the curious and mischievous expressions on the women around her she was going to need some serious fortification, and she'd never been a wine girl.

She spied some kind of fancy longneck in front of Gabe and figured, what the hell. "You got any Bud Light?"

"I think I can swing that." He grinned like he'd had a direct line to her thoughts and shot her another one of those winks she felt in places she shouldn't. "The girls will take good care of you."

With that, he was gone, leaving her alone in a sea full of *Oh, my God, how do I do this?*

Not waiting even a beat, Ninette backed against the counter next to the massive stove, anchored her hands on the edge of it and grinned huge. "So, now that we're alone...tell me about your hottie friend, Rex."

"Oh, my God, Ninette," Vivienne said. "You're gonna

run her off before she can catch her breath. Are you purposely trying to make sure Axel kills us?" She snagged her wine glass off the table and motioned Lizzy toward an empty seat at the table. "How about you take a load off and tell us how you got started playing music? Jace says you're phenomenal on stage."

Lizzy glanced at Natalie still stirring whatever was in the bowl and Sylvie just finishing stacking lemon bars on a plate. "You sure you don't need some prep help?"

Like maybe running an errand?

Or blending into the background so you don't make an ass out of yourself?

"Oh, that's already done, lass." Sylvie bustled to the far counter and stacked the empty tub with a row of others already lined up. "We had most of it done last night. Natalie's just finishing up the ambrosia."

"Yeah, but don't tell the guys we're not slaving away," Gabe said. "Half the reason we're able to keep them outside is they're afraid we'll put 'em to work if they're in here." A knowing look moved across her face and she dipped her head toward the chair Vivienne had indicated. "Seriously. It's okay. We only give the guys a hard time."

Gia let loose an unladylike sound that was utterly incongruous with her Southern Belle perfect appearance. "Um, I seem to recall every single one of you ganging up and dragging me to a cooking lesson."

"Oh, that was fun and you know it." Either Ninette sensed Lizzy's hesitancy, or she was just as no-nonsense and to the point as her son, because she intervened, led Lizzy to the table and took the last open seat next to her. "So, tell us. How'd you end up on stage?"

Lizzy shrugged and settled into her own seat. "Rex

gave me a guitar when I was little, taught me how to play and things just kind of…took off."

"Do you write your own music?" Darya asked.

"Not at first," Lizzy said. "I played covers in book-stores and parks and stuff until I was twenty-one. Then I figured out I needed my own music to get any real trac-tion. Turns out, I enjoyed doing that, too."

"That's how Axel was." Sylvie turned from the pantry and shut the door behind her. "Begged and pleaded for a guitar he'd seen in a pawn shop until I gave in. Took to it like a fish to water and wrote some of the prettiest songs I've ever heard."

"Whoa, boy," Ninette murmured. "Here we go…"

Sylvie zeroed in on Ninette. "What? Lizzy likes music and so does Axel. I'm just commenting on the common-ality. Plus, the boy sings like a damned angel."

Natalie spooned the last of the ambrosia into a clear glass bowl. "Not sure you can put *angel* and *Axel* in the same sentence, but I have to admit, hearing him at Christ-mas shocked the socks right off me."

"Exactly," Sylvie said. "I don't give a damn if he doesn't get up on stage like Elizabeth, but to keep his gifts under wraps is a bloody shame."

"I don't get it," Lizzy said. "Why'd he quit?"

The room got scary quiet, and Ninette and Sylvie eyed each other with the focus of two people who didn't need words to communicate. Sylvie pinched her lips together like it was all she could do not to forge into more dan-gerous territory, then sighed and padded toward Lizzy. "The details aren't pretty. Nothin' he'd want me to tell ye yer first day with us seein' as he wants to make a good impression on ye, so I won't.

"But I will tell you this." She stopped right beside

Lizzy's chair and motioned to the room around her. "Everything you see here—all the security and comfort Ninnie and I have today—came because our boys wanted us to have an easier life. The rest of the lads do the same for their women so none of us ever have to worry about wanting or needing a thing."

"I'm not sure I understand how that ties with music."

"Because making music was his dream. Playing it. Writing it. Singing. The whole thing. But he gave it all up to keep me safe. That's the kind of man my boy is. The kind of men they all are." She smiled a wistful smile and rested her hand on Lizzy's shoulder. "And from what I see, Elizabeth, Axel's decided to take care of you, too."

Chairs creaked from people shifting in their seats and the muted laughter of Levi and Mary outside seemed discordant in the thick silence.

Vivienne picked up her wine glass and cleared her throat. "Well, that wasn't an awkward and intense overshare for the new girl on her first day, or anything."

Gabe snickered and raised her fancy beer in salute. "Don't worry. You'll get used to it."

Lizzy wasn't so sure about that. Granted, she didn't have a heck of a lot of time under her belt hanging with women in general, but these ladies were either the most laid-back, welcoming and transparent women on the planet, or they'd sucked back a lot of booze before she got here. "Not sure there's anything to get used to. Axel's just a possible business connection."

Gia chuckled and the sound that came out of Ninette was almost a dead ringer for the unladylike snorts Lizzy always made around the guys.

"Mmm hmmm," Natalie said. "We all said, 'Just business,' once upon a time."

"Oh, don't tease her." Ninette reclined back in her chair and crossed one tanned leg over the other. "She'll figure it out soon enough."

Since Vivienne seemed to be the most level-headed of the bunch, Lizzy focused on her. "Figure what out?"

Vivienne smiled, a gleam in her eyes that seemed almost contagious in this house. "Out of all the men you've met today, there's not one of them that wouldn't relocate mountains or take hostages if they thought it would make us happy. And you, whether you realize it or not, appear to have caught the attention of one very determined Axel McKee." She lifted her glass in a mock toast. "Or, said more succinctly, 'Welcome to the family.'"

Chapter Eight

Talk about a long game. Their whole damned life, Axel and Jace had tackled some hellacious projects together, but Axel had a feeling not a one of them was going to be as challenging as winning Lizzy's trust.

Seated snuggly between Lizzy's thighs on the edge of a poolside lounger, Mary squealed at successfully strumming another chord and beamed a huge smile up at her mentor over one shoulder. The body of the classic Martin D-28 he'd brought down from his room covered all of her little torso and the only way she'd managed the solid sound with the thick neck was Lizzy helping her press the strings against the frets, but she'd been in hog heaven for well over half an hour. Levi was right there with them, plunked down at the end of another lounger and fixated on Lizzy's every word.

Kicked back in swim trunks and nursing a Bohemia Weiss, Zeke watched the trio from their haphazard huddle in the outdoor living area with the same languid approval as all the rest of his brothers. "I'm surprised the band cut out when they did."

"No shit," Beckett said. "Between the amount of food we had and the way the moms doted on them, I thought they'd be more inclined to spend the night."

Jace shook his head and lifted his Scotch off the armrest of his own chair. "Nope, they did it on purpose."

Not much could've drawn his attention from Lizzy working with the kids, but that little tidbit sure as shit did. "I thought Skeet said they had to help a buddy move." At least that's what Skeet had said in between the main course and dessert when he'd casually asked Axel if he could drop Lizzy at home later.

"Yeah, I'd have bought that line of shit, too, if I hadn't overheard the four of them congregated in the back hallway when I went to get Viv a jacket out of my room."

"Well, that's convenient." Knox snagged his own beer and waggled his eyebrows at Axel. "Sounds like you've got partners in crime."

He didn't doubt it. The mere fact that Lizzy had shown at all today was likely in part to all four of them strongarming her all the way here. Plus, Skeet had been full of questions about what kind of ideas Axel had for getting Lizzy attention, which said they were more for the idea of him stepping in than against it. "Rex was in on it, too?"

"Yep. He made Skeet be the one who reached out to you out of loyalty for Lizzy, but they know what you're offering's a good deal for her."

"A stranger off the street would know this was a good thing for her," Trevor added. "The moms might have doted on her crew, but I think the women have made it their sole mission to find a way to the heart of her."

Ivan tipped his head toward his daughter. "From the looks of that, I'd say Mary's gettin' there the quickest."

Danny huffed out a chuckle. "That kid's got every damned one of us wrapped around her little pinky. No way Lizzy's not gonna fall for her, too."

He was right. In the time since he'd left Elizabeth with

the women, he'd watched her struggle to make sense of his family's dynamic. How she'd watched every person with avid curiosity during the banter at dinner. How her gaze had lingered on each of his brothers in the tender moments they showed their wives. The wistful look on her face when he'd caught her watching him hug his mother.

But the second the kids had gotten her alone after her crew left? Yeah, she'd totally melted. Completely given up the armor and let the vulnerability he'd glimpsed in those early music clips shine through.

He wanted that openness aimed at him.

Wanted it in a way he'd never wanted anything else. Not even a career in music. Which was insane given he'd done nothing more than steal a casual touch here or there all damned night long.

Definitely a long game.

A stealthy no-holds-barred game of cat and mouse that would likely have him climbing the goddamn walls before he finally claimed a kiss.

Beckett's voice cut through his thoughts. "Oh, he's totally fucked."

Axel rattled what was left of the ice in his Scotch and scanned the rest of his brothers. "Who's fucked?"

Jace snickered and kicked his feet up on the wicker coffee table. "Brother, we've been talkin' to you for five minutes and you didn't hear a word we said."

"I was thinkin'."

Knox's chuckle was as evil as they got. "Oh, we know."

"So, when's rally?" Trevor said.

Okay, maybe he had been a little out of it if he'd missed a discussion that required rally. "Come again?"

Beckett dipped his head toward Lizzy. "The way

you're lookin' at her, I'm thinking there's more to what's going on than just business and, frankly, I've lived for the day you actually fall and claim a woman."

"Amen," Knox added.

A claim.

It was odd hearing it in reference to him. And oddly lacking, too. For months Lizzy had been a growing presence in his thoughts. A constant focus that underlined every other activity. A thought or need he couldn't quite shake. Hell, if anything, she'd been the one to claim him the first time he'd seen her.

But taking this step was a huge risk. A deal that might well be beyond his capacity to close.

Lizzy smiled down at something Mary said and smoothed her hand in a comforting stroke down the back of Mary's head. Protective. Patient. Tender.

What would she be like with her own kids?

With his *kids?*

The thoughts thunderbolted through him, rattling every fear and challenging them at the same time.

He kept his gaze on Lizzy, an anchor as the startling truth bubbled up. His voice was low enough it rumbled in through his chest, but with every word that itchy sensation that had driven him nuts for months finally began to settle. "Everyone's here. Don't need a basement and a gavel to state she's mine."

No one moved a muscle. Hell, it was probably the quietest he'd ever heard them in his whole life. The mid-June night pressed soft around him, the wind still as if it was just as shocked as his brothers.

"Does she know that yet?" Jace said.

No way in hell. Lizzy Hemming might be a badass on

stage with a take-no-prisoners approach to life, but he wouldn't win her by beating her over the head.

No, his Elizabeth needed time. A slow burn and build up to take a risk the likes of what he had in mind.

And they were going to start tonight, which meant it was time to wrap up Mary and Levi's lesson and get some alone time with his woman.

He stood and set his empty tumbler on the coffee table. "Not yet, and odds are good she'll fight me every step of the way." He straightened and locked eyes with Jace. "But I'll wage war to make it happen. And I'll win."

Chapter Nine

Lizzy couldn't decide what was crazier—the fact that the guys all thought she'd bought their excuse about having to bail to help a friend move, or that she'd willingly given up escaping along with them.

Oh, don't bullshit yourself, Lizzy. You wanted to stay.

She bit back a sigh and scowled out the passenger window of Axel's fully restored Mustang Shelby. Okay, so yeah. She'd wanted to stay. Wanted to watch just a little more of the interactions with Axel's family and soak up the laid-back atmosphere a little longer.

And see if Axel would touch you again.

This time she did sigh and shifted in her seat, the whole tough love routine from her inner hussy about as comfortable as a tack-lined seat cover.

Axel's rich voice blended with the soft strains of Angus & Julia Stone's "Draw Your Swords." "Either my driving's making you uneasy, or the wrestling in your head's overtakin' your body." He glanced at Lizzy long enough to zing her with those striking green eyes of his, the color more accented by the streetlights lining the road. "You want to talk about it?"

"Your family's nice."

Axel chuckled. "They are, and they seemed to think

well of you, too, but I'm not thinking my family's what's got you so jumpy you need a second seat belt to hold you in." He steered them to the exit lane, downshifted, then covered one fisted hand in her lap. "Breathe."

One touch.

Not too bold, but not soft either. Just a comforting connection thick with warmth and confidence, there and gone again too fast as he shifted gears and turned the corner that led to her apartment complex.

But it worked.

Quieted her rioting thoughts and left her body poised and focused on only the moment at hand.

Why?

How could someone she barely knew impact her so keenly with a simple word and a casual touch? She didn't want to want someone so close. To crave the sound of their voice. The feel of their eyes on her and the anticipation of physical contact. She'd embraced that craving before and look what it had gotten her. Lost and broken. Trapped in a sick and twisted place that had taken her months to resurface from.

But here she was again, foolishly dancing on the edge of temptation and entertaining foolish risks.

Outside, the storefronts, houses and complexes painted a much different vibe than the posh neighborhood where she'd spent her afternoon. And yet, Axel seemed unaffected by the scenery. Utterly comfortable as he pulled into the parking lot filled with cars and trucks that made his look like a Rolls-Royce in comparison.

She pointed to the building at the farthest corner of the lot, suddenly way more sensitive to how plain and unappealing the structure looked. "That one's mine."

He dipped his head in acknowledgment and whipped his hot rod into a vacant slot right up front.

As soon as he put the shifter in neutral and yanked the brake, she went for the door handle.

"Keep your hands in your lap, Elizabeth." Volume-wise, his voice was on par with the muted rumble of the Shelby's engine, but pure steel punctuated every word.

"Excuse me?"

His lips twitched, and while he managed to keep his smile in check, the humor he obviously fought was right there in his eyes. "I opened the door for you when you got in. I'll open it for you when you get out."

Not waiting for a response, he killed the engine and got out. Which was good because it took the time between then and when he made it to her side of the car for her brain to scramble its way out of dumbfounded and rally a defense.

"You're kind of bossy," she said the second the heavy door swung open.

He chuckled and held out his hand. "More so than you know. But it won't ever be for anything other than your safety." He pulled her to her feet, keeping his body within inches of hers, swung the car door shut, then murmured low beside her ear. "Or to give you pleasure."

Holy hell.

The shiver that snaked through her on the heels of that thought was so potent it nearly knocked her off balance—a considerable thing considering she'd forgone heels for once and had only dared the one beer before dinner.

Axel must have noted it, too, because he steadied her with a hand at her hip. His warm breath whispered against the tender skin behind her ear. "Easy, pet."

Another tremor. This one dragging her eyes shut on a

nearly silent sigh as the odd endearment moved through her. Which was insane because no woman should like being called such a thing. Let alone feel pleasure from it.

Well, you *certainly did.*

And it's not much of a surprise is it? Not for a little slut like you.

Her eyes snapped open, shrill sound of her mother's voice ringing in her head. She cleared her throat and forced herself to put an arm's length between them. "I'm not a pet. I'm not Elizabeth either. I'm Lizzy."

Axel studied her, a poised hunter patiently gathering information from its prey. "I'm not so sure you know who you are, lass. Or maybe you do, but are just too afraid to let her out to play."

Before she could even wrangle her thoughts around his statement, he moved in close enough to steer her toward the building with a hand low on her back. "Come on. Let's get you inside."

She sidestepped his touch and faced him. "You don't need to walk me up. I'm fine."

"I'm not walking you up. I'm following you up. And after you unlock the door, we're going to sit down and take a minute to talk about business without your band hanging over your shoulder, or my mothers driving us both crazy."

Axel McKee.

In her apartment.

Without anyone to run interference.

As bad ideas went, it had to rank at the top of the heap. Especially with the echoes of one of her mother's taunts floating around in her head. "I have to get up early in the morning."

"We're talkin' business, lass. Nothing else. You'll be tucked up in bed all alone in under an hour."

Business.

Right.

And going to bed alone was the smart thing. She should be happy at least one of them realized that.

"Business," she said.

He cocked an eyebrow. "Well, now if ye want something else, I'll not turn ye down. But I think we'd be smart to go slow."

She snorted before she could catch it, spun on her heel and marched toward the staircase. "Oh, give it a rest, you dirty Scot."

His low chuckle and the leisurely pace of his footsteps followed behind her. "Now, lass. You've got no cause to call me dirty. Not yet, anyway."

Nearly to the top of the stairs, she aimed the drollest look she could muster over one shoulder then dug her keys from the bottom of her purse. For once, the lock didn't give her grief, though, how she'd actually managed to slide the key home as easily as she did with him pressed so close behind her was a miracle for the ages.

She turned the knob, pushed through the door for much needed breathing distance and flipped the wall switch.

The lamp at one end of her tan couch and the little fairy lights she'd strung on a chrome ring and hung in the corner for a poor girl's chandelier fixture filled the room with a soft glow. The space wasn't much, and the simplicity of her belongings had never bothered her before, but after spending the day at Axel's house, her yard sale specials and second-hand store bargains were kind of a downer.

She waved him toward the couch. "Not nearly as fancy as your place, but it's comfy, and none of my neighbors creep me out. Plus, Rex is close, so I know I've got someone's door to go knock on when I get sick of my own headspace." She kicked off her sandals and turned to find him scrutinizing her instead of her meager space. "You want something to drink? I don't keep any Scotch, but the guys are over enough I keep a decent amount of beer on hand."

He shook his head and settled in the corner of the couch with the light behind him. With one arm stretched along the couch back and the other resting on the side edge, he looked like a king comfortably ensconced on a throne. "I'm good. Better if I keep my wits around you anyway. You might talk me into a deal I'm not comfortable with."

"I highly doubt anyone could talk you into anything you didn't want to do." She sat in the other corner, curled one leg underneath her and crossed the other one over it. "So, you wanted to talk business. Tell me what plans a man who's never managed a band before has for manning a high-maintenance singer like me."

His frown and sharp yet carefully modulated words were the last thing she'd expected. "Well, the first thing we're gonna work on is ditching the self-deprecation."

"Come again?"

"You've got quirks. We all do. But you're an artist, too, so added quirks are a fucking job requirement. The fact that you know what you want and have exacting standards, means you've got drive and taste. Not that you're high-maintenance."

She blinked.

Several times.

But the repeated act didn't do a damned thing to help her brain generate a response. "You're joking, right?"

"Not even a little bit."

Everyone called her high-maintenance. Joffrey especially—unless of course, her high-maintenance benefited him, and then she'd *been a real doll*. "You haven't worked with me yet."

"Not directly, no. But I've worked with high-maintenance types and I'd bet my half of Haven you're not one of them."

"What's Haven?"

"A ranch Jace and I bought on the outskirts of Allen. The moms live there with the two of us, though there's enough room all the brothers and their families can come out and stay if they want to." He smiled. A soft one that said the topic touched on something special or sacred. "I'll take you there someday."

Why she sensed a critical importance beneath the simple statement, she couldn't quite pinpoint, but it was definitely there. A hidden promise beyond her comprehension. One she wasn't altogether sure she wanted to understand. "I doubt Haven has much to do with the music business, so maybe we'd do better to focus on what plans you have in mind."

That deeply amused grin he seemed to wear more often than not around her crooked one corner of his mouth. "All right." He stroked the line of his jaw with his thumb, a thoughtful gesture she suspected he didn't let show with just anyone. "For starters, I'm not interested in just being your manager. I'm not interested in working with other bands, or being involved in your career only at a surface level. I want a partnership. Involvement in the whole process from production to promotion and marketing."

"Not to sound like a complete pessimist, but when you say *partnership*, I hear *control*."

"Then I'd say that's the context you've experienced it through in the past. But in my world, it's collaboration." He paused and cocked his head. "You spent the afternoon with the people I spend the vast majority of my time with. Did anything about that experience come off as heavy-handed or controlling to you?"

It hadn't. Heck, if anything she'd been as comfortable with the people he called family as she was around Rex and the band. "It was a barbecue. Not business."

"Sweetheart, what you saw today is my life *every* day. Surrounding ourselves with people we can trust and be ourselves with is how Jace and I accomplished all we've done so far. I think you and your crew are a good fit for ours. If you weren't, we wouldn't be talking. I damned sure wouldn't risk upsetting the foundation of my family."

"You act like they'd be part of our business arrangement, too."

His smile turned devilish, a secret she couldn't quite discern floating behind those sharp eyes of his. "You get me—you get them. It's a package deal." He cocked his head. "Have you ever considered what it'd be like to have that much family at your back, lass? That much support from people who only asked you to be who and what you are at your core?"

"This is business. Not family."

"For us, they're one in the same."

"Sounds like the mafia."

The snarky quip earned her an ear-to-ear smile. "Not far off the mark. Only we're a lot more laid-back and we avoid bloodshed unless someone fucks with one of our own."

He shared it as an equally flippant retort, but something told her that last part wasn't a huge exaggeration. "Okay, so let's assume this is a partnership. What's the goal?"

"I told you. Make it so you can do what you love full time and draw a big enough income you can pick and choose what you do and when you do it going forward."

"How?"

She'd known Axel had a head for business. Had been surrounded by the by-product of his creativity and savvy intellect an awful lot in the last forty-eight hours, but in that second, she got the full impact of him in tycoon mode. A swift shift from easygoing to laser focus—and he didn't even move a muscle. "No text book ideas. The old standard most managers, promoters and labels try to use these days is completely lost on the reality of people today. I want grass roots. More indie thinking."

"Indie takes a whole lot of money and connections."

"I've got plenty of both." He cocked his head and narrowed his gaze. "You ever heard of the Listolizer app?"

"The one that looks at all your music and movie playlists and tells you other stuff that's like it?"

"Yeah, that one."

Fuck, who hadn't heard of it. For people who wanted to binge on a particular style of music, or movie genre, it was a gateway drug. "What about it?"

"Knox wrote it." He chuckled, and his expression softened a little. "Actually, Darya's taken it over in the last six months. Said it needed a woman's touch. But the foundation is all Knox."

"No shit?" That app was huge and, as far as she knew, none of the other music or movie services had been able to beat its recommendations. Still… "What's that got to do with indie music?"

Axel's expression turned wicked. Utterly unrepentant and devious. "Because when Knox heard what I wanted to accomplish with you, the first thing he suggested was leveraging his algorithms to give you a leg up."

Whoa.

Talk about your inside track. Having that kind of connection was kinda like having a contact with Homeland Security when you needed to track down someone's bank account number. "That sounds like a guerilla tactic."

"Lass, when it comes to business, guerrilla tactics are the best ones, and I'm not afraid to leverage any of them—so long as you come out squeaky clean on the other end."

For once, her cynical past lay silent. Stupefied and frozen in place by the magnitude of what he was suggesting. "And what do you get out of it?"

He shrugged, a cavalier action that was grossly disproportionate to the dumbfoundedness rattling through every inch of her. "Satisfaction."

Bullshit.

No one offered the kind of support and involvement he'd just outlined without wanting something significant in return. "That sounds like an evasive answer."

He studied her a moment, the intensity behind his gaze such that it seemed he was measuring out the consequences of his response. "You've got your secrets, Elizabeth. I've got mine, too."

"Do they have to do with you not playing like you used to?"

"Aye."

Nothing more. Just a simple acknowledgment that left

something inside her grasping for more. But digging deep would only encourage him to want the same in return. And while this afternoon had given her a pretty good idea he wasn't a slime like Joffrey, she wasn't anywhere near ready to relive her past. "So, let's say I agree to a partnership. What would you do first?"

His gaze shifted to the side, grew distant for a beat, then refocused on her. "Outside of a few live clips on-line, I couldn't find any of your studio music available."

"That's because studios cost money."

"You don't have any recorded?"

"Nothing new."

He rubbed his thumb through the scruff at his chin and his gaze narrowed. "And the old stuff?"

She ducked her head, the past striking like a dull axe to the back of her neck. "I can't use it."

"Why not?"

For years, she'd tried to answer that question. To come up with some kind of rationale that didn't leave her feeling like she did in that very second. She'd never found one other than the obvious. "Because I was stupid."

Overhead, the air conditioner sent cool air whooshing through the vents, and the muted drone of traffic on the street outside pushed through the thin windowpanes.

Axel sat forward, his elbows braced on his wide knees and his hands clasped loosely between them. With her head down, she thankfully couldn't see the expression on his face, but she felt the weight of his gaze all the same. "If I'm gonna help you, lass, you're gonna have to give me more to go on."

He was right. And, if she worked with him, he'd eventually find out anyway. Better to face reality now than let him get blindsided later.

She looked at him, the tightness stretching across her collarbone and neck so potent it was hard to speak. "I didn't copyright them."

"Recording them *is* a copyright."

The nasty burn that came just before tears danced across the bridge of her nose. She swallowed around the lump in her throat. "Not if someone else heard them beforehand and copyrighted them on their own before any recordings are made." She shrugged. "At that point, it's one person's word over the other's, and a twenty-three-year-old girl with no money doesn't have much of a leg to stand on."

He sat upright, a frightening comprehension giving a dangerous edge to his features she'd never seen before. If she'd had any doubt about his potential for bloodshed before, looking at him now eradicated it. "And your new stuff?"

"I was stupid and gullible at twenty-three. Not at thirty. Everything I write today I file with the government before I play it anywhere. Even in a studio."

"You filed them yourself?"

"Well, I sure as hell wasn't going to hire an attorney to do it. Do you know what they charge? Besides, it's pretty straightforward online."

He nodded, but the hard edge in his demeanor lingered. "I changed my mind. Getting you in a recording studio comes second. First order of business is Jace making sure everything you've registered is ironclad."

What?

Of all the things he could have said in that second, Jace doing legwork on her behalf was the last thing on the list. "Why Jace?"

He chuckled at that, a good chunk of his tension ebb-ing away along with the rich sound. "Believe it or not, that hard-looking bastard is a helluva attorney. And I think we've already established, when you work with me, you work with all of my family and the tools we've got at our disposal." He paused a beat and cocked his head. "So, what do you think. Are you in, or are you gonna make me work for it a little more."

"We haven't talked terms."

"Terms are easy. I'll front all the money you need including a salary. Once income starts rolling in, you pay yourself and your band a base so you can focus on making this work. I get ten percent of what's left after the base is covered and original expenses reimbursed. Then we move to a straight fifteen percent."

"That's insane. It's all slanted in my favor. What if I never make the money back?"

"A moot point because you'll not only make it back, but you'll make us both a hell of a lot of money on top of it."

Why?

Why her? Why now?

The sheer certainty behind his conviction just wouldn't compute. Not unless he had some alternative motive she couldn't reason out.

His voice dropped to that velvet pitch he'd used when he'd steadied her beside the car and coiled firmly around her. "Do you want what I'm offering, lass?"

"Anyone in their right mind would want that offer. I just can't figure out why you're offering it."

He stared at her for long seconds, utterly motionless. When he spoke the sincerity behind his words resonated with incredible power. "Because I believe in you. And because if I give you this, I'm giving myself a second chance, too."

Truth.

Absolute, unvarnished truth.

No matter how bad Joffrey had burned her—no matter how many lies she'd missed in the past—there was no way she could miss the honesty in his statement.

"Stop thinking so hard, Elizabeth. Take the leap. Say yes."

It was a huge risk. One she'd sworn she'd never take again. But if she kept her eyes wide opened and kept things platonic between them, she'd be nuts to say no. Not to grab on with everything she had. "I'll agree on one condition."

"Name it."

Her body recoiled even as she forced the words past her lips. "Only business. We keep it purely professional."

He huffed out a short chuckle and hung his head, clearly trying to get a hold on his response before he spoke. When he lifted his head, most of his smile was under control, but his eyes were still full of laughter. Only when he'd held her gaze long enough it was hard for her not to fidget did he finally speak. "I suspect you've not had a wealth of honesty in the past, lass, but with me that's all you're gonna get. So, I'll straight up tell you right now—that's one condition I can't give you."

She opened her mouth to argue.

He kept going before she could finish drawing breath. "I won't ever push you. Won't ever expect or try to take anything not freely given." He paused as if to add more weight to the rest of his message. "I'll give you what you want for now. But one day, Elizabeth, there *will* be more than business between us. The only thing at question is timing."

Yes.

One single thought her body fervently agreed with. And yet, that damned reluctant harpy inside her was the first to speak. "That's bold."

"That's honest. And you know it's how things will play out as well as I do. You're just afraid to admit it."

"You're also cocky."

"That I am." He stood and smiled down at her. "Time for you to get some shut-eye. Come lock the door behind me."

Apparently, her brain was too log jammed to process physical movement while it tried to untangle everything he'd said, because she was still sitting on the couch with her mouth hanging open when he stopped at the front door. "The door, lass. I want to hear the bolt slide home when it shuts behind me."

"You know, I've been taking care of myself for years and haven't suffered any long-lasting injuries yet."

His expression sobered. "If I thought you'd admit it before the sun came up tomorrow, I'd debate whether or not that's true, but you can rest assured, it's not gonna happen again. Not on my watch." He motioned her forward with a quick crook of his fingers. "Come on. It's late and you've got a full day ahead of you tomorrow."

Tomorrow *would* be a long day. A boring string of tasks that did nothing to fulfill her laden with empty interactions with strangers.

And yet, the last thing she wanted right now was to bring tonight to an end and go to sleep knowing she had no concrete plans to see him in the future.

Totally stupid.

The same kind of happily-ever-after bullshit thinking that had gotten her into the whole mess with Joffrey.

She shoved to her feet and all but stomped to the door. "You're wrong about the whole connection thing outside of business. All we've got is a mutual appreciation of music."

"That so?"

Rather than answer, she crossed her arms over her chest and raised her eyebrows in a silent *Absolutely*.

He smiled. "Care to give that resolve of yours a test?"

Fuck no. She was barely hanging on to what she had as it was. But she also wasn't about to cede any ground if she was going to be working with him for the foreseeable future. And not working with him for the foreseeable future given what he was offering was just plain stupidity. "What? You think you can kiss me until my knees are weak and make rainbows and daisies appear in little cartoon figures around me?"

"Ah, lass." The way he dragged the response out, it sounded like she'd all but waved a red cape in front of him. "I don't need to kiss you to do that."

The sharp laugh that pushed past her lips was a pure defense mechanism. A nervous response generated on instinct to cover an involuntary sigh and the fact that her knees weren't altogether steady. "I'll give you one thing—you're not lacking in confidence."

"And you're stalling. Yes, or no?"

Nope. Not stalling. More like trying to figure out how she was going to make it through whatever he had in mind without tossing good sense out the window and jumping on a train guaranteed to shuttle her back to her past. "Sure." She shrugged and tightened her arms across her chest like that might add a layer of defense. "Go for it."

His gaze dropped to her arms, then back to her face. "It's unsettling, isn't it?"

"What is?"

He inched closer, the added span of her forearms between them doing nothing to impede his efforts. "How strong it is—this thing between us."

The words didn't make sense. Wouldn't process with the onslaught of sensory input overloading her system. His scent—subtle yet reminiscent of a sultry summer night and utterly masculine. His unrelenting stare. The heat from his body and the crackling energy that sparked between them.

And, *oh, my God*, the feel of him against her. She could've no more kept her arms crossed and kept from pressing her hands to his pecs than she could've willfully stopped breathing. He was all muscle, his physical presence every bit as powerful as the demeanor he carried himself with.

He skimmed his hands from her elbows to her shoulders, the combination of his soft, yet confident touch and calloused palms sending goose bumps out in all directions. Rather than stop and lean in for a kiss as she'd expected, he splayed his hand just above the hollow of her throat. The angle of it should have frightened her. Should have fired every survival instinct she had.

Her eyes slipped shut and she sighed instead, the sheer possessiveness in the touch and the protective sensation it built stilling everything inside her. No harping from the shitty committee in her head. No nasty barbs carried on her mother's voice.

He traced her pulse with his thumb, the humming bird rhythm of her heart no doubt unmistakable. "Do ya feel that, lass?"

Feel was the only thing she could do. Feel and forget everything else in the world except the depth of his voice, his touch and the bliss it created.

"That's not cocky," he said. "That's me being in tune to you and what you want and being brave enough to take us both where we need to go." His warm breath danced over her face, and her lips tingled with the nearness of his. His voiced lowered further, a rumble that waterfalled through every inch of her. "Whatever you need to accept this thing between us, I'll help you get there. But it *will* happen. And in the space in between, we'll put an end to you ringing up groceries and get you on stage full-time, so you can spend your life doing what it is you love."

A vow.

A promise so infinite it resonated to her soul.

"Open your eyes, Elizabeth."

She couldn't. Looking meant leaving the haven he'd created and facing just how fully he'd proven his point.

He traced her lower lip. "Look at me, pet. I want your eyes on mine when you hear this."

Whether it was the tender command in his voice, or the teaser he'd added to prompt her curiosity, she couldn't say, but it forced her weighted eyelids open.

"We're doing this. And we'll do it all in a way that's genuine to you. But we're doing it together." He eased back, keeping one hand braced on her shoulder as though giving her time to steady herself before he let her go completely and opened the door. "Think on that. When you're ready for more, you let me know."

No rubbing in how thoroughly he'd accomplished what he'd set out to do.

No gloating.

No superiority of any kind.

Hell, if anything he looked like he was as loathe to leave as she was to see him go.

Because he's real.

The thought ripped her out of her stupefied state and two steps toward the door before she stopped herself from following him out with a hand on the jamb. "Axel?"

He stopped and faced her, just the openness in his expression unlocking a truth she'd barely admitted to herself.

"I can't do personal. I don't know how. Not and stay whole in the process. I lost myself once and I'm not sure I can live through it again."

Understanding swept across his features and a tender smile tilted his lips. "My sweet Elizabeth." He ambled back to her and cupped the side of her face. "You can't lose yourself, lass."

"You can't know that."

"Yes, I can."

"How?"

His smile deepened, and he stroked the line of her cheek with his thumb. "Because we only lose ourselves when people extort more than we're willing to give. But the only thing I want from you is your time and trust. You give me that, and I promise you—you'll not only stay whole, but that part of you you've tucked away where you think no one else can see it can step back out into the light." With one last lingering gaze at her lips, he winked and stepped away. "Sleep well, Elizabeth."

Chapter Ten

Whoever said patience was a virtue was fucked in the head. Either that, or they'd never tried to win the trust of a woman like Lizzy Hemming.

Gaze rooted to the room's plush carpet, Axel paced the length of the recording studio's control room and focused on Lizzy's voice rolling through the speakers mounted opposite the wide sound board. Same fantastic delivery. Same powerhouse vocals.

But the emotion was missing.

No, that wasn't right. The emotion was there. It was just the *wrong* emotion. A strained frustration that made the feel-good song they'd been trying to capture all day sound more like an angry battle cry. Which kind of made sense given the sexual tension both of them were fighting.

For three weeks Lizzy and her bandmates had busted their asses, taking on every gig Axel booked and squeezing in recording time in between. Through it all, that potent awareness he'd wrestled since the day he'd laid eyes on her had taken on a life of its own. Made concentrating on anything outside of her career, or her in general, fucking impossible.

A slow burn. Exquisite and torturous by equal parts. And from the sound of things, Lizzy had reached her boiling point, too. Why he'd gone and promised her he wouldn't push anything between them he still couldn't figure out, but it was a mistake he was just about ready to rectify.

Perched on the edge of a chair behind the board, Lizzy motioned for the engineer running controls to kill the playback. "That's absolute shit." For a second, she just sat there, her jawline tense and body rigid. Then she sighed and hung her head. "I don't know what the hell is wrong with me."

"Yeah, you do," Rex said from the oversized stuffed chair in the corner. "You're just too damned stubborn to admit—"

Lizzy's head snapped up, all signs of fatigue replaced with a warning glower that would have given even a crazy man pause. "Shut it, Rex."

Not the least bit fazed by the bite in her response, Rex just chuckled and anchored one ankle over his knee. "Little girl, I've been listening to your rants since you were five. That look doesn't work on me." His gaze slid to Axel for all of a beat, then shifted back to Lizzy. "Got a feelin' it's not gonna work on him much longer either."

For the most part, their sound guy, Sam, had kept his head down and focused on the task of capturing the best tracks possible, even ignoring the band's jibes and antics as they'd laid the instrumental pieces earlier in the day. But on that cryptic remark, he cast a quick *what's that about?* look at Axel.

It was a damned good question. One Axel was ready to start prying out of one or both of them when Lizzy stood and marched toward the door that led to the sound booth. "Sam, back it up, and let's do it again."

"No." Volume-wise, Axel's voice barely carried across

the room, but he'd put enough command behind it Lizzy stopped dead in her tracks.

"What do you mean, 'no'?"

"I mean you're exhausted and beating your head against a wall, so we're calling it a night."

"No, we're not. We need this done."

"The only timetable we've got is the one we set for ourselves, and you need a break." He shifted his attention to Sam. "Pack it up. Let me know what your schedule looks like over the next few days and we'll get another run set up."

"No, don't." Lizzy retraced her path, the stride behind her steps almost making it look like she was prepared to strap Sam back in his seat if push came to shove. "It's only a little after six. We've got plenty of time. I'll get it."

"There's a time to work, and there's a time to play," Axel said. "For you, it's time to play, so get your purse and get ready to go."

"I'm thirty years old. I don't play anymore."

Axel bit back the chuckle that wanted to push free, but not the quip that went with it. "Think that's part of the problem, but we're gonna fix it."

Rex pushed to his feet and cleared his throat. "While I'd love to stay and see how this skirmish plays out, I think I'll duck out now and save myself the shrapnel." He held out his hand to Sam. "Good talkin' to you."

Sam wisely took advantage of the moment and used the man-to-man farewell to escape his place behind the console. "You, too, man." He looked to Axel and jerked his head toward Lizzy. "I'll let you two finish up. I'll come back and shut things down when you're done." Which was basically man speak for *Once the battlefield is cleared.*

Rex grinned liked he'd interpreted the same thing, zeroed in on Axel and offered his hand to him as well. "Thanks for letting me hang. Always wanted to spend some time in a place like this." As soon as Axel clasped his hand, he leaned in and lowered his voice. "Glad to see you takin' this off dead-center."

Lizzy snorted behind him. "I heard that."

Rex's grin morphed to a huge smile full of teeth and he raised his eyebrows at her over his shoulder. "Really? 'Cause you haven't listened to a damned other thing I've been telling you for three weeks." He shot Axel one last commiserating look before he moseyed out the door. "I'd say 'have fun,' but I think you're gonna have your hands full."

Axel held his silence and watched Lizzy glaring daggers at the one man she seemed to trust without question— but only until the control room door snicked shut. "Not sure if I should ask what all that was about, or steer clear entirely and focus on getting you someplace where you won't injure innocent people when you go off."

"What is it with you guys?" she snipped with more venom than he'd ever heard. "A woman has a rough day and every man thinks it's their business to smooth out our ruffled feathers. Well, I don't need mine smoothed. I need to finish that track so we can get on with business."

Oh, yeah. His Elizabeth was well past frustration and itching for a fight. If they were past the initial tango and on better personal footing, he'd give her one just to glory in her fire then fuck her until she was nothing but pliant, smoldering lava. As it was, he'd have to diffuse her temper another way. A much more drawn out way that would take an awful lot of patience and stood a good chance of making him crazy in the process.

He held his ground and slid his hands into the front pockets of his dress slacks. "Oh, you need smoothing, pet. Plenty of it and over an extended time period. Preferably tied down where you can't give me sass or try to run in the middle of it. But I made you a promise to wait until you asked for more. If I can't give you what you need the way you need it, then I'll get creative." He dipped his chin just enough to add a little glower of his own. "Even if it means throwing you over my shoulder and lugging you out of here like a sack of potatoes."

"You wouldn't dare."

At that, he couldn't have stopped his smile even if he'd wanted to. "Try me."

Oh, that look.

A mix of wide-eyed shock, feminine consideration and just enough of a flush across her cheeks to let him know he'd hit a few buttons with his comments. And Christ, he couldn't wait to figure out which ones they were. He softened his voice and added a gentle push to his words. "Get your things, lass. Let someone else have the wheel for the rest of today. You might find it's just what you need to get centered again."

Watching her process his words was a delight in and of itself. Anger. Disbelief. Hope and surrender. They all washed across her expression in mere seconds, leaving that same vulnerable woman he'd walked away from three weeks ago standing in their wake.

She fidgeted as though uncertain what to do then braced her hands on her hips. "Where did you have in mind?"

Poor thing. Fighting for control even as the longing behind her blue eyes said all she really wanted to do was let go. "Relax, Elizabeth. Get your things and let me take care of you. Just for tonight."

Whether it was the last of her control grappling for purchase, or that the mere idea of someone taking care of her was too much, he couldn't say, but she ducked her chin so he couldn't see her eyes. "Fine." She spun for the sound booth with the same attitude of a teenager who knew they'd been bested, but weren't quite ready to acknowledge their defeat. "But I'm hungry, so food better be somewhere on your agenda."

It took him fifteen minutes to get her out of the building and just short of a takedown to get her in his Shelby instead of letting her follow him in her own car, but after that she settled into the drive, happily commandeering his radio and changing stations as it suited her.

The first Carrolton sign whizzed by and Axel shifted to the exit lane.

Lizzy twisted in her seat. "We're going to Carrolton?"

"Maybe. Could be I'm just driving with no destination at all in mind just to keep you guessing."

She harrumphed and crossed her arms, but otherwise didn't complain. Just kept her sharp focus trained on the stores and streets around them, obviously trying to figure out where they were headed.

Ahead, the old-fashioned marquee that marked their destination drew closer, its vivid yellow background and cowboy caricature on the front one that usually sent Levi and Mary hooting the second it came into view. Axel slowed and turned into the drive. At this time of day, there were more people driving off the property than lined up for the tollbooth-style entrance that led to the park, but Axel was good with that. The less people to deal with, the shorter the lines—which meant more fun for Lizzy. And given the stupefied look on her face as she stared at the amusement park sign straight ahead, this was going to be a completely novel experience for her.

She looked at him, then back at the entrance. "You're joking, right?"

Axel scoffed and rolled down his window to pay the attendant. He laid on the accent and added a mock stern face to boot. "A Scot never jokes about fun and games, lass. We take our fun very seriously."

He handed off the cash for their tickets, fully expecting either a grumble or one of those adorable little snorts that always snuck out at the funniest times and always seemed to embarrass her.

What he got instead was a full laugh. One so genuine, light and utterly unexpected that he nearly dropped his change when the clerk handed it over. Her eyes were light, too, the flash of happiness behind the vivid blue enough to leave him stunned senseless. Yeah, he'd heard her laugh before, but it was always with her band and usually from a distance.

But this one was for him.

His first.

A black truck pulled in behind them.

Beside his Shelby, the attendant waited patiently for him to get things in gear and move along to the parking lot beyond.

But fuck if he gave a damn.

Lizzy didn't seem to care much either. Just held his gaze as her laughter died off, a shyness in her expression that said she'd surprised herself by letting go almost as much as she'd surprised him. She ducked her head. "You're looking at me funny."

"Not looking at you funny, pet. I'm marking down

every detail so I can analyze it and draw that sound out of you again."

The attendant crouched for a better look through window. "Everything okay?"

"Yeah." Axel put the gearshift in first and nodded to the man. "Everything's perfect." He eased off the clutch and steered them toward the parking lot, a whole new layer of resolve burning through him.

His first laugh.

Finally.

What had caused her to finally let go, he didn't have the first fucking clue. But it was a start. A good one. And he was by God going to make the most of it.

Chapter Eleven

"You're out of your mind." Lizzy looked from the attraction in front of them to Axel beside her. "I've had two corn dogs, half of a funnel cake and cotton candy. There's no scenario where bumper cars is a good idea with what's in my stomach."

"It's a grand idea." Axel hefted the ridiculously large teddy bear he'd won her out from underneath her arm and urged her forward with a hand low on her back. "Half the fun of an amusement park is goin' until you're green around the gills. Ask Levi and Mary. They've perfected the art."

"I take it you bring them here a lot?"

Axel handed the man at the front of the line their tickets. "A few times the last year. Made a family deal out of it both times." He grinned at her and winked. "You haven't lived until you let loose with my clan."

Good grief. Just imagining his family unrestrained in this environment sent her head spinning like the Tilt-a-Whirl they'd tackled an hour ago. Yeah, they'd been polite the first day she'd met them. Laid-back and unpretentious despite the multi-million-dollar home they'd welcomed her into. But there'd been an underlying energy between them, too. A connectedness and sense of safety that would make just about anyone feel free enough to throw their hands up in the air and enjoy the hell out of life.

"I see that got you thinking." Axel sat her teddy bear on the ledge out of harm's way and guided her to two cars at the far end of the platform. "You could have seen them in action for yourself yesterday if you'd come to family night."

"I'm not family."

He grunted and motioned her into the red car. "You're the only one who thinks you're not. And you're lucky they're givin' you as much distance as they are."

"What's that mean?"

"It means they're exercisin' restraint and givin' you time to wrap your head around things because I asked them to, but if you don't get there soon, then the mountain's likely gonna come to Muhammad."

"I still have no idea what you're talking about." She crawled into the tiny space and twisted to both sides, scanning the interior. Outside of a foot pedal, a comical looking steering wheel and a flimsy seat belt that looked like it'd been around since the 1970s, there wasn't much to the inside. "And how's this thing work?"

She looked up and found him crouched beside her car, staring at her with that same dumbfounded expression she'd earned in the car. "You've never played in bumper cars?"

For some reason, she felt like he was asking about more than just this particular ride. Or maybe she was just reading too much into it.

She shrugged and focused on wrangling the too-large seat belt. "I went to the fair a few times with some friends in high school, but I've never been much on rides."

Not entirely the truth, but no way in hell was she admitting the only reason she'd been able to pay for the fair admission was Rex slipping her cash beforehand. Back then, she'd been too young to hold a job and earn her own money, and asking either of her parents for money was just more pain and trouble than it was worth, so tickets for rides had been out of the question.

Axel pulled the seat belt from her fingers, adjusted the strap and slid the buckle home.

She dared a peek at his face just as the click snapped.

Resolution.

Pure male determination punctuated by the hard focus he kept on the buckle and the stern line of his lips. His gaze shifted to her hand resting on her thigh and he covered it with his own, the intensity he seemed to be wrestling settling with the simple contact. "Nothing to it. You just floor the pedal and try to steer the car while people are ramming into you."

"But there's no brake."

He met her gaze and squeezed her hand. "No, Elizabeth. There's no brake. You gotta just go with it and enjoy the ride."

A flutter and swirl that had zero to do with cars crashing into each other or a new experience took flight in her belly, and her voice came out a little unsteady. "Are we still talking about bumper cars?"

"Applies to everything. You let go and roll with it, I'll make sure you don't care there's not a brake." With that, he stood, ambled to the car behind her and folded his big body into the tiny space, leaving her a jumbled mess of nerves, giddiness and hope.

A grating buzzer ricocheted around them, and a mix of whoops, giggles and cheers from the riders lifted up behind it. A loud click sounded and the cars around her started moving.

From there, it was pure, delightful chaos. Picking up speed. Trying to steer with a wheel that was only marginally responsive while other people knocked you completely off course. Slamming into people you didn't know and watching them laugh as they circled around to return the favor.

It was fun.

Simple, uncomplicated *fun*.

And through it all, Axel stayed close. Not once taking advantage of the many chances her poor navigating left him open to a clear attack, but more often than not blocking those who tried.

By the time the cars stopped moving, her heart was thumping at a steady jog and the muscles in her cheeks ached from smiling. She popped the buckle and stood, the lingering adrenaline making her bobble a little as she tried to step out onto the smooth platform.

Axel caught her with an arm around her waist and steadied her. "Easy, lass."

She leaned into him, either gravity or sheer instinct driving her actions as she braced her hands against his pecs. Even as she gloried in the closeness, her mind urged her to step away. To regain the distance that would keep her safe. She focused on his sternum and tried to catch her breath. "Sorry."

His arm tightened around her and his voice dropped to that low rumble she'd replayed in her mind for days. "I'm not."

She wanted to ignore the crowd. To snuggle against him and feel both of his arms around her. To breathe that summer scent of his into her lungs and feel his heartbeat beneath her cheek.

But before she could give into the impulse, he laced his fingers with hers and guided her toward the bear waiting on the edge of the platform. "Come on. Mary says snow cones are mandatory at amusement parks and she'll scold me for days if she finds out I brought you here without getting you one."

So much life all around her.

Kids racing from one ride to the next. Parents either smiling or utterly exhausted from trying to keep up. Everything from country to rock music on the adult rides clashing with the distant drone of the merry-go-round near the front of the park. The ding-ding-ding of someone winning a prize behind them.

But the only thing that mattered—the only thing her brain could focus on beyond putting one foot in front of the other—was the feel of her hand in his. Not forceful. Not demanding. Not intended to control her actions or put on a show for the people around them. Just a confident, protective grip that made her feel like he was simply happy to be with her.

She'd never had that. Not once in her life.

And it felt really, really good.

Axel slowed near a green metal bench along the garden walkway that circled the park and motioned her toward it. "Take a load off. You want cherry, grape or strawberry?"

Loathe as she was to release him, her body was absolutely on board with some time to even out. "Cherry sounds good."

Axel smirked. "Yeah, it does."

She barked out a sharp laugh that made a couple lingering near the garden fence look their way. Lizzy schooled her features and lowered her voice. "Stop it with the innuendos. And besides…that particular cherry's long gone."

"Innuendos are fun. Kind of like foreplay for the mind." Not the least bit daunted, he sat the teddy bear right next to her, leaned in and braced his hands on either side of the bench at her shoulders. "And once you give me the green light, I'm willing to bet I can find a few firsts beyond bumper cars you haven't tried yet."

Grinning like he'd taunted the devil himself, he straightened, winked and sauntered to the row of vendors opposite her bench.

The couple next to her still hadn't shifted their attention away, so Lizzy dug out her phone to have something to do other than think about their curious scrutiny.

No new emails.

No new texts.

No new anything to help her take her mind off Axel and the dangerous places he kept steering her thoughts.

As she had countless times the last week, she thumbed up the last text conversation she'd had with Rex and stared at the last message he'd sent her.

Safe is overrated.

He hated texting. Said it was a poor excuse for communication and usually called her rather than type, but this time he'd actually replied and cut right to the heart of the matter at hand—a rebuttal to her on-going concerns about letting things go too far with Axel. Lizzy had probably re-read the thing a thousand times since he'd sent it. Like some part of her thought if she read it just one more time the letters might shift into a more concrete directive. An assurance from the universe that she wasn't poised to swan dive off into a shallow pool and certain death.

With her hair pulled back in a ponytail, the soft evening breeze whispered against her bared neck. What would it feel like if Axel touched her there? His fingertips, or his lips? She'd never kissed a man with a beard either. Five o'clock shadow yes, but not a beard like his. Would it tickle? Annoy her?

She tapped the edge of her phone and refocused on the message.

Safe is overrated.

In all the time she'd known Rex, he'd never intervened in her life. Not even when it was obvious he'd hated Joffrey as both a manager and a person. Had carefully kept his boundaries and adhered to the principle of *live and learn* where she was concerned unless she explicitly asked his advice—and even then, he often wouldn't comment.

But this time he had.

Had squarely put his stamp of approval on Axel and dared her to jump with three little words.

After what she'd been through with Joffrey—after how much of herself she'd given up chasing the approval of someone she'd so blindly trusted—trusting herself and her own judgment was impossible.

But she trusted Rex.

She trusted her band.

Not once had any of them shown hesitation about Axel. If anything, they'd thrown her headlong in his direction with their schemes, sly looks and blatant encouragement.

A delighted child's giggle and a woman's panicked shriek ripped Lizzy from her thoughts. She lifted her head just in time to see Axel step between a little girl who'd darted out into the main walkway and a cluster of teenage boys who had no clue they were about to mow the child down. More impressively, he did it with a snow cone in one hand and managed to make the girl squeal with glee and clap her hands.

Lizzy was on her feet a second later, the boys casting clueless glances at Axel and the mother who'd already scooped her away and buried the child's face in her neck. Lizzy's breath was a little choppy like she'd sprinted the distance between them rather than simply weaving through a crowd, and the uncomfortable buzz that always came after some kind of near miss skimmed beneath her skin. "Everything okay?"

It was the mother who answered, casting an exhausted but grateful smile at Axel. "Yes. For a two-year-old she's pretty fast on the getaway. Thank you for stepping in." She chuckled when she'd realized what she'd said. "Literally."

"Happy to do it." Axel handed Lizzy her snow cone and gave the little girl one of his charming smiles. "Have to keep the wee ones safe so they can grow up and wear there mommas out doing other things."

The little girl beamed an equally endearing smile back at him, pointed at Lizzy's snow cone and said, "Momma, that."

"Right. More sweets." The mother groaned and rolled her eyes, but hugged her daughter just a little tighter.

"Thank you again." With that she turned back for the vendors.

Axel chuckled, accepted his snow cone from the vendor still waiting in the window, then took a bite. If he noted all the bystanders watching them, he didn't show it.

"That was nice of you," she said.

He looked at Lizzy, obviously a little startled by the comment. "It wasn't nice, lass. It was common decency. No person in their right mind is gonna let a wee thing like her get run over."

And that right there was the difference in Axel McKee.

He was a genuinely good person. A man who lived by an innate moral compass and surrounded himself with others like him.

That was what Rex had been trying to tell her. What that quiet voice had been urging her to recognize and accept even as the screaming pain from her past tried to drown it out.

"Elizabeth?" His low voice reached through her wandering thoughts. Where he'd been utterly at ease seconds before, now his features were pinched with concern and awareness.

"I'm fine." She smiled, still a little shaken by the simple realization dominoing through her reality for it to be as steady as she wanted, but a smile nonetheless. She lifted her snow cone. "And thank you for this."

Axel studied her for a second, a hesitancy in his expression that said he was considering the wisdom of letting things go versus digging for more answers. He dipped his head once as though coming to a decision. "You want to sit for a bit and eat it, or walk through the garden?"

Walking was good. Especially if it gave her time to get

her bearings. Maybe figure out what to do next. "As much crap as I've eaten today, I think walking's the smarter choice."

His lips twitched. "All right then. Walking it is."

The walkway was quieter. A plain concrete path that meandered through the park's garden lined on either side by a wrought iron fence. During the day, the sun probably made the bold reds, yellows and pinks of the varied flowers pop, but with the sun already below the horizon and the old-fashioned streetlights beaming soft white circles on the pavement, it was more of a dreamy environment. A hidden place to simply unwind and relax away from the midway's chaos.

They ate their snow cones in silence, the cherry syrup on her tongue as potent and sharp to her senses as the thoughts zinging through her head. What would it look like if she stepped into something more with Axel? Would it change things on a professional level? For the better? For worse? And what happened if things didn't work out well for them personally? What if they tried for something more and it ended up sabotaging a golden chance professionally for her and her band? Just thinking of all the permutations and risks was exhausting. Let alone actually tackling them in real life.

Safe is overrated.

Rex had been front and center last time. Had witnessed how far she'd fallen and been the one she'd clung to as she'd scrambled to put her life together, and yet he'd still encouraged her.

Axel was quiet.

No pressure to say or do anything she didn't want to say or do. No expectations to be anything other than what she was. Not now or any other time she'd been with him. With the dregs of the snow cones discarded and the night's sultry air all around her, it seemed like the whole world was poised and alert. Waiting for her to wake up and take her chance.

The back of his hand brushed hers. An accidental touch brought by proximity and their meandering gait alone. And yet it nudged her forward in a way that felt right. Inspired in its simple innocence.

Keeping her gaze facing forward, she pulled in a shaky breath and touched her fingers to his. Tentative at first and then carefully curling so they were loosely laced with his.

As if it were the most natural action on Earth, Axel solidified the grip, easily taking over in that confident, protective way he had before. His steps slowed, and his deep voice moved through her with the same provocative sensation as the night breeze against her skin. "How did that feel?"

She could have pretended not to understand, but it seemed disingenuous in the face of the chance she'd taken. "Terrifying."

"Mmm." His thumb shuttled back and forth in a soothing arc along the back of her hand. Ahead, an alcove created for pictures and resting in the shade during the day sat in shadows, well apart from the soft glow of the walkway lights. He steered them that direction.

Her heart tripped then took off at an awkward jog, a heady mix of anticipation and anxiousness making each step feel lighter. Only when they were well out of sight and surrounded by the lush bushes and ornamental grasses did he stop and face her, keeping her hand in his. "Tell me what you want, Elizabeth."

God, she wished he wouldn't do that. Every time he

used her full name, her brain seemed to unplug from all processing save whatever words he voiced next. "I don't know how to answer that."

"Yes, you do." He took a step forward. Then another. Slowly inching her backward until the iron railing pressed against the small of her back. "You were brave enough to take the first step." As if he sought to add a visual reminder, he lifted their joined hands and moved in tighter. "Tell me. Not what you think I want to hear. Not what you think you *should* say, but what you want."

She swallowed hard. Or at least tried to. No easy task considering her words felt knotted up at the back of her throat. "I've got a long list of shoulds."

"I gathered that. And I'd guess you've got a load of hard lessons and disappointments that helped you build that list, but I've a mind to help you start ditching them— starting right now." His gaze moved across her face, an acute study that made her feel like he saw all her secrets. Every shred from her past and all the shame that went with it. He leaned closer, his strength, scent and breath curling around her until the rest of the world didn't exist. "Tell me what you want. Say it out loud."

Just do it.

Throw it out there and get it over with.

Now or never.

Just go!

"I want to try."

"Try what?"

"This thing. With you."

His gaze focused on her lips and his voice dropped to a husky rasp. "Not clear enough, pet. Say it so there's no misunderstanding."

Fucking difficult men. Stubborn, infuriating, diffi-

cult men. "I want you. Personally and professionally."
Her lungs burned beneath the frustration and the unsteady breaths she'd managed, and her heart hammered
so hard behind her sternum it physically hurt. But what
the hell—in for a penny, in for a pound. "And I want you
to fucking kiss me already."

His mouth crooked in a wicked smile, one suited for
pirates and devils who'd just stumbled on bounty untold. He untangled his fingers from hers and guided her
palm to his chest. "There she is. My sweet Elizabeth." He
cupped each side of her face, the unabashed confidence
in his touch unwinding her tension and drawing all of
her attention to his mouth so close to hers. "I want you,
too. Have since the day I laid eyes on you." His fingertips pressed more firmly against her and his lips whispered against hers. "And you're going to get a hell of a
lot more than just my kiss."

Contact.

Heart-stopping, mind-seizing contact. Bold and com-
manding. A siege against all her senses that eradicated
everything beyond his kiss. The firm, yet sensual press
of his lips as he coaxed hers apart. His rich taste mingled
with a hint of cherry. Each decadent glide of his mouth
against hers and the encouraging groan she earned as
she opened for more.

Anything.

Though vague on the surface, the single thought swept
through her with startling clarity. A judgment handed
down from someplace so deep inside herself she hadn't
even been aware it existed until that moment.

But it was awake now. Awake, freed of the darkness and
ravenous for more of what he offered. Ready to beg, steal
or borrow whatever it took to protect its newfound life.

The fervency behind the drive should have terrified her. Should have sent her scrambling for the nearest exit considering the mistakes she'd made in her past, but the sentiment felt inordinately *right*. She *would* do anything. Her body knew it. Accepted his touch and yearned to simply surrender.

It didn't make sense.

But with the hard press of his body against hers and the steady thrum of his heart beneath her palm, she didn't care. Not one fucking bit.

He wrapped one arm around her waist, splayed his hand high on her ass and pulled her hips flush against his even as he cradled the back of her head and deepened the kiss.

And holy smokes, was he ready for business, his rock-hard cock an insistent press against her belly.

She was lost. Floating on pure desire and so unplugged from anything other than him and the alternate reality he'd created, surfacing wasn't even an option. More of an obstacle to be avoided at all cost.

The low cadence of approaching voices tickled the edges of her mind. A warning some distant part of her said she should heed and take action.

Not more than a second later, Axel dragged his mouth from hers with a frustrated growl. Though, rather than release her entirely, he used his grip at the back of her head to tuck her cheek against his chest and wrapped her up tight. "Should have known you'd give me the go-ahead in a place where I'd have to behave myself." His chest rose and fell with the same haggard rhythm as hers, but the soft shuttle of his thumb along the back of her neck was featherlight.

She shivered beneath the tender touch and clung to

his broad shoulders, shock and the overwhelming impact of what they'd shared leaving her legs unsteady. "Wow. Just…wow."

His low chuckle vibrated through her. "My poet is finally speechless." He pressed a tender kiss to her temple, his beard whisper-soft against her cheek. "I'll take that to mean I made a good first impression."

"You could take us someplace where you don't have to behave." The hushed suggestion was out of her mouth before she even fully processed the thought, the uncomfortable prickle of shock and embarrassment that rose up in its wake urging her to push away from his strong embrace and run.

His arms tightened around her before she could try as much. Not giving even an inch with his hold, he lifted his head and studied her face. A slow, lingering perusal that burned to the very heart of her. "Much as I want that, you're not ready yet. Not for what I want from you."

So ominous. And yet, a part of her unfurled beneath the mysterious promise behind his words. "I'm not sure how I should take that."

"Take it the way I mean it." He traced her jawline with his thumb, the featherlight touch a stark contrast to the barely restrained strength behind his voice. "That the first time you feel my cock inside you, you'll know you belong to me."

A shiver too strong to hide slithered through her and goose bumps that defied the summer evening heat fanned out in all directions. "That sounds frighteningly possessive. Almost creepy."

His grin was utterly unrepentant. "Like I said—it's too soon." He pressed a kiss to her forehead, then pulled

away and laced his fingers with hers, guiding them back
to the main walkway. "But you'll figure it out."

"Figure what out?"

He stroked the pulse at her wrist and kept walking,
but there was a certainty in his stride. One of a man
with a clear and unstoppable purpose. "What it means
to be mine."

Chapter Twelve

Foreplay had always been a thing for Axel. A practice he insisted on no matter who his play partner was or how long he'd known them. But a long, drawn-out seduction of a passionate woman like Lizzy?

Nothing better.

He took the exit off Highway 35 and headed for the private airport where Trevor based his executive fleet. Lizzy sat quiet in the passenger seat, her focus concentrated on the buildings whizzing by outside.

For three weeks, he'd bided his time. Taken advantage of sessions in the studio and regular gigs to get her accustomed to the idea of them as a couple. To touch her and spoil her. To introduce her to luxuries he knew damned well she'd never had the benefit of in her meager life. And not once in that time had he done more than kiss her.

He'd wanted to.

Badly.

But fuck—watching her squirm and try to anticipate what delicious surprise was going to come next made the constant hard-on he'd battled worth it. Unquestionably the best torture of his life.

He pulled into a wide drive between two white hangars and stopped in front of the twelve-foot iron gate topped with electrified wire holding sentry. In the distance, a moderate-size private jet came in for a landing. Perfect timing.

Lizzy sat up a little taller in her seat and followed its descent, that cute little furrow between her brows digging in deep. An expression that was completely out of context to the high, sleek ponytail and black form-fitting dress she'd worn. "You said we had some kind of publicity thing to do. This is an airport."

"Aye." He rolled his window down.

"So, are you going to tell me why we're here?"

Keeping his voice modulated to a matter-of-fact tone instead of giving way to the laughter inside him was a challenge. "No."

The speaker mounted outside his window crackled to life with a cheery feminine voice before Lizzy could prod him further. "Good morning, Mr. McKee. Good morning, Ms. Hemming. Mr. Raines has everything powered up and ready to go. Head on in and the porter will meet you on the tarmac."

"Thank you, lass." With a smile and a nod to the camera mounted just above the speaker, Axel powered up his window and put the stick back in first.

The gate began to open.

Lizzy whispered like someone could still hear her talking. "She knew my name."

"Of course, she knew your name."

"How?"

Yeah, anticipation with his Elizabeth was a heady thing. And it was about to get even better. He eased his car forward. "Because I gave it to her, pet. Hard to fill out a flight plan without all the names of the passengers who're going to be on board without it."

Just as the last of his words slipped out, they rounded the white metal hangar blocking her view and brought the full impact of where they were headed front and center—a white Gulfstream with maroon stripes along its side and a phoenix emblazoned on its tail.

Lizzy's jaw slackened, and her awed voice was just barely over a whisper. "Holy shit."

This time he let the chuckle loose, remembering all too well how he'd reacted the first time Trevor had introduced him to one of his prized babies. "Been flying with my brother more times than I can count, and it still hits me when I see it."

She blinked a few times and frowned like she wasn't altogether sure her brain was piecing together information the way it was supposed to. "This is Trevor's charter service? I thought it would be like…you know. Those small planes or something. These are like…"

"Really fucking big jets for people who like to travel in style and have the money to do it," Axel finished for her. He parked his Shelby next to the red carpet at the base of the jet's stairs and faced her. "Today, you're one of those people."

Getting Lizzy out of the car was a hoot. Only when she was forced to pay attention to keep from bumping her head or tripping in her four-inch heels, did she pry her attention from her surroundings. Every single detail she treated with the utmost attention. From watching the porter in his clean, yet functional coveralls driving his car away, to the buildings, the red carpet and the plane itself, her focus was all consuming.

And he'd given it to her.

Which only made him want to bust his ass, bend over

backward and move whatever mountains were necessary to make it happen over and over again.

From the quick glance he stole toward the jet's windows, he wasn't the only one enjoying her response. It had taken him forever to talk Lizzy into joining him with his clan on family nights, but once she'd agreed, both his mom and Ninette had thrown themselves into making her feel welcome. Accepted and loved as only they could. The first time, she'd kept as silent as she'd been at the barbecue, but last week, she'd loosened up. Even dared to spend some alone time with his mother in the kitchen.

Which was why when they'd heard about today's trip, Ninette and his mother had insisted on being along for the ride.

He splayed his hand at the small of her back, a touch she no longer fought, but readily accepted by leaning slightly into him. "Come on, lass. Time to get you airborne."

Her pace up the stairway was hesitant. Almost reverent, as though committing every second to memory.

Trevor met her at the top, his blue button-down rolled up to his forearms and a smile on his face that said he was tickled shitless he'd left yet another person shell-shocked by one of his babies. He held out his hand to Lizzy. "That look never gets old."

"What look?" Despite the question, Axel wasn't so sure she'd be able to process the answer. Not if the way she was looking around the plane's interior was any indication.

Trevor must not have thought so either, because he skipped a response entirely and focused on Axel. "I take it you went with the surprise approach?"

"Wasn't sure I'd get her in the car if I'd shared the full agenda."

His mom hustled to the front of the cabin, her smile bright enough to give the early August morning sun outside a run for its money. "It's a big day for you, Elizabeth! Are you excited?"

"Easy," Axel interceded before his mother could ruin the rest of the surprise. "I haven't shared all the details yet, and you're not goin' to either." He guided Lizzy farther down the aisle. "Have you flown before?"

Lizzy's gaze drifted from the dove gray leather-lined ceiling to the glossy mahogany cabinetry and the butter-soft couches and chairs lining each side of the interior. If she'd gotten past the classy aesthetics long enough to factor in Jace, Vivienne and Ninette watching her with amused expressions, she didn't show it. "Only twice. Roundtrip to Florida to bury my dad last year." The breathy tone in her voice was pure wonderment. "It was *nothing* like this."

Behind them Trevor chuckled. "Nope. Never gets old." He nudged Axel's shoulder. "Show her the head and get her settled. Got a decent headwind so we gotta get wheels up if we're gonna get you to New York on schedule."

Lizzy snapped out of her stupor. "New York?"

"Jesus, Mary and Joseph," Axel grumbled under his breath. "Remind me not to clue the lot of you into surprises the next time around." He aimed a scowl at Trevor. "Get your bloody arse in the cockpit. We'll be ready in five."

Trevor didn't seem to give two shits about what he'd let slip. Not if his grin was any indication. "Right. Five minutes." With that, he dipped his head in that laid-back cowboy way he'd used to wrangle all number of women before he'd met Natalie. "Enjoy the flight—and the surprises."

As it turned out, five minutes was more like fifteen with Lizzy's fascination over the bedroom, the fact that the plane had not just a fancy bathroom, but a shower, and all the fancy gadgets in the galley kitchen. Thankfully, everyone had been so preoccupied with coaching Lizzy through the taxi and takeoff process, they'd avoided spilling any more details about their destination and all the other details he'd saved until they were well on their way to New York.

As soon as the plane leveled out, Ninette unbuckled her seat belt and meandered to the kitchen. "I'm getting a drink. Anyone want something?"

A round of responses went out, but Lizzy stayed quiet, that wide-eyed look on her face still that of a woman who wasn't quite sure she was fully grounded in reality.

Seated next to her on the leather couch along one wall, Axel shifted his arm from the couch back to her shoulders and hugged her a little closer. "You all right, lass?"

Her smile was adorable. Shaky, but so innocent he halfway wished he'd put his foot down and insisted they travel alone. At least then, he'd have been able to pull her into his lap and cuddle her the way he wanted. "The one trip I took on a plane felt like a huge luxury. I never in a million years imagined I'd fly on a plane like this."

"Yeah, me either." Seated on the opposite side of the cabin in one of four leather chairs that surrounded a high-polished wood table, Vivienne tidied up a stack of papers she'd pulled out of her briefcase shortly after takeoff. "It's surprising how quickly you get used to it, though. No security checkpoints. No waiting in line. No waiting for baggage."

"And let's not forget how much easier customs is," Sylvie added. Per usual, she'd kept herself close to Lizzy and settled on the far end of the couch. She reached over and patted Lizzy's leg. "We'll have to make that your next surprise. Maybe we'll take you to Scotland and I can show you the Highlands. No prettier country anywhere."

Lizzy let loose one of those adorable snorts. "I've been to Florida and Texas and only drove through the states in between. Scotland seems like another planet."

Ninette looked up from emptying a mini can of Sprite into a crystal tumbler. "Do you drive when you visit your mom in Florida?"

In an instant, Lizzy sobered, the soft and innocent wonder that had surrounded her dowsed with hard revulsion. "I don't visit my mom. Not if I can help it." As if she'd belatedly realized how strong her words had come out, she let out a small sigh and lowered her voice. "She's not exactly fond of me. No point in going where you're not wanted."

For a moment, everyone froze, and the steady drone of the jet's engines filled the cabin's awkward silence.

Axel moved first, using his arm around her shoulders to pull her in close for a kiss to the top of her head. "More time for me."

"More time for us," Sylvie added with a definitive grunt and sharp nod.

Jace grinned and lifted his tumbler of Scotch in salute. "Can't argue on that score."

Vivienne's smile was softer, a knowing look on her face that openly reflected memories of those early days when she'd first stumbled into the family fold. She held Lizzy's gaze for several moments, a silent show of support and understanding, then shifted her attention to

Axel. "So…maybe now would be a good time to talk business?"

Lizzy jumped on the topic change faster than he could get a word in. "You mean like the fact that we're on the way to New York and I have no clue why?"

"The trip's just a by-product of the plans, lass. What Viv's talkin' about is the fact that your full album went up for preorder on Tuesday, your first single's live and we've got a five-month tour with major US cities that kicks off at The Green on Labor Day weekend."

Lizzy stared at him. Then at Jace, then the moms and Vivienne, before she landed back on Axel. "My album's live?"

"Your album's on preorder," Axel said. "The single's live."

"And doin' damned good on both counts according to Knox this morning," Jace added.

Lizzy frowned. "How would Knox know?"

The grin on Jace's face was the same devious one he always sported when one of them undercut the competition and came out on top. "Because he and Darya changed their Listolizer algorithms over the weekend to prime the pump and have been watching sales on all the major outlets since it dropped."

"We should have a party." Sylvie shifted in her seat for a direct line view of Ninette who'd settled into the chair opposite Vivienne at the table. "A big tour launch party."

"And an after-party," Ninette said.

Vivienne smiled. "Axel's already got me on it. He's scheduled radio remotes from all the top regional alternative stations and the bigwigs from satellite stations." Her eyes got big and she held up a finger. "Oh, and get this…" She flipped open the briefcase tucked beside her in her chair, dug out a handful of papers and handed them to Jace to pass on to Lizzy. "We've even got merchandise. T-shirts, posters, backstage lanyards, buttons…" Her expression turned a little sheepish and she wrinkled her nose. "Honestly, I might have gotten a little carried away on the promotional stuff, but Axel said to have at it."

Lizzy stared down at the flyers, flipping through the pages like she'd been handed a stack of lottery tickets rather than a bunch of mockups on concert paraphernalia. Once she got back to the top of the stack, she sat absolute still, her gaze locked on the images, yet distant. "I didn't do anything to help."

"Well, you've been a little busy," Ninette said. "The good thing about family is you can spread out what needs to get done and cover more ground faster."

Lizzy ran her thumb along one side of the top page and cleared her throat, but when she spoke it was still aimed at her lap. "What's in New York?"

Axel smoothed his hand up her spine and cupped the back of her neck. In all the time since he'd known her, he'd yet to see her with her hair completely down—a fact that he fully intended to rectify sooner rather than later. But right now, he was glad for direct access to her skin. "I leveraged a contact I made about a year ago with SiriusXM. I played 'em your first single and told 'em we were launching this week. They picked it for this week's Critical Cut and wanted you to fly up for an interview."

Finally, she lifted her head, but angled it so only Axel got a straight-on view of her face. Her eyes were wet and her shaky voice barely audible over the engines. "You're flying me to New York to interview on a nationwide radio station for my first single."

Not a question so much as a need for confirmation,

and with it so much raw vulnerability the words seemed to knife between his ribs.

"Aye, Elizabeth," he said just as quietly. "That's what we're doing."

She swallowed hard. Tears welled a second before she averted her gaze back toward her lap, her hand pressing to the top of the merchandising images for a beat before she hastily stood. "I think I need a minute."

She was through the galley and in the bedroom with the door shutting behind her before anyone could react.

Not surprisingly, it was his mother who was on her feet all of a heartbeat later and headed after her.

Axel stood as well. "No, Ma."

Sylvie spun, her green eyes so much like his own sparking both fire and concern. "Don't you tell me, 'no,' boy. The lass needs someone to see to her."

"And that'll be me," he said, his own brogue thickening in response even as he lowered his voice. "You care for Elizabeth, and for that I'm grateful because I'm bloody damned certain she's had far too few people in her life who have. But she's proud, and I all but stripped her armor off and laid her bare in front of a crowd. I'll be the one to make sure she has what she needs to put herself back together again."

"Ye dinnae strip the lass bare. We're family. We're takin' care of her."

"But she doesn't know what that looks like." The cold, hard fact shot out sharper than he'd intended. He'd known it, and he'd still miscalculated and sprung the news on her in front of everyone.

At the stark sadness in his mother's expression, he moved in and pulled her into a hug. "It was my fault, Ma. I'll fix it. And then we'll teach her how family works."

Never one to pass up a hug from her son, Sylvie wrapped him up and held on tight—but only for long enough to let him know she understood. Then she stepped away, swiped the underside of one eye and shooed him toward the bedroom. "Well, get on with it, then. The poor thing's probably lookin' for a parachute and an escape hatch by now."

Not likely. If he knew Lizzy, she'd probably already whittled one of her stilettos down to a killing point and was halfway through honing the second one. Still, he'd learned at a young age not to keep his mother waiting and that wasn't a practice he was going to change today.

Fortunately, either Trevor hadn't deemed locks on the bedroom door a necessity when he'd tricked out the Gulfstream, or Lizzy had been in too much of a hurry to escape, because the handle turned easy. The room was opulent even though short on space and was decorated in ivory and maroon with clean, contemporary lines.

It was also empty.

A sniffle sounded through the partially opened bathroom door.

Fuck.

Definitely too much too fast. A fact he'd have remembered if he hadn't been so damned caught up in getting things moving with her career the last few weeks. The thick ivory carpet silenced his footsteps, and while the door prevented him a full view of her, the six inches it stood ajar showed her braced behind the sink with both hands on the counter and her head hung low. The second he splayed his hand on the door and pushed it open, she straightened, swiped the back of her hand across her cheek and pushed her shoulders back. Her eyelashes were spiked and her cheeks a mottled red. She tried for a smile, too, but it completely missed the mark. "Hey."

"I see I gave you too much."

She cleared her throat and put a whole lot of show into checking her outfit in the mirror. "Too much what?"

"Too much time. If I hadn't had to beat my ma back to keep her from comin' after you, I'd have made it in here before you could get your armor back in place."

She bristled at that enough to forgo the nonchalance routine and met him eye to eye. "I'm not putting on armor."

"No? What would you call it?"

Her mouth pressed into a hard line, and the way she held her breath, he'd bet good money she was fighting back a fresh wave of tears. When she spoke, her voice came out tight. "I made a complete ass of myself in front of your family."

"In front of *our* family."

"Don't say that. They're nice people, but they're yours. Not mine."

Maybe it was the conviction behind her words that did it—or maybe it was just that the Dominant in him had fucking had enough. Either way, he snapped and had her pinned with her ass to the sink and her arms clamped behind her back in one of his hands before she could get in a solid gasp. If she'd thought about fighting back, she swallowed back the action the second his growled words rolled free. "Those people went to bat for you. They're out there worried because they know you're hurting. That's what family looks like."

"Well, I haven't had family." As soon as she realized how loud and aggressive her answer had come out, she lowered her voice and eased back from the nose-to-nose posture she'd volleyed back with. "I might have had a mom and dad, but I've never had anything like what you've had. Not outside of Rex. So, I don't exactly have an image to work from."

Finally, the crux of the matter. And with her, admission her body softened enough she allowed him to pull her flush against him and tuck her cheek against his chest. He smoothed his hand up her spine. "Well, you have it now. We're not going anywhere. And more than that, every one of us is going to stay on your ass until it sinks in, so you might as well start accepting you're stuck with us."

She pushed against his chest until he relented and let her meet his gaze. "Why? Why all the effort? All the persistence? They don't even know me. Not really."

His sweet Elizabeth. So keen on the details of everything around her except the ones that pertained specifically to her. "Because they see what I do. A woman with talent. A woman who lives large and has the capacity for love even if she hasn't had many chances to use it."

"They've known me what? A month?"

"Six weeks." He cupped the side of her face and smoothed his thumb along her still damp cheek. "But you're not giving yourself enough credit, lass. They knew inside a few hours what kind of woman you were. If not for the fact that I'd already made it plain you were special, then by the way you interacted with them. A real person who didn't put on airs or try to be someone she wasn't. Who sat at the dinner table with them and bothered to learn a little about each one of them when it would have been easy to stick to the sidelines. A woman who sat down with two kids overdosed on sugar and shared your time without a single complaint."

"That was good manners."

He squeezed her hip and slid the hand at her face so he cupped the back of her neck. "Stop arguing, pet. We outnumber you and we're a persistent lot. Or as Knox would say, 'Resistance is futile.'"

Her mouth quirked in a shy smirk. "That's a *Star Trek* quote. Not a Knox quote."

"See? The fact that you know that proves it." He pressed a soft kiss to her lips then pressed his forehead to hers. "You fit, Elizabeth. Me and my family. The only one fighting it is you."

She sighed and slid her hands up from his chest so her arms circled his neck. "Okay, fine. I'm honorary family."

"Family," he corrected. "And probably only five minutes away from having two highly protective mothers invade your privacy and show you just how invasive being in one can be." He pulled away enough to frame both sides of her face with his hands. "Now, are ya ready to head back out and face the troops?"

She wrinkled her nose. "I don't know. Do you have any other news you should tell me in private before I do?"

He grinned at that. "You mean, besides the fact that me and my brothers leveraged every contact we've got to get your single included on every music service we could find?"

She stilled, and her expression sobered in a flash. "You mean like Spotify?"

"That one and every other service like it. At least all the ones that count."

"Holy shit. That's huge."

It was huge. It'd taken a whole damned rally with all seven of his brothers wracking their brains for contacts and a solid few days of making phone calls to pull it off, but it'd worked. "Damn straight it is. Now, are you comin' out of this bathroom so we can celebrate properly? Or shall I send the mothers in after ye?"

Her smile was brilliant, what was left of the red on her cheeks making the expression that much more adorable. "I'm coming out and I'm celebrating."

Chapter Thirteen

It was mighty damned hard for a girl to speak intelligently about music and her plans for the future when she was smack dab in the middle of the most surreal moment of her life. Of course, nothing since she'd gotten off the elevators at the SiriusXM office had looked like what she'd expected it to look like. But then, late night *WKRP in Cincinnati* reruns didn't exactly prepare a girl for real-life radio.

At first glance, the place had seemed just like any other high-end office—a fancy glass entry, a receptionist up front and lots of cubicles in neutral dove gray that housed people with their heads down and hard at work. It was what came after the front office that had been the biggest shock. She'd expected lots of machines and huge rooms filled with CDs and platinum albums on the wall—especially for a nationwide satellite place like this one—but the reality was that every station's control room was barely more than the size of a small bedroom at best. And, in some cases, more on par with an over-sized closet, a feat possible thanks to digitized music and the wonders of computer automation.

The people were super cool, though, with everyone

right up to the program director she'd met dressed in jeans and T-shirts.

Beside her, Skeet sat on the edge of a fancy metal bar-stool, the heel of his boot anchored on the top rung and his hands gesturing with an uncharacteristic wildness as he answered the DJ's latest question as to what time in the studio for the new album had been like. "Working with Lizzy live has been a wild ride from the get-go. There's just an energy she brings to the stage you won't find with a lot of artists. But in the studio?" He glanced at her and shot her one of his ornery grins before he faced the DJ again. "Man, she's a machine. The second she stepped foot in the building, she was unstoppable. A lot of the songs we've played live for a while now, but she came up with some brilliant ideas that completely revamped the overall feel."

The rest of the guys nodded their heads and murmured their agreement, then Tony launched into his own per-spective of the recording experience.

Fuck, but she was glad they were here. Yet another unexpected surprise she hadn't seen coming thanks to Trevor's fleet and an earlier flight time, and a definite plus for those moments when she'd found herself tongue-tied.

Leaning against a window ledge with his ankles and arms crossed, Axel watched from the far edge of the room, his *GQ* attire and powerful build combining to give him an edge that made everyone they'd encoun-tered stand up just a little taller. Hell, even the program director had perked up and stepped a little quicker in Axel's presence, which was funny as hell to watch con-sidering it was them looking for a leg up instead of the other way around.

"So, Lizzy…"

Her name on the DJ's lips jolted her thoughts back into focus.

"…we talked your team into sharing a few other cuts from the album for us to highlight this week as well, and I gotta tell you, I'm stoked to hear the full release. 'Burning Heart' was utterly inspired. Any chance you could give us a little insight on what prompted you to write it?"

Yeah, this was what she got for zoning out in the middle of a really freaking important interview. Especially, when the topic at hand was one as up close and personal as the inspiration behind her lyrics.

She cleared her throat and locked gazes with Axel, who smirked back as if he knew she'd been caught daydreaming. "You know, one of the things I love most about music is how every song is open to interpretation. The two of us can both listen to the same thing and come away with entirely different responses because we each bring something different to the table. So, I'm always hesitant to share too much of how a particular lyric comes into being. But I will say this…

"I wrote 'Burning Heart' at a really dark time in my life. One of those black periods where hope and sheer stubbornness was about the only thing I had going for me. So, that's what I focused on. Rebuilding myself. Digging myself out of the hole I was in and redefining who I was."

The DJ, Grant Tempe, smiled huge, the lopsided slant of it pairing with his stylishly disheveled blond hair to give him that sexy nerd look. "Man, whatever you did— it worked. A killer first album, a solid first cut and a tour comin' up…it's like every musician's dream come true."

Without meaning to, Lizzy's focus drifted to the people standing in the production booth opposite the wide window that separated the two rooms—Rex, Jace, Vivienne, Sylvie and Ninette. Not surprisingly, the two mothers were front and center and looking at her with such pride in their eyes it made the space behind her sternum ache. The burn of barely contained tears fanned along the bridge of her nose, and she tried to steady her voice, but it came out a little scratchy anyway. "Yeah. In so many more ways than just music."

If Grant noticed the emotion behind her voice, he didn't cop to it. Just shifted right into introing the song. "Well, we're gonna give our listeners an extra dose of what we're talking about with an exclusive you won't hear anywhere else. Here's 'Burning Heart' by Lizzy Hemming and Falcon Black."

A few button pushes later and the first strains of the song filled the speakers overhead. He peeled off his headphones and held his hand up to Lizzy for a high five. "That was perfect. Direct. Clean. Easy for people to relate to." From there, he focused on the guys in the band, fist-bumping and hand shaking while a few other men she hadn't met before swaggered into the room and started glad-handing with Axel.

No more pressure. Just an unguarded moment where she could catch her breath and let it all soak in.

Her first interview.

Her song playing through the speakers and streaming live into God only knew how many other people's lives. *Un-fucking-believable.*

Rex's voice sounded behind her, the tone of it soft and laid-back like when he'd coach her through how to make a chord all those years ago. "Lizzy, girl. You did great."

Yeah. She'd done pretty damned good. Definitely a

long way from the girl who used to hide at her neighbor's house just to avoid another rant from her mother.

She faced him, her body so pumped up on awe and excitement it was a wonder she didn't float right off the ground. "You were right. This was the right thing to do. Not just because of the opportunity, but because of the people."

With that know-it-all smirk of his firmly in place, he grabbed her by the back of the neck and jerked her up next to him for a bear hug. "Mark it down. Lizzy Hemming admitted I was right on August third in the year of our Lord 2018."

She mock punched him in the gut and pushed herself away. "Yeah, well don't get used to it. I just admitted to people all over the nation I'm stubborn. Not gonna blow my new rep right out of the chute."

Rex barked out a laugh, not the least bit worried about his bold response with all the hand shaking and business talk going on around them.

"She's grinning like a loon and I missed whatever caused it," Axel said sidling up next to them and wrapping a possessive arm around her waist.

"She admitted I was right," Rex said. "It's a goddamn miracle."

Axel studied her with a curious grin. "Indeed." He squeezed her hip and hugged her tighter to his side. "You'll have to let me know how you pulled that off. Something tells me I might need that skill once or twice in the future."

"Hey, Axel." The DJ paused in the doorway, his lanky body leaning against the light-stained door to hold it open while her bandmates filed into the hall in front of him. "I'm gonna show the guys the production room and grab a download of the interview for you. You guys wanna come along?"

"Hell, yeah," Rex answered first and headed out after them.

Axel guided her forward. "You bet."

Waiting in the hallway just outside the door, Vivienne, Ninette and Sylvie stood to one side, patiently waiting.

When was the last time she'd actually had a girlfriend? Like a *real* girlfriend to do things with or just shoot the bull with?

Um, like never. For cryin' out loud, even your own mother was a distant acquaintance.

"You know what?" Lizzy stepped out of the flow of traffic and motioned Axel forward. If she was gonna go all in and really try to believe in the concept of family, she might as well do it full bore. "Why don't you go with the guys? I'm gonna hang here with the girls and catch my breath for a minute."

The look on Axel's face said he was just as surprised hearing the plans as she was saying it. His gaze slid to the women behind her, then back to Lizzy. His lips tilted in that soft, understanding smile she'd come to crave. "I think that's a fine idea. We'll meet you up front in the lobby." He leaned close and gave her a quick but tender kiss. "Try not to let 'em corrupt you too much while I'm gone. I want to handle that job all on my own."

In the handful of seconds it took for everyone to meander down the hallway, the space around them went from sounding like a Super Bowl watch party, to a hushed atmosphere more appropriate to a corporate office.

"Men and their toys," Ninette said. "Give 'em a chance to push buttons or take something apart and they'll light up like little kids every time."

"God, isn't that the truth?" Vivienne rolled her eyes and started toward the entrance. "What do you bet it'll be a solid thirty minutes before we see hide or hair of them again?"

Sylvie moved in right beside her, letting Vivienne and Ninette lead the way. "Who cares! Lizzy's an official celebrity! And did you see the two big executives hobnobbin' with Axel?"

Vivienne lowered her voice and glanced back over her shoulder. "How do you know they're executives?"

"Because they came out of that big corner office over there," Sylvie said dipping her head to the huge space with glass walls. "More than that, I heard 'em talkin' when they went past. One of 'em mentioned Lizzy's name and *feature spot* in the same sentence."

Having reached the lobby, Lizzy stopped dead in her tracks. "You got all of that out of a moving hallway conversation?"

"Honey," Ninette said, "Sylvie has the hearing of a hound dog and could ferret secrets out of a covert double agent over tea and scones, and they'd never be the wiser. The only damned reason we were able to keep our boys out of jail growing up is she overheard half of their conversations before they had a chance to actually carry out their plans. If she says she heard it, you can pretty much bank on it being accurate."

Vivienne waggled her eyebrows at Lizzy. "What do you think they mean by 'feature spot'?"

"Are you kidding me? You know more about my promotional plans than I do right now. I'm doing good just to put one foot in front of the other and not make a total ass out of myself. Let alone figure out how all the pieces fit together."

A smooth and highly cultured masculine voice sounded almost directly behind her. "Well, I'll be damned. Lizzy Hemming all dolled up and in New York City."

Not just any voice.

Joffrey's voice.

I made you. You will do what I say, when I say to do it, or I will ruin you. Do you understand me? Do. You. Understand?

It'd been seven years since he'd shouted them at her, but the words were still fresh. The physical blows he'd dealt with every word still aching beneath her skin.

A cold sweat broke out across her forehead and along the back of her neck. Her heart tumbled in an awkward rhythm and the once soft dove gray carpet beneath her feet now seemed closer to quick sand.

Breathe. Just breathe. He can't hurt you anymore.

The same words Rex had told her over and over again when he'd found her after the fact and carted her back to his house.

She forced herself to turn, her knees so unsteady it was all she could do not to brace a hand on Sylvie's shoulder. "Joffrey."

God, what had she ever seen in him? Yeah, he was handsome on the outside—dark hair, even darker eyes and swarthy skin that hinted at Latin or Greek descent. But beneath all that there was an ugliness she'd missed all those years ago. That her innocent eyes had completely glossed over at first then made excuse after excuse to ignore the deeper in with him she fell.

She saw it all now. The arrogant way he carried himself. The contempt in his eyes. The cruel tilt to his lips.

His gaze slid to the women next to her, that superior tone he'd used to criticize and berate her in the last few months they'd been together pairing with his smug smile. "Let me guess. You and your girlfriends won some kind of giveaway and you're here to pick up your tickets?"

Before Lizzy could fully register the meaning behind his statement, the women closed ranks with Sylvie and Ninette flanking either side of her. Ninette's frigid tone made Joffrey's passive-aggressive maneuver look like amateur night. "Well, aren't you just the pompous prick to top all others?"

The group of mostly men that had come in behind Joffrey grew still, only the hushed twitters of what appeared to be groupies breaking the awkward silence.

If she'd been a bystander watching the interaction, the shock on Joffrey's face and the uncomfortable way he smoothed his hand down the front of his heavily starched button-down would have been comical. As it was, keeping herself upright and breathing steady was a challenge.

Joffrey scrutinized each of the women close to her once more, this time focusing his gaze as though looking for some clue he might have missed the first go-round. "I'm sorry?"

Ninette didn't miss a beat. "You clearly know Lizzy, and yet you can't think of a reason why a talented singer and songwriter would be at a radio station other than to pick up concert tickets?" She pinned him with a look that would shrivel any man's nuts. "If that's not a pompous prick move, I don't know what is."

Joffrey smiled, but there was a quaver behind it. "I… uh…think you misunderstood my meaning." He glanced over his shoulder, scanned the watchful group behind him and powered up his salesman expression. "Lizzy and I go way back. Just razzing an old friend."

The air around her shifted and the fine hairs on the

back of her neck prickled a second before a wall of heat pressed against her back.

Axel.

Even if his summer scent hadn't wrapped around her at the same time his hands pressed against her hips, she'd have recognized him on sheer presence alone. A crackling energy that drew attention from every single person in Joffrey's group and grounded her with startling force. His low voice sounded in her ear, his brogue thick and laced with a dangerous bite she'd never heard before. "Is there a problem?"

"Apparently, this is an old *friend* of Elizabeth's." Sylvie eyeballed her son over one shoulder. "Joffrey, I think she said his name was."

Axel's fingers tightened at her hips. "Indeed."

Voices sounded behind them, the deep masculine chatter and chuckles as Jace, Rex, Skeet, Tony and D approached from the hallway. Apparently oblivious to the awkward tension, the DJ stepped into her line of sight and held out a thumb drive. "There you go. Your own copy of the interview. I told Axel I'd send a soft copy, too, along with the schedule and channels it'll run on." He shifted his attention to Axel. "Did you tell her she's gonna be this week's Critical Cut?"

As deeply gratifying moments went, watching Joffrey's eyes get huge while the crew behind him looked envious shot damned near to the top of her list.

Ninette crossed her arms and eyeballed Joffrey with a satisfied smirk.

Sylvie harrumphed and lifted her chin to rival a queen.

Axel shifted to one side of her and acted like Joffrey didn't even exist. "That I did." He held out his hand. "Have to tell you, I appreciate all you've done to support Lizzy's release. Look forward to seeing you at tour kickoff at The Green on Labor Day. Let me know who you're bringin' with you and when you want to fly out, and we'll get your flights set up."

"Awesome, man. Appreciate it." Grant stepped back and waved them through. "Lookin' forward to getting the rest of those album cuts, too. Y'all have a great flight back." He spied one very dumbfounded Joffrey and his crew behind him and froze. "Oh, hey. You guys need some help?"

To his credit, Joffrey rallied quick. He held out his hand. "Joffrey Reynolds. Miramar Records. You must be Grant Tempe." He motioned to the men behind him. "These are the guys from Hip Pocket. They've got an interview with you this afternoon."

For the first time since she'd met him this afternoon, Grant lost his laid-back demeanor and looked like he'd just been busted with a mother lode of weed. "Oh, shit man." He glanced at the receptionist who'd long since written everyone in the lobby off and had gone back to focusing on her computer screen. "Yeah, I think we've got a problem." He looked back to Joffrey. "We had a schedule change up today. Didn't anyone call you?"

The guys from Joffrey's band shot him a mix of perturbed and altogether angry looks.

Joffrey puffed up his chest and pulled his phone out of his pocket. "No. No calls at all, and my secretary confirmed this afternoon."

"Wanker," Sylvie muttered under her breath only loud enough for Lizzy and Axel to hear. "Bloody bawbags like him always blame the bloody secretaries."

Axel hung his head to hide his smile.

Lizzy fought back a snicker.

"Right." Grant corralled the lot of them up toward the receptionist's desk. "I gotta jet here in about ten, but how about we get our promotions people up here, and we'll figure out a reschedule." He pointed to Axel. "Thanks again, man. Safe flight home." And then he was all hustle and focus getting the receptionist to help him find someone else to handle the scheduling fubar.

Rex, the band and the rest of their motley crew moved in around Lizzy like a defensive line and ushered them out into the elevator landing. The glass door hadn't even finished whooshing closed yet when Jace chimed in. "Anyone else wanna punch that numb nuts in the mouth just on principle?"

"The fact that I never have is nothing short of a miracle." Rex punched the elevator button and aimed a pointed look at Lizzy. "I still think the cock sucker needs a crowbar to the head."

Lizzy shook her head. "Not now, Rex. Let it go."

"Who is he?" Vivienne said.

"An old manager," Axel answered, though his voice was soft and his sole focus on Lizzy. He cupped the side of her neck and pulled her in close. "You okay?"

Where the giggle came from she couldn't say. And the sheer fact that she could actually make such a sound after the terror that had flooded her at the sound of Joffrey's voice only made her want to laugh harder. "I just saw the man who stole at least ten of my songs and gave them to other artists get shut down in front of me. And that was after he learned SiriusXM is supporting my release. I'm a hell of a lot better than okay."

"Stealing songs ain't all that fucker did to you," Rex muttered.

Lizzy spun as far as Axel's hold would allow. "Don't. Not now."

Rex held her stare for a minute, shifted his gaze to Axel for another heartbeat, then scoffed and faced the elevators.

Sweeping the faces of everyone watching, she sucked in a big breath. "Really. I'm fine." She met Axel's gaze head-on and gave his shoulder a reassuring squeeze. "I'm great. Ready to fly home and celebrate."

Something in her statement wiped the concerned scowl off his face and replaced it with a shit-eating grin. "Hate to disappoint you, lass. But you're not flying home." He dipped his head toward everyone watching them. "The rest of 'em are, but you're grounded in New York City for the weekend."

"What? Why?"

"Because you had your nose pressed against the limo window the whole drive over from the airport. No way we're not hanging around and giving you time to explore. Trevor'll send a plane back for us Monday."

She blinked.

Then did it again, waiting for her brain to cough up some kind of response she could use. When nothing came, she looked to the women. "I can't stay the weekend. I don't have any clothes. No makeup. No nothing."

Sylvie smiled a smile to rival her son's and clapped her hands together. "Jace, call Trevor and tell him we'll be late getting back." She looked to Ninette and Vivienne and the smile got bigger. "We've got shopping to do!"

Chapter Fourteen

He was addicted.

A complete goner.

Hell, if he was honest, he had been from the start. But seeing Elizabeth tonight—watching her walk into the elite restaurant in the classy bold blue dress the women had talked her into wearing and the awe-struck wonder on her face—Axel accepted it. Embraced it and committed himself to finding any and every way possible to give her every experience she'd yet to have.

Lizzy stared down at the varied sushi options the waitress had just laid out between them. It'd taken a whole lot of cajoling from his mother and a direct command from him, but her dark hair finally hung loose past her shoulders, perfectly framing the curiosity and wariness in her expression. "You're sure this stuff is safe to eat?"

The waitress smiled and poured the sake, keeping her silence.

"I've got more than just money invested in your well-being, lass. I'll push you in ways you've never dreamed, but I'm not ever gonna do anything to put you in harm's way."

The cryptic statement brought her gaze to him. "What if I don't like it?"

"Then we'll ask the nice lady to cook you up a steak. Either way, you'll be well sated before the night's over."

One second and her expression shifted, her soft pink lips parting and her eyelids sinking down just a fraction before she ducked her chin to hide the response.

The look the waitress shot him said she was either envious or willing to assist. "May I get you anything else?"

Axel shook his head. "I think we've got plenty for now. Thank you."

Lizzy waited until she was gone before she looked up again, her features schooled even though the line of her shoulders and way she angled her torso closer to the table still belied her tension. "So? How do I do this?"

So cute. Adorable really. And sushi was just the tip of what he planned to show her tonight. What he wanted to show her every fucking day from here on out. He pointed to the rolls to start. "These are pretty basic. Makizushi. It's got crab, cucumber and avocado in it."

She checked her plate and the space around it. "Where's the silverware?"

"You don't need it."

After a quick glance at the chopsticks, she frowned up at him. "I don't do chopsticks and I saw how much the stuff you ordered costs. I'm not risking fumbling something on the floor."

"Easy enough to fix." He stood and moved his chair to her right.

"What are you doing?"

"You don't want to fumble with the chopsticks, so we'll tackle learning those another day. Today, I'll feed you."

She glanced over both shoulders. "You can't do that."

"Elizabeth, I paid good money to give us all the privacy we need and there's not a soul outside our curious waitress who's going to see past those shojis." He settled into his seat and shifted the rolls, shoyu and ginger closer. "Besides, if I'm close enough to feed you, I'll be close enough to tease you, too."

She shot him that wary, disbelieving look he was growing so fond of. "You wouldn't."

"Oh, pet. You'd be surprised at the things I'll do for you." He rested one arm along the back of her chair and teased his thumb along her shoulder. "Or to you."

There it was again. That heated yet wary expression of a woman thoroughly tempted, yet uncertain how to proceed.

She'd know the lay of the land soon enough, though. Both in terms of what she meant to him and his family, and exactly how to grab onto the dynamic between them and make the most of it.

He picked up a portion of the roll and dipped just a bit of it in the shoyu. "Now, open up."

She stopped him with a hand on his wrist. "You're picking it up."

"That's how you do the rolls. A lot of people use their chopsticks, but some hardcore enthusiasts say otherwise."

"Well, I could've done that."

"You could've, but where's the fun in that? Now, open up."

She wrinkled her nose and stared at the roll for a beat, then tentatively opened her mouth and accepted the bite.

Axel watched. And waited.

Her brows dipped inward as she chewed and her gaze shifted to the table, the distant focus behind her eyes that of a person more attuned to their inner thoughts than their surroundings. Finally, she lifted her head, an almost comical consternation pinching her features. "Okay, that wasn't as bad as I thought."

One tiny step forward—with miles of exploration left to go before the night was over. He dipped his head toward the rolls. "Now you. Dip the flat side into the shoyu, but not too much."

He waited until she followed his instruction then did the same. "You said something on the flight here—something I'd like to know more about."

In her usual no-nonsense way, she shrugged. "Shoot."

"Why do you think your mom's not fond of you?"

"Oh, I don't think. I know." She wiped her fingers on the napkin in her lap and reclined against her chair back. "I was an accident, so I had a handicap from the start. But the fact that I cramped her style just by being a responsibility made things worse."

"Cramped her style how?"

She frowned and shifted her focus to the New York City streets stretched out twenty stories below them. "Mom likes men. Lots of them." Her gaze slid back to him. "Harder to keep your stable active when you've got a kid to look after. So, I got the bare minimum. Rex kind of filled in the rest."

"What about your dad?"

"Oh, Dad loved Mom. Would have given her anything. *Did* give her anything. And turned a blind eye every time she picked up someone new on the side."

Interesting. And it sure explained a lot about her reaction to his mom's and Ninette's enthusiasm on the plane this morning. To everyone's enthusiasm. Though, that still hadn't been exactly the answer he'd been looking for. "I meant, what about your dad taking care of you."

"Ah." She carefully picked up another bite of roll and

skimmed the surface of the shoyu. "He tried for a while, but Mom doesn't like to share. The more Dad tried to fill in the gaps she left hanging open, the more she took out her shit on me." She popped the bite in her mouth. "In the end, I think Dad just chose to give me a break by keeping his distance."

"Then I'm glad you had Rex."

She smiled at that, a soft one that spoke of many fond memories and untold stories. "Yeah, me, too."

The rolls gone, he moved the next plate closer. "Now, this is nigiri-zushi. You can tell it's that by the finger of rice the fish sits on."

She shifted a little in her chair. "What kind of fish, exactly?"

He pointed to each option. "This one's maguro, or tuna. This one's salmon. And this one's eel."

It wasn't often he'd seen Lizzy hold so still, but the way she eyeballed the pieces he'd pointed out, she might as well have been a statue. "You realize this is a huge stretch for me."

"I do." Not giving her time to balk, he flipped the tuna on its side and picked up the bite with his chopsticks. "Now, with nigiri-zushi, you'll hear different guidelines on the right way to eat it. Some say fingers are fine, and others say chopsticks are a must, but they all agree, you don't dip the rice in the shoyu. Only the meat." He did just that and held it up to her mouth. "Open up, pet."

She shook her head.

"One bite of each. If you don't like it, you don't have to eat more. If you do, well, then…you eat more. Either way, you've tried something new and learned something about what you like and what you don't."

Her lips firmed to the point he halfway expected her to

stand up and march to the front door. Instead, she sucked in a short breath, said, "Fine," then opened her mouth.

He set the bite on her tongue.

She held his gaze and chewed.

Confusion settled on her face. Then surprise. "It's kinda… I don't know. Just okay? Not bad, but not knocking my socks off either."

"Mmm hmmm. A lot of sushi enthusiasts will tell you tuna's overrated. We'll work our way up." He took a bite for himself and ventured toward the next landmine on his agenda. "So, tell me about Joffrey."

Unlike the response to his question about her mother, this one locked her up tight. "What about him?"

"When I walked down the hall and found you staring at him, it looked like you'd come face-to-face with a demon."

Rather than answer right away, she took the next bite he offered willingly. Only when she'd finished and he didn't readily offer up the next portion did she answer. "I guess in a way, I had."

He let that settle and offered her a pinch of ginger from his fingertips. "We're in a relationship, Elizabeth. That means I want to know about you. Want to know what fears and experiences you bring to the table so I can do my part to respect them."

She fiddled with her napkin. "I don't like talking about it."

"Why not?"

"Because it reminds me how stupid I was. How much of myself I lost when I was with him."

Axel nodded. "That's twice now you've said that about being with him. Tell me what it means."

Whether she realized it or not, her shoulders relaxed a

fraction at the lowered tenor of his voice and she leaned her torso closer to him. She drew in a long, steadying breath. "I was really happy when things started out. To a woman with no relationship experience and almost no life experience, he seemed to know everything. Was larger than life. Knew tons of people."

"And he was offering you your dream."

She nodded. "It was more than that, though." She paused for a few moments, her gaze aimed at her lap. Pensive. "Rex talked me into seeing someone to help me process what happened at the end. You already know I trusted Joffrey more than I should've. That I made it easy for him to steal my music and claim it for his own. But the therapist I talked to said, the core of everything was grounded in family of origin issues. That I was so desperate to find love and acceptance from someone in my life—someone on an intimate level—that I sacrificed my own needs and wants to keep what I thought I'd found."

Part of him wanted to leave it at that. To leave the ugly secret he sensed sitting between them untouched where it couldn't hurt her.

But if he did that, he risked stumbling on it later and there was no way in hell he was going to risk greater harm if he could face it now. "What happened at the end?"

"It was a pretty messed up relationship from the start. Dysfunctional. Emotionally abusive. But at the end, it crossed a line."

"Crossed a line how?"

A stillness as cold and dark as a cemetery at midnight gripped her. "He hit me. Several times, actually. Bad enough it freaked him out when he was done and he ran. I called Rex. He came, got me and my stuff, and I never saw Joffrey again."

Axel didn't dare move. Only focused on keeping his expression masked and carefully modulated his own breathing.

But Joffrey Reynolds was fucked.

When or how Axel would extract punishment on Lizzy's behalf wasn't yet clear, but that day would come. And it would come with an unforgiving iron fist that son of a bitch would feel for the rest of his fucking life.

Still locked in place, Lizzy stared unseeing at the table.

"Elizabeth, look at me."

It took a solid two heartbeats, and when she finally did as he said, the movement was painfully slow.

"I'm not blind to the similarities between your meeting him and your meeting me." He leaned a fraction closer and lowered his voice. "But I'm not him."

"I know that," she all but whispered. "I didn't at first. Couldn't get past the common elements, but I get it now."

"Good." He nodded, silently vowed to find at least fifty more ways to prove it just so she'd never doubt it and pulled the last platter closer. "Then we'll shut the door on that and not bring it up again unless it's something you need to talk about."

He lifted the first bite of sashimi up with his chopsticks.

She ignored it entirely. "Thank you."

"For what?"

For several seconds, she held her silence and simply held his gaze. "For just being you."

Mine.

The thought roared through his head, the fervency

behind it so powerful he nearly fumbled the bite to the table. "You don't have to thank me, lass. Not for anything. I spend my time with you because it's where I want to be. Where it feels right to be." He lifted the bite a little higher. "Now, open up."

Her attention shifted to it and a sly look settled behind her eyes. "Only if I get a secret from you."

Oh, now that was a promising proposition. Not to mention, a good way to navigate them out of choppy waters. "Food first. Secrets second."

She smiled as if she'd won a major victory and opened up. The second she swallowed, she shifted in her chair as though settling in for a good story. "Okay. Spill."

"Is there a particular secret you're after, or am I just grabbing random ghosts?"

She hesitated only a second. "Why don't you play or sing anymore?"

He chuckled despite the difficult answer her question required. He should have known that would be the first one out of her mouth. But after what she'd given him tonight, she deserved the truth. "You know Jace and I have been friends since we were little boys."

She nodded.

"Well, we were friends because our mothers were friends. They shared the same occupation."

"Why do I have a feeling I'm not going to like what that occupation was?"

"Probably because you get they haven't always had it as easy as they have it today." The old frustration he'd fought for years after learning how his mom and Ninette put food on their table knotted up his gut just like it had when he was nine. "They were prostitutes. No pimps because they didn't want anyone fucking with them, but that also meant they had no protection. That's how Jace and I found out about what they were doing—a john followed Ninette home one night and things got nasty."

A sadness crept into her expression, but he kept going before she could comment. "They did it because they had to. Neither of them had an education and took raising their boys and giving us what we needed seriously. Once Jace and I learned what they were doing, we made a pact. We'd do whatever it took to make it so they could get out of their predicament and never have to even consider it again." He stroked the bare curve of her shoulder, the touch a much needed comfort as he shared the rest. "A man can't make a stable living with music starting out, and success without significant backing is a hell of a gamble."

"You gave up your dream to take care of her. So, you're giving me mine instead."

God, she was quick. Nimble as a fucking cat. "Something like that." He handed her sake. "Some people say you shouldn't drink it until after your sushi's gone, but after that story, you look like you could use it."

She sniffed it, then jerked back enough to study the contents. "What is it?"

"Sake. It's made from rice." He lifted his own ceramic cup and inhaled. "Take a small sip. Let it linger in your mouth for a minute and then swallow."

Mimicking him almost perfectly, her eyes popped wide a split second after she swallowed. "It's sweet, but really strong."

"Indeed."

She took another sip, though this one was much bigger than the last and when she set her cup down she added a satisfied *ahhh* along with it.

Axel moved her cup out of reach, then took another sip of his own.

"Hey." She eyeballed his serving, then hers. "Why'd you take it away?"

"Because the alcohol content is a lot stronger than wine or beer and I have plans for you tonight."

That shut her up quick. Though, not for long. "What kind of plans?"

"The kind where I want to be sure the only thing muddling your mind is me."

She pursed her lips, just a hint of a smile tugging at the corners. "Care to elaborate?"

Oh, he was going to elaborate all right. And it was highly probable she'd use those incredibly long legs of hers to hightail it out of the building before he could finish.

Still, better to lay it all on the table now. All of it. Starting with being completely honest about who he was and what he wanted.

He picked up a bite of sashimi and dipped the tip of the squid in the shoyu. "The last eight months have been different for me."

"Different how?" Clearly, the topic was enough of a distraction from what he was about to feed her that she didn't even balk from opening her mouth when he lifted the bite to her lips. Convenient considering what he was about to share.

"I love sex. Every fucked up, kinky, twisted variety you can think of. So long as the right energy and dynamic are there, I'm game."

Yeah, she didn't have a clue she'd just swallowed down raw squid. Wasn't even sure the texture or taste had even registered. She swallowed the bite, lifted the napkin from

her lap and dabbed her mouth. "Um…" She folded the
napkin back into place and cleared her throat. "Aside
from some hot make-out sessions, I've barely been able
to get you past first base for three weeks. Now you're
telling me you're…what?"

Okay. Not exactly the response he'd anticipated, but
he'd take it all the same. "Not much a fan of labels, but
the short version is, I'm anything but the run-of-the-mill
vanilla in the bedroom. Ropes, chain, impact play, sensation play, mind fucks—I love it all." He paused a beat
and let the full breadth of what he'd just shared soak in.
"If you need a label, I'm a Dominant."

One heartbeat.

Then another.

She licked her lower lip and, while there was a cau-
tiousness in her expression, her breathing sped up and a
pretty flush began to spread along her collarbone. "Like
a BDSM thing?"

"About a thousand different flavors that fall under
that umbrella, pet, but for the purpose of this conversation, yeah."

Ducking her head, she smoothed her hands along the
silky blue fabric covering her thighs. Her voice was quiet,
barely loud enough to travel the distance necessary for
him to hear and loaded with disappointment. "I'm not
a submissive."

Such a sweet thing. So soft and tender beneath that
tough exterior she donned for the rest of the world.
Watching her drop that armor and step into that quiet
place she was right now on a larger scale was going to
be a beautiful thing to behold. To be a part of. "On the
stage and day-to-day? No, you're not." He hooked his
finger beneath her chin and guided her face to his. "But

Elizabeth—with me, you're very much a submissive. You have been from day one."

She bristled at that, the same battle-ready demeanor she'd taken with him that night with Vic the Dick rearing forward in a second. "No, I'm not."

"You are. And if you think about it, you'll see it's true. That first night you followed my lead when Vic pulled his shit with you. You did the same the night I drove you home. And again, the night at the amusement park. From day one, I've led and you've followed. A natural dynamic that's as easy to both of us as breathing."

The furrow between her brows softened, but the intensity behind her blue eyes said there was still a mighty debate going on inside that head of hers.

He smoothed her hair away from her face, the soft strands tempting him to spear them deeper and hold her steady while he kissed her worries away.

But he couldn't do that.

Not here.

Not yet.

Not until she knew everything he'd set out to share tonight. "Whatever you're thinking right now, I want you to put it on pause and consider something for me."

She hesitated only a second, then dipped her head. "I'm listening."

"If Skeet sang a melody with you instead of singing harmony, would it sound as good?"

"Why would he do that?"

"Right. There's no point because it doesn't add anything." He jerked his head toward the dance floor. "And if you and I were to head over there, how would it turn out if both of us tried to lead?"

Both of her eyebrows snapped upward. "You dance?"

"Oh, lass. I'll dance with ya. On and off that dance floor." He leaned in just enough to ensure she felt his words as much as heard them. "And you can bet that prime ass of yours, I will *always* be the one who leads."

She swallowed.

Hard.

Then broke their eye contact in favor of a solid perusal of the empty platters in front of them. She smoothed both palms along the table's edge. As if she needed contact with something solid just to see if the world around her was real.

Axel reclined back in his chair. "That's who I am, Elizabeth. I thrive on being the one in charge. In finding whatever kink or sweet spot it is that works for my partner and taking full advantage until they're so sated they can't talk. That's what gets me off."

She cocked her head and frowned, that distant yet intently focused narrowness to her eyes that said she'd just hooked a few stubborn puzzle pieces together. "You only met me a few months ago. What changed eight months ago?"

Clever girl. Always thinking. Though, he had a mind to help her find a few ways to turn that brain of hers off. Eventually. "I saw you. A show you did over in Fort Smith. My being there was a complete fluke. I'd checked out another band at a different venue, but they were a complete bust. I was taking the long way home and saw your name on the sign out front. They had a good number of cars in the parking lot, so I pulled in." He leaned in and crossed his arms on the table. "Best detour of my life."

"Why'd you take so long to talk to me?"

He chuckled at that. "Good question." He twisted his

sake glass like it might somehow dial up the right combination of words. No small feat considering it'd taken him nearly all that time to figure it out for himself. "Not an easy thing for a man like me to process the kind of reaction I had for you."

"What kind of reaction?"

Overwhelming.

All-consuming.

Life changing.

Just thinking about those first moments he'd watched her on stage still made him feel like he was trapped in a giant's fist. "It wasn't about the sex anymore. Not about the next scene, or the next thrill." He met her gaze head-on. "It was about you."

He'd thought she'd balk at such a revelation. Maybe be stunned speechless. God knew, he'd been for months.

But no—not his Elizabeth. Instead, her lips twitched like it was all she could do not to bust out laughing. "You're telling me your kinky mojo dried up?"

Little minx.

Though, if he was honest, the sass was one of the best parts to her personality. And Christ, he couldn't wait until she learned what that sass would earn her. "Oh, no, lass. It's well stocked and loaded with a decade's worth of fantasy. Only difference is they're all geared toward you."

Her smile shifted, the snark shifting the curve of her lips to one significantly softer. Shyer. Her voice was quiet. Almost reverent. "Lot of big secrets covered tonight."

Before he could answer, the waitress approached the table. "How is everything? Can I get you anything else? Dessert?"

Axel shook his head. "I think she's had enough exploring for one night and dessert's already planned."

The waitress smiled. "Excellent. I'll be right back with the check."

When she was out of earshot, Axel picked up where they left off. "The best relationships don't have secrets, Elizabeth. Unless me or my brothers take on something that might backfire on you or the other women in our family, I won't keep things from you. Not ever."

She frowned at that. "What the hell would you take on that might backfire on us?"

And there it was. The last bridge to cross served up as simple as could be. "Whatever we need to. Business interests or protecting one of our own. Or, like you've seen, promoting one of our own. At the end of the day, we play by our own rules. Rules founded on our own sense of honor. Sometimes that falls within the law, sometimes it doesn't. But you, our moms and the other wives—you all stay safe. At any cost."

He covered her fisted hand on the table and smoothed his thumb along her pulse point. "The last two months— none of it's a fluke. I'm in this. My family's in this. For your career and for you."

Her voice was little more than a whisper. "Why are you telling me this now?"

Part of him was tempted to wait and simply answer with actions. But that wouldn't develop the kind of trust he was after. Not to mention, it robbed him of a chance to build the anticipation.

He skimmed the back of his knuckles along her chin and took his time soaking in every detail. The contrast of her dark hair against her creamy skin. How soft it felt beneath his touch. Her softly parted lips and the way her eyelids hung heavy over her vivid blue eyes. "Because, Elizabeth, I'm done waiting, and I wanted all my cards out on the table before I make you mine."

Chapter Fifteen

Lizzy stared up at the intimidating pale stone facade of the Four Seasons, the tinted windows of the limousine doing nothing to dampen the impressiveness of the towering building as it stair-stepped to the sky. "I thought we were getting dessert."

"We are." Axel stepped out into the muggy New York City night and offered his hand to help her out. "It just so happens we're going to do it alone where I can see to you myself."

I'm done waiting.

Apparently, he hadn't been kidding around with his proclamation. And while her body was still humming at the promise of finally getting something more than his devastating kisses and heated looks, the travel time between the restaurant and the hotel had given her mind plenty of time to circle back to some of the secrets he'd shared. "Right." She took his hand and carefully alighted, her legs way too unsteady for the heels Sylvie had talked her into buying. "Dessert in a hotel room alone with you."

"You sound a little wary."

"Wary?" She waited until they were past the doorman then lowered her voice. "More like envisioning stickiness in places I've never been sticky before."

With the towering ceilings and marble and stone walls all around them, his chuckle seemed larger than life. "I see your mind's had too much time to process since we left the restaurant." The elevator door swished open and he ushered her inside. As soon as she was tucked close to his side, he squeezed her hip and murmured, "Stop thinkin', lass. Just breathe and stay in the moment."

She snorted, and for once in her life, she didn't give a fig that she'd done it in front of someone—which was either solid evidence she was well in over her head, or she'd reached a frightening level of familiarity with the man next to her. Odds were good, it was a little of both.

Stepping into the suite had no less of an impact than it had before and after their shopping trip. Space-wise, it was at least four times that of her apartment and boasted a living room, dining room, kitchen and a sprawling bedroom— every inch of it decked out in the finest décor in neutral colors with gold accents. From every room, views of the New York City skyline stretched out fifty-two floors beneath them. It'd been impressive in the daylight, but with the towering buildings and the city aglow, it was breathtaking.

Axel tugged the small clutch from her fingers barely two steps past the front door. "Shoes off." He set her clutch aside on the entry table along one wall and motioned to the opposite side. "Leave them there."

Huh. Odd.

A relief though, considering how unsteady the adrenaline had left her balance. She peeled the straps off the back of one heel, slid the first one off and sighed the second the cool marble touched her bare feet.

Axel waited, one shoulder leaned against the ornate entry wall with his arms crossed in front of him, the fine cut of his black button-down stretched across his broad shoulders.

"What?" she said as she worked the other shoe free. "Something wrong?"

His self-satisfied grin didn't budge. "Quite the opposite." As soon as she set the shoes aside where he'd indicated, he pushed upright and guided her toward the living area. "Now, let's get you ready for dessert."

"Are you kidding? I was ready for dessert before the waitress showed up with a week's catch worth of raw fish."

Rather than head toward the dining area like she'd thought, he kept going toward the bedroom. "You haven't said what you thought of it."

She glanced back at the dining room table with its fancy chandelier that reminded her of something from Superman's Fortress of Solitude—only probably made from something a lot more expensive than ice. "Shouldn't we eat at the table?"

"Let me worry about dessert. Tell me what you thought of the sushi."

Sushi. Right. Because that was an important topic at a time like this. "It was okay. I'm not gonna up and encourage you to take me out for it again any time soon, but I won't hide if you say that's where we're eating either." She shot him a mini-scowl. "I'd have probably been more enthusiastic with more sake."

He drew her to a halt and smiled. "Then next time we'll have more sake." He kissed her forehead and turned her around so she faced the bed. On it sat a medium-sized white box with a pink tulle bow wrapped around it. "Now you change into that and I'll get your dessert ready. Come join me when you're dressed."

"What is it?"

Moving in behind her, he cupped her shoulders and teased the shell of her ear with his lips. "Open it and find out." With that he turned and prowled toward the door.

For some stupid reason, the scene where Morpheus offered a blue pill and a red pill in *The Matrix* came to mind.

Blue pill?

Red pill?

"Elizabeth?"

She kept staring at the box. "Hmmm?"

"Nothing else goes on but what's in the box. You've got five minutes. If you're not changed and at the table ready for your dessert, I'll come in and help you."

A shiver worked through her, the tone behind his message indicative that help wouldn't mean unzipping her dress and waiting politely while she ducked into the bathroom.

"All right, then," she muttered to herself and snatched up the box. "The red pill it is."

Her march to the bathroom was probably a long way from anything even remotely sexy and it took her a precious thirty seconds glaring at the pretty pink bow before she garnered the nerve to untie it. When she finally popped the lid off, there was still a good amount of delicate tissue paper to dig through until she found— "Oh, fuck no."

She held up the robe, a bubblegum pink to match the bow that had adorned the box and sheer enough when worn to offer a hint of what waited beneath. "There's no way I can wear this. No way." She glanced up at her reflection in the mirror like her other self might have some words of encouragement. When she didn't get it, she stepped farther away from the vanity and let the full length spill out to the floor.

It was beautiful. Classy and daring all at once with silk edging that lined the hem, sleeves and neckline.

And your favorite color.

Not that anyone knew that. She'd given up any pretense of being fit to wear such a romantic, girly color long ago—somewhere between her mother behaving as just short of a whore and accusing her of being the same.

It's been two minutes.

Just try it on.

She rubbed her thumbs along the silk. So incredibly slick. Cool and soft.

If she didn't like it, she could always put the dress back on and tell Axel she wasn't ready to take things to the next level. He'd honor that. Of that much she was sure.

Yeah, but you are *ready. Try to lie to yourself all you want, but you know better.*

It was the truth. Just remembering the things he'd shared about his sexual interests at dinner stirred something inside her. A part of her she'd tried desperately to ignore for fear of turning out like her mother.

But she wasn't her mother. No more than Axel was Joffrey. And here she was, standing in a hotel room that probably cost five grand or more a night with a man that made her body sing with just a look. Why not explore? Just a little taste. One time to see how it felt.

You're wasting time, Lizzy.

Right. Time to throw a little *why the hell not* into the equation and dive in.

Zipper down.

Dress folded.

Robe on.

She cinched the silk belt and finished it off with a bow, all too aware of the massive mirror on her right.

Don't look. Better not to look. Just go.

And how long had it been anyway? Four minutes? Five? Did grace periods for overages apply in a thing like this?

The bedroom was quiet and the door stood open the same as when she'd disappeared inside. "Axel?"

"You've got fifteen seconds, pet." Not a scolding comment. More of a subtle nudge laced with a decent amount of humor.

Just before crossing through the doorway, she hesitated. Checked her belt. The neckline of her robe. Her hair.

"Elizabeth."

One word, but she felt it everywhere. Inside and out. A stroke that filled her with courage and fired a whole layer of anticipation. She stepped through the doorway.

Axel waited at the dining room table, the chandelier above him casting a soft circle around the intimate space as the lights of New York City wrapped around him. He stood as she approached and openly raked her from head to toe with a heated, appreciative look. "Beautiful."

Funny. She could stand in front of a massive crowd and sing her ass off without so much as a flinch, but keeping her chin up and her shoulders back for his leisurely perusal instead of snuggling in close for a hug took everything in her. "Pink's not my color."

The look he gave her said he wasn't buying it, which made no sense. There wasn't a stitch of the stuff in her closet to give him any other indication. He held out his hand to her and crooked his fingers. "Come here. I'd say you've more than earned a reward."

She laid her hand in his, expecting him to guide her into the chair he'd vacated, only to have him resume his seat and pull her into his lap. So startled by the maneuver she giggled like a little girl and bobbled awkwardly until she was tucked tight against his chest. "What are you doing? I can't eat dessert like this."

"Sure, you can." He took full advantage of the moment and kept her cradled tight to him even when she tried to push herself upright. "Now settle down and relax."

"Easy for you to say. You're not balancing your 140 pound body on someone's lap in a silk robe with nothing on underneath."

"And the more you wiggle the more I'll get to see what's underneath."

She stilled in an instant. Sure enough, the neckline had gone from a respectable V to something more appropriate for a nightclub and the lower portion had split up above her knees.

He cupped the side of her face, the pad of his thumb softly fanning along her cheekbone. "Good girl."

Ah, hell.

The mother of all phrases that should've fired every bullet in her feminist arsenal, but unleashed a whole host of butterflies in her belly and sent pleasure spearing straight between her thighs instead. Even worse, the grin on his face said he knew damned well how they'd affected her. "Stop looking at me like that."

"Like what?"

"Like you think you've got me all figured out. I just want my dessert and I'm not above playing games to get it."

His grin grew, that devilish smile that always did her in showcasing a whole lot of teeth. "Well, then. Can't keep you waiting can I?" He pulled an ornate cover off a dish waiting on the table with all the flourish of a waiter in a five-star restaurant.

"Oh, hell. You got me turtle cheesecake."

He slid the plate a little closer and snagged the lone spoon beside it. "Of course, I did. It's your favorite."

"Well, yeah, but how'd you know?"

"Because you scarfed two slices of my mother's at the barbecue, and I heard you tell her you'd take it over any other dessert every time." He spooned up a bite. "Ma would tell you it's not as good as hers, and she's probably right, but we won't offend the chef downstairs and tell him that."

He held the bite up to her mouth.

Rather than open, she said, "I'm surprised you heard me say that. You were across the table talking to your brothers."

"I was across the table pretending to listen to my brothers. I was far more interested in you." He circled the spoon. "Open up, pet."

She did, if for no other reason than to have a few minutes to wrangle her thoughts. Not that it did much good, because the second the bite was down, she opened her mouth and blurted, "What else have you noticed?"

This time his smile was more serene. That of a man with secrets not yet revealed. He held up another spoonful. "I know you love your heels, but the first thing you do at home is take them off and set free one of those sweet little sighs I adore." He pulled the spoon free of her lips. "I know you say pink isn't your color, but your eyes lingered on every single outfit that exact color at least five times while we were shopping today, and you've painted your toenails that shade at least twice since that night at Vic's bar."

She swallowed.

Hard.

"You don't miss much, do you?"

"Not where you're concerned, pet. Not for a second."

He kept feeding her, one unhurried bite after another without a single one for himself. Through it all, he watched her, so thoroughly immersed in the simple act of feeding her it seemed he lived for the simple task. That he genuinely enjoyed the act.

She stopped him two-thirds into the slice with a hand on his wrist. "No more."

He cocked one questioning brow.

"Seriously. I'm stuffed. Plus, it really isn't as good as your mom's." She motioned toward the slice with her chin. "You eat it."

He set the spoon beside what was left of the slice and pushed the plate away.

"What? You're not going to eat any?"

Before she could grasp what he was about, he shifted and firmly cupped the side of her face. "Oh, I'm getting a taste. I'm just picky about how I take it."

And then his mouth was on hers, his kiss as implacable as his arms around her. In the weeks since that night at her apartment, he'd kissed her plenty. Soft, tender ones. Hard ones. Long, drawn-out heated ones that left her toes curled and her sex aching.

But none of them had been like this.

This was a promise.

A vow of everything he intended to give her and a declaration of what he intended to take all rolled up into one. Lips. Tongue. Teeth. He used them all. Held her firm for every wicked stroke and nip and consumed her with a single-minded determination.

And *wowza*, was she on board with giving him whatever the hell he wanted. She gripped his shoulders and hung on for dear life. Met each swipe of his tongue with one of her own and reveled in his taste. She was just about to say to hell with staying put and straddling his lap—the lack of anything under her robe, be damned—when he broke the kiss and rested his forehead on hers.

It took all she could do not to sink her nails into him and beg him to pick right back up where he'd left off. "Why'd you stop?"

For once, he wasn't quick on a comeback. Just pulled in one heavy breath after another for a solid three heartbeats. "Oh, I'm not stopping, Elizabeth." He lifted his head and met her stare head-on. "Just putting things on pause while we cover a few basics."

Basics? "Didn't we already cover that with the whole *I will* always *be the one who leads*, business?"

His lips twitched and his eyes fired with what looked like all kinds of wicked ideas. "Those aren't basics, lass. Those are facts. I'm talkin' about safety."

"Oh."

She said it in a way that indicated she understood exactly what he meant, but somehow, she still felt like she was standing in the middle of some deserted country road with no clue which way was north.

"How long's it been since you've been with a man, Elizabeth?"

Oh. *That* kind of safety. "Ummm." She focused on her knees and pulled the robe so it covered them. "I went out with a guy Rex set me up with last year. Haven't really been much on dating since Joffrey."

"Did you fuck him?"

The crude verbiage got her gaze back on his in a second. "No."

His lips quirked in a crooked smile. "Did you use protection with Joffrey?"

"No. But after everything that happened with him, I figured it was smart to get tested and I'm fine."

"No one since then?"

She shook her head. "I'm not much on sleeping around. Not after watching my mom."

Axel nodded, slipped a hand in his pant pocket and pulled out a single folded piece of paper. He handed it to her. "I have slept around. A lot. But I've always used protection and been judicious about my partners."

The text on the paper was simple. A long list of medical jargon and columns that didn't make a whole lot of sense on first glance. "What's this?"

"My latest tests. With my lifestyle, Zeke's always kept a close eye on me, but I had him run a full spectrum again a few weeks ago, just to be sure."

She studied the form again, the paper crinkling inside her shaky fingers.

"No issues, lass. Not a single one."

Folding it back the way he'd handed it to her, she kept her gaze averted. "I don't have anything like that."

"I don't need anything like that." He took the paper and tossed it to the table. "You said you were tested. You haven't been with anyone since and I trust you. So, unless you tell me you're uncomfortable with it, I'm taking you tonight without protection."

The shiver his words triggered might have been subtle enough he'd missed it, but the catch in her breath wasn't.

"You're sure? I mean, if you haven't up until now, then maybe—"

He silenced her with a stern look. A freaking *look*. Nothing more. "You're mine, Elizabeth. The only thing different about tonight and every other night since the day we met at Vic's is the physical manifestation of that claim and I plan to stake it without a single thing between us."

He teased his fingertips along the tops of her feet, then up between her shins.

The front of her robe from her knees to her ankles parted, the delicate silk whispering against her skin as it fell to either side of her legs, leaving a good span of her thighs exposed.

He inhaled deep, an appreciative masculine sound that made her squeeze her knees together on reflex. Teasing the seam between them, he skimmed his big hand up her thigh then dipped beneath the fabric to squeeze her hip.

And wow, did it feel good. The power of it. The confidence behind his touch and his unwavering focus he kept on her face.

She was spellbound. Utterly rooted in place and he'd barely done anything yet.

Oh, yes, he has, and you know it.

More than that...

You like it.

As if he'd been privy to her thoughts, the stern line of his mouth softened and he slid his hand free. "Stand up."

The look on her face probably would have been enough to convey her confusion, but her mouth got in on the act anyway. "What? Why?"

"Because I said so, pet. And for every second you make me wait, I'll make you do the same at a time you won't like very much."

Wait? When would…

Oh.

Then.

Pure obstinacy kept her locked in place a few seconds, her gaze locked with his in what felt like an erotic battle of wills. "Okay, fine. I'll play along, but only because I'm curious." She stood, praying the maneuver didn't look as clumsy as it felt. "I'm still not buying the whole submissive thing."

"You don't have to buy anything." He stood as well, splayed his hand just above her ass and guided her to the bedroom. "You don't even have to play along. Anytime you're not comfortable, all you need to do is say so."

Mmm hmmm. Like there was any chance of that happening when just the depth of his voice did wonky things to her insides. Still, letting a man like Axel know how far gone she was didn't seem prudent. When he stopped her about five feet from the foot of the bed and turned her so her back was to it, she quipped, "Are you gonna tie me up now, or something?"

Moving in close, he ran his knuckles along her collarbone. "I do love rope." He teased a path along her sternum. "Love watching a woman respond to the rasp of it against her skin. The different patterns I can leave on her body and how vulnerable she is when she's tied up."

Patterns made no sense at all, but imagining the sensation he described and what it might be like to be truly powerless against a man like him made her breasts grow heavy and her nipples pebble against the gauzy weight of her robe. She dragged in a shaky breath, the rise and fall of her chest further heightening the erotic response.

He circled behind her. His heat whispered against her back, not quite touching, but close enough to tempt. Gently, he rested his hands on her shoulders, then skimmed them down her arms until his fingers banded firmly around her wrists. His voice was a low delicious rumble at her ear. "I'm also fond of cuffs. I've got a brand-new leather set for your wrists and ankles, just for you. Soft and supple, but stout enough no amount of wiggling will get you out of them." As fast as he'd gripped her, he released his hold and stepped away. "But no. No bondage. Not tonight."

Dear God, what was wrong with her? Her robe was still on and he'd touched her absolutely nowhere to generate any kind of a sexual response, but her breath was sawing at a deep, unsteady pace, her heart was thrumming and her body was strung tight enough she could probably make herself come with little more than a few strokes of her clit.

Speaking of…why wasn't he touching her? She waited until he paced back in front of her again and tried prodding his male ego. "You sure your mojo's not dried up?"

His lips twitched. "Keep it up, lass, and I'll show you how good it'll feel when I paddle your ass."

She froze. "You wouldn't."

"Actually, I *will*." Taking advantage of her gasp, he moved in close and traced his thumb along her lips. "I have a feeling I'll have to keep a ball gag handy for that mouth of yours, too."

Her breathing shallowed and a whole different level of awareness prickled beneath her skin. "Not sure I'm liking this."

"No different than dinner lass. Trying new things. Exploring. Seeing what works. What doesn't." He kissed her. A slow, tender press of his lips to hers that spoke of care and patience. He pulled away only enough to murmur against her mouth, "No way I'm gagging you tonight, though. I'm gonna see how many different sounds I can get you to make."

Sounds? Maybe. Words? Doubtful.

He lifted his head and stared down at her. "Need you to take a deep breath, Elizabeth, and really listen to me."

A deep breath.

Right.

A normal function.

Easy.

She could do that.

Holding his gaze, she inhaled. Then repeated it.

"If you get uneasy about anything, or something doesn't feel right, you say *yellow*. If you want me to stop—no matter what's going on or why—you say *red*."

"What's wrong with stop?"

His lips lifted in a deviant grin. "Because there will be times you'll beg me to stop and I absolutely won't because I'll know you'll give me more." He sobered for the rest of what he had to say. "But you say *red* and everything stops on a dime. No matter what."

"What about *green*?"

The grin whipped back into place. "Sweet girl, your body's humming with more energy than they capture at the Hoover Dam and we haven't even started yet. I think I can read your *greens* just fine."

Boy, that was the truth. The last time she'd had this much of a buzz going on, she'd drank one too many Red Bulls. Though, that hadn't felt nearly this good. She dipped her head once. "*Yellow* if I'm nervous. *Red* to stop. Got it."

"Good." He cupped the back of her neck and teased her lips with his. "That's the only thing you need to remember. Everything else, I just want you to enjoy." He licked the seam of her mouth. "Relax." Another kiss. This one longer and dragging her deeper with the sound of his voice. "Nothing for you to do except what I ask and learn what you like as we go. Nothing else."

She could've floated there for hours. Stood inside the comfort of his arms and simply savored each brush of his mouth against hers and the soft whisper of his beard against her skin.

Too fast, he stepped away.

The room's chill swept in with his absence and left her trembling and lost. On sheer instinct, she sought him out. Tracked his trajectory toward the bed and started to face him.

"Don't move." His command wasn't overly harsh, but there was no questioning the steel behind it. An implacable order he fully expected her to carry out.

Oddly, she obeyed without question, and a lick of pleasure so utterly foreign, yet profoundly sensual pooled low in her belly.

The soft swoosh of weight against the mattress sounded behind her, followed by two muted thunks against the thick carpet. His shoes, maybe? A slithering sound came next—leather against fabric. Then a soft metal clink against wood. Soft footsteps rounded the foot of the bed and the mattress shifted once more. "Turn around."

Such a simple direction. Even simpler words with the clearest meaning. But what she heard was, *And now we begin.*

She shifted, looking first over one shoulder to find him sitting at the foot of the bed right behind her. His feet were bare, and while his button-down was still tucked in, he'd rolled his shirtsleeves up to his forearms. He'd also taken off his belt and left it coiled on the nightstand.

Facing him, she took a tentative step forward.

"No. Stay where you are." As soon as she stepped back in place, he lifted his chin toward her. "Take the robe off."

Oh. Fuck.

"For real?"

"Did I sound uncertain?" He cocked an eyebrow. "You're also making me wait. We talked about that."

"We didn't talk. You made a statement."

"I did. And yet you didn't balk when I said it, did you?" His gaze narrowed. "And you're still stalling."

Part of her wanted to stomp her foot, jerk the sash free and toss the damned robe at his head. Instead, she tugged the silk free as slowly as she could.

The robe parted down the center, no more than a few inches, but sufficient enough cool air slipped beneath the fabric and tickled her belly and thighs. Lifting her hands, she trailed her fingers along the exposed skin at her neckline.

Axel waited and watched, his eyes locked not on the movement of her hands or her body, but on her face. As if he knew she needed the visual connection to step fully into what he asked.

She peeled the robe off her shoulders.

Gravity took over and the silk whispered against her arms, hips and thighs, pooling softly at her feet. Goose bumps lifted across her skin and her nipples tightened to the point they ached.

And still he held her stare. A predator and a protector poised to fill whatever need she exhibited. "Feet apart."

Another push. A nudge further into his world where control met surrender. This time, she did as he asked with only a flicker of hesitation, bracing her feet shoulder-width apart.

And wow.

She wouldn't have thought such a simple pose could make her feel more exposed than she already quite literally was, but it did.

Finally, he stood and prowled toward her, his perusal of her as languid and purposeful as each step. He stopped right in front of her, no more than six inches between them. "Wider. I want to be able to touch what's mine wherever I want and not have anything blocking my access."

What's mine.

Fuck, but that was hot. No matter how much her common sense and self-preservation railed against it, the rest of her resonated from it like a thoroughly struck tuning fork.

She took two more incremental steps out.

He cupped the back of her head, his fingers loosely combing through her hair as he slid it to the back of her neck. "Good girl."

Her pussy clenched.

Not a flutter, but a full-on mini-gasm that nearly made her knees buckle. Hell, they might have actually done so if it hadn't been for his hand holding her steady.

Given the smirk on his face, he not only knew the effect it had on her, but had anticipated it. "Something else you need to learn—when I tell you to do something, you acknowledge it with *Yes, Sir.* Understand?"

Another mini-gasm swept in right behind the last and a moan slipped past her lips.

"Elizabeth?"

Looking at him wasn't an option. Not if she had a

prayer of holding herself in check. She focused on his shoulder instead. "Hmmm?"

"I asked you a question, pet. What do you say?"

Oh.

Shit.

She licked her lip, the surface of it uncomfortably dry. An irony considering she was pretty sure her sex was drenched. "Yes, Sir."

The response was barely audible, but it whipped between them like an electric current. The urge to lean into him—to rub herself against him like a damned cat—was nearly overpowering. Like her body somehow knew he could not only further quiet the noise in her mind through his touch, but ease the ache he'd created, too.

"Beautiful." He smoothed her hair off her shoulders, teasing his fingertips along her skin in the process. "How'd that feel?"

"Weird."

He smiled at that. "And?"

Just tell him. There's no shame in it. Not with him.

And yet, forcing her lips to move, she still felt like she was headed into a confessional. "I liked it."

"Good." He skimmed his hands over her shoulders. Smoothed one calloused palm across her belly. Traced the curve of each hip and raked his fingers along the front of her thighs.

So erotic. Tempting and delicious despite the fact that he got nowhere near the pleasure points she craved. When he ran the backs of his knuckles between her breasts, her eyes slipped shut and she covered his hand with her own.

"Hands behind your back." Unlike his other commands, this one was sharper. Unbending enough to make her eyes whip open.

His demeanor was just as intimidating. His height. His stern, unblinking stare. The fact that he was clothed while she stood naked before him.

"But I want to touch you."

The candor must've reached him, because his features softened in a second. "Oh, trust me, lass. You'll have your time. But not until I say. And when you want something, you ask permission."

"Ask permission, how?"

She hadn't thought his eyes could get any more heated. Any deeper in color or ferocity.

She was wrong.

He traced her lower lip with his thumb. "*May I touch you, Sir?* usually works. A soft *please* thrown in for good measure probably wouldn't hurt either."

A mixed groan and chuckle slipped out. "I'm screwed then. I've been doing what I wanted when I wanted since I was sixteen and my mother would tell you I don't understand the word *please*."

"Your mother can kiss my ass. And I'm thinking you'll get the knack of asking permission faster than you think you will." His gaze dropped to her arms, then shifted back to her face.

"Right." As soon as she said it, she self-corrected and folded her arms behind her back. "I mean, yes, Sir."

She'd expected another *good girl*. Or maybe one of those devious grins that said he was inordinately pleased. Instead, he cupped the side of her face and kissed the top of her head. Praise and tenderness all rolled into one.

A long, welcome sigh pushed past her lips and her muscles uncoiled.

He rounded behind her, resuming his leisurely exploration with his hands. The length of her spine. Her sides. The curve of her ass. "Christ, Elizabeth." His warm breath danced along her shoulder and his fingers lingered along the crease where her legs and ass met. "I've always appreciated your ass in clothes, but seeing it bare makes me hope you'll fuck up sooner rather than later so I can turn it pink with my hand."

The visible shiver that worked its way through her belied her words. "There's no way I'm gonna like that."

He moved in tighter, the blatant press of his cock against her lower back shocking a gasp out of her. "Gotta take a bite before you decide you don't like something, pet. You taste and something's not for you, we'll set it aside." The press of his hand against one asscheek firmed and his voice dropped to a delicious rumble. "But something tells me you're gonna like the slap of my hand right here when the time comes."

This time she gave into the urge to lean into him, consequences and expectations be damned, a sound somewhere between a groan and a growl fueling her movement as she reached back with both hands to pull him closer.

Not that she got far. Before she'd even had a chance to make solid contact, he had both of her wrists in his hands and her arms crossed in front of her at her waist. "It doesn't work that way, pet. Not with me." His arms tightened around her. "Trust me to give you what you need when you need it."

Trust.

Was that what this was about? Yes, he was exercising control, and so far, she'd yielded it. But none of it had been about putting his needs above hers. Or about using her without thought to her pleasure. Quite the contrary. Every single second—every touch and word—had been

for her. A mental, verbal and physical dance geared solely
for her pleasure.

Like a gear settling into its matching groove, she relaxed into his hold. Rested the back of her head against
his chest, surrendered both mind and body and breathed
in acceptance.

This was right.

Natural.

Safe even as the unknown stretched thick with uncertainty before her.

"Yes, Sir."

The sincerity in her words must have registered because his hold shifted. A reassuring grasp intended
to comfort and support rather than hold her confined.
"That's my girl." His lips skimmed her temple and his
chest rumbled against her back as he spoke. "My sweet,
Elizabeth."

Back and forth, he rocked her. An almost impercepti-
ble motion paired with the steady in and out of his breathing that lulled her deeper and deeper. She was floating.
Drifting in a sensual place beyond anything she'd ever
imagined. She could have easily stood there forever. Simply savored the strength of him. His scent. His heartbeat.
His warmth.

"What you feel right now," he murmured. "That's only
the start. The raw dynamic between us. The more we
step into it, the stronger it'll be. You just need to trust it.
And me." He loosened his hold and stepped away, holding her steady with hands at her shoulders. As soon as
he seemed confident she was good to hold her own, he
circled back in front of her. "Undress me."

Not much could have snapped her out of the happy

space he'd created for her, but the unexpected directive did the job in a jiffy. "What?"

His ornery grin crept back into place. "You wanted your hands on me." He lifted his hands. "Now's your chance. Do your worst."

Axel McKee.

Naked and at her mercy.

She might be new to the whole Dominant/submissive thing, but this was terrain she knew well enough to do some serious damage.

Forgoing the formal stance he'd put her in, she stole forward and smoothed her hands from his belly to his chest. Like all of his clothes, the cotton was the finest money could buy and slid soft beneath her fingers. "Finally."

"Put you off too long, did I?"

She worked the first button loose. Then the next. "Just felt a little out of balance with you fully dressed and me as naked as the day I was born."

"Mmm…" Rather than touch her while she worked, he kept his arms at his sides, making her actions seem that much more formal. "You'll get used to it."

The comment gave her pause on the last button. "You're saying me naked while you're dressed is going to be a common theme?"

"I'm saying you're a beautiful woman and I'm a greedy man with a bossy streak a mile wide. If you don't think I'll take full advantage and enjoy your body every chance I get, you don't know me at all."

"Well…" She dipped her fingers beneath his shirt. "You've been a little slow on the uptake since I met you." She stroked upward, his hot, hard flesh and the soft dusting of hair along the way tickling her palm.

God, he felt good.

So strong. Solid as only a man like Axel could be. More than anything, she wanted to press herself against him. To feel his warmth and weight against her while she drowned herself in more of his drugging kisses.

But he'd taken his time with her. Shown her how intense simple touch could be. Maybe she could do the same for him.

"Needed to wait until you were ready, lass. Couldn't have exactly introduced you to a night like tonight right from the start, now could I?"

Lost in peeling his shirt from his broad shoulders and savoring every inch of the skin she'd unveiled beneath, it took her brain a second to catch up. Once it did, she laughed. An unhindered full-belly laugh that filled the room with its richness. "I'd have likely punched you or taken a guitar stand to your head."

"Probably both." His words were heavy with a wry drawl, but his eyes glinted with mirth. Only once a beat or two of silence settled between them and her fingers lingered at his waistband did his expression sober. "Finish it, lass. We've waited a long time for tonight and I'm not up for a minute more."

Her fingers shook, the clasp of his tailored slacks far more complicated to release than it should have been. The zipper was a near silent hiss. Barely audible over the sound of her heightened breathing and the thrum of her own heartbeat. Her fingertips brushed the tight cotton beneath and she hesitated, her gaze locked on his sternum as an odd, yet also comforting idea took root.

He kept his silence, but gently caressed one shoulder. As if he sensed her mind had stumbled onto something important and needed space and the time to process it.

It was probably a silly idea. Especially to someone like Axel who'd clearly experienced far more sexually than she'd ever dreamed of exploring.

But it felt important.

A simple gift she could share without being asked.

She lifted her gaze to his, fought for another shaky inhalation, then slowly dropped to her knees.

His expression shifted in a second. Darkened even as he reverently cradled the side of her face with one hand. "Oh, Elizabeth. You've got no idea how much that pleases me."

She had some idea. And if it was anything remotely close to how she'd felt kneeling in front of him, it was mighty powerful stuff. Enough so she pushed for a little playfulness in her reply just to ease some of the impact. "I didn't like…trigger some secret BDSM code and swear lifelong obedience, did I? 'Cause that's just not realistic."

His mouth crooked in a lopsided smile. "No. I only want what you give me of your own free will."

Right. Freaking. Answer.

She hooked her fingers in the waistband of his slacks and black boxer briefs and carefully inched them downward together.

And holy schamoley, did she get an eyeful. Axel McKee wasn't just well-proportioned. He was fucking *endowed*. Like to the point she felt it prudent to circle back to the topic where she might as well be a born-again virgin. Trying not to gape at the thick length straining tall and proud toward his belly button, she shoved his pants to his ankles. The way she figured it, she had two options—play the direct approach, or fall back on humor.

Humor.

Always humor.

Better that than wave just how worrisome his size might prove to be in his face.

She waited for him to step out of his slacks, then met his stare. "Do you, um…" She nodded toward his cock. "…need a license to carry that thing? I mean, I'm pretty sure it could be categorized as a weapon."

One second, his head was thrown back and filling the room with his deep, bold laughter, and the next, she was in motion, the room spinning while his powerful arms held her close. Her back hit the mattress in a decadent swoosh, but Axel cradled the back of her head in his big hand before it made contact as well. His body still shook with laughter and his beautiful green eyes were as bright as she'd ever seen them.

"Christ, woman, but you're a wonder. Only you could kneel at my feet, make me laugh like I haven't in years and look sexy as fuck doing it."

A wonder? Really?

Under normal circumstances, she'd have reveled in such praise a little longer. Maybe replayed the comment a few times and tucked away the details that went with it to cherish later. But with his massive body pressed fully along one side of hers and their legs intimately tangled, her mind wasn't too keen on sidebar processes.

Somehow, she did manage a snappy retort. "Not a buzzkill, huh?"

He smiled down at her, one full of pure pleasure and devious intent, then pressed his hips more firmly against hers.

His cock prodded her hip, a hot, insistent weight. "That feel like a buzzkill to ya, lass?"

"No." Her eyes slid shut, her brain all too eagerly coughing up ideas on how it would feel when he pressed inside her. Beneath her palm, his heart thudded a steady, strong rhythm, and his wild russet hair tickled her arm crooked around his upper back. "I think you're still good to go."

The last of his chuckles shifted to a deep moan of appreciation. "My sweet Elizabeth." Much like he had before, he skimmed his hands along her thighs, her hips, and up along her ribs. His thumb fanned out along the side of one breast. "I think the last three weeks have been as hard on you as they have been on me."

"Frustrating," she said, forcing her eyes open so her memory banks could add visuals for later. "At least until I could get home and take the edge off. I think my vibrator's had more action in the last month than it's had since I bought it five years ago."

His expression took on a calculating glint and his voice hinted at a man up to no good. "Has it now?"

Oh, boy.

She'd definitely stepped in a trap. Though, how or where, she couldn't be sure. "Come on. Don't tell me you haven't done the same."

He lowered his head, his voice a delicious growl that whispered against her lips. "Been jerkin' off to thoughts of you so often I'd make a fifteen-year-old boy look lazy." He teased his lips against hers. Nowhere near enough to sate what she wanted. What she craved. "But fair warning— you're about to learn a new game."

"A new game?"

"Mmm hmmm." He nipped her lower lip and chuckled. "Probably gonna piss you off, but if you play along, you'll see—it'll be worth it." Much to her dismay, he pulled away enough she lost most of his weight. He skimmed his hand up the inside of her leg closest to him.

"Why am I suddenly very suspicious?"

"Nothing to be suspicious about." He hooked his hand behind her knee and lifted her leg so his hip held her splayed open. He tapped the inside of her opposite thigh. "Spread wider for me, pet. I always want access to what's mine."

She shivered even as she growled. "I should hate that."

"Hate what?"

"*Mine*. It sounds like something a Neanderthal would say, and I kind of want to punch you in the gut when you say it."

He chuckled and teased his thumb high along the inside of her thigh, his gaze openly taking in her exposed sex. "But it also feels really damned good and makes you wet."

Her lips lifted in encouragement, the so-close touch making the ache between her legs narrow tighter on her clit. "Oh, would you shut up and touch me?"

"No."

That got her eyes back on him quick. "No?"

"No." He guided the arm she'd had wrapped around his back out from around him and shifted enough to give her full motion of both her arms. "You said you got yourself off the last month or so." He dipped his head toward her bared sex. "Show me."

"Okay, that's a new one."

His smile was swift. "Just the first of many, pet. Now, get busy. Show me how you touched yourself when I dropped you off at home."

Easy enough. Not exactly foreign terrain. And she performed for people all the time, right? "Just like I do at home?"

"Exactly the same. The only rule while you do it—enjoy every second of it. Remember every detail."

Yeah, like her brain was going to forget anything from this night. Not freaking possible.

She let out a slow breath. Shifted on the bed until she was comfortable. Then closed her eyes.

It was easier than she'd thought. The proximity of his body to hers, his summery scent and physical warmth wrapping her up in all of those fantasies she'd eagerly nursed each night. She caressed her breasts. Skimmed one palm down her belly. Gently teased the tip of her clit. Before she knew it, her fingers were drenched and release hovered close. She circled her swollen clit, ready to let herself fall over the edge.

"Stop." Axel circled her wrist with his fingers and tugged her hand away.

"Are you nuts?" She tried to sit upright, but Axel was too fast, maneuvering his leg so he held her leg closest to him wide and pinning her hands over her head beneath one of his. With the other hand, he pressed her unpinned leg up and wide.

"Not crazy in the slightest, pet." His voice was pure primal male, the rumble of it moving through every part of her. "Did you remember? Every touch? How it felt?"

"Of course, I did. I'd have felt it better if you'd let me come."

There it was. A wicked grin from the devil himself. "That's the game, Elizabeth. You don't come by your own hand anymore. Not unless I give you express permission to do so. Your orgasms belong to me, Only me."

Her sex spasmed hard, just the thought of being denied something so simple—so fundamental—and placing it in the care of someone else dragging release so close she thought she could come from a single touch. "Holy shit."

"Do you want to come, Elizabeth?"

"Yes."

He tightened his hold on her wrists. "Yes, what?"

Another spasm, this one so harsh it was a wonder she didn't just spill over into the orgasm she craved. She bucked against his hold, her hips lifting as if it would get the hand he pressed low on her belly into motion. "Yes, Sir. Please."

In an instant, his grip around her wrists gentled. He didn't release them, though.

Not that she was remotely interested in fighting him anymore. Not with his fingertips teasing her swollen labia. Teasing the tip of her aching clit.

She rolled her hips.

His touch disappeared. "Don't move."

"Fuck!" If she'd had laser vision in that second, she'd have likely blasted his head straight off with the glare she shot him. "Don't stop."

The sadistic son of a bitch just smiled down at her like he had all the freaking time in the world. "Are you giving me an order, pet?"

Okay. Maybe demanding Mr. Bossy Pants at a critical time like this wasn't the best plan. Granted, she could just say *red*, tell him to mind his own business and take care of business herself, but man…nothing she'd ever given herself had promised to be this big. Nothing she'd ever experienced *ever*. Her lungs churned with all the subtlety of a sprint runner at the finish line and there wasn't a muscle in her body that wasn't strung tight, but she forced herself to stay motionless. "Please?"

His smile deepened, pure satisfaction crinkling the

skin at the corners of his eyes. "You're learning." His touch came back. Light and slow at first. An exploration and a relentless tease that only built her need higher and higher. Slowly, he added more. Deepened his contact. Drew the wetness weeping from her core up and around her clit and circled in confident, demanding strokes.

She closed her eyes. Focused on the rising tide. The press of his thick, strong fingertips against her soaked and straining flesh.

"That's it, Elizabeth. Take what I give you. Know that I'm the one giving it to you. The only one who will." His touch shifted, the heel of his hand now pressing against her clit while his fingertip circled the mouth of her sex. "And after you come for me, I'll bury my cock right here and make you do it all over again."

The second he pressed inside her, her world imploded. Shattered into a thousand tiny shards until there was nothing left but pleasure. Sweet, back-bowing, world-stopping pleasure so powerful and overwhelming it ripped a ragged cry up the back of her throat and sent her reeling. Writhing against his hand. Begging for more with words and noises that likely made no sense.

And she didn't care.

Not one damned bit.

Only knew that if this was the response he was capable of wringing from her, she was definitely on board. An eager enthusiast willing to pay any price for admission.

He shifted, giving her more of his weight, then worked another finger inside her. He changed the angle of each thrust so the pads of his fingertips brushed the sweet spot along her front wall. "Again."

Again?

Was he insane?

After that?

Eyes squeezed tight, she shook her head and wrestled the combatting sensations of the climax still pulsing through her and the impending rush his fingers began to build. "I can't."

"You don't tell me *no*, pet. You say, *Yes, Sir*, and come for me when I tell you to."

Apparently, her body agreed because as soon as the words were out of his mouth, a whole new layer of contractions gripped her. Sent her pussy spasming around his demanding fingers and her thoughts scattering like weightless particles on a wild gale.

"That's mine," he growled above her, the warmth of his breath whispering against her lips. In and out his fingers pumped, a promise of what was still to come and a tether to keep her grounded as she soared. "Every time you come, I'll claim it. Remind you who gave it to you and how they all belong to me."

His thighs wedged her own wider and the steady glide of his fingers disappeared. "Eyes open, lass."

A heartbeat later, his cock pressed against the mouth of her and her eyes snapped open, the abrupt reminder of his size yanking her back to reality. "Axel…"

"Shhh…" He released his hold on her wrists in an instant, cupping the side of her face with a patient tenderness that belied the tension gripping his powerful body. "Hold on to me. Hands on my chest. Legs around my waist."

Like he'd have to ask twice. His heat was a balm. His scent and the weight of him against her a welcome anchor.

"You'll take me." He inched forward, the slow but delicious stretch that came with the motion firing a whole new cascade of flutters through her sex. "Every inch."

Deeper.

Fuller.

A consuming connection that blocked out everything else save the hard glide of him pushing farther and his unwavering gaze on hers.

"You belong to me, Elizabeth. Feel it. Accept it. Own it." He slid to the hilt and she shuddered, the feel of him completely seated inside her so well suited her body seemed to rejoice. Two people, perfectly pitched. Resonating on a level she'd never dreamed existed.

His hips moved against hers, his thick shaft slowly shuttling in and out of her pussy. Then building. Dragging the flared head of his cock against her sensitized flesh and nudging her back to the peak.

She was lost. Drowning in the feel of him. His hard to her soft. Each flex and release of his muscles as he worked himself inside her. The dusting of hair across his chest that teased her breasts. Every ragged and rumbling exhalation he made and the slick, wet sounds of his shaft tunneling inside her.

But his eyes held her steady. Promised everything. Laid every unspoken emotion bare for her to see.

No lies.

No pretense.

Only Axel.

And he belonged to her every bit as much as she belonged to him.

"Yours." Just whispering the word whipped the fire higher. Breathed new life into an already raging storm.

"Aye, lass. All mine." With a wicked and deeply satisfied smile, he braced one hand beside her head and pinned one of her knees high and wide with the other. The angle took him deeper. Amped the pressure of his pelvis against her clit so every rock of his hips was like a living pulse insider her. "Now take what you want. Come for me so I can feel your sweet pussy squeezing my cock."

Words and sensation collided. Exploded in a frantic rush that swept her up and over the peak once more. Her sex fisted his shaft. Grasped and milked the thick length in a greedy clutch she felt clear to the arches of her feet.

He powered deep. Ground his hips against hers and growled his own release, each pulsing jerk of his cock inside her forcing aftershocks that rippled through her already spasming muscles.

Perfect.

Utterly perfect and so damned profound it seemed as if her whole world had been reset. Long cemented points of view rearranged to show a whole new landscape. New realms of possibilities and futures wrapped up in vivid color fueled by a wealth of emotion.

She clung to his shoulders. Rolled her hips and savored the feel of him inside her. The slick glide of his hard flesh inside her. His muscled torso against hers. Breathed in each of his ragged exhalations as he skimmed tender lips against hers.

"My sweet Elizabeth." Slow and steady, he moved inside her. Dragged each moment out as she surfaced with reverent devotion. His touch. His kiss. His complete focus. "Fucking knew it would be like that with you."

How she could laugh at such a moment was a wonder, but a husky chuckle rumbled up from low in her belly. She wrapped her arms around his neck and tightened her legs around his hips. Savored the feel of his hard body flush against hers and the warm intimacy that seemed to wrap them in a secret cocoon. "Really? Because I didn't even know something like that was humanly possible."

She'd expected him to laugh. To unleash that rich baritone she loved so much and cast that smiling gaze that made her feel like she was the most beautiful woman alive down on her.

Instead he stared at her. Anchored himself above her on his forearms, framed each side of her face with his hands and studied her with an intensity that stole her breath.

Her heart kicked uncomfortably. "What's wrong?"

The intensity didn't ebb, but a softness crept into his expression. A tenderness that matched his gentle touch. "Waited a long time to earn that laugh from you. Got it on a night when you gave me your body and opened yourself up to something you weren't sure about. Got it with you soft beneath me and me still inside you." He pressed a soft kiss to her lips and murmured, "Gonna fight to keep that. Whatever it takes—whatever you need—I'd kill to keep that laugh and the woman who makes it in my life."

Whoa.

As confessions went, it wasn't exactly eloquent. More of a warlord staking his claim than any romantic hero making his vows.

But the sincerity rocked her. Wrapped an already perfect night laden with new experiences and discoveries in soft-spun gossamer stronger than steel. "I'd fight for you, too."

It came out whisper-soft and totally unexpected. A vow she accepted as solemn truth as soon as the words crossed her lips.

His lips curled in a smile she'd never seen before. One so open and vulnerable, she could almost see the boy he'd been once upon a time. "That's never gonna be necessary, lass. Though I pity the woman who goes up against you. They'd end up shredded to bits and left in a burning heap of ashes in under thirty seconds."

Damn right they would. Although, if they'd earned her wrath by putting their hands on Axel, she might well leave their hearts beating so she could repeat the process a few more times for good measure.

While she didn't share the thought out loud, her expression must've conveyed the sentiment because she finally got the bark of laughter from him she'd been looking for to begin with. He rolled to his back, taking her with him as he chuckled and tucking her tight to his side, guiding her head to his chest and leaving their legs tangled. His cock pressed still semi-hard between them and his come tickled the inside of her thigh.

"Umm…" She wriggled in his arms and tried to push upright.

His chest still rumbling on the last of his laughter, he tightened his hold and kept her locked in place. "Where do you think you're goin'?"

"I…ummm." Seriously? "I need to go cleanup."

He combed his fingers through her sex-mussed hair at the back of her head and murmured, "Does it bother you?"

This time she must have caught him off guard, because she managed to prop herself up on one elbow. "What? No. I just…well, I thought I was supposed to. I mean—" She swallowed Joffrey's name back before it could come out and ruin the moment. "Isn't that what everyone does?" Because Joffrey had hated it when she didn't.

He cupped the side of her face and pulled her closer. "Just fucked you for the first time, came hard doing it and marked you in the process. Unless you're uncomfortable, I like that mark right where it is."

The muscles between her legs shouldn't be able to move after the night she had, let alone flutter the way they did at his comment. But low and behold, they couldn't seem to get enough of Axel any more than she could.

She nestled back down against him and sighed. "Okay."

Another chuckle, this one paired with an affectionate squeeze from his arm around her back.

Beneath her ear, his heartbeat thrummed a steady beat and the memories he'd given her stretched out like magic lampposts. Markers she'd either missed in her past or simply had never noticed before.

His breathing steadied and the quiet surrounded them.

"Axel?"

"Mmmm?" A comfortable sound. A man replete with satisfaction.

She grinned, both delighted and terrified at the words on her lips. But what the hell. She'd come this far hadn't she? And now she had a whole new world to explore. With Axel. "I think I might be on board with the whole submissive kinky thing after all."

He brushed a kiss to the top of her head, the growled acknowledgment her statement earned her not sounding the least bit surprised. "That's good, lass. Because you're gonna get a lot more of it. And often."

Chapter Sixteen

On a scale of one to ten, Axel was humming at about a hundred. He loved his job. Loved his life. But nothing in the world topped waking up in his bed at Haven for the first time with his Elizabeth curled tight next to him.

Headed down the main staircase that led to the main living room and the massive kitchen beyond, he glanced out the huge transom over the double front doors and confirmed what he'd already suspected—his brothers were here already for rally and he was seriously late. No doubt, that'd earn him more than his share of shit round the table, but after the weekend he'd had with Lizzy in New York City, he didn't give two fucks.

The house was mostly quiet, only the muted voices of his mom and Ninette from the kitchen filling the silence, and the scent of coffee and breakfast already past lingering on the air. He padded into the kitchen on bare feet and found both women seated at the round kitchen table, each of them with a coffee mug within reach. "The guys already in the basement?"

Ninette looked up from her computer, gave Axel's faded T-shirt and jeans a once-over and grinned. "Looks like someone had a full weekend."

"We didn't get in until after two in the morning."

Her grin got bigger, the shit-eating quality to it a dead ringer for the one her son usually sported. "Wasn't talkin' about your travel schedule, son. Was talkin' about the fact that you look like you caught and ate a whole slew of canaries."

Sylvie pushed from her seat, snagged her coffee and headed toward the coffee maker. "Where's Elizabeth? Does she want breakfast?"

"She's still out. We had a full weekend."

Ninette had gone back to her computer, but she still chuckled. "I'll just bet you did."

The grin his mother shot him said she'd thought the same thing, but was doing her best to avoid prying for details on at least that part of the trip. She popped open the top of the single-brew machine, dropped in a pod-thing and punched go. "So? When are we moving her in? I bet we could get her things here in under a day if we coordinated everything right."

Moving in behind her, Axel cupped her shoulders and kissed the top of her head. "Haven't broached that topic with her yet."

She spun so fast, she nearly elbowed him in the gut. "What? Why not?"

"Easy, Ma. She's not goin' anywhere. We just had a few other things to talk about first. I'll tackle movin' just as soon as I get a few other issues under wraps."

Ninette's once pleasant and easygoing voice turned droll and icy. "Hope one of those things is Joffrey Reynolds. Never met a bigger prick in my life."

Uncanny the way his family worked. Hell, he wouldn't be the least bit surprised if, by the time he made it downstairs, Jace hadn't already given the rest of his brothers a recount on the scene they'd walked up on at the radio station and launched a campaign to sink Joffrey's career. "*Prick*'s too kind of a word."

The machine hissed and sputtered as it finished, a sound that seemed appropriate for the laser-focused looks his comment garnered from both women.

"I take it you found out more about her ex after we left?" Ninette said.

His mother knew better than to ask and cut straight to the point. "If he hurt her, I'll gut the bastard with ma own bloody hands."

Axel nabbed his mug from the brewer, cupped the back of his mom's neck and pulled her in for a hug. "Nothin' for you to do but take care of her and show her what it means to have family. And by that, I mean real family. Not that fucked up shit she grew up with."

Ninette grunted, stood and paced toward him. "Sounds like you found out more than just about Joffrey. So, when are you gonna share the details?"

Letting his mother go, he blew across the top of his coffee. "I'm not. When Lizzy wants you to know, she'll tell you. But suffice it to say, I owe Rex a debt for keeping her whole and sane until I found her."

The mention of Rex shifted Ninette's demeanor in a heartbeat. "Oh, yeah?" Her gaze shifted to Sylvie long enough to give her a wink, then she refocused on Axel. "Does this mean your hands-off policy is null and void? 'Cause I'm willing to volunteer for the gratitude committee."

Well, that was one way to shift the mood. He took full advantage of the opening, leaned in and gave the woman who'd been a second mother to him nearly all his life a kiss on the cheek. "Think we're past the good impression stage now. If you think he'll make you happy, I say go for it." He turned and headed for the stairway just off the kitchen that led to the basement. "I told Lizzy I was headed down, but I only got a garbled murmur back from her." He opened the door and his brother's voices rumbled up through the opening. "You two good takin' care of her while we talk business?"

Ninette planted both hands on her hips, a scolding brewing behind those ice blue eyes of hers. "She know about rally yet?"

"Rally, no. But she knows we don't fuck around when it comes to taking care of our own, and right now, I need to take care of one of our own."

Sylvie shooed him on. "We'll take care of her. Go, hurry up so we can know the plan."

Fat chance in hell that was going to happen, but he'd think of something to tide her over before he came back up the stairs. He nodded and headed down.

Oddly, it was Danny who started in with the razzing when he hit the bottom stair and came into view. "Wow. A Monday morning and he's not just late, but wearing T-shirts and jeans."

"And barefoot, too," Zeke added.

Jace aimed that wicked smile of his at Axel. "Guess Don Juan finally met his match."

"Oh, get it right up all yer arses." Axel spun the big barrel-style chair with its ruby red crushed velvet around, dropped into the worn thick cushion and rested his arms on the rounded sides. Every man around the table had their own seat—something chosen to mark a time or event in their life, or simply something they needed to remember. His was undoubtedly the most garish of the group. Something better suited for a 1970s porn flick. But he and Jace had picked it up for a song at an estate sale not long after they'd moved into their first apartment and those had been some of the best days of his life.

Or had been—until this weekend.

He swept the men gathered with a hard look, then landed on Jace at the end. "You fill 'em in yet?"

"That Joffrey Reynolds needs to have his nuts shoved down his throat?" Jace shook his head. "Didn't need to. Sylvie and Mom covered that over bacon and eggs before I got a word in edgewise."

"Yeah, but they didn't have details," Trevor said, "and given the look on your face, I'm thinking there are a lot of them."

"Enough, that I want to know everything there is about Joffrey Reynolds. Who he works for. What his weaknesses are and every fucking secret he's got."

"How bad is it?" Beckett asked.

Axel spilled it all. Reiterated the copyrights Joffrey had stolen and used with other clients he'd signed. Lizzy's family dynamic. How it set her up for Joffrey's head games and how she'd taken his shit emotionally before it finally escalated to physical violence. "Rex is the one who got her out. She was in bad shape, but he packed her up, took her to his place and then got her help."

"That why he moved here when she did?" Knox said.

Axel shook his head. "Think that's more because he's the closest thing to a father she's ever had. Her mom likes men. Didn't care she was married or what it did to her own man. And more than that—she was jealous of Lizzy. Made it so her own dad never paid her any attention to save her from more blowback and filled her head with all kinds of bullshit. If it hadn't been for Rex, she wouldn't have had anyone." He paused a beat, the same gratitude that had done nothing but build since the day he'd met the man swelling bigger in his gut. "I owe him. Big-time."

"Easy enough to pay it forward for a man like that," Jace said. "The bigger question's what you've got in mind for the ex."

The same fury that'd hit him when he'd learned how bad things had gotten for Lizzy rushed him all at once, his face hot with the power of it and his hands itching to wrap around the man's throat. "Death's too good for that cock sucker. I want him to hurt, and I want it to drag out so long he never forgets."

Usually the quietest one of the group, Zeke weighed in. "The way Jace described the guy, seems the best way to do that is to hit him on the financial side."

"Fuck that," Beckett said. "If a man took a hand to my woman, I'd maim the son of a bitch and do it in a way no one ever looked at him again without flinching."

Danny chuckled. "Ya mean kinda like what you did to good old Judd?"

Beckett's expression turned wicked, the mere mention of the man who'd nearly destroyed Gia's career reigniting his temper. "Exactly like that."

"Do both." This from Ivan and delivered in an understated tone that was equally ice cold. "A man lays a hand on a woman, he deserves whatever he gets."

An understandable sentiment coming from him considering his sister had died at the hands of a man who'd beaten her. An event that had mysteriously ended with the boyfriend going MIA and the man Ivan had been back then disappearing at the same time.

Axel nodded. "Exactly that."

Jace leaned forward and crossed his arms on the table, the big black coffee mug he'd brought down with him in easy reaching distance. "You wanna do this right, it's gonna take time for research."

"You're point?" Axel fired back.

"My point is, you look like you're ready to rip this fucker's head off and piss down his neck. You think you're gonna be able to hold your shit in check long enough for us to build all the traps?"

Oh, he'd wait. And he had his own plans to put into action while he did. "That scunner stood in front of *my* woman and played her off like a worthless piece of shit. Did it in front of me and my family. That means I'll not only bide my time to make the revenge I hand her worth it, but I'll use the space in between to build Lizzy up so damned high he'll choke on his words on the way down."

The comment garnered a swell of grins, chuckles and nods around the table, each man clearly in agreement. It was Knox, though, who spoke. A game maker ready to engage. "Guess I'm not just diggin' for dirt this week, but bumpin' those algorithms to a whole new level." He threaded his fingers and cracked them with a dramatic flair. "We got us a star to make."

Chapter Seventeen

"Goddamn, Lizzy. This is huge."

Rex's gravelly voice behind her was low enough none of the other people in the VIP tent to one side of the stage could hear it, but it was also thick with the same degree of awe she'd been wrestling with for hours.

Out in front of them both, throngs of people filled the wide-open space in front of Dallas's most popular outdoor venue, a year-round music stage dubbed The Green situated in downtown Dallas's Klyde Warren Park. The sun was just making its final descent, the soft yellow, golds and mangos of the western horizon etched with the city's skyline. Up on stage, the opening band worked it for all they had, pouring out their heart to the people standing, sitting in lawn chairs or sprawled out on blankets along the sides.

And she was up next.

Lizzy Hemming.

A headliner for the first time.

And not just on any weekend either. But a Saturday night Labor Day show that had drawn a maximum capacity crowd.

"Baby girl," Rex said still in his hushed and dumbstruck voice, "you've hit the big time and you've done it huge."

All those negative thoughts she'd wrestled with since she was a kid, most of them delivered in her mother's voice, for once were silent. Struck stupid and speechless by the sight in front of her and the day she'd had. "It's pretty wild, huh?"

"Wild?" Rex shifted out from behind her and motioned to the VIPs behind him with his longneck. "Lizzy, you've got people here from every one of Dallas's rock stations, the dude who interviewed you on the alternative station and a rep from one of those music video channels ridin' Axel and his brothers for more exclusives. You've got a VIP tent that'd make any headliner proud and your band's so giddy from all the attention and photo ops they've been pulled into, I'm not sure they're gonna know an A chord from a solo ride. I even heard some chick from a guitar magazine scheduled an interview with Skeet."

"Wow." Lizzy scanned the crowd for any sign of her guitar player. "Really?"

"Really. And you'd have thought Sylvie, Ninette and Viv were born for this shit the way they're workin' the guests. Pretty sure everyone with one of those fancy laminated things around their necks walks away from them thinkin' you're the next big thing since Elvis."

Lizzy tried not to make a face, but it didn't work. The whole Elvis-as-a-measure-of-success discussion was one they'd debated for years. "You're comparing me to a dude who wore rhinestone jumpsuits and capes and died on the toilet."

Rex got mock stern in a heartbeat. "Don't knock The

King, baby girl. He had style. He had the voice. And he had the moves—just like you."

"Oh, give it a rest. You were only fourteen when he died."

"Old enough to know a legend when I saw one and grew up cuttin' my teeth on his music."

Axel's warm voice laced with a heavy amount of amusement registered a second before his heat blanketed her back and his hands rested on her hips. "Not sure there's any time I've seen the two of you together you're not locked in some kind of debate." He kissed her cheek. "What's the topic this time?"

"Elvis," Rex answered before she could. "Told her she was a legend on par with him in the making."

Lizzy twisted enough to meet Axel's eyes. "Rex is a little overwhelmed with all the pomp and circumstance today. I'm tryin' to bring him back down to reality."

Axel grinned at that and kissed her forehead. "Hate to break it to you, pet, but—with the track you're on—this is your new reality."

Rex raised both eyebrows, looked down his nose at her in one of those *told-ya-so* looks, then took a pull off his beer.

Ignoring him, Lizzy leaned back in Axel's hold enough to study his face. "What's that supposed to mean?"

That smug expression that usually preceded her being shocked stupid or blown away by yet another toe-curling smile settled on his face. "Just got the word from Knox. *Billboard* rankings are out. Your single's in the top ten."

"Whoa!" Not giving two shits she was still semi-wrapped up in Axel's arms, Rex swooped in and pulled her to him for a huge bear hug. "Now, that's what I'm talkin' about." He squeezed her extra tight then released her almost as fast as he'd grabbed her and focused on Axel. "What number?"

"She's at eight and Knox says signs show she's only gonna track further upward. Pre-orders for the full album are trending up and building steam."

The driving bass and steady kick from the drums on stage matched the wild rhythm of her heart, and where the den from the crowd and guests in the VIP tent had been fairly prominent before, now it all meshed together like she was underwater.

"Hey." Axel's low voice pulled her back to the surface, his firm, yet gentle palm against once side of her face a lifeline in an unexpected storm. "You okay?"

She swallowed hard and met his gaze, the burn behind her eyes threatening tears.

Don't cry.

Not now.

You gotta sing.

You gotta make people happy, not freak them the fuck out.

And Axel would definitely freak. To the point of canceling the whole freaking show if he thought she needed it. Contemplating how it would impact the moms wasn't wise in any capacity. "I'm fine. I just…" What the fuck did someone say in a moment like this? "You're sure?"

His concern evaporated, the white of his teeth appearing in the wake of his huge smile. "I'm sure, lass."

"*Billboard*? Not some local chart?"

"It's *Billboard*. Heard it straight from a rep who's here and wanting an interview."

"Fuckin' A," Rex stated from beside her with all the attitude of a sports star talking smack. "Baby girl's gonna interview with *Billboard* fucking magazine. Get a load of that!"

She giggled, the full weight of what she'd learned finally plowing through her initial shock long enough to let Rex's enthusiasm carry her past her shock and fear. Or at least it banked her fear right up until she realized how close they were getting to her turn on stage. "Wait. An interview? Right now?"

"No, lass. Not until after the show. Got about four of 'em I've managed to put off until you're off stage and we'll do those back at the after-party."

"Oh, yeah," Rex said. "Ninette said they got ya set up at the Adolphus. Fancy digs."

Fancy indeed. The first time she'd stepped foot in it a week ago, she'd felt like she'd shot back to a time when women wore nothing but long dresses and met for afternoon tea every day. "I still don't see why we're doin' it there. Renting that swanky bar downstairs was money we didn't need to spend."

"It's all about appearances," Axel said. "Speaking of…" He nodded to the also completely unnecessary line of tour buses lined up off to one side of the VIP tent. Though, with the Texas summer heat still hanging on for dear life, having some good old fashion AC to escape into from time to time had been a blessing. "Time for you to get your ass in there and do whatever it is you've got to do. Your opener's gonna be off the stage in one more song and the crew's gonna have your gear set to go thirty minutes after."

"Right." She squared her shoulders and tried to ignore the butterflies swarming her insides. "Showtime." Not caring that it probably ruined her badass image in front of the other people around them, she leaned in and planted a solid, yet tame kiss to Axel's lips. "Thank you," she whispered. "For everything."

She'd planned to pull away and head to the bus, but he held her fast and whispered right back against her mouth. "Don't have to thank me, Elizabeth. It's not just your dream anymore. It's ours." He gave her another, shorter kiss, let her go and swatted her on the ass. "Now, get your ass in there and get ready."

In the end, she'd had closer to an hour to get ready, but it still felt more like fifteen minutes. No doubt part of the reason being she'd changed her outfit four times, the last switch putting her back in the first pick she'd started with—rocker jeans, killer black heels and black fitted vest that zipped up the front. Cool enough the weather wouldn't kill her by the end of the night and fitting for an outdoor show, but still edgy and badass enough to fit the vibe she was after.

The trip to the stage went by in a blur, the only real constant that kept her grounded and centered the steady presence of Axel by her side and the chatter from her bandmates around her. The sun was fully gone, only the royal blue of the western sky leaving any reminder of the day that had past. The open park area that stretched a good football field long in front of the stage was packed with even more people than before and the classic AC/DC piped through the speakers seemed to have them energized and ready to go.

Well out of view from the crowd on the side of the stage, she adjusted her guitar hanging over her shoulder and gripped the neck. Roadies hustled this way and that, so focused on getting their job done right under Axel's watchful eye they barely spared her or her guys a glance. Hell, they'd even tuned her guitar for her beforehand. A luxury she'd never once had in her life and, standing there with nothing to do and a whole lot of nerves to wrestle, she wasn't altogether sure she liked giving up.

A soft hand touched her forearm. A tentative contact so soft it startled Lizzy out of her stupor. Carefully so as not to whack anyone with her guitar, she turned and found Sylvie waiting just behind her. Oddly, her partner in crime, Ninette, was nowhere in sight. "Oh. Hey." She glanced back at Axel who hadn't yet seemed to notice his mom's presence, fully planning on letting him know she was there.

Before she could, Sylvie chimed in. "Leave him be. The lad's focused on taking care of you right now, as he should be." She moved a little closer, a necessity given the activity around them considering how low she spoke next. "I'll not keep ye. I just didn't want ye to set foot on that stage without knowin' how proud I am of you. How proud we all are."

She'd learned a lot about Sylvie McKee in the last two and a half months. That she was an insanely gifted cook—especially when it came to desserts. That she had no compunction about flirting up any man that caught her eye, and that her laugh was truly one of the most joyful sounds God had put on this earth. But in that second, Lizzy realized she also had one of the most amazing hearts and the same uncanny instincts as her son. Instincts driven to protect and stand steadfast behind the people she cared about. "You have no idea how much I needed that right now. This is all…" She scanned her bandmates. The massive stage setup. The waiting crowd. "It's a little intimidating."

"It is that, lass. But you'll conquer it. And you'll do it as only you can." She leaned in and gave her the best hug she could with the guitar between them, her voice in Lizzy's ear just a little gruffer than seconds before. "You go be you. We'll be out there cheering you on and will be waiting when you're done." She backed away, her eyes bright with what looked like threatening tears, though she hid it well with her bright smile. "And tomorrow we're going shopping to celebrate. I'm thinking I may have to try my hand at an outfit like that and see if I can pull it off."

Oh, she'd pull it off. With her personality and the life she'd lead, Lizzy had a feeling Sylvie could pull off anything she had a mind to and make it look easy. "It's a date."

"What's a date?" Axel said, finally distracted from his oversight enough to notice his mother's presence.

Sylvie waved him off. "Just a girls' day out. You take care of our girl. I'm headed out to join the family."

And then she was gone, strutting her way down the stairs and through the VIP tent with the same kind of attitude Lizzy felt on stage.

"What was that about?" Axel said.

I'm in this. My family's in this. For your career and for you.

His words from their first night in New York City blasted crystal clear through her memories. He'd convinced her his part of it was true, and she'd known his family was supportive of the two of them being together, but in that second, she realized what he'd claimed all along was the real deal—they were her family now, too. Supportive. Steady. And in her brief, yet simple visit to the stage, Sylvie had given her the one thing she'd never had in her entire life.

A real mom.

Maybe not by blood.

But in all the ways that counted.

On stage, the same guy who'd interviewed her strolled onto the stage and greeted the crowd, an act that earned him a swell of applause and cheers.

Axel ignored it. Just kept his focus on her, waiting for an answer.

Lizzy smiled huge, a huge swell of happiness pushing out all the fear and leaving only pure joy in its wake. "I'm thirty years old and I just got my first go-get-'em speech."

Axel's eyes warmed, a soft understanding settling behind his deep green eyes. "Yeah? How'd that feel?"

"Like I'm ten feet tall and bullet proof."

He chuckled at that and moved in tight. "Good thing, pet, because it's time for you to kick some rock-and-roll ass."

Sure enough, the DJ was in the final throws of his wind up, the crowd giving it their all as he drove them higher.

The guys strolled onto the stage.

Lizzy held her place, waiting for the final intro. That beautiful hum that always fired beneath her skin just seconds before the first chord was strummed kicked into high gear and her belly dipped and swirled like she was seconds away from leaping from a plane. Except this time was different. This time she had Axel beside her and her family waiting out with the crowd.

He'd given her everything. A chance at her dream. A real family. Passion like nothing she'd ever experienced before. Constancy. Affection.

Him.

She moved without letting herself think too much about her actions, grabbed both sides of his face and gave him a firm kiss just as the DJ started her intro. She lifted her head, but held on tight and let all the happiness she felt in that second fuel words she might regret later, but couldn't have held on to in that moment if she'd tried. "I love you, Axel McKee. You and your family."

"Everyone—give it up for Lizzy Hemming and Falcon Black!"

Axel's eyes heated and his hands at her hips squeezed tight. His words were nearly swallowed up by the crowd's roar and they came out on a sexy growl. "Gonna paddle your ass later for giving me that at a time when I can't give you back an answer you deserve."

Tony counted out the first song and the band struck the first chord.

Stepping away like it took everything in him to pull it off, Axel swatted her behind and jerked his head toward the stage. "Get after it, lass, or I'm gonna keep you here for myself and end up refunding a whole lot of tickets."

Not a rebuke.

No shock.

No fear.

Nothing but ready acceptance, a whole lot of fire behind his gaze and the promise of more to come.

Lizzy grinned and sauntered onto the stage, but glanced back, winked and yelled over the music, "Yes, Sir."

Chapter Eighteen

This was not the time for business. One glance at his woman staring pensive out the window of the limo's window and there was zero doubt in Axel's mind that he needed to be off the phone and focused on untangling whatever was mucking up her head.

But some business couldn't wait. Not if it meant keeping Lizzy's career on track and tying up loose ends. He forced his mind back on track and tuned into the last of Jace's update.

"...and according to Knox, preorders jumped by another twenty percent by halfway through the show. This keeps up, she might debut in the top five when it goes live on Tuesday."

Definitely good news. "That's what we want. The bigger the bang coming out of the gate, the faster we'll roll from there." Axel gently squeezed Lizzy's hand where it rested in his lap, but she didn't look away from the window. Just kept staring unseeing as the lights on Highway 75 swept overhead. "Trevor get Grant Tempe and his girl headed back to New York all right?"

"They were wheels up thirty minutes ago. According to Trevor, the guy vowed to be a lifelong supporter of all things Lizzy Hemming before they even got the door locked for takeoff."

Another bonus. Which meant there was just one last item to make sure they'd effectively crossed off their list. "And the other thing?"

Footsteps and motion sounded in the background, a dead giveaway that Jace was having to get out of earshot before he could cover the day's biggest pain in the ass. "Joffrey Reynolds might be a persistent mother fucker, but he never made it near any of our guests."

Persistent was an understatement. The man had tried every maneuver under the sun to get backstage, in the VIP tent before the show, or into the after-party at the hotel—none of which Beckett's men had let happen. What he couldn't yet tell was if Lizzy had spied Joffrey during those attempts, or if she'd managed to stay blissfully unaware. He'd felt pretty confident of the latter until she'd clammed up on the ride home. "Any clue what he was after?"

"Never said and didn't seem to have any cronies with him to hit up for info either."

"He have any idea it was us road blockin' him?"

Jace chuckled at that. "Nope. He just thinks we've got stellar security. Though, Beckett tells me Ivan fucked with his head a little when they nearly frog-marched him out of the Adolphus parking lot." His chuckles died off and his voice got serious. "You know, a man acts that determined, you can bet it's not gonna be his last attempt."

"Oh, I'm counting on more. Already covered bases with Beckett to make sure she's covered 24/7." The burning push for vengeance billowed up like bile in the back of his throat. "How much longer till we shut this shit down for good?"

"Knox is on it. Hasn't found the level of dirt we need to make a solid play, but you know he'll come up with something. Then we'll shut him down."

Not fucking fast enough for his taste. But Lizzy was safe for now. Too fucking quiet for a woman who'd not only kicked ass and taken names in front of nearly twenty thousand people and wowed an army of press after the fact, but safe.

And alone with him.

Finally.

"Right. Anything on that front breaks, you know where to find me. Otherwise, I'm shutting down for the night. From the looks of things, I got a woman with something on her mind and that doesn't bode well for the celebration I had in mind."

That got her attention quick enough, not to mention a perplexed scowl.

Clearly, Jace had learned enough in the three years he'd been married that the look he was talking about was one he was familiar with because he barked out a sharp laugh. "Better get on that quick, brother. You'll be tried and well on your way to executed if you don't."

Axel grunted, draped his arm around her shoulders and pulled her tight against him. "If I'm not in tomorrow by two, send in a search party." With that he punched the end button, shoved the phone in his pocket and kissed the top of her head. "You wanna tell me what's goin' on, or you gonna make me find creative ways to make you talk?"

Her scowl turned to playful wariness. "The last time you got creative I ended up wearing nothing but rope."

That'd been a fun night. Not only had she responded to the feel of jute against her skin and the intimacy Shibari created, she'd come so many times it'd taken her a solid thirty minutes to form complete sentences. "And you looked beautiful in it." He cupped the back of her head. "Now talk, Elizabeth. Something's doing cartwheels in your head and I want to know what it is."

Sure enough, she tried to look away.

Axel used his grip to hold her firm and stared her down.

She huffed out a frustrated breath. "I'm scared, all right?"

Of all the things she could have said, that was the last on his list. Or at least a good distance from the top.

Unless she'd actually seen that dickweed ex of hers today. In which case, he wasn't so sure he'd be willing to wait for physical vengeance anymore. "Of what?"

She held his gaze a second longer, then let her eyes slip shut and let lose an exhausted sigh. She relaxed into the crook of his arm and dropped her head against his shoulder. "Do you have any idea how big today was for me?"

"Pretty much the textbook outcome of every rock-and-roll fantasy I had growin' up, so yeah, I think I can hazard a decent guess."

She traced a button on his shirt, quiet for three whole heartbeats before she whispered, "How am I going to top that? I mean…" She pushed against his chest and met his stare. "Everything that's happened the last few months— the recordings. The interviews. The tour. The pre-sales. It's all been great, but what if I can't live up to it? What if the album drops on Tuesday and everyone hears it and it sucks? Or worse, what if they love it and then I have to make another one and it sucks?"

So, no Joffrey on the mind. A plus, considering how bad of a mood just thinking about the jackass put him in.

That said, hearing that much doubt coming out of Lizzy's mouth said she'd been gnawing on her insecurities for a lot longer than he'd realized. "First off, you're worryin' about shit neither one of us can control. We can plan. We can circumvent. We can play dirty and fight. But at the end of the day, life's gonna have what it wants no matter what we do. So, the only real play we've got is soakin' up every drop of right here and right now. The rest'll work itself out the way it needs to."

Her mouth twisted in a wry smirk. "You make it sound easy."

"Fuck, no, it's not easy. Felt the same damned things when Jace and I got our scholarships. When we started seein' success in our clubs. My first thought right out of the chute was wonderin' how long it was gonna last until the rug got ripped out from under us. It's normal. Especially, when you've fought and clawed for all the good in your life.

"But here's the thing, lass. We're fighters. You, me, my family...it's why we work together the way we do. We know how to take a punch and have the support to suck it up, stand tall and get back in the fight after it happens. Your career's gonna be no different."

The limo slowed and veered off the Knox-Henderson exit, a shift that swiftly diverted Lizzy's attention and drew a sharp frown. "Where are we going?"

"Had to share you with too many people the last few days. Not up for sharin' tonight. Not with that gift you gave me today still ringing louder than Skeet's amplifiers."

The driver took a left and steered them through the bustling nightlife toward the elite neighborhood where his home was located. Even if the shadows had done a better job at hiding her blush, she couldn't have hidden the shyness behind her eyes if she'd tried. "That was probably too much to say."

"You try to take it back, I'll make that playful paddling you got last week look like a tickle."

She bit her lip and her chin hitched downward like she was really fighting holding his gaze, but she pulled it off. "I didn't say I wanted to take it back."

God, she was sweet. A playful kitten hiding behind the facade of a vicious black panther.

And she loved him.

Him.

A no one who'd grown up in a trailer park with a whore for a mother.

They came to a stop in front of his house—a moderately sized home compared to the rest of those in the neighborhood and so heavy on the contemporary design it looked like it'd popped right out of the future. At most, he'd spend three or four nights a month here, but it gave him a private space to retreat to when he needed it and it fit him better than Haven's décor.

Lizzy shifted closer to the door and gaped out the window. "Whose place is this?"

"Mine."

She spun just as the driver opened the door. "You've got *another* house? Why?"

Chuckling, Axel stepped out of the car and helped her out. "The Compound's a place we use for out-of-town guests and parties. No telling who's going to be there. Haven's home with lots of space to spread out no matter how many of us are there, but sometimes a man's just got to have space away from everyone else."

Lizzy paced up the winding flagstone walk and scanned

the front facade. The lines were clean—tan sandstone so pale it was nearly white, a slate gray aluminum roof, and loads of deeply tinted windows. "It's pretty. Simple, but classy."

"It's nothing in size compared to Haven or the Compound, but I didn't need much. Just an escape." He unlocked the front door, pushed it wide, and motioned her in. "I've got a lady who takes care of it for me when I'm not around. She came over this morning and freshened the place up for us, and Ma left us a care package for the night."

Inside, only the two lamps on either side of the charcoal flannel sofa and a soft overhead light from the kitchen to the left of the living room offered any light. The moon was full, though, spilling through the massive windowed-wall that looked out into the backyard.

Gaze roving in all directions, Lizzy padded across the thick gray rug that covered much of the dark, hand-carved wood floors and gently set her purse down on the glass coffee table. "They should do this place up in one of those urban living magazines."

"You like it?"

"Hell, yeah." She hurried over to the window and peeked outside. "I mean Haven is awesome, and the Compound looks like it belongs in a mob movie, but this place is slick."

Interesting. Almost everyone in his family had given him a hard time for buying the place, but they'd really piled on the ribbing once he'd fitted out the insides.

Beyond the window, his property stretched for another half-acre—no small feat in this part of Dallas. All around it, a nine-foot stone fence surrounded the heavily manicured lawn and lagoon-style pool. He didn't pay attention to a lick of it. Just kept his gaze rooted on Lizzy's reflection in the window and the wonder on her face.

He kept his distance, though pulling it off was a Herculean feat considering how bad he wanted his hands on her. "Shoes off, pet."

In an instant, her expression shifted. Where she'd first started her sexual journey with him heavy on caution, now she seemed insatiably curious. A kitten who'd learned the joy of tugging and swatting at every string he dangled in front of her and took pleasure in each and every game.

"You know the protocol," he said. "The second you're through the door, the shoes come off." Protocols were a practice many Dominants used with their submissives—simple rules designed to strengthen their dynamic and meet each of their needs. With Lizzy, he hadn't instituted many, but this one had brought her pleasure the first night, so he'd kept with it.

"I didn't know the rules applied to this house."

"Well, now you do." He nodded to her feet. "And I'm still waiting."

Challenge flashed behind her striking blue eyes. A single beat of defiance bred from years of having to stand up for herself when no one else would.

And then she softened.

Lowered her gaze and let out a shaky breath as she worked the first shoe free. Her words today had been a gift. A surprise he'd never dreamed he'd earned this quickly.

But this—seeing the depth of her trust and willingness to surrender to him when they were alone—was love and trust in motion every single time. As raw and vulnerable as a woman could be. And she'd stepped into it fully.

Embraced every new sensation—every experience—
with the same passion and abandon she shared on stage.

She straightened from her task, the fitted black tunic
dress she'd changed into after the show for her interviews
a mix of sex kitten and runway model. Without him having to give further direction, she unwound the loose braid
that hung over one shoulder, holding his stare as she did
and then shaking it free.

Another protocol. One only required when they were
alone, but that she'd come to appreciate when she realized it meant he'd spend ample time with his hands in
it, combing through the thick strands until she all but
purred next to him.

And his Elizabeth definitely loved to be petted. He
stalked toward her. "Much better." Capturing her hand,
he pulled her close, one hand cradling the back of her
head and the other low on her back. "Do you need anything? Food? A drink?"

"I've spent all but the two and a half hours I was on
stage today with your mother. If I eat anything else, I'm
going to have to go up a dress size."

He grinned at that. "If that workout on stage didn't
counter all Ma's power snacks, then what you'll get tonight should do the trick."

She cocked an eyebrow at that. "We're trying something new tonight?"

Oh, he had something new in mind. Something that
promised to rattle him at the deepest level. But if she was
strong enough to put herself out there, then he could, too.
She deserved that much, and so much more. "Something
like that." He ran his nose alongside hers. Breathed her
in and allowed himself a moment to simply savor the energy that always flowed between them. Two beings in

perfect symbiotic rhythm. "If you need anything, tell me now, because we're both going to be too spent to move, let alone make it to the kitchen before I'm done."

Her fingers at his shoulders tightened and her lips whispered against his. "All I need right now is you. To not think. To not worry. Just to feel and let go."

Christ, she was a wonder. Every time he thought they'd reached a place they couldn't get any closer—any more tightly synced—she'd go and say something like that and rearrange everything he'd thought possible. "Lass, if you can think or worry from this point forward, I'm not doin' my job right." He sealed his grumbled words with a firm kiss, then forced himself to step away before he could change his mind and take their night on a completely different course.

He captured her hand, laced his fingers with hers and led her toward the stairs. "Come on. If I'm gonna do this right, we gotta go where the tools are."

"The tools?" She kept pace beside him, but a definite inquisitiveness spun through her voice. "Are you telling me you've got kinky furniture, whips and crops, or something?"

Saucy damned woman. "No. Never had a need for any of that before. If I played, I did it at a club, or with toys I carried with me." They rounded the landing halfway up the stairs and headed for the second floor. "Though, the way we're working through things, I'm thinking I may have to re-think my strategy to keep you entertained."

Her smile was pure delight. A highly sexual woman's equivalent to a kid who'd been given the keys to Candyland. "Bet you'd have a hard time explaining that one to the moms."

Probably less than she'd think. Neither his mom nor

Ninette had ever said boo to him about the rumors they'd
undoubtedly heard. But then again, they knew what it felt
like to be the center of trash talk.

At the top of the stairs, he paused, pulling her to a
stop beside him. Moonlight spilled through the many
open windows, casting shadows on the dreams he'd left
behind. He hadn't been joking when he'd said the house
was nothing in size compared to Haven. Where the upstairs had once offered three moderate-sized bedrooms,
his renovations had turned the entire space into one large
area more reminiscent of urban lofts. A space devoted
to his first love.

Music.

He flipped the wall switch and a floor lamp nestled
in the far corner of one end and two lamps on either side
of the bed at the other cast the spacious room in a soft
white glow. While the ceilings had once been uncomfortably low, now the height of the room soared and exposed the beams he'd had replaced with chunky gray
patina wood. The wood floors had the same hue, only
lighter, the oak planks reclaimed from some farmhouse
or barn his decorator had found in New Hampshire. Rugs
in cream, taupe and dove gray rounded out the modern
space. A bohemian touch to what might have been a cold
tapestry without them.

A decorator's dream. But that wasn't why he loved
the place. And it took Lizzy all of a second to register
the real importance to him, the significance poignant in
her soft gasp. "Jesus." She slipped her hand free of his
and reverently padded toward the center of the room, her
gaze lingering on each instrument. "It's like a guitar col-
lector's Mecca." She glanced back at him, her eyes wide.
"No wonder you didn't flinch when Mary wanted to use

your guitar at the Compound. That Martin was just a drop in the bucket to some of these."

She wasn't wrong there. Though, he'd probably still let Mary have a go with some of the ones here even if they were worth four or five times those at the Compound. He scanned the Fenders, Gibsons and one D'Angelico that cost as much as a luxury sedan. "I might have given up the dream, but I never gave up the love. Every one of them sounds amazing."

She all but tiptoed closer to them, lifted her hand to touch one of the Martins, then hesitated. She looked back at him. "Can I play one?"

Yep. Kid in a candy store. And he was about to make it better. "Seeing as how they're yours just as much as they are mine, you can play any damned one of them you want." He started forward. "But not until tomorrow. Tonight's for something else." He motioned her to the black leather loveseat. "Sit right there."

Confusion marked her face. "What do you mean they're as much mine as yours?"

"Just what it sounds like." He fixed her with the stern look that usually got her hustling when nothing else would. "Sit down, pet. Don't make me say it again."

It wasn't often she balked anymore, but in that second, it looked like curiosity was pushing her to do just that. Screwing up her mouth in a cute little mew, she finally redirected to the loveseat and sat on the edge, her hands curled around the edge. "Okay. Now what?"

Now, he bared himself in a way he rarely did for anyone anymore. No one but family.

He studied the guitars, his gaze lingering on each one as if the visual contact might give him both inspiration and courage. The '36 acoustic Gibson with its deep-stained edges and starburst center hung mounted near the bottom of the display, nowhere near as valuable as most of the others above it, but it'd been the first in his collection. A huge step up from the pawnshop version he'd learned on. He plucked it from its holder and settled on the end of the wide leather ottoman that doubled as a coffee table. As steady as the temperatures were in his house, tuning it took almost no time, and just having the instrument against him—the solidness of the neck resting in his palm and the press of the strings against his fingers—calmed him. Centered him in much the same way Lizzy's presence did, only more familiar. An old friend.

Lizzy held completely still. Didn't budge so much as an inch. Which, considering her penchant for fidgeting when she was uncertain, said she'd intuited just how important this moment probably was for him.

He strummed a chord.

The guitar's rich sound filled the space, the subtle vibration of the strings a perfect mirror to the nerves he barely kept in check. He met her stare and set free the words that had danced around in his head all night. "You gave me something important today, Elizabeth. Laid yourself out in a way no one's ever done for me before." He strummed the same chord. "Of all the dreams I've had for myself, that's one I never thought that could be mine."

"Axel—"

He shook his head to cut her off and began to play. A classic by today's standards, but he still remembered the first time he'd heard it.

Van Morrison's "Someone Like You."

When he'd first heard it, he'd sat down and learned to

play it under an hour, and wondered what kind of woman could make a man write a song like it.

Now he knew.

The lyrics spilled out. The notes comfortable. A message shared in the most sincere form available to him. By the time he reached the final verse he was lost. Fully immersed in the moment and connected with her in a way he suspected few others ever experienced.

"Someone exactly like you."

The last chord rang then softly faded to nothing.

Lizzy watched him. Studied him as though seeing him for the first time, utterly shocked and fascinated.

A quip as to how he'd obviously found a new way outside of sex to leave her tongue-tied sat on the tip of his tongue.

Before he could launch it, her awe shifted to a tender smile. She slowly shifted to her knees in front of him, her touch tentative atop each of his thighs. "Me, too."

Such a simple response. But it was perfect. He cupped the side of her face, the swell of emotion he felt in that second so thick it was nearly impossible to speak. "Not a thing I wouldn't do to keep you in my life, Elizabeth. No expense I wouldn't bear. No act I wouldn't take if it meant keeping you safe and with me." He soaked in every detail of her face. Traced the line of her cheekbone with his thumb. "That's what a man does when he's in love."

"I didn't say it expecting anything back."

"And I'm not sharin' it because I think you did. I'm sharin' it because it's time and it's right." He tightened his grip. "And just so we're clear, as soon as we get your tour behind us, you're marrying me."

She jolted and cocked her head, her eyebrows popping high. "You're asking me to marry you?"

"No. I'm telling you we're getting married. You're already mine. Putting a ring on your finger is just a way for me to make sure every other man knows it and to make sure you're protected in every possible way." He pulled her closer and all but growled against her lips. "Everything I have is yours, Elizabeth. My money. My property. Businesses. Me. My fucking soul if you want it."

He'd meant to give her soft. Wanted to. But the soft rasp of her sharp inhalation at his vow snapped his control.

He fisted her hair at the back of her head and took her mouth. Consumed her kiss and swallowed down her pleasured groan.

Fuck, but he loved the taste of her. Sweet and sultry, just like the woman. Loved the way her body unfurled with his touch. How her breath mingled with his. How her hands roamed his chest, shoulders and arms and she leaned eagerly against him as though desperate for more. For all the discipline he'd been able to call upon since the night he and Jace had learned about their mothers, tonight it was almost nonexistent. A nearly empty well that left only primal drive and instinct to guide him. A beast without benefit of conscience and only a primitive urge to guard and take what was his.

Remember what she gave you.

The memory of the smile she'd given him in the seconds after she'd told him she loved him rushed in after the thought. Her blue eyes bright despite the shadowed corners of the stage. The complete abandon she'd put behind each word.

He forced his hands to relax and gentled his kiss. Glided his lips against hers and breathed her in. "Need you to stand up, lass."

"Now?"

"Yes, now." He nipped her lower lip. "Otherwise, you're gonna be naked and under me in another ten seconds, and that's not how I want tonight to go." He forced himself to lift his head and let her go. "Now, up you go."

The look on her face said fighting the gravitational pull was just as much of a challenge for her, but with a wrinkle of her nose, she did as he asked.

He leaned the guitar against the sofa to his right and stood. "Stand at the foot of the bed. Facing me."

"Yes, Sir." It came out cuddly-kitten soft. A sweet sound he doubted any other man had ever heard slip past her amazing lips and damned sure wouldn't ever be shared with another going forward.

He followed her more slowly, openly appreciating every inch of her. When he finally made it to her, he smoothed his hands from her elbows to her shoulders and down again. "You have one rule tonight, pet."

"Only one?"

Under normal circumstances, he'd have swatted her ass just for fun. But tonight wasn't a normal night. He settled his hands on her hips and inched the hem of her dress upward with his fingers. "One rule until morning." With the fabric bunched beneath his palms and her legs bared, he teased the outside of her thighs with his fingers. "You stay only in the present, you feel and you let go. No thoughts of tomorrow. No thoughts of tours. No thoughts of anything except us and what's going on between us."

"You just told me I'm getting married. Gonna be hard for me to let that one go."

He slipped his hands beneath the fabric and palmed her hips, the only barrier between him and her skin the delicate lace of her panties. "You have a problem with marrying me?"

"No."

No hesitation.

Zero.

And while the simple answer had been more whisper than solid voice, the emphasis behind it was significant.

"Then I'll amend my rule—you stay in the present, you feel, you let go and know beyond the shadow of a doubt that the things you're gonna feel I'll give you so long as I'm drawing breath." He paused long enough to let his words sink in. "Think you can handle that?"

She held his stare, an emotion he couldn't quite identify dancing behind her blue eyes. "I think with you next to me, there's not much I can't handle."

His hands tightened of their own volition at her waist, the raw sincerity in her words dragging free his own. "Well, then, you're set to conquer the world, lass, because I'm not going anywhere."

He peeled the dress up and over her head.

God, she was beautiful. Strength, grace and femininity combined perfectly. Since their night in New York City, he'd spent ample time appreciating her body. Learning every inch of it. Finding which sensations made her moan and which made her cry out. Tonight, his search was far more important. A goal he'd never once dared to reach with another woman—touching the heart of her. Peeling back every emotional barrier and forging a link neither of them would ever want to break.

Her dress slipped from his fingers, unheeded, to the floor. Tempted as he was to rid her of her delicate panties in a far more primitive fashion, he peeled them past her hips until they pooled around her ankles and held her steady while she stepped out of them.

Crouched in front of her, he looked up and found her watching him with an expression he'd come to adore. A genuine curiosity fueled by that nonstop mind of hers as it scrambled to try and figure out what he was up to.

That was the thing about his Elizabeth. Her thoughts were always working overtime. Either trying to figure out how to do whatever task was at hand better than she already was, or trying to ferret out how to get in front of obstacles she hadn't even learned about yet. One of the first things she'd told him the morning they'd woken up in New York was the quiet she'd found in following his commands. The mental stillness and focus that came in the wake of each one and how rich every sensation had felt without the weight of everything else to drag them down.

Tonight, he wanted to give her that tenfold. To burrow beneath all the worry and memories of her past and give her something to hold on to no matter what the future handed them. He stood and kissed her forehead. "You're thinking."

"I'm wondering."

"Same difference." He backed away enough to squarely meet her gaze. "Close your eyes."

Again, with the pinched brow and pensive look. Though, this time she paired it with a tiny huff as she did what he demanded.

"Good girl." When he was sure she was steady, he got to work, retrieving a single hank of jute and rigging a slip knot over one of the exposed beams. His dresser sat along one wall, parallel to the beam, the monstrosity of a mirror mounted above it something he'd called a bloody waste of money and space when he'd first seen it.

He was eating those words now. The placement was perfect for what he had in mind. A prime palette to leave his woman with an image she wouldn't soon forget.

Once satisfied, everything was ready, he sat on the bed, toed his shoes off and tossed his socks on top of them.

It was all of three seconds after he'd stood and begun to unbuckle his belt that she broke the silence. "You know I could have helped you with that."

"With what?"

"Your clothes." She dipped her chin and turned her head enough to show her eyes were still closed, but was actively tuned into her sense of hearing. "Normally, you have me undress you."

"And you like that?"

Her smile was quick and filled with genuine joy. "Better than when you have me dress you."

"And why's that?"

The smile softened and a shyness crept into her voice. "Because I like the times when we're alone with nothing between us. Putting them back on you means that time is over."

So sweet. How that tenderness inside her hadn't shriveled up and died at the hands of her parents and Joffrey was a miracle.

Out of his shirt already, he shrugged out of his pants and briefs, tossed them to the bed behind him and took her by the hand, careful to make it the only point of contact. He guided her forward. "Eyes stay closed. Just follow me."

Once he had her lined up with the rope and centered in the mirror's reflection, he gathered both wrists and crossed them. "I have you dress and undress me for a reason, pet. Do you know why?"

At the first scrape of the soft rope against her skin, she gasped, a welcome knowing painting her features even as a mischievous smile tilted her lips. "Because I've inflated your ego too much and you know the more I touch you the hotter I get?"

He chuckled at that and adjusted the rope, slowly pulling her bound wrists high above her head. Not so much she had to strain, but enough she could use the tension to hold herself upright when he gave her cause to lose her balance.

Because he was definitely planning on making her lose her balance. And soon.

He moved in close and cupped the side of her face. "I have you undress me because it helps set the dynamic." He skimmed his lips across her cheek. "Because I know it helps you focus and find that quiet place you love so much." He trailed his lips lower, dragging the line of her jaw and letting his beard rasp against her skin. "But also because I'm selfish and it makes me fucking burn seeing the look on your face when you do it."

Her breaths accelerated. Grew shallow and left her voice at barely above a whisper. "That doesn't explain why you have me dress you."

"Ah, pet." He kissed the curve of her neck. "I like that best of all."

A tiny frown marked her face. "Wh-why?"

He touched the hollow of her throat. Skimmed his knuckles down the valley between her breasts and on to her belly button. "Because when I'm without you during the day, I can remember your hands on me. Know that you were the one who armed me up to face the day and did it with those sweet looks and lingering touches that promise more when I see you again."

A shaky exhalation whispered past her lips. As foreplay went, every point of contact had been simple. Almost innocent. And yet, she came alive beneath it. Shifted from the easy stance of seconds before to one of heightened awareness. A pliant lightning rod primed and ready for another lick of electricity.

He gave her exactly that. Subtle touches along the lower swells of her breasts. Her thighs. Her hips and up the ticklish stretch at her sides. He circled around her. Offered the same soft caresses along her shoulders, down her spine and over the perfect curve of her ass.

With every second, her breaths grew shallower. The trembling in her body more pronounced. Pressed tight against her back, he circled her waist, slowly ghosting his palms up along her belly until he gently cupped her breasts.

Her head dropped back against his chest, the delicate line of her neck beautifully exposed. He skimmed his lips along the juncture where her neck and shoulders met, then grazed the tender skin with his teeth. "Who do you belong to, Elizabeth?"

"You." She arched her back, silently begging for him. "Only you."

Intoxicating. Every time he touched her it was sexual artistry in physical form, but tonight it was more than that. A sacred communion between two souls ideally suited to each other. Oxygen and flame swirling and feeding off each other until there was only heat and an all-consuming need. He tightened his hold. Ground his hips against hers and let her feel how hard and ready his cock was for her. "Feel that, pet. Just thinking of you can get me there. Even when you're not in the bloody damned room." He teased her nipples, slowly rolling and tugging the tight points as she hissed and wiggled her pert ass against him.

"Axel…"

"I know, baby." He slid one hand lower, teasing the top of her mound. "The ache won't go away will it? Even when we're not together it's always there. Just beneath the surface. Asleep, but alive. Just waiting for a chance to run wild again."

She whimpered her agreement and undulated toward his hand. Rather than slip his fingers lower like she wanted, he splayed his hand low on her abdomen. "Be still."

This time the sound she made was closer to a groan, and she wound her fingers around the rope that held her wrists as if she needed the extra support to keep herself in check.

"Good girl." He paired the praise with a kiss to the back of her neck, taking his time to savor the soft skin just behind her ear. He locked his gaze on their reflection in the mirror, poised to capture her response to the image that waited. "Open your eyes, Elizabeth."

She obeyed without the slightest hesitation, her eyelashes fluttering open and her breath stuttering on the sight that greeted her. The exhale that followed was pure sensuality. A pleasurable *Oh* he felt like a stroke along his cock.

He gave himself free rein. Relished the smooth glide of her skin beneath his rough palms. Plumped her full tits in his hands. Pinched her hard nipples. All the while feeding her mind with his words. "Tonight I want you to see what I see. Know exactly the memories I carry around with me every day. How beautifully you respond to my touch. How your body reaches for my touch. Answers every demand I make."

He dragged his thumb down her cleft, barely skimming the top of her swollen clit. "Legs wider, pet. I want room to work."

She made quick work of his request, her gaze riveted to his fingers and the way he teased the seam where her thighs and sex met.

He collared her throat with his free hand and pulled her flush against him.

Her eyes shot to his in the mirror, the possessive hold stilling her completely save for the shudder that rippled through her body.

"You're going to come for me, Elizabeth. Over and over while you watch every second. Until I'm sure it's burned in your brain." He stroked between her slit. Coated his fingertips in the wetness and dragged the silky juices up to her clit. Circled the tight, swollen nub, feeding her just the right amount of pressure to push her to the edge, but not enough to go over.

Back and forth, he worked her. Built the rhythm. Followed the subtle pulses of her hips and the tension building in her body. "You're *mine*. Mine to protect. Mine to pleasure."

"Axel, please."

His cock jerked against her back, the need to slide his length between her thighs and take her the way he wanted nearly breaking his resolve. "Please what?"

Her gaze lifted from his where he worked her. A slow, erotic perusal that promised no detail went unnoticed. The contrast of their skin. The breadth of his body compared to hers. Her curves and soft skin braced against his strength. Her stare locked with his. "Please, let me come."

So sweet. Her body thrumming with the need to let go and her blue eyes dark with passion. "Come."

One word paired with a steady pinch of his fingers low on her clit.

Her head dropped back and her throaty cry rang out, her hips rocking against his hand.

"Eyes open, pet. I want you to see it all." He kept the pressure and held her firm against him, taking the bulk of her weight while her legs trembled. "How your back bows for me. The flush that covers your chest and how those perfect nipples of yours practically beg to be stroked and sucked. The eager way you move against me and try to wring out every sensation."

Shadowed by the heavy weight of her eyelids, the blue of her eyes seemed closer to black, but she took every detail in. Surrendered physically to his embrace and set free a contented, sexy sigh. Only when her movements slowed and softened did he resume his explorations, slicking his fingers through her drenched folds and teasing the mouth of her sex. With every pass, her muscles contracted. Fluttered from the contact in their heightened state. "I think you're ready for another."

She groaned and rolled her head against his shoulder. "I'm still enjoying the last one."

"That's the idea, pet. Keep you coming and make you watch every one of them until you can never forget where your home is. Where your heart is."

He took her up again. Stroked, teased and pressed. Gauged every expression and sound she made and leveraged every technique to pleasure a woman he'd ever learned. The second round, her cry was softer. More ragged and desperate in its depth. Her clit pulsed beneath the steady pressure of his fingers and her legs trembled, but her eyes stayed open. Weighted with the power of her release and glazed, but open and absorbing every second. Panting and writhing against his hand. Riding the storm they'd created. "Axel, please." She rolled her hips again and whimpered. "Let my arms down. Let me touch you."

"Your arms hurt?"

She shook her head, the wildness behind her eyes warning her judgment might not be all that reliable. A quick check of the rope around her wrists and the color of her hands, though, promised she was good for one more. One chance for him to taste her and burn an indelible vision in her head. Careful to keep her steady as he moved, he crouched in front her. "Then we're not done here. Not yet."

As soon as her mind registered his intent, she groaned and tried to wriggle out of his grip. "I can't."

He chuckled at that and held her firmly in place. "I seem to recall a particular night with a vibrator where you told me the same thing, but I proved you very wrong."

She stilled in an instant. "You wouldn't."

"You keep usin' that phrase with me, lass, and by now I'd have thought you'd have learned I'll go to great lengths to make you come." He nuzzled her mound and growled against her cleft. "Not usin' a vibrator this time, though." He met her dazed stare and licked a slow circle around her clit. "I'm usin' my mouth."

She jolted on contact. Shouted and fought his unrelenting hold even as her hips bucked against his mouth. He licked. Sucked. Nibbled and teased her sensitized flesh. Lapped up every inch of the sweet cream she'd given him already then worked his fingers inside her, priming her for more. Her body went bowstring taut and her breath caught—and then she was pulsing around his fingers. Clenching and releasing around each upward stroke as a grated yet beautiful sound rolled up the back of her throat. A unique and deeply sensual noise somewhere between a sigh and a groan, reserved for when she was lost in the moment.

He loved it. Craved it almost as much as the taste of her release. The scent of her sex in his lungs and on his skin. The passion behind her blue eyes as she held his stare and floated in the moment.

"Please." So soft and yet thick with need. She undulated her hips against his mouth and sucked in a ragged breath. "Please let me feel you."

"I'm right here, pet. From what I can tell, you're feeling me just fine." He teased the base of her clit with his tongue and triggered a beautiful aftershock. "See there? Still responsive. Ready for more."

The sound that came out of her was part shout and part mangled curse, her jerky movements that of a woman poised for a major fit. So much so that, if she'd still had on those heels of hers, he'd have been in a dangerous proposition crouched as he was in front of her. "You know what I mean. I need you. Inside me." She fisted the rope stretched over the beam tighter. "Now."

"Are ye askin' or tellin', lass?" Slowly, he stood, taking his time along the way to skim his palms along each curve. "Because it sounds a lot like yer tellin' me and you don't look to be in a bargaining position."

This time her voice broke on a needy sob. "I'm asking. Begging." She looked up at his face, her brow misted with sweat and a pretty flush dotting her cheeks, neck and chest. "Please. Let me feel you inside me."

One jerk and the quick release knot he'd bound her with slipped loose. Her arms were around his neck all of a beat later, the straggling ends of the jute slithering down his back as she speared her fingers through his hair and cupped the back of his head, consuming his mouth with complete abandon.

He lifted her with hands at her waist.

Her legs wrapped around his hips unerringly, the sweat-misted press of her breasts and belly against his torso and the wet glide of her cunt against his straining cock testing his restraint. Dropping her to the bed, he gripped her thighs, dragged her ass so it met the edge of the mattress, hooked her legs so they draped his upper arms and palmed her hips. He rolled his hips against hers, coating his shaft in her slickness as he clawed for some remnant of control. "Waited too long. Wanted to give you slow."

His cockhead notched just inside the mouth of her. Natural. A perfect fit and a welcome home all in one easy movement.

She gasped and lifted her hips to meet his, angling for more of him, but failing without more leverage at her disposal. Her nails dug into his shoulders and her husky voice worked him like a velvet touch around his nuts. "I don't want slow." She tried again, the wild need behind her gaze as she tried to claim more of his length as primal as the drive clawing inside him. "I want you. Raw. Alive. Everything you've got."

It was more than he could take. A challenge offered with featherlight delivery that shifted all balance in a snap. He buried himself inside her. Unleashed every emotion and let them fuel every movement. Every thrust. Every touch and every kiss.

It was savage. Pure animalistic instinct married with the most intimate exchange of energy he'd ever experienced. In that second, he didn't exist without her any more than she existed without him. There was only one perfect union. Primitive and utterly uninhibited, but faultless in its construct. Their combined scents. Every ragged breath and grated moan. The brush of her soft and giving curves against his straining muscle. He was lost to it. A slave to anything save the moment and the woman giving it to him.

He shifted forward, deepening each thrust so he filled her to the hilt. He palmed her throat. "Mine."

Her lips parted, and beneath him her body softened further. A sweet and silent surrender.

"My woman. My pet. My *wife*."

"Yes." A whisper, and yet it filled him like a shout.

He growled and thrusted faster. Let the beast inside him have free rein and take its due.

Her breath hitched and her sex fluttered around his cock.

"There it is." He gave her more of his weight so each brush of his pelvis against hers worked her swollen clit. "I want one more. Want to feel you come on my cock."

She whimpered and eagerly rolled her hips, riding the rampaging storm for all she was worth. Her back arched and her heels dug into his back, the strain in her voice that of a woman on the brink of an earth-shattering release. "Please."

He wanted to draw it out. Hold her on the edge a little longer and build a bigger release. One she'd never forget. But one look at her—back bowed, muscles taut, dark hair splayed out on the bed and her glorious tits bouncing with every stab of his hips—it wasn't happening.

His balls drew up tight and his cock swelled inside her. "Come, pet. Show me who you belong to."

Her body obeyed in an instant. Bowed down to his command and left her bucking against him. Her sex fisting his shaft in a pulsing, greedy clutch even as his own release jetted inside her. Marked her in the most fundamental and primitive way.

His Elizabeth.

His heart.

His everything.

Skin to skin and heart to heart, he brought them down. Gave her his weight. His touch. His kiss and all the words of encouragement and affirmation she'd gone most of her life without. "So sweet." A gentle nip of her earlobe. A lick to the sensitive spot just beneath it. "So beautiful." He continued his path down her neck to the hollow low on her throat, slowly pumping his shaft inside her to draw out the pleasure for them both. "So passionate and wild." Only when her breathing evened out and the last of her spasms subsided did he cup the side of her face and meet her eyes. "I waited a long time for you, Elizabeth. Years I wish we could have spent together." He skimmed her lips with his own. "But I'd have waited twice as long if I knew you were my reward."

Tears welled in her eyes in a heartbeat, but her smile was blinding. A conqueror's prize and supplicant's blessing. "You need to warn me before you turn sweet."

"Sweet?"

She laughed at that, the jerky motion sending her tears spilling down her temples. "Yes, sweet." She tightened her arms and legs around his neck and hips. "You've got the heart of a poet hiding behind all that brawn and manly bluster."

The space behind his sternum swelled and his throat got tight. For all the comparisons she could have made, she'd naturally zeroed in on one that secretly mattered. He'd never match her skills, but he'd always wanted to. Always wanted to craft words that touched another person's soul. "And you find my sappy words sweet, do you?"

Her smile softened. "Very." She smoothed his hair away from his face and studied his features. Soaked in every detail as though committing them all to memory. "One minute you're an iron fist and the next you're a velvet glove. I love them both, but when you turn sweet on me without a warning, I get all soft and mushy." She skimmed her fingertips through his beard. "So, give a girl a warning, will ya?"

A warning.

The woman was a loon. A joy and a talent to be sure, but she had her bizarre moments, too. He grinned and kissed the tip of her nose. "Are ya feeling grounded now?"

Her gaze turned playfully wary. "Why?"

He smiled and traced her lower lip with his thumb. "Because I love you, Elizabeth. Love seeing the heart of you. The wild in you, and everything in between. Which means, no, I'm not giving you any warning because I'm a fan of your soft and mushy and then I'd risk missing it."

A fresh wave of tears filled her eyes and her lips trembled. "I'm not used to showing that side of me."

"I know that, lass." He pressed a tender kiss to her lips, letting his mouth linger whisper light against them as he spoke. "But your days of having to hide it are over. No matter what it takes, I'm gonna make it so you're safe and you've always got a place to set it free."

Chapter Nineteen

It'd been years since Axel and Jace had opened Cross-roads. The renovation that had turned the massive build-ing into Dallas's premier hot spot had taken nearly a year and a whole lot of painstaking attention, but it'd been the cornerstone of their enterprises ever since. The biggest hurdle cleared in their professional journey that had given them unstoppable momentum.

And it had started right here. In this conference room.

Granted, the former storage room between his and Jace's third story offices hadn't been much back then. Just a dusty room with unfinished walls, banged up metal shelves and cheap gray industrial tile that'd probably been the last dregs of a closeout sale somewhere. But he and Jace had hauled a cooler full of cheap beer up to this very spot the day they'd closed on the property and lobbed all kinds of far-fetched ideas between each other on what they wanted to do with the place until the beer was gone and they were spent.

It'd become their home base.

Their ground zero.

Or at least it had been until they'd bought and built the house at Haven and the rest of the guys had joined the family. Now, the sleek room with its contemporary feel and black and maroon décor was mostly just for show. A place they could interview potential new managers, or a quick huddle space the guys could use if they had an urgent topic that couldn't wait until everyone could drive to Haven.

Today, though, it was going to be center stage.

The arena for what he suspected was going to be the first foray into war.

Seated around the massive table, all of his brothers traded bullshit stories from their workweek while they waited. Beckett punched a few buttons on the laptop in front of him and frowned, clearly not liking the inactivity reflected back in the camera feeds from the front of the building.

At Beckett's right side, Danny glanced at the screen then eyeballed Axel. "You sure the fucker's gonna show?"

"Oh, he'll show." No way Joffrey was going to pass up one-on-one time with Axel. Not after he'd nagged Axel's office manager nearly nonstop for the last week and a half with calls and drive-bys to get a meet. "The wanker's shown at every one of Lizzy's gigs since she played The Green."

Beckett grunted, reclined back in his leather chair and crossed his arms across his chest. "Never got past us, but he's tried to tail her a time or two."

Axel zeroed in on Knox. "Not likin' bein' on defense with this guy. You got anything on him yet?"

"Outside of the fact that the guy's up to his eyeballs in debt with no sign of living within his means anytime soon, he's squeaky clean." Knox braced his hands on each armrest and cocked his head, that perplexed look he got whenever a pattern didn't quite make sense pinching his eyebrows into a deep V. "I did notice something last night, though. Not sure if it's worth chasing down, but might be worth a shot."

Jace stroked his beard at his chin. While his words were for Knox, his stare was locked on Axel. "Thinkin' anything's worth a shot if we wanna keep Axel from guttin' the guy in broad daylight."

Some of his brothers chuckled, but even the light-hearted sounds had an edge to them. Like they not only felt his frustration, but were eager to get off dead-center as much as he was. "What'd you find?"

Knox scratched his cheek. "Remember how you said he stole a bunch of Lizzy's copyrights?"

Axel nodded.

"Well, he's got a lot of songs registered under his name."

"I saw that, too," Jace said. "Got at least sixty plus under his name when I checked Lizzy's new registrations."

Trevor set his longneck on the table. "So, he's got a lot of songs. Not sure how I get that's a thread we can pull."

"Yeah, that's what I thought," Knox said. "Until I noticed the dates they were registered."

The room got quiet, each man looking from one to the other.

Knox sat forward and crossed his arms on the table. "What hit me funny was all of his registrations were chunked together. Ten under one date. Another ten or twelve under another. So, I did some checking. Pulled up some other big artists and compared patterns. They've got dates close to each other—songs on the same album getting recorded with dates inside a week or two—but not all of them the same. And, if you know the registration process, it makes sense. Every song's got its own record, and every record gets reviewed and finalized one at a time by someone in the copyright office."

"Bulk entries," Danny summarized in his gruff voice. "Something outside the standard process."

"Right," Knox said. "And the only way you could pull something like that off is if someone hacked into the system, or you knew someone on the inside with access to the apps database."

"You're thinking he did the same thing to other people he did to Lizzy," Zeke said.

"Makes sense," Ivan said. "You pull something off once, you feel brave enough to do it again." He shifted his steady stare to Knox. "Any copyrights before Lizzy?"

"Four. Recorded about a year earlier."

"How far apart are the registrations?" Trevor asked.

"Six months to a year."

"It's a pattern," Danny said. "He promotes people for a living. If we can tie new entries to the times when he took on new clients, we might have something."

"Might want to do some digging with past clients, too. See what they think about the guy and if they recognize any of the songs listed under his name."

Jace's low voice cut through the room. "There's a more important angle."

The room got scary quiet, every man's gaze locking onto Jace. "This guy works for a big label. If we tie him to stealing copyrights, ASCAP could get him for fraud or falsification of federal records at a minimum. But if he had other bands record songs he stole like Lizzy said he did with her, it'd be a much different story."

Zeke shook his head at Jace. "Brother, I can crack a sternum and squeeze someone's heart without breaking a sweat, but you're gonna have to dumb this one down for me."

Axel gave the answer instead, a righteous buzz building steam behind his chest. "He's with a huge label." He scanned each man at the table. "Stolen copyrights passed off to other artists signed to that label and making money? He wouldn't just be fucked legally. He'd be taking a label down with him and they're gonna do whatever it takes to scrape him off rather than let that happen. He'd be screwed for the rest of his professional life."

"So, all we've got to do is connect the dots." Trevor grinned and stretched his legs out long under the table. "Sounds like fun."

Ivan grunted and palmed his beer. "Don't mind a good puzzle now and again, but I'm personally lookin' forward to the beatdown that fucker earned hurting a woman."

"Everything in good time," Jace said, though his grin was wicked enough to indicate he was looking forward to it, too.

Beckett sat forward, gaze narrowed on his laptop. "Yeah, well, put a chokehold on that motivation for a bit." He spun the laptop toward Axel. "Your guy just showed."

On the screen, Joffrey paused as Shelly intercepted his trek through the main lobby.

"A suit and tie at four o'clock in the afternoon on a Sunday." Zeke chuckled and swiveled toward Axel. "Looks like he needed armor."

Likely a spot-on assessment. Which was ironic because Axel had intentionally gone with his oldest pair of jeans and a Black Sabbath tee so faded you could hardly make out the design anymore. With his hair loose and the rest of his brothers dressed just as casually, Joffrey would get one look at them and assume they were nothing more than a bunch of bikers or thugs who'd gotten lucky financially at best. "He's gonna need more than armor when I'm through with him."

Elbow braced on the arm of his chair, Ivan opened and closed his fist. "How're we playin' this?"

"Don't know what he wants, so I'm wingin' it," Axel said. "What I do know is, whatever he wants, the answer is probably no, and him getting shut down in front of an audience won't feel good."

Trevor chuckled and finished off his beer. "This might well be the most entertaining part of my weekend."

"Bullshit," Jace said. "With Levi gettin' spoiled rotten at Haven since Saturday morning, I think the most entertaining part of your weekend happened last night."

Trevor's smirk was completely unrepentant. "Last night wasn't entertaining. It was fucking inspired."

Despite the low laughter that followed, the heavy chunk of the steel door downstairs rattled like the pump of a shotgun.

A tense quiet followed, every man waiting. Readying for whatever lay ahead while Shelly's soft footfalls and Joffrey's heavier ones traveled up the staircase just outside the hall. Even Shelly kept her silence, avoiding the usual banter she kept with visitors when she walked them up as if she'd somehow cottoned on to the fact that she was leading a man into the lion's den.

She stepped through the doorway only a few moments later, sweeping the men on either side of the table with a familiar, yet awkward smile before she faced Axel. "Joffrey Reynolds is here to see you."

He could have gotten up. Would have if it'd been someone he even remotely respected. But in this case, Axel figured the guy would live longer if he stayed well out of choking distance. He nodded to Shelly. "Thanks, lass. Go ahead and head home. We'll see Mr. Reynolds out."

Her smile slipped and she glanced at Joffrey as if she wasn't altogether sure if his exit would be facilitated on his own two legs, or hauled out as deadweight thrown over one shoulder. God knew, in the years she'd worked with him and Jace, she didn't doubt the latter scenario was a possibility. "Thanks." She glanced at the rest of the guys, waved and slipped back into the dark stairway.

Joffrey watched her retreat and rubbed his hands in front of him like he wasn't quite sure if he'd be smarter to follow her back down, or dive headfirst into the shark tank.

Jace made the decision for him. "Understand you wanted to meet with us about something?"

Curt, ice cold and straight to the point.

Eyes wide, Joffrey's gaze shot to Jace, then to the men around the table. He frowned at Axel for a beat before refocusing back on Jace. "I had a meeting with Axel."

"Nothin' you can say to me you can't say to them." Axel swiveled in his chair enough to casually stretch his legs out in front of him, cross them at the ankles and rested his elbows on the arms of his chair as if he had not a care in the world. "I'd offer you a place to sit, but we're out of seats and in the middle of a meeting, so what's say we get to it? You wanted to talk. I'm listening. So are they."

Hands still clasped in front of him, Joffrey rubbed his palms together, seemed to realize what he was doing after the fact and then stuffed them in his pockets. His smile was that of a car salesman who'd sold a lemon to a mob boss and had just been backed into a dark alley. "Well, I was rather hoping we could have a dialog."

"Kinda depends on the topic."

Again with the nervous glance from Joffrey up and down the table. His gaze snagged on Beckett and he frowned. "I saw you at Lizzy's tour kick off at The Green."

Beckett smiled in a way he might as well have held up a switchblade at the same time. "I run her security."

Comprehension settled on his face. "I see."

Fucking Knox chuckled under his breath, enjoying the awkward moment a little too much.

Joffrey being the jolly yet foolish trooper he was zeroed back in on Axel and kept going anyway. "Well, you may or may not know, but I used to represent Lizzy."

"You don't now." Yeah, it was a harsh response, but the sooner the guy realized he was tap-dancing on a landmine and got the fuck out of here, the sooner Axel could stop detailing out the different ways he could torture the bastard.

Clearing his throat, Joffrey pasted one of those slick smiles on his face and smoothed his already perfectly aligned tie into place. "Right. Well, that's a detail I just happened to find out a few days ago."

"Saw me with her in New York. You didn't think to maybe find out if it was me representing her after that? Or for that matter, just to see if anyone else was backing her before you opted to show up at a show unannounced? You workin' for Miramar, I can't imagine you don't have resources to research a detail like that."

"Under normal circumstances, absolutely."

"And this situation falls outside the norm how?"

"I…uh…" Joffrey dipped his head and scratched the top of his nose. "Well, part of the conversation I wanted to have was business, but I was also looking forward to catching up with Lizzy on a personal level."

Axel held absolutely still. Barely even drew a breath.

But the room went laser focused and super-charged with a deadly edge in a second.

His voice was low and grated when it came out. A warning only an idiot would miss. "Lizzy's got nothing personal to say to you. Not a damned thing." He forced himself to take a breath. To keep his ass in his chair. "Do I make myself clear?"

Joffrey swallowed hard, his body frozen in place as if he'd just heard the subtle click of a pulled grenade pin. "I didn't mean it at that level. I just wanted to catch up with her for old-time's sake and share a business opportunity."

"Your past with her is over and done with. Any business you want to share goes through me. Now, you gonna get to that point, or are we done?"

There it was.

The flare of indignation behind Joffrey's eyes.

The straightening of his spine and squaring of his shoulders that said the line from general game play to all out warfare had been crossed. "I'd intended to talk to you about Lizzy's future and an opportunity with Miramar, but I'm guessing by the tone of our conversation such an opportunity would fall on deaf ears." His disdainful gaze flicked to his brothers then back to Axel. "Unfortunate, because my label has unlimited resources at its disposal for a talent like her."

"Lizzy's doing just fine."

"As things are now, yes. But luck can only run so long. She needs someone who can back her for the long haul."

"Someone?" Axel cocked his head. "Are we still talking about Miramar? Or you? Because the way I hear it, you're not the kind of person anyone needs for any long-term plan."

Joffrey's greasy smile disappeared altogether, replaced with a hard line that made his already too-thin lips even thinner.

Jace cut through the brewing tension with a sharp, "I think this conversation's gone as far as it's gonna go. Beckett, how about you make sure Mr. Reynolds doesn't get lost on the way out."

Axel held Joffrey's stare, kept his breathing even and added a deadly smile. He kept it in place until Beckett moved between them and herded Joffrey out the door with a none too subtle hand at his shoulder.

Everyone held their silence.

The steel door at the bottom of the stairs chunked open then slammed shut only seconds later.

"Knox…" Axel said not taking his eyes from the doorway.

Knox was up and out of his seat before Axel could finish his sentence. "Yeah, yeah. I'm all over it."

Axel tried again. "Knox."

His brother stopped mid-threshold, the anger in his own expression a living presence.

The fire Axel had barely tamped down surged hard and thick behind his sternum, nearly choking his words. "I'm done waiting. You don't find something on this bastard soon, I'm gonna handle things one-on-one."

Knox shook his head. "Brother, that's a fucked-up approach and you know it. You wanna ruin this guy long-term, you gotta table anything physical until our play is in the bag and tied up tight."

"He's right," Jace said. "You hang with Lizzy at Haven

for a few days, or take her somewhere completely off the grid while we work, but you do *not* want to go there yet."

The pressure inside his chest mushroomed up until it noosed around his neck and clamped down hard. Beyond the shadow of a doubt, he knew the other men in the room understood what was driving him. The barely restrained violence trying to claw its way free. But it didn't make voicing his truth any easier. "I need her safe."

"And we'll make her that way," Jace said with an equal conviction. "He'll get his due and, when he does, we'll make sure the pain never ends."

Chapter Twenty

It was weird the things you missed when your life changed on a dime. Her POS Toyota was clean, but the dash was pretty beat up and the carpet worn. The black leather seat was heavily worn on the driver's side and only marginally better for the passenger's seat. The headliner was also loose enough it billowed in the wind—which was pretty much all the time between March and late October in Texas since the AC didn't work worth a damn.

But it was familiar.

Comfortable in its simplicity.

Which was exactly why, after a week of the plush life, she'd snuck to the eight-car garage at Haven while Sylvie, Ninette and Viv were busy prepping for dinner to indulge in a little joy ride. A reminder of who she was and where she'd come from.

She paused at a four-way stop just a few miles from the ranch and let the car idle. The engine emitted more of a determined buzz than the throaty growl of Axel's Shelby, but it suited the hum skittering under her skin. A quick check of the side and rear-view mirrors showed not a single car anywhere nearby.

Alone for the first time in…well, hell. Almost three months.

And look at how much had changed.

Yeah, you're a walkin' talkin' dream come true. But for how long?

She grunted at the negative thought, snatched her purse off the passenger's seat and dug out her phone. Just because shit had gone south for her before didn't mean it was going to this time. And truth be told, the happy times she'd felt with Joffrey had been an illusion. A mirage he'd created to manipulate and use her that she'd happily bought into to escape her mundane life.

Axel wasn't like that.

Axel was real.

His family was real. Good people who genuinely cared about the people around them and bent over backwards to make each other's lives better. Kind of like her band, only with a hell of a lot more personality and better time management skills. Though, she'd noticed the guys in the band hadn't been late to a single gig after the first time they'd done it with Sylvie in attendance. For a woman who could smile to rival the sun, she could also rip four men a new one with only her words and never let her smile slip once while she did it.

Double-checking to make sure there was still no on-coming traffic first, she punched in a text to Axel.

Felt like a drive. Got the tunes up and out tooling around. Might swing by Rex's and say hey. Be home before you.

She hit send and stared at the screen.

Oh, what the hell. She'd gone goofy and stupid with the man already. Might as well go for broke.

XOXO

The little bubbles that promised an incoming reply started up.

Who's with you?

Yeah, that part of her top-notch fantasy come true she could have done without. One thing about Beckett Tate, he didn't fuck around with security. And for whatever reason, he and Axel felt she needed it all the time. As in every single time she stepped foot outside of Haven.

No one. Just out driving. Need the quiet. I'm good. Promise.

She put the shifter in first and eased off the clutch. At twenty till five on a Monday she was twenty kinds of crazy headed anywhere near a highway, but the more she thought about heading to Rex's house and just chillin' with a beer, the more the idea grew on her. As much as she'd been on the road, she'd done good to see him once a week and every one of those visits had been at family night with all of Axel's family around her. Yeah, she'd been tickled they'd deemed him part of the family given how tight they were, but it wasn't the same as just sitting and shooting the shit like they used to.

She needed that.

Craved just a little of the old to balance out the *wow* of the new.

Her phone rang not ten seconds later, Axel's name big and bold on the screen. She punched the green answer button and tucked the phone under her ear. "I told you, I'm fine."

"You got no one with you, lass. I don't like it."

"Axel, I'm going for a drive. That's it. I get some of my best ideas when I'm out driving around. Besides, Rex'll be home in another thirty minutes. I wanna run by his house and say hey. See how he's doin'."

His voice dropped to that tone reserved for when he was either in full Dom mode or dead serious about getting a point across. "Your life's not like it used to be. You've seen how people act at shows. How close they wanna get. The way you interact with the crowd and the kind of songs you write, they feel a connection, and not everyone's sane enough to know where that connection ends."

He wasn't wrong there. People who came to her shows at bars had always treated her like she was a long-lost friend or someone they sincerely wanted to get to know, but in the three weeks since her tour had kicked off at The Green, she'd experienced a whole different kind of response. An eagerness at meet and greets that varied from elation to outright creepy. Especially when the meet and greets happened after the shows. "I promise. Just a trip to Rex's house, then I'll head home. No stops in between."

Axel grunted, but otherwise the line hummed with silence for a solid five seconds before he spoke. "Compromise. I'm sending a man to Rex's house. He'll keep his distance, but follow you home. No stops on the way."

Stubborn man.

Not that she was complaining. Having someone besides Rex to look out for her—a whole family that genuinely seemed to care about her and that she could reciprocate with in kind—was the best part of her new life. "Why do I get the feeling you're only using the word *compromise* to make me happy and you've already got a text spun up for Beckett?"

A few sharp clicks of a keyboard sounded in the background. "Probably because you've got good instincts and you know I protect what's mine." The subtle groan of soft leather and movement sounded through the phone. "Only got a few more hours here. You wanna leave your car at Rex's place, I can pick you up on the way."

"And miss the joy of navigating this four-cylinder wonder that's well past its prime on Dallas's fine highways? Where's the fun in that?"

Again with the grunt, though, this time there was humor behind it. "On that thought, it's time we go car shopping. If you're gonna go out toolin' around, I wanna make sure you're in something that's got a decent chance of getting you back home to me."

"Ugh, I hate car shopping. Besides, I was thinking I'd wait until we see how my first month's sales do. If they're good enough, I wanna talk to Danny and see if he'd build me a custom ride."

He chuckled at that. "Sweetheart, if you want a custom job, it's not gonna matter what your sales look like. Danny's not gonna take a penny from family. But you behind the wheel of a souped-up classic is hot. I'll let him know you're interested."

"But I want to pay."

"Wanting to and getting to are two very different things, pet. Now focus on driving and dream up some new ideas while you're doin' it. It'll be time to hit the studio again before you know it."

She harrumphed, traded a playfully petulant goodbye for a chuckling one from him, then tossed her phone next to her purse on the passenger's seat. Definitely a dream come true. Domestically, romantically and professionally. Hell, she was the damned trifecta of reality lottery wins.

The drive to her old complex was a lot less packed with traffic than she'd anticipated, the only slow-down that gave her any grief when she hit the High Five at LBJ and Highway 75. Unlike Axel's Shelby, her car was too old to handle any music streamed by Bluetooth and only had the free local stations to listen to, but she caught a solid streak of classics and sang along to every one of them.

What kind of car would she get if Danny agreed to do a custom for her? A Vette?

No. Too cramped. Although, Beckett still managed to fold his big body into his. Maybe he'd let her take his for a test drive. Or, better yet, she and Gia could go for a girls' night out in it.

But Zeke's Camaro was another option. The way Gabe worked an engine, she could have a ride that looked and ran as wild as she was on stage.

Getting a little ahead of yourself, aren't you? Just because he said he was going to marry you doesn't mean he will. Men will say anything—do anything—to get you where they want you.

The barbed diatribe cast an unwelcome chill on the warm and happy daydreams she'd nursed on the drive over. One of many that had slowly tried to push its way through the blissful life she'd been enjoying for the last few months. The more she ignored them, the more frequently they'd pounced. Which kind of reminded her of how her mother always seemed to up her antagonistic ante the more Lizzy had tried to put distance between them.

Odd.

Now that she thought about it, all of the negative thoughts that went through her head always sounded like one of her mom's clipped and bitter rants. No doubt, her therapist would have a field day with that correlation.

She pulled into the parking lot and circled around to Rex's building. When they'd first moved from Tampa, this complex had been the only one with two one-bedroom apartments available inside their price range. The fact that they'd been across the courtyard from each other had been an added bonus. They'd have saved a fortune if he'd given in and agreed to rooming with her in a two or three bedroom instead of two separate units, but he'd been adamant that she needed her own space.

He'd been right. But then again, Rex usually was.

She found an open parking spot about midway back from the building, nabbed her purse and headed to the walkway. This late into September, a few tenants had started to make use of the somewhat cooler nights and were grilling on the free charcoal grills in the courtyard, but the grass was still a haggard brown from the lack of rain and the fact that the complex owners hadn't bought into the idea of landscape irrigation.

In her black slip-on Chucks instead of heels, her footsteps barely registered on the concrete, only the muted thump of her hand bag swooshing against her hip mingling with the laughter of a little girl swinging in the playground.

"Lizzy, hold up!"

Her heart lurched and she nearly tripped on the panicked surge that followed when she registered the harried voice. Part of her wanted to run, or at least keep going and pretend she hadn't heard Joffrey's voice. But just like that weird drive people got when they rubbernecked at an accident, she turned instead and foolishly met his gaze as he jogged in her direction from the parking lot.

His usual smile was in place, but there was a discomfort behind it tonight. One of those looks a man had when he was trying to show a brave face, but was sorely worried they were about to get their ass handed to them. Which made no sense. After all, he'd been the one with the right hook, not her.

He slowed to an uncharacteristically awkward amble until he got within talking distance and shoved his hands in the pockets of his cargo shorts. "I've been looking for you."

For once in her life, not a single snarky comeback bubbled to her lips, the sheer disbelief at why he would even remotely want to talk with her clashing with the shock of seeing him here. "Why?"

One unguarded word and that overdone charm that had once sucked her under slipped into place. A dark Prince Charming mask to cover the snake underneath. "What's wrong with just wanting to talk to you?"

"Joffrey, you never wanted to talk to me. Not even when we were living together. All you wanted was a puppet who did what you said when you told them to do it."

The Mr. Suave routine sputtered. "Now, that's not entirely fair. No relationship is perfect. I admit I was probably too demanding for how young you were back then, but I had a lot on my plate. I didn't handle the pressure well."

"No. Three cracked ribs, a fat lip and a face so bruised it took four weeks before I could go without makeup in public is pretty poor stress management." She scanned the parking lot, for once wishing she had her shadow in tow. "If it's all the same to you, I'll pass on the conversation."

She turned for Rex's courtyard and got all of one step in before Joffrey clamped his hand on her shoulder and spun her back around to face him. "Hold up."

"You *did not* just touch me." Despite the low volume she delivered her words with, there was a palpable menace behind them. A tone she easily channeled with a powerful glare and a few threatening steps forward.

Joffrey held his hands up palm out. "Hey, hey." He backed up a few more steps for good measure. "Hear me out. I need to talk to you. It's important."

"Then you make a fucking appointment like everyone else. You don't track me down in a parking lot, act like you're here for old times' sake and put your hands on me."

"That's what I need to talk to you about. *I've tried* to get ahold of you. I've been to every show and went through your manager, but he's stonewalling me. Wouldn't listen to a thing I said."

"Then I'd say he's figured out you're a douche and you should leave me and him alone."

"Lizzy." He ventured a step closer, his hands held in front of his chest like he was trying to calm a wild animal. "Babe, you gotta listen to me. That guy is a thug at best. No real experience in the biz and nowhere near the financial backing a real label could give you. The ride you've got going with your career right now is pure luck and luck won't last forever. You need someone with experience. Connections."

Her barked laughter echoed off the apartment buildings around her. "Like you?"

"Miramar is one of the biggest labels out there. They

know what they're doing. Have deep pockets and solid connections."

"They're also locked into old-school playbooks and wouldn't know how to customize a marketing plan for a specific artist if someone gave them a crystal ball." She leaned in enough to make sure he got her point. "If Axel's not interested, I'm not interested." She jerked her head toward the parking lot. "Now, you've got your answer. You can go."

A dark gray Chevy truck that looked like it'd just rolled off the showroom and had every chrome upgrade on it pulled into the parking lot and sped in her direction.

Joffrey aimed a scowl at the truck for all of a beat then refocused on her. "Lizzy, I don't think you realize how bad this guy can be for you."

"Bad for me?" Her incredulous laughter rose over the truck's revved engine. "That's rich coming from you. You left me used, bruised and broken. I can't think of anything he could do to me you didn't do worse."

"I'm worried he's screwing you over." He glanced back at the truck and lowered his voice. "A lot of artists get scammed by guys like him. They sign a management agreement and learn later they signed away their copyrights, too. I was worried about you, so I checked your registrations. His name is listed on all the songs under your new album."

Mother. Fucker.

Her stomach pitched like she'd downed a fifth of Vodka on an empty stomach and the world around her took on a detached, hazy focus.

Well, what did you think was going to happen? Did you think he actually liked you? That this was going to be some kind of happily ever after?

The fast-moving slap of footsteps against concrete jolted her out of her stupor just before a mountain of a man moved between her and Joffrey. "Sir, gonna have to ask you to step away."

As big as the guy was, Joffrey was completely blocked from Lizzy's view, but his voice was pure outrage. "Are you kidding me? This is a public place." He darted far enough to one side of the guy he caught Lizzy's gaze for all of a second. "Do you see? This is why I couldn't talk to you."

See? Right now she was having a hard time breathing. Let alone combat the screeching negativity in her head and deal with a man who'd caused her emotional and physical harm.

"Tell him you're fine," Joffrey said. "He can wait in the parking lot or something, but we need to talk."

The big guy kept himself between them, but twisted enough to meet Lizzy's gaze, an unspoken request for guidance written on his expression.

I'm in this. My family's in this. For your career and for you.

Why she remembered Axel's words at dinner that night in New York in that moment, she couldn't say, but they calmed her in an instant. Axel was many things. Clever. Ruthless in business. Utterly unstoppable once he put his mind to something.

But he wasn't a liar.

Or a cheat.

Joffrey, however, was both of those things and a bully to boot.

With one last look at her ex's pathetic face, she pinned her bodyguard with a hard look and shook her head. "I'm not talking to him. Not today or any day after that."

Chapter Twenty-One

Axel was right. She should have stayed home. Or at least have been sure to take one of her shadows with her. If she had she wouldn't be holed up in the corner of Rex's sofa staring at a half-full Corona on the end table next to her wondering why Joffrey's ambush was bothering her so badly.

Kicked back on the opposite end of the sofa, Rex propped one foot on the edge of the custom coffee table he'd welded as one of his art projects and motioned to her beer with his own. "You sure you don't want another one? Pretty sure that one hasn't been drinkable for thirty minutes."

"Nah. No point wasting a beer." She snatched the long-neck, took a drink then shuddered as the too-warm brew went down her throat. She stood, padded to the kitchen and poured what was left down the sink.

Rex chuckled in that affectionate way he did with no one else. "Change your mind?"

"No. I just decided I've got enough on my mind and don't need to torture my taste buds while I'm at it."

Grunting, Rex set his beer on the coffee table next to his foot then stretched out his arms on the couch arm and seat back. "Can't believe that fucker tracked you here."

"I can. Joffrey's not a big fan of the word *no*, and from the sound of things, he's heard it a lot from Axel." She moseyed back to her seat and curled both legs underneath her. "He saw you with me in New York. With Axel blocking him at the shows and me not showing up with a Dallas address anywhere, he was out of options."

"I knew I shouldn't have stopped for a pack of smokes on the way home."

Lizzy frowned at him. "What does that have to do with anything?"

"If I hadn't stopped, I'd have been here when that fucker was and I could've stepped in before Axel's muscle did. Been wanting a chance at that bastard for years."

She dropped her head back on the cushions and studied the popcorn ceiling with its drab white paint. "That's not gonna solve anything. Guys like Joffrey always find a way to play shit to their advantage. He'd probably find a way to get you arrested and squeeze a promotion out of it. Maybe run for office and build a political campaign on pity and crime prevention."

When all her snark earned her was silence, she lifted her head.

Sure enough, Rex was staring her down with that look that said there were words parked on his tongue he had every intention of sharing, but wasn't exactly looking forward to it.

"What?" she prompted.

The clipped question aired with the attitude of a sassy teen earned her a lopsided grin. "I can share it, but you ain't gonna like it."

She snorted and stretched her legs out on the coffee table to match his. "Not like that's ever stopped you before."

For a good ten seconds, Rex stared at his jean-clad legs. "You get how hard it's been for me to hold back with Joffrey all these years."

"I get that pounding Joffrey's face until he can't see isn't going to undo what he did to me or how I allowed it to happen."

"No, it wouldn't. But it might've made him think twice before he did the same to another woman."

Regret.

It wasn't often she'd heard it color Rex's voice, but in that second, his words were loaded with it.

"You can't change men like Joffrey. We've talked about this."

"No, you asked me not to act, and I honored what you asked because I wanted you to make your way in this world the way you want to do it. But I'm thinking maybe I'd have been smart to share a little about what a good man processes when they're faced with protecting someone they love."

"What's that mean?"

He lifted his gaze to hers, that stern look he'd first shared with her the one time he'd dared to overstep and offer his opinion about Joffrey early on reflected back at her once more. "It means some men won't let a wrong go unanswered. Won't take the high road."

Axel.

Deep down she knew it. Had felt the deadly current in him even as she'd experienced tenderness at his hands.

"That day in New York," Rex said, "you were looking at Joffrey, but I was looking at Axel." He paused a beat. "He was furious then. Ready to do battle and leave Joffrey bruised and bloodied. But after this? Now that you've told him what that dickhead did to you? He's gonna wanna kill him."

"Oh, come on. Joffrey's a dick and a bully, but he hasn't—"

"Lizzy." One word and her mouth snapped shut. He took good use of it and lowered his already gruff voice for extra emphasis. "What I'm sharin' isn't up for debate. It's a fact. I *saw* what was in Axel. I know the man he is and what he's capable of. You need to wrap your head around the same reality and you need to do it quick because I promise you, something is going to happen."

"Not if I don't tell him."

His lips twitched. "That's a shit move and you know it." He snagged his beer off the table and chuckled. "Not gonna be an option anyway 'cause his muscle's probably already told him you had a run-in."

Fuck.

She'd been so damned busy trying to stuff her past back where it belonged and figure out why the hell Joffrey would concoct such a bullshit lie about Axel, she hadn't thought about Mr. Muscle reporting back to the mother ship. Shoving to her feet, she paced the open space in front of the coffee table and fisted her hair on top of her head. "So, what am I gonna do? I can't let him get into it with Joffrey. Axel's too high profile. It could impact his business. His family. I can't let that happen."

Rick flat out laughed at that one. "Baby girl, you're acting like this is something you can actually control. What I'm trying to tell you is you don't control a man like Axel McKee. The best you can do is trust his judgment and hang on for the ride." He cocked his head to one side, eyes narrowing. "You do trust him, right? You know that shit Joffrey said is just that—absolute shit."

Yeah, she knew it. At least the sane part of her did. Unfortunately, the shrew masquerading with her mother's voice hadn't shut the fuck up since she'd escaped into Rex's apartment forty-five minutes ago. "Of course, I know it's shit. I wouldn't trust Joffrey as far as I could throw him."

"You sure?"

Absolutely.

Aside from all the fear pushing up through the tiny fissures from her past like noxious gas. "I'm not stupid. Axel's not like Joffrey. Not even close. I'm just wigged out at the thought of what my life's gonna do to his family."

"*Your* family."

She stopped her pacing and glared at him, something close to a growl rolling up the back of her throat. "I get that particular reminder from Axel enough. I don't need it from you, too."

"If it takes both of us stating the obvious, then maybe you *do* need it."

"Pfft." She spun and took another lap. Fucking men. Always beating their chests when they should be figuring out how to get on with things. She stopped in front of the window. No longer blocking traffic like it had been during her showdown, the gray truck was now parked in the row closest to Rex's building with Mr. Muscle calmly standing near the front fender. Nothing said intimidation quite like a six-foot-six behemoth Adonis in a T-shirt that left none of his muscles hidden and his arms crossed over his massive chest. "What am I gonna do?"

"Aside from coming clean with your man, what makes you think there's something you have to do."

She spun. "Because this is *my* shit show. Axel's already done enough for me. I need to handle this and if I tell him, he's going to want to."

"No, he *will* handle it. Big difference."

She frowned and paced back toward the kitchen, seriously reconsidering a fresh beer. "You're not helping."

"Sure I am. I'm keepin' it simple. You tell Axel, you let it go, game over. Nothing else to do and no other problem to work through…unless you're feeding me *and* you a load of bull and you're seriously considering Axel might have done what Joffrey said he did."

Sighing, she plopped down next to Rex, the backlash of the last hour, the weight of her thoughts and the uncomfortable panic skittering beneath her skin dropping her like a stone in a world with double the gravity. Perched on the edge of the cushion, she hung her head. "I know Axel couldn't have done it. I know he's not that kind of man. But what Joffrey said just brought it all back up to the surface." She lifted her head and met Rex's patient stare. "It's like it's all right there again. Fresh, like it happened yesterday and reminding me how stupid I was all over again. You know?"

"Yeah, I think I get it. But you weren't stupid, Liz. You were human. We all are. We fuck up. We fall. We get back up and we try again. That's what we're here for—along with having some fun and laughing while we're at it." He studied her face, that knowing look that always made her feel like he could see straight through to her thoughts narrowing his focus. "What else is goin' on in that head of yours?"

That was the thing. She couldn't quite put her finger on it. Only knew that there was something she needed to get. Something she needed to see or tie together. "Why would Joffrey accuse Axel of taking my copyrights? I mean, that's not the kind of thing Axel could do without my consent. Joffrey would have to know I'd be able to look online and see my name's still there. So why even try that ploy?"

Sadness tainted with regret moved behind his eyes. "You understand what kind of work Knox is capable of, right? How he has a history of getting into things most people can't?"

"Yeah, but he wouldn't do that either. Not to me. Not to anyone he cares about."

"No, he wouldn't. But what I'm tryin' to remind you of is that Knox isn't the only one with that skill."

Her sharp laughter ricocheted around the sparse room. "You're joking, right? I mean, Joffrey does good to turn a computer on. Let alone hack into a system."

One corner of his mouth lifted in an ironic grin. "Surprised that son of a bitch even knows how to work his dick, so not surprised he can't operate a computer either." His expression sobered. "Doesn't mean he couldn't find someone else with skills, though."

Shit.

Rex was right.

And Joffrey was extremely skilled at making and keeping connections with all kinds of people. After all, one never knew when they'd need to use someone to his best advantage. "You think he found someone to make the change?"

"Don't know. For all I know, he was just blowing smoke to stir trouble. Easy enough for you to pull your registration up online and see what's showing and debunk it if that's all it is, but you're right. He could be up to more." He dropped his foot back down to the floor and leaned forward, anchoring his elbows on his knees.

"Whatever it is he's up to, you gotta trust that the people around you today are solid. More than that, it's not your job to fix it or go the path alone. Not anymore."

Three sharp raps bounded off the front door, the impact so forceful compared to Rex's low and heartfelt voice Lizzy's heart jolted.

Rex didn't seem the least bit startled. Just casually checked the time on his watch and huffed out a muted chuckle. "Surprised. I thought for sure he'd have shown fifteen minutes ago. Traffic must've been hell." He stood and ambled to the front door.

Her brain still scrambling from her run-in with Joffrey, her conversation and Rex's cryptic comments about his visitor, Lizzy stayed perched on the sofa. "Who?"

"I told you, baby girl. Axel's a man of action." Rex smirked and met her gaze over his shoulder. His voice was low enough it wouldn't carry beyond the door, but it was also loaded with male satisfaction. "And from the sound of that knock, I'd say it's showtime."

Chapter Twenty-Two

Axel waited. Glared at Rex's front door and focused on his breath. Trusted that Beckett's man parked in the parking lot was right and Lizzy was safe on the other side.

He wouldn't push her.

Wouldn't lock her up and coddle her the way he wanted to while he contemplated Joffrey's murder. She'd wither up if he did that. Would fight such confinement with even more passion than the grace she surrendered with.

But fuck it all if he wasn't going to stay right next to her until his own frustration and panic downshifted to something less than DEFCON five.

The paint on the door in front of him was gray and weathered to the point it matched the overcast skies. Behind the builder-grade metal, Rex's voice rumbled closer, the words too low to make out, but with a humorous tone.

Humor was good. Per Beckett's telling, Lizzy had not only held her own with Joffrey, but had been practically in his face when her guard had pulled into the lot, but that hadn't stopped Axel from worrying about how she'd handled the aftermath the whole drive over. All he'd been able to think about while stuck on LBJ was how rattled she'd been the last time she'd seen Joffrey. How distracted and on edge she'd been for hours. But if Rex was laughing, that was a good thing. Less reason for Axel to kill Joffrey the first chance he got.

You do not *want to go there yet.*

Jace was wrong on that one.

Axel *did* want to go there. Badly. But in the last week they'd made enough discoveries to make Joffrey's life a living hell, so Axel was hanging on to his brother's advice with all he had in him.

The knob rattled and the door chunked open. Rex stood in the opening, the look on his face one of those man-to-man *I get it* expressions that said he wasn't gonna stand between Axel and Lizzy for long. "I take it traffic was bad?"

Yeah, Rex totally got it. Which was why Axel and his brothers had already launched plans to jump-start Rex's fledgling art career. "A total bitch. Two ambulances and three overturned cars."

Rex nodded and stepped out of the way. "I figured as much."

Lizzy sat dead-center on the old gray-blue sofa. She'd clearly slipped out of the house for nothing more than a joy ride, because she was dressed for comfort more than style in her favorite Halestorm tee and cutoff Levis. She was also completely void of makeup and had left her hair loose. Normally, there was a vibrancy to her. An eagerness that made her pretty blue eyes as bright as a summer sky. But right now the only read he got from them and her posture was sheer fatigue. "Hey."

All of his plans, positive thoughts and good intentions wavered with that one simple word. She wasn't just fatigued, she was shaken. Which meant whatever Joffrey had said to her had struck clear to her heart.

You do not *want to go there yet.*

You do not want to go there yet.
You do not want to go there yet.

Axel fought back the growl lingering at the back of his throat. Rather than stomp toward her like some brute asshole and throw her over his shoulder, he forced a calm gait and a steady voice. "Heard you had a run-in with the asshole. How're you holding up?"

One of those cute little snorts she always made when her snark took over blended with a chuckle. "Well, I didn't come up with any ideas for a power rock ballad today, but I've got a few hate anthem possibilities to run with."

And there was the humor. Rex had definitely done his thing while Axel had been dodging Dallas traffic. Plus, his woman was honed on indomitable spirit and faultless feminine steel. "You gonna give me shit when I tell you I'm reneging on my compromise and am drivin' you home?"

"You gonna give me shit when I tell you I'm not up for replaying Joffrey's visit?"

Beside him, Rex shook his head, ambled toward the kitchen and muttered something Axel couldn't make out beneath his breath. Which meant odds were good Rex knew damned well what'd gone down between Lizzy and her ex in that parking lot. It also meant Rex and Axel were going to be having a heart-to-heart soon if Lizzy didn't volunteer the details before then.

Axel nodded. "Deal."

Getting gone from Rex's place was an exercise in the mundane. A familiar handshake with Rex. Lizzy slinging her purse over one shoulder and wrapping Rex up in a familiar hug. A stop by her car to snag her shades and lock the heap up. All of it done with the energy of a kid who'd hit a wall after a nonstop day at an amusement park on nothing but sugar and adrenaline. Even the drive to Haven was eerily quiet, Lizzy keeping her gaze locked on the road in front of them without her seeming to see a thing.

Only when Vivienne's dog, Ruger, came barreling toward his Shelby and barking for everything he was worth did she snap back from wherever her thoughts had taken her, her breath catching as if she'd been startled from a light sleep.

Axel pulled into the garage, killed the engine and yanked the parking break.

Lizzy went for the door latch, but he caught her free hand and gave it a solid squeeze before she could make contact. "Hold up."

While she didn't say a word, her expression said plenty. Mainly that she was tired as fuck, wary and uncertain as hell.

He fanned his thumb along the back of her hand. "I made you a promise. I'm not gonna badger you about what went down, but I've got needs, too, and distance isn't gonna work for me. Not today. Not until I know you're solid."

For the first time since he'd laid eyes on her at Rex's, her lips lifted in a soft smile. "I don't want distance." She laced her fingers with his and her voice slipped to that husky pitch that worked his dick like a physical stroke. "I don't want to think either."

He squeezed her hand tighter, the urge to drag her across the center console and claim her mouth right then and there a need as vital as breathing. "Sweetheart, once I get you in the house, the only thing you're going to do until you fall asleep is feel." He lifted their joined hands to his lips and kissed her knuckles. "Everything else, you leave to me."

Something flickered behind her eyes. Comprehension, maybe, mingled with fear. "Just let it go. The only way Joffrey could hurt me anymore is through the people I love, and I don't want anything to happen to you, or the family."

Warning prickles danced along the back of his neck and shoulders. Whatever that fucker was up to, he'd somehow managed to leverage Lizzy's connection to him to do it. Which meant Axel would be upping the plans he and his brothers had made for Joffrey Reynolds just as soon as his woman was well sated and sleeping soundly in his bed. "Nothing's going to happen to any of us. Trust me on that." With that, he released her hand, got her out of the car and into the house.

Not surprisingly, the moms, all of his brothers and most of the wives were milling in the kitchen when they came through the back door, the lot of them making a poor play at pretending to linger over what was left of dinner. No point in dancing around why they were there at this point. Lizzy might not have had much of a family to butt into her business before, but she did now and she'd have to get used to it. He squeezed Lizzy's hand reassuringly and stuffed his keys in his pocket. "I see the grapevine's been hard at work," he said to the gathering at large. "Lizzy's fine. Just needs a little downtime to regroup and decompress."

Ninette didn't take the hint, but tossed her kitchen towel to the counter, planted one hand on her hip and pegged Lizzy with a stern stare. "Did he touch you?"

At first, Lizzy's eyes widened like a high school kid busted coming in well past curfew, but she shifted gears and whipped up her own brand of attitude just as fast. "I held my own."

That earned her a smile and a few harrumphs from the women, but Ninette still looked to Axel and proclaimed, "That boy needs a lesson."

Thankfully, Jace interjected before Axel had to. "I wouldn't worry about it. Things have a way of working themselves out." He shared a silent vow of support with Axel for all of a heartbeat before his gaze shifted to Lizzy and softened. "Go take a load off with your man. We'll make sure the women stay contained and don't head out on a castration mission."

"At least not without you," Zeke added with a wink.

That same indecipherable look Lizzy had aimed at him in the garage swept across the people in the room. "Honest to God, I'm fine. The best way to irritate Joffrey is to ignore him and move on."

At best, she got a few grunts and nods, but not a one of them looked like they believed it. In fact, if anything, he'd bet everyone around the table would start plotting as soon as she was out of earshot. Just another part of family life she'd have to learn.

He hugged her close to him, kissed her temple, then steered her toward the living room and the main staircase beyond. "Come on, lass. You've earned a little spoiling tonight."

Located far from the core of the house, his suite was nothing but quiet. Shadows cast by the setting sun muted the already somber gray and black décor, the only light other than what was left coming through the French doors coming from the bathroom.

Lizzy slowed near the bed and eyed the tousled white sheets and thick crocheted comforter as if hiding beneath them and surrendering to sleep was a serious contender for her time.

He moved in behind her, wrapped her up at the waist and pulled her tight against him. "You want to crawl in now, or spend some time soaking in the tub?"

She dropped her head back on his shoulder and peered up at him. Her smile might have been dimmer than it usually was, but it was still full of memories. "I haven't soaked or showered alone since I moved in here."

"And you're not gonna start today."

"So you're telling me it'll be you soaking and me washing all those glorious muscles again? Because the last time we did that, we ended up with more water on the floor than in the tub."

"No, baby." As natural as could be, his hand went to her throat, the grip on the slender column gentle, yet firm. "No games tonight. Just you and me."

She sighed and turned in his arms, loosely cupping the back of his neck. "He really didn't get to me. Not in the way you think."

"Sweetheart, you're standing here in front of me, looking like you've done battle for three days straight. Don't tell me he didn't strike a nerve."

"Shame." She paired the admission with her unflinching gaze. "Every time I see him, I remember how foolish I was. How careless I was with my work and how much of myself I gave up. And yes, he told me some things about you that pissed me off."

"Such as?"

"What he said doesn't matter because I don't believe a word of it. What pisses me off is that he tried to drag you into things just to get his way. I love my life. I love you. I love your family."

"*Our* family."

She rolled her eyes in that way reserved for women who were at their wit's end with men. "All right, I love *our* family. Enough that I don't want anything rocking the boat. Something always rocks the boat eventually, but I don't want it to happen yet, and him pulling that shit runs the risk of doing exactly that. So, I'm asking you—let it go."

Agreeing with her would be easy. Definitely more compassionate in the short term.

But honesty was what she deserved and the only thing he'd ever give her. "I can't do that, Elizabeth. I won't." He cupped both sides of her face. "But what you need to get is there's not a damned thing that man, or anyone else in this world, can do to rock the boat you're in now. You're in it with me. With my family. You and Rex. And bein' in that boat means you don't have to worry or keep your guard up to keep other people from stealing what's good in your life. It's here and it's staying."

Tears welled in her eyes and the raw vulnerability that went with them knifed straight through his gut.

Not once in his life had he wanted to hurt a woman. Not like he wanted to hurt Lizzy's mother in that moment. And God help the woman if Ninette and Sylvie ever caught the selfish bitch alone. "I get growing up you couldn't count on anyone but Rex, and I get that the first time you tried to count on someone in a relationship he ended up being a dick, but those days are over. No amount of rattlin' our cages is gonna shake us, Lizzy."

Her lips trembled and her voice came out ragged and scratchy. "I really need for you to stop being sweet and kiss me."

There she was. His sweet, sassy woman hanging on

for all she was worth. "Gonna do a lot more than kiss you, pet." He leaned in and teased her lips with his. "But if you wanna start there, I'm happy to oblige." He swallowed her gasp. Held her steady with a hand at the back of her head and feasted on her mouth the way he'd wanted to since seeing her perched on the edge of Rex's couch.

Fuck, but he loved the taste of her. The tiny moans from the back of her throat. The feel of her hands exploring his shoulders, pecs and abs. How she met every glide of his lips and tongue with her own. So natural. A dance performed to perfection every single time.

And she was hungry. The ravenous almost desperate energy behind her touch and her kiss as wild and scorching as an untamed blaze. Any other night he would have bound her. Would have pinned her hands behind her back and taken control until she met the pace he set and surrendered. But not tonight. Tonight she needed something else. A release grounded in control and thick with confidence.

"That's it, lass." He forced his fingers to loosen their grip at the back of her head and at the small of her back. Willed his straining muscles to relax and murmured between each kiss, "It's all you. Whatever you need, it's yours."

With impatient jerks, she tugged his shirt free of his slacks, her breath escalating as she worked each button. She nipped his lower lip and grunted when the last button refused to cooperate. "Fuck." She yanked too hard and the button snapped, flying to God only knew where. For a second, she stared at him like a guilty teen waiting for her sentence, then shook it off and splayed her hands against his bare chest. "I'll buy you another one."

Christ, her hands felt good. Always did. The same

passion and devotion she put into every note on stage flowing with every physical touch. "Sweetheart, you just gave me incentive to buy by the case. Don't stop now."

It was just the fuel she needed. Incentive delivered with a light touch that unleashed the last of her restraint. Belt. Shoes. Socks. Pants. She ridded him of them all. A woman on a mission. Focused and clinging to something she could tangibly control when the outside world and the memories of her past refused to cooperate. When he tried to peel her tee up her torso, she uttered a frustrated grunt, batted his hands out of the way and pushed him backward. "Bed."

He chuckled at that, but went with it, dropping onto his back on the mattress and cocking his knees wide so she'd see the full impact her wildness had on him. He stroked his cock. "Can't remember the last time I let a woman get bossy with me in the bedroom, but where you're concerned it's hot as hell."

Her gaze locked on the action and her whole demeanor shifted. She might have been hungry before and grappling for the upper hand, but now she was a huntress. A purely primal being focused on one need and a target to unleash it on. She kicked her sandals off. With the grace and sensuality of a seasoned Domme who knew full well the impact of her movements on her prey, she straightened, pushed her shoulders back and peeled her tee over her head. In only faded cut-off Levis and a lacy black bra, she was every man's naughty-girl-next-door fantasy.

She unhooked the clasp on her shorts and shimmied them past her hips. When she straightened to let him look his fill, her dark hair spilled around her creamy shoulders, a few of the strands dipping toward the valley between her breasts.

Forcing intelligible words past his lips instead of growling was a challenge, but she was pure fire and he was eager to see what happened when he poured some extra nitro on the flames. "You gonna tease me with the visuals all night, or make it worse and give me some hands-on torture?"

She smiled at that. A tentative, yet wicked grin that said she'd not only picked up the gauntlet, but was ready to whip him with it if he didn't give her what she wanted. She nudged one bra strap off her shoulder. Then the other. The way she paired unpinning the clasp at the back with her husky voice was erotic as hell. "Oh, I don't know. You've gone to great pains to make me wait a time or two since New York." She teased the lower swell of one breast with her fingertips while the other hand dipped beneath her panties. While the lace blocked a visual confirmation, the way her head dropped back and the low groan that rolled up her throat said her fingers had zeroed straight to her clit.

"Elizabeth." It was a command. One he hadn't meant to utter, but fuck if he wasn't desperate for the feel of her. The taste of her. "Get your ass up here and take care of your man."

She lifted her head, eyes opening slowly to reveal both heated need and blazing feminine power. For a second, he thought she'd balk. Thought she'd use the opportunity to push the envelope and glory in her control a little longer.

But the hunger won out. Her hips swayed as she prowled to the bed, the way she crawled over him that of a feline predator snaring her prey solely on her sensual prowess. She straddled him, bracing her hands on either side of his head.

He palmed her hips and ground his cock against the lace between her legs. "You forgot the panties, lass."

Her lips lifted in a devious grin. "Oh, I didn't forget." She undulated against his length, the soft rasp against his shaft delicious, but nowhere near what he wanted to feel. "I just don't take direction well."

"Now, pet. You and I both know that's a load of shite." He tightened his grip enough to still her movements and pressed his cock squarely against her clit. "You take every direction I give you and are primed and ready for me to take you before I even lay a finger on you." He punctuated his statement with a roll of his hips.

Her eyes slipped shut and a shaky sigh slipped past her lips. She smoothed one hand along his sternum. "God, how do you do that?"

"Do what, baby?"

"Send me floating." She opened her eyes, the weight of her lids over her blue irises the sexiest thing he'd ever seen. "One minute I'm in my head and the next I'm just lost in you. In everything you're giving me." She tried to wiggle and gain control of the motion.

He held tight and upped his thrusts. "That's not me, sweet girl. That's us. The energy that's always there."

Her legs shook and the need in her gaze shifted to pure desperation. "Axel."

God, he loved the sound of his name on her lips. The hunger in it. "Bet you wish you'd left those panties off right about now, don't you, pet?"

Her nails dug into his shoulder, the sharpness perfectly paired with the frustration in her words. "Fuck, you're an evil man."

"No, lass. Not evil. Just solidly tuned into my woman." He shifted his grip just enough to get a handful of her panties at each of her hips. "And I think it's time you got what you need."

One jerk and the lace was gone, the remnants of her panties tossed to the floor with the rest of their clothes. He was in her a second later, her hot wet sheath accepting all of him. Her contented sigh ringing in his ears. Her shoulders back and tits bouncing with every upward thrust.

Gorgeous.

Wild.

Completely uninhibited.

Alone they were each strong, determined people. Driven and talented in their own ways. But together they were unstoppable. A unique dynamic he still didn't fully understand and was done with trying to, but was absolutely committed to protecting. To building and forging the rest of his life around it.

She was his.

His woman.

His heart.

His Elizabeth.

The need for release gripped him. Pooled tight and heavy in his nuts and forced his thrusts faster.

But he wasn't taking it. Not until she took her own and dragged him along with it.

He angled her pelvis with his grip at her hip, nudging that sweet spot along her front wall with the head of his cock.

Her breath caught. "Axel…"

"I know, baby." He slid one hand inward and teased her slick and swollen clit with his thumb. "Just ride it. Feel it all and let it take you where it wants to go."

Another tremor, this one mirrored in the muscles tightening around his cock. "Please…"

Beautiful.

Absolutely, fucking beautiful.

Inside and out.

He circled faster, thrusting to the hilt with each stab of his hips. "That's it, lass. Right there." He pressed low and upward on her clit. "Come for me."

Her shout was a glorious sound. Triumph, gratitude and sheer bliss filling the room as her cunt fisted around his cock.

And then he was right there with her. His growl mingling with her groans and his come filling her. Marking her as surely as she'd marked his soul. He'd never get enough of her. Never spend enough time hearing her talk. Enjoying her laughter and those adorable snorts. Feeling her body against his and drifting in the aftermath of the sensations they created together.

With a whimper, she collapsed against him, her pussy still fluttering around him and her hips languidly moving against his own. Her heavy breaths whispered against his chest and her hair spilled across his shoulder. "Wow."

The playful, yet surprisingly short commentary ripped an unexpected chuckle from him. "Wow?" He palmed the back of her head and savored the silky glide of her hair against his palm. "Must've done something right if my girl's short on words."

The comment earned him a delicate snort. "Well, I think my brain short-circuited when you ripped off my panties."

"Liked that did you?"

"Mmmm." Her fingers drifted over one pectoral, her

voice softening to match her touch. "Makes me not feel so bad for ruining your shirt."

"Sweetheart, you can rip my clothes off anytime."

She lifted her head enough to shoot him a playful grin. "Ditto."

Yeah. Utterly beautiful inside and out. He tightened his grip at the back of her head, intent on pulling her in for a kiss.

But she fought the movement with a gentle press of one hand at his chest. Her expression sobered. "I'm glad you came to get me today."

"I'll always be there when you need me, lass. Might take me a minute or two to pull off whatever it takes to make it happen, but I'll get there as fast as I can."

She swallowed hard. "You don't need to do anything to Joffrey. You being there for me was enough." Her lips tightened for a second as though she was fighting sharing whatever else needed to be said. "But I get it. You're you and you'll do whatever you feel like you have to do." She hesitated a beat then added, "I trust you."

Three words, but for a woman who'd been hurt and disappointed as many times as Lizzy, they were more valuable than gold. A gift beyond measure. And one he'd made damned sure stayed safe.

He pulled her to him. Wrapped her up tight against his torso so she could feel his vow as well as hear it. "I'll never let you regret that, Elizabeth. Not giving your love or your trust." He closed his eyes, savored the feel of her skin and her steady heartbeat against his, and breathed her in. "You're mine, and I'll do whatever it takes to keep you and your heart safe."

Chapter Twenty-Three

It's not your job to fix it or go the path alone. Not anymore.

Utterly languid in Axel's bed and naked as the day she was born, Lizzy stared out the French doors that lead to the balcony off Axel's suite. At nearly ten in the morning, the skies were just as overcast as they'd been the day before and offered zero guidance on what to do next. Yeah, she knew Axel was probably already digging into Joffrey and doing whatever it felt like he needed to handle the situation, but she just couldn't let it go. The whole experience had left her out of sorts and uncomfortable. Like in seeing Joffrey again and having him wave the reality of what he'd done to her all those years ago in her face had ripped the veil off the mistakes of her past and forced her to really look at how she'd handled things. How she'd meekly tucked her tail, accepted all of the blame and restarted her life.

But she wasn't the only one to blame.

Yes, she'd given up too much of herself. Ignored all the warning signs Rex and her subconscious had tried to spell out for her and trusted a man she never should have given the time of day, but Joffrey had used her. Emotionally and physically assaulted her.

It wasn't right.

It never had been.

But she'd taken the passive way out. Done exactly what she'd asked Rex to do then and was asking Axel to do now.

And then you nursed your part as a victim.

Wherever the thought came from, it pulled no punches in its delivery. The difference was in the voice that carried it—her own. Not shared in a negative or condescending way, but with the gentle honesty of an empowered woman willing to really see herself and own her mistakes.

Because you know what that looks like now. How women who own their lives and their choices operate and conduct themselves.

The images of the women who'd been waiting for her last night replayed in her head. Every one of them was beautifully unique in both appearance and personality, and yet fundamentally the same in their strength. In their courage and willingness to share their collective wisdom.

And they'd accepted her as one of them. Pushed right past her defenses without so much as an *excuse me* and pulled her into the fold.

So why couldn't she be as bold and unflinching as them? Actually, *do* something this time and stand up for herself?

She was out of bed, dressed and hustling down the main staircase, her loose hair undoubtedly a rat's nest and yesterday's tee and shorts a rumpled mess.

But they wouldn't care. They always saw behind a person's exterior to what lay underneath. And they were quick in getting there, too, because Ninette and Sylvie had called Joffrey's character in under thirty seconds of meeting him.

Ninette's husky voice sounded from the kitchen, the volume behind it pitched for casual conversation and too low to make out the actual words. Eager to spill her new-found thoughts on her, Sylvie and maybe even Viv if she was working from home today, Lizzy rounded the main entry and all but skidded to a halt.

Every single woman in the family sat seated around the table, a mix of coffee mugs, iced teas and juices situated in front of each of them. More importantly every eye was locked on her.

"What's everyone doing here?" The second her blunt question hit air, she winced. "I mean, was something going on today and I missed it?"

Sylvie stood and waved Lizzy into the chair she'd vacated. "No, lass. We just thought some girl time might be in order after yer run-in with yer bawbag of an ex yesterday." She opened the warming oven built into the kitchen island and pulled out a tray. "Gia went on a pancake marathon this morning and ye can't have pancakes without bacon, so we saved ye a plate."

"Better that than when she tried to make oatmeal," Natalie said. "I swear that stuff was like concrete. Took two days to get the pot clean."

"Hey, I'd never used a pressure cooker before!" Gia said. "How was I supposed to know you had to cut the cooking time by a third?" She frowned at Lizzy. "Besides, pancakes are better anyway, right?"

All heads turned to Lizzy, expectant expressions on every face.

"It's Tuesday," she said.

Clearly, her response wasn't what they'd planned on hearing because they all looked from one to the other.

Ninette shifted in her chair for a straight-on stare at Lizzy. "It's also creeping toward ten thirty in the morning and it's too damned hot for the end of September." She cocked her head and narrowed her gaze. "Are you thinking you've slipped into a time warp, or is there something we're missing?"

"Girl time is Wednesday. Always the same day as family night."

From the perplexed looks the comment garnered, most of the women still didn't get it.

But Ninette's face softened and a knowing smile tilted her lips. "What makes you think we can't have a special day when one of our own needs it?"

The space behind Lizzy's sternum got so tight she could barely breathe and the air around her seemed to lighten. As if gravity had thinned enough in mere seconds to let her body float above the earth. "It was just a run-in with an asshole."

"Oh, haud yer wheesht," Sylvie said coming up beside her with a fully prepared plate. She grabbed Lizzy by the arm and firmly walked her to the table. "We saw ye when you walked through the door last night, so that shite's not flyin' today." She planted a hand on her hip and nodded to the food. "First order of business is breakfast."

"Then, after that," Ninette added, "you can tell us what had you hauling ass in here with a determined look on your face."

"I need you to help me teach Joffrey a lesson." The statement shot out of her mouth with all the subtly of a cannon and left the women around the table openly stunned. Even Ninette and Sylvie who never seemed to get rattled by anything stared at her with wide eyes and slack jaws.

Interestingly, it was Gabe—usually the quietest of the bunch—who spoke first. She picked up her coffee mug and blew across the top of it, sending steam dancing around the edges. "So much for breakfast being on the agenda."

"Personally, I like topic number two better anyway." Gia sat forward and crossed her arms on the table. "What kind of lesson are we talking exactly?"

Viv aimed one of those stern teacher looks at Lizzy. "Might not be a bad idea to backtrack and explain the why behind the lesson in question while you're at it."

Tricky.

As tight as the family was, there was no guarantee one of them wouldn't go off half-cocked and tell one of the guys, and if that happened, Axel was guaranteed to act.

No, wait.

Rex had said point-blank that Axel would make it a priority to take action no matter what. So, what difference did it make if they said anything? And besides, this was about her doing something to vindicate herself. About purposefully putting the past to right and moving forward without any regrets.

She scanned the women around her. Strong women. Smart women. Every one of them there today because they cared and wanted to support her. The words came out fast, every detail rattled out as rapid-fire as her thrumming heartbeat. How Joffrey had tried to make it sound like Axel was trying to take advantage of her. Manipulate her by keeping Joffrey away. How he'd said her early success with Axel wasn't much more than beginner's luck and that she'd need a label like the one he worked for to sustain her long term.

It was when she'd shifted gears and shared how Joffrey had not only stolen her copyrights years ago, but had implied Axel had done the same that the room got scary tense and quiet.

"You can't seriously think Axel would do that to you?" Gia said.

Sylvie sat beside her, her mouth clamped in a hard line, but her sharp gaze obviously asking the same question.

"God, no," Lizzy said. "I mean, yeah, after what Joffrey did to me back then, my knee-jerk response was to find Axel and raise hell, but it only took about five seconds after that for common sense to settle in. Axel's nothing like him. He wouldn't do that. And even if he did want to fuck me over, he's smart enough to not do things the exact same way Joffrey did."

"Well, clearly, Joffrey doesn't know that you know what he did with your copyrights," Vivienne said. "If he did, he wouldn't dare try to pin the same scheme on Axel."

"Oh, I don't know," Natalie said. "Wyatt was so fucking arrogant he thought he could get away with anything, and from the way you guys have described Joffrey, he's every bit the narcissist my ex is."

Darya grunted an agreement that came off surprisingly feminine and locked gazes with Lizzy. "Have you checked online yet?"

"For what?"

"The copyright listing," Gia said. "If he was just bluffing and we're looking for a way to put him in his place, we'll have to find something else."

A smile that would have given an axe murderer pause

lifted Ninette's lips and her voice was chilling in its delivery. "Ah, but if he actually found a way to do the dirty work like Rex suggested, we'll have an insta-ready way to hang the bastard."

Chapter Twenty-Four

Patience had never been an issue for Axel. When he wanted something he laid out the steps to take it and executed the plan. Simple. Easy. Methodical. From buying the building that had become Crossroads to seeing Lizzy on stage for the first time, he'd always had an undercurrent of calm that tethered his plans and kept him grounded. But waiting to take his due on Joffrey Reynolds, that well had finally run out.

12:09 PM showed at the bottom of his computer screen. Twenty more minutes until he'd have the chance to let his long legs stretch and take the long way through the inside of Crossroads to the back parking lot where he, Jace and his key staffers parked. He'd also have the light midday traffic to the airport, which meant he could let his Shelby have some room to run and take out his aggressions on the highway, too.

For the fourth time in fifteen minutes, he refocused on the P&L on the screen and tried to focus.

The harsh ka-chunk of the secured metal door at the bottom of the staircase outside his and Jace's office rattled through his open door, followed by soft footfalls.

He switched his screen to the live feed of the main office. Shelly and her new assistant sat behind their desks, neither of them appearing to talk about anything work related given the wild arm gestures Shelly paired with her words. If it wasn't them, then whoever was on the way in had to be family, because they were the only two non-Haven women who had a prayer of getting past Knox's hand scanners.

The *who* got crystal clear all of four seconds later when his mother meandered through his door. Usually, she wouldn't leave the house without full hair and makeup in place, but today she was makeup free with her hair pulled back in a low ponytail.

Manners ingrained from as early as he could remember had him on his feet as soon as she crossed the threshold. "I can count on one hand the number of times you've climbed those stairs in the last two years, so either you've won the lottery, or you and Ninette are havin' a rare fight and you're out to find a henchman to take her out."

She walked into his outstretched arms and wrapped him up in a hug like she always did. No matter what their living circumstance, one thing about his mother that never flagged was her capacity to love. "What? A mother can't come by just to visit with her son without an agenda?"

"Sure she can. But considerin' the two of us spend most nights under the same roof, I'm not thinkin' you'd make a thirty-minute drive when we could shoot the bull tonight." He kissed the top of her head, palmed her shoulders and pulled her away enough to meet her eyes. "Now, tell me what's got you out of the house without that unnecessary war paint on."

She rolled her eyes, playfully swatted his shoulder and turned for one of the chairs positioned in front of his desk. "Pfft. Yer just like yer father. Too smooth with the words to be safe around women."

"I'm nothin' like that bastard."

The *harrumph* his comment earned was one he'd heard plenty of times over the years. "I've told ye before, sweet boy. Yer father's leavin' wasnae a loss for me or for ye. He gave me you along with a year's worth of memories and that was enough."

"He left you with a baby and no income."

She crossed one leg over the other, a move she made look elegant even in her jeans and T-shirt. "He barely brought in an income even before ye were born. Not thinkin' he'd have brought in much more after and there was another mouth to feed. I got what I needed then, and I'll get what I need tomorrow."

Damned right she would. He and Jace had made sure of it.

Rather than argue further, he grunted and ambled back to his chair.

"You know," she said, "it didn't go unnoticed by Ninnie and I how you boys changed after what happened to her."

An odd change in topic. Not exactly miles away from where they'd started, but not exactly a subject they were fond of straying toward. But then a john with above average stalking skills nearly killing his best friend's mother didn't exactly make for pleasant conversation.

"We saw how your focus changed," she said. "Talked about it a lot. In the end, we decided the drive would make life easier on you both and chose to play along, but we saw it for what it really was—two young men impacted by something frightening and coping with it by taking control of what they could."

Oh, yeah. His mother was on a mission all right. The question was—what was her target. "Ma, it's been almost thirty years since Ninette's thing happened."

"A very long time, and you've made an impressive life for yourself."

"Not my life I'm curious about, but why you're bringing the topic up now."

Her mouth twisted in one of those cute little mews that said she definitely had a message to deliver and wasn't quite sure how to get it said. An uncustomary occurrence considering she normally just blurted out whatever was on her mind. "I guess because I never felt like I needed to explain why I did what I did to make money. I made my peace with it before I picked up my first john."

"But you suddenly need to explain it to me now?"

"No. I'm still comfortable with my reasons…" She frowned and tapped one finger atop her folded hands. "It's just…sometimes for a woman to truly put her past behind her, she needs a chance to stand up for herself. Not to have someone else do it for her, but to take the bull by the bloody horns, look him in the eye and prove to herself she's not afraid anymore. That she's not a victim to be trampled."

Lizzy.

His gut twisted on the thought and an uneasiness on par with handling an unpinned grenade hit him like a right hook. "Stop fuckin' around, Ma, and cut to the chase."

"I know you, Axel. So does Ninnie. Neither you, Jace or any of the other boys would ever in a million years let a man like Joffrey get away with messing with one of our own."

"You'd be right, but I'm still not seein' how that ties with what you're taking too damned long in telling me."

She smiled. A soft one that spoke of easy feminine pride. "You're too stubborn and proud for your own good sometimes, Axel McKee. What I'm tellin' your daft self is that a woman like Lizzy's not gonna let it go either. And, if you're not careful—payin' attention and seein' to what *she needs* instead of your own drive—the two of you might well collide."

A warning.

A vague one to be sure, but the women had their own code, too, and if she was dancing a line of loyalty, she'd need to be. He stood fast enough his chair nearly toppled behind him and waved her out of her seat. "Where is she?"

"They're all at Haven."

She'd barely gained her feet when he grabbed her arm and gently but forcefully guided her through the conference room to Jace's office. "They?"

"All the wives. Ninnie's doing her best to keep them corralled while I'm allegedly at the grocery store, but Gia's already gone out to do some legwork. Something about finding a witness to corroborate changes made to a federal database?"

"Bloody fucking hell!" He whipped out his phone just as the two of them barged into Jace's office, quickly yanking Jace's focus off the screen in front of him.

Before Jace could ask what was up, Trevor answered. "You bein' here any sooner than one o'clock isn't gonna make this flight go faster. Only make my crew antsy."

"Switch the flight plan," he said to Trevor holding Jace's stare. "We're gonna have to delay takeoff by an hour maybe an hour and a half." He shifted the phone enough to direct his next order to Jace. "Get on the phone with Miramar and ASCAP. Push the meet back to three."

"Brother, you're asking a lot. They barely gave us the one o'clock slot." Jace glanced at Sylvie then back to Axel. "What the fuck's going on?"

"Gotta be a doozy if you're moving the time back willingly," Trevor said, clearly hearing both sides of the conversation.

Axel jerked his head toward his mother. "She's not sharin' details, but I'm thinking the gist of it is, the women aren't waiting on us to handle shit this time and are on a nut-crushing mission that might derail our own."

Jace scowled at Sylvie and snatched up his phone. "I'm on it."

"Yep, me, too," Trevor said. "You gonna tell the rest of the guys, or do you need to delegate."

Axel nodded to Jace and steered Sylvie out of his office, down the staircase and toward the parking lot. "I'll handle them on the drive to Haven. Probably the only thing that's gonna keep me from givin' Lizzy a heads-up I'm on my way."

"Roger, that. We'll have the bird ready."

The line went dead, leaving only their quick strides to fill the silence. Oddly, Sylvie didn't seem the least bit upset with his response. In fact, if anything, she looked downright pleased with herself.

He opened her car door and stepped back to let her slide behind the wheel. "You wanna look like you're really at the grocery store you might oughta be a good thirty minutes behind me."

She reached for her seat belt and beamed up at him. "If I'm thirty minutes behind you, does that mean I miss the flight to LA?"

"Yes."

Nodding, she buckled herself in and fired up the engine. "Then I'll go straight to the airport and meet you at the plane."

Axel was just about to swing the door shut, but drew up short at her words. "You sure? You took a lot of pains to make sure you didn't cross the line on outing Lizzy in this ruse today. If you're waiting at the plane, she's gonna know you interfered."

Her smile softened, one of those gentle looks aimed up at him reserved for precious moments that—to his estimation—she hadn't had nearly enough of. "She's our Elizabeth. And while she might not have had a mother to look out for her before, she's got two now. She'll figure out why I did what I did eventually and forgive me, but she's not goin' into this without me there to back her up."

Fuck, but he loved his family. Every meddlesome one of them. "Right." He leaned in and kissed her cheek. "Best thing I ever did in life was choosin' to take care of you." He pulled away and winked. "Be sure you call Trevor. Tell him to add you and Lizzy to the flight plan. We'll meet you at the plane in an hour."

The drive to Haven went by in a blur, the scenery and a dangerous amount of the traffic utterly ignored through the calls he made on the way—Beckett to alert him that Gia was out doing legwork that would no doubt overlap with their own, and Knox to see what part Darya was playing. He finished up with a follow-up call to Jace to have him alert the rest of the guys and get a confirmation he'd pulled of a scheduling miracle with Miramar.

Inside the house was way too quiet, not a single soul in the kitchen or even the usual murmur of the huge TV in the entertainment room giving him a clue where to start.

Soft footsteps sounded on the catwalk that stretched across the massive living room.

Axel strode into the room just in time to see Ninette duck into Jace's office, though she did manage a second of eye contact and a subtle wink before she closed the door behind her.

Figured they'd be holed up where the computers were, which meant Darya was involved up to her eyeballs and possibly already catching an earful from her husband.

He took the stairs two at a time. The closer he got, the more their voices became recognizable—Vivienne, Darya, Natalie and, yes, Lizzy. But unlike their normal casual tones, their delivery was focused. Sharper and urgent.

He opened the door at the same time Natalie spun from the window with the phone held up to her ear and said, "She's not answering." Her eyes shot wide and she jerked the phone away from her ear, quickly ending the call. "Oh, hey, Axel."

"*Oh, hey*, indeed." He scanned the room, noting that all the other women were in attendance as well, and nodded to the phone in Natalie's hand. "If you're trying to reach Gia, odds are good she's on the phone with Beckett learning that one Annette Jonas is already on a plane and headed to Los Angelas."

Where Natalie had been the primary one with a guilty expression up to that point, the look ended up mirrored on the rest of the women in the next heartbeat. All of them, that was, except Lizzy who straightened from where she'd been looking over Darya's shoulder at the computer. "You know about Annette?"

"I know about her, how Joffrey's used her as an in with the copyright office, and the ten other musicians

Joffrey's been stealing music from in as many years—
everyone of which is ready to testify against him when
the ASCAP lawyers take our case to court."

"What case?"

He couldn't quite decide if the look on her face was
one of shock or disappointment. Maybe a little of both.
Kind of like a kid who'd thought for sure they'd slid one
past their parents, only to find out Mom and Dad had
been wise to them the whole time. "The one we've been
building for the last two weeks."

A few of the women ducked their heads trying to hide
their knowing grins. The rest aimed a mix of rolled eyes
and grunts in his direction.

He ambled to Lizzy, needing the contact to wipe
away what was left of the uncomfortable buzz that had
hounded him the whole drive to Haven. "I told you in
New York, lass. We take care of our own." He pulled her
flush against him and squeezed her hips. "That includes
making sure men like Joffrey pay for what they've done."

Her mouth quirked in a wry, half smile. "Rex reminded me as much."

"We all reminded you," Vivienne said from her place
on the sofa. "You just weren't content with letting them
do the dirty work."

Ninette winked at Lizzy, but otherwise held her tongue.

And there it was. The need to vindicate herself rather
than have someone else do it for her. And he'd almost
robbed her of the chance without realizing she needed it
to put her past to rest. "You wanted to be the one to take
him down," he said as gently as he could.

"Wouldn't you?"

Hell, yes, he would've. As it was, it'd taken everything in him to wait as long as he had on Lizzy's behalf.

"I get it, pet. It might have taken me a stroll down memory lane and a stern talking to, but I get it." He pulled her in tighter and kissed the top of her head, not giving two fucks about the audience watching them. "So, if I told you the plane's waiting and you could be there as the primary person bringing charges against Joffrey, would that be enough to put you in the driver's seat? Not like you didn't already figure out the ins and outs of what he's been up to on your own."

She pulled back in his arms enough to meet his gaze. "You'd do that?"

His sweet Elizabeth—always surprised when people stepped up to give her what she needed. He'd fix it so that surprise faded over time. Him and all the rest of his family. "In a heartbeat." He leaned in and gave her a soft kiss that lingered a beat longer than it should've with everyone watching. "But you'd better hurry up and get those ass-kicking stiletto boots of yours on. The plane's waiting and you've got a bull to grab by the horns."

Chapter Twenty-Five

Los Angeles wasn't really everything music videos and movies made it out to be. No one told you about the dingy haze that hovered over the city, and while there were palm trees scattered here and there, the downtown area still had the same concrete and high-rise landscape as Dallas. In fact, so far as Lizzy could tell, it was just a place with better temperatures and better proximity to a beach.

Outside the limousine's tinted window, perfectly dressed women in fashionable outfits and men in suits to rival some of Axel's strode between buildings. Yeah, she'd seen a lot of walking in New York City, but this was different. More like they were there to be seen and meet a culturally expected behavior than the pure function of getting from point A to point B.

On the bench across from her, Sylvie sat engrossed in a romance novel that looked like it'd been read at least twenty times already. Several pages were dog-eared to the point Lizzy was confident she could find all tasty parts in under five seconds. In fact, if she wasn't mistaken, Sylvie had jumped from one of the easy to find spots between when they'd disembarked from the plane to the time they'd shifted to the limo.

Now that Lizzy thought about it, she had a few books

of her own she'd been meaning to read downloaded on her phone. But that would require trying to focus her mind on something besides the face-off only minutes from happening and the odds of remembering anything she read at this point was probably nil.

Axel's hand rested on her thigh, cradling her own. His thumb skated along the back of her hand a second before he spoke. "Miramar's in the big high-rise at the end of the next block."

A tilt of her head brought the tallest of the buildings into view. A circular building lined with nothing but blue-tinted mirror windows and a sharp point on the top that made her think of lightning rods. "You mean the one that looks like it belongs on *The Jetsons*?"

"That's the one." Unlike her, Axel looked like he was headed into work on a normal day, only today he had on a full navy blue suit that was unquestionably custom-made. Only the top part of his hair was pulled back into one of those messy buns most women bungled, while the rest of his red hair hung loose to his shoulders. No jitters. No tension. Hell, if anything he looked bored.

Lizzy smoothed her hand over the faded skin-tight jeans she'd picked to go with her black stilettos and fitted black top. The woven bracelets interspersed with teal and cinnabar beads were the only color to break the rest of her outfit. "Maybe I should have gone with a skirt."

Sylvie peeked up from her book. "The jeans are perfect. You're not playing into their norm. It'll make you stand out more."

Axel gave Lizzy a sidelong head-to-toe and grinned. "She's right. You're perfect. One thing these people understand, it's how to hold a crowd, and you do it even when you're not trying to." He nodded at the building ahead. "You'll do fine."

Fine as the primary artist who'd brought a host of federal crimes committed by one Joffrey Reynolds and, in conjunction, Miramar Studios, to light with ASCAP and a whole team of federal agents scheduled to meet them at the label's office in fifteen minutes. Originally, Axel had planned to keep Lizzy as distanced from the proceedings as possible—an effort he'd apparently insisted on to keep her career unaffected by any negative press. But in the space of the two-hour flight to LA, Axel and Jace had not only shifted the overall delivery to make her look like a rock star ready to wreck vengeance, but an avenging angel on behalf of all beleaguered artists everywhere. "There's no way I'm gonna remember everything you told me."

"You don't need to. You just tell your story. The evidence and the ASCAP attorneys will do everything else." The car came to a stop outside the building just as Axel met her eyes. "All you gotta do is walk in there like you do on stage, let things happen and enjoy the hell out of the show."

A man and a woman stood to one side of the elevator landing, both blending in with the rest of the executives coming and going through the lobby. Axel dipped his head in their direction. "Those are the attorneys." His gaze shifted to another trio exactly opposite the attorneys—two men wearing sub-par quality suits and the other clearly some form of law enforcement, complete with sidearms and cuffs anchored on his utility belt. "Those would be our Feds."

The attorneys and Feds noted Axel and Lizzy's arrival and moved in for a round of handshakes and introductions.

The female attorney, Olivia Trudeau, zeroed in on Lizzy and smiled the kindest smile she'd seen since stepping foot on California soil. "Ms. Hemming, if you're ready, we'll head upstairs."

In the time she'd been singing she'd been known to forget her lyrics a time or two. Had even gotten so lost in her own thoughts while performing she'd surfaced in time to realize she didn't know if she was headed into the first chorus or the second, and had to wing her way through getting her bearings again without letting anyone be the wiser. But this was a whole different ballgame. A seven-second delay she had no hope of bluffing her way through. Instead of trying, she nodded and squeezed Axel's hand in hers. "Ready as I'll ever be."

They crowded in the elevator. Where the ASCAP team seemed alert, on-point and ready to do white-collar battle, the Feds stuck to the rear of the car and looked like they'd drawn the short end of the stick on criminal detail. Lizzy couldn't blame them. Stickin' it to some pompous asshole who'd stolen intellectual property from a host of people wasn't exactly a thrill ride compared to trading down drug lords and international espionage. The hottie with the cuffs kept himself off to one side and projected a suitably badass image, but she'd bet he was counting down the hours to a midweek happy hour with his buddies.

Turning toward the elevator doors, Sylvie leaned close to Lizzy and whispered, "You're not too awfully mad at me are ye, lass?"

Mad? How could she possibly be mad at a woman who'd not only dared to champion her needs, but had been willing to risk Lizzy's wrath to do it. Lizzy wrapped her arm around Sylvie's shoulder and hugged her as tight as the elevator confines would allow. "No, I'm not mad. Glad actually. Maybe even relieved. This could've been a shit show if you hadn't intervened."

Sylvie leaned forward enough to catch Axel's eye. "Well, we could've just worked together from the start and avoided the near collision altogether."

Axel grumbled something unintelligible under his breath, punched the button for the forty-fifth floor, then anchored his arm around Lizzy's waist.

The silence as the elevator swept upward was awkward. Stifling to the point it felt as if someone had sucked all the oxygen from the cramped space. The tasteful ding announcing their arrival was a blessed relief, and her lungs rejoiced at the cool, conditioned air that swept in as the doors parted.

Axel gave her hip a reassuring squeeze, then shifted his hand low on her back and nudged her forward. "Time to find your swagger, lass. It's showtime."

He wasn't wrong. From the second they stepped into the posh elevator landing with its gray and black contemporary décor and chrome, white mirrored accents, she got the sense she'd just walked on stage. Two receptionists sat behind the wide black desk just ahead of them, both of them sporting perfectly styled hair and expert makeup. Another woman dressed in a tasteful yet sexy white sheath dress and nude pumps stood to one side, pointing to one of the computer screens.

All three women noted Lizzy and her motley crew's arrival at the same time and aimed polite, yet empty smiles their direction.

But they weren't the only ones watching. On either side of the floor-to-ceiling wall that separated the entrance from the main office area stretched a sea of low-walled cubicles filled with eager young workers clamoring for one of the closed office spaces lining the far wall—and every one of them looked on with avid curiosity.

Surprisingly, it was the female attorney that approached the receptionists rather than Axel. "Olivia Trudeau to see Mr. Belmont. Our one o'clock appointment was rescheduled to 4 PM."

Professionally delivered, but with a sharp enough edge no one would dare not take her seriously.

The women at the reception desk scanned Axel, Lizzy and Sylvie, then the rest of the crew behind them. It was the woman in the white dress who intervened. "I don't believe Mr. Belmont anticipated a group appointment." Her gaze lingered on the badass with the cuffs and sidearm for an uncertain beat then shifted back to Olivia. "What should I advise him you're here to talk about?"

"You should advise him the topic is such that he wouldn't want me sharing it with you, or within hearing distance of the twenty or so people watching right now." She dipped her head toward the open conference room with the glass walls open to anyone who cared to keep an eye on things. "If that's the only conference room available, I'd also recommend meeting in Mr. Belmont's office unless he's looking for a promotional nightmare."

As a mechanism for short-circuiting any bullshit, Olivia's frank approach worked wonders because the woman in white straightened as tall as her tasteful pumps allowed and she pasted on a glacial smile. "Certainly. I'll let him know you're here."

The two receptionists looked at each other, then up at Lizzy. The friendlier looking of the two dared a sheepish smile. "You're Lizzy Hemming, right?"

Why the recognition still caught her off guard even after the last few months, she couldn't imagine, but the question jolted her out of the tension that had gripped her since they'd landed. "I am."

The woman's smile got bigger. "I'm a huge fan. My boyfriend and I scored tickets to see you play next month in San Diego."

"Those tickets went fast," Axel interjected, giving Lizzy time to gather her wits. "The amphitheater's got a lot of seats. You get good ones?"

Her smile wilted a little and she wrinkled her nose. "Not great. We could only swing the back section, but at least we're in the center."

Axel gave her that charming smile he'd no doubt fine-tuned wrangling his way into way too many panties growing up and slid his hand into the inside pocket of his suit jacket. He pulled out a card and handed it over. "We've got a few set aside closer up for friends and family. Shoot me an email and we'll see if we can't get you and your man a better view."

She was on her feet and snatching the card from Axel's outstretched hand so fast, Lizzy nearly missed the corner office door swinging open. "Thank you." She looked back to her colleague, clearly fighting back a squeal inappropriate for an uptight office when she said, "Bobby's gonna lose his mind."

The colleague rolled her eyes and shot Axel a wry smile. "You realize I'm gonna hear about this for the next month."

While Axel had clearly clocked the older man who'd emerged from the office and was headed their way with an unhurried yet determined stride, Axel's charming grin never wavered. "That's the way it works, lass. Give a little, get a lot."

"You should add the lass and one of her friends, too," Sylvie said to Axel. "More fun for the ladies that way. They can plan their shenanigans while they're supposed to be working."

Both receptionists aimed huge smiles Sylvie's way, but the excitement was cut short the second Belmont rounded their desk. He swept the lot of them with a pointed, appraising look. His attention snagged Sylvie first, a flash of interested curiosity registering a second before he shifted his focus to Lizzy. Recognition flared and he zeroed in on Olivia. "Ms. Trudeau, I'd assumed your visit was to arrange this year's program grants, but it seems you've brought some guests with you." He frowned over her shoulder at the federal trio, particularly at the badass. "Will I be needing to contact my attorney to join us?"

Olivia's coy smile could've charmed a snake. "How about if I share the information we have for you and then you can determine where you'd like to go from there?"

Belmont's gaze volleyed between Axel and Lizzy. "All right." He stepped back and waved Olivia forward. "If you'd like to join me in my office?"

"Of course." Olivia paired it with all the graciousness of a Southern Belle, but her eyes glinted with sharkish delight as she walked beside him through the field of cubicles. Her partner moved in step behind her, the Feds and the badass moving in next to leave Lizzy, Axel and Sylvie at the end.

Lizzy leaned into Axel and murmured, "I really like her."

"Of course, you do. She knows her business and

doesn't take shit from anyone." He beamed down at Lizzy and winked. "Kind of like my Elizabeth."

And just like that, all the tension and worry she'd wrestled the whole flight over unwound.

My Elizabeth.

No matter how many times he'd said it, or how often he looked at her with the pride on his face that was there now—it never got old. Still had the power to hack reality off at the knees and leave her totally floating in a blissful bubble. "You keep saying things like that and I'm going to end up with a permanently goofy grin on my face. Vivienne will have to rework my entire image. I'll be the rocker who went soft and traded in her high-heeled boots for wearing white sundresses and daisies in her hair."

"Sweetheart, if anyone could pull that image off and still rock the house, it'd be you." He pulled her in closer just as they crossed the threshold into Belmont's office and growled low in her ear. "Just don't take those boots off yet. You're about to get to dig them into Joffrey's throat."

Rather than sit in one of the three chairs stationed in front of Belmont's desk, Olivia and her partner stood to one side and waved Lizzy, Axel and Sylvie into the seats. Olivia rested her tasteful briefcase on the edge of his desk and pulled out a few folders while the Feds and the badass lined up behind Axel and Lizzy's chairs.

"I appreciate you working with us on scheduling today," Olivia said. "You know our primary concern at ASCAP is representation of artists like Ms. Hemming and, considering the impact our information has had on her and several other artists, we felt it was important she be here as a witness so she can feel confident the matter is being addressed appropriately." She laid a thick file in front of Mr. Belmont. "Before we begin, I'd like to ask you to call in one of your employees. One of your artist reps by the name of Joffrey Reynolds."

For the first time since he'd appeared this afternoon, Belmont's expression turned wary. His gaze slid to the badass then back to Olivia. "Something I should be concerned about?"

"Indeed. But we'll cover that in detail while Mr. Reynolds is on his way in."

It took two seconds. Two heartbeats at most before Belmont appeared to deem Joffrey on his own for whatever it was he'd done. He picked up the phone, punched a single button and clipped a sharp, "Find Joffrey and get him in here." He laid the phone back in its cradle with admirable calm and eyeballed Olivia. "All right, now cut to it and tell me what's going on."

The smile that tilted Olivia's lips was one that would've made Ninette proud. She also did exactly what Belmont had demanded and cut straight to the heart of things with all the sensitivity of an upper cut. "We have irrefutable proof and testimony from eleven individuals—one of which is Elizabeth Hemming—that your employee is guilty of conspiracy, fraud, falsification of federal records, forgery and theft of intellectual property rights. These crimes were committed both before and after he became an employee of Miramar Records. Many of the songs he allegedly wrote and gave rights to Miramar artists to record on your label actually belong to other individuals who had no idea their copyrighted information had been stolen, thereby putting Miramar Records at fault as well. All evidence has been reviewed and warrants for Mr. Reynolds's arrest issued." She motioned to the Feds.

"These gentlemen are here to present those warrants and take him into custody."

She waited a beat, letting the full breadth of what she'd smoothly unveiled sink in. "Will that be a problem, Chad? Or will Miramar be supporting ASACP in holding Mr. Reynolds accountable for the crimes committed and rectifying the wrongs done to the artists in question?"

Behind Belmont, the Los Angeles skyline stretched in a bold, artistic line, topped by an exquisite blue sky. A cosmopolitan paradise shared only by the elite blessed enough to live in such a city. The peaceful view made the building fury on Belmont's face that much starker. A utopian backdrop for a volcano swiftly rumbling toward a mammoth explosion.

Despite the deepening red behind his tanned face, his voice came out surprisingly soft. "Miramar has long prided itself on the longevity of our artists and supporting their rights. Assuming what you claim is true, naturally we will provide our full support in making full restitution."

"Oh, the claims are unquestionably true." She nodded to the file on his desk. "Documented there, you'll find technological evidence that shows Mr. Reynolds not only blackmailed a long-time copyright office employee to enter records he never had rights to claim, but recently leveraged his contact to falsify existing records in an effort to pressure Ms. Hemming into leaving her current manager, Axel McKee, in favor of signing with Miramar."

From there, Olivia expertly outlined every shred of evidence, her partner cleverly playing to her delivery with extra details that made the two of them look like life-long sportscasters paired for the sporting event of the century.

By the time they got to the end of the file, ten minutes had passed and the anger on Belmont's face had shifted to something closer to indignant outrage.

A knock sounded on the door a second before it opened.

Joffrey took two steps in, swept the room with his greasy smile, locked gazes with Lizzy—and froze.

What possessed her to do it, she couldn't say. Maybe instinct. Maybe just the driving need to finally face her past and make damned sure it stayed anchored squarely behind her. Whatever it was, she stood, prowled out from between the desk and chairs and faced the man she'd allowed to control far too much of her life. "Hello, Joffrey."

Her words had barely died off before she felt Axel and Sylvie move in behind her, a quiet yet unmistakable show of support that fortified her resolve with an impenetrable steel.

To Joffrey's credit, he didn't shoot straight to his smarmy demeanor, but shifted his focus to his boss instead. "What's going on, Chad?"

Behind her, the legs of Belmont's impressive leather chair swooshed against the thick carpet, followed by his soft footfalls. "I believe you already know, Ms. Hemming and Mr. McKee. They've brought a few of their associates with them to share some information with me, but maybe you'd like to share the nature of your background with Ms. Hemming with me first."

Joffrey's attention cut to Axel and for the first time ever, Lizzy half expected Joffrey to turn on his heel and take off running. He swallowed hard and met Belmont's stare. "We lived together."

"And, in that time were you privy to the songs she wrote?"

Comprehension settled in Joffrey's features. His mouth hardened. "Of course. We were in a relationship. We shared everything."

"You were in a relationship, but not married," Olivia clarified. "And the extent of your cohabitation was just under one year. Certainly nothing to suggest common-law marriage or rights to her music in any way."

Joffrey clenched his fists at his sides. "I have no idea what you're talking about."

"They're talking about how you took my songs, recorded them and registered them with the copyright office as your own."

"I did no such thing." Despite his denial, his voice shook. He looked to Belmont. "I don't know what these people have told you, but Lizzy and I didn't part on good terms. She's never been able to let things go between us and is just trying to manipulate some form of revenge."

"Revenge?" Propelled by years of frustration, she took one slow step forward after another. "Why would I need revenge? I didn't do anything wrong. But you did. You took not just my music, but other people's, too. You stole them. Claimed the rights, gave them to other people to record and have been banking the royalties the whole time to line your own pockets." She stopped right in front of him. "And when you figured out I'd done well for myself without you and might be able to further your career a little more, you decided to use that poor woman at the copyright office to stick her neck out a little more and get your pawn back." She cocked her head. "That doesn't sound like revenge to me, Joffrey. That sounds like setting things right."

The Feds might not have seemed too eager to participate in the day's activities up to that point, but they took a cue like nobody's business and picked that exact moment to step forward. Badass took a precautionary place by the office door and folded his arms across his chest.

The taller of the two agents held a folded piece of paper in his outstretched hand. "Mr. Reynolds, I'm Special Agent Taylor Damon with the Federal Bureau of Investigations. You're under arrest for charges of conspiracy, fraud, falsification of federal records, forgery and theft of intellectual property rights. You have the right to remain silent. Anything you say can and will be used against you in a court of law. You have the right to an attorney…"

Agent Damon droned through the whole speech.

Through it all, Joffrey's face slowly shifted. Confusion. Utter shock. Disbelief. Uncontainable rage.

She'd seen that last one before.

Had felt the wrath that came with it—verbally and physically.

You need to move.

Now.

The thought came too late, Joffrey's scathing, "You bitch!" ringing through the room even as he drew his arm back, his hand fisted and perfectly aimed toward her face.

She flinched and tried to duck out of the way, but firm arms clamped around her and pulled her to the side.

Not Axel.

Sylvie. The familiar scent of Chanel No. 5 cocooning her as securely as Sylvie's arms even as a sickening thud sounded in front of her. The next thing she knew Joffrey dropped like a stone to the dove gray carpet.

Axel stood above him like an avenging giant. Gone was the civilized man that was never rattled, replaced with a well-dressed god of war primed for deadly battle.

"Get up, ye bloody scunner!" He shoved Joffrey to his back with a foot to his shoulder. "Get the fuck up and try that shite again so I can gut ye with my bare fuckin' hands."

No one moved. Not the attorneys. Not Belmont. Not even the Feds or the badass.

"I said get the fuck up!" Axel roared, his shoulders heaving under the blast of adrenaline and pent-up frustration.

Joffrey only moaned and rolled back to his side, curled in a fetal position.

But Axel wasn't having it. He fisted the back of Joffrey's once pristine high-dollar haircut and yanked him upward.

The threat of bloodshed and possible homicide got the Feds and the badass in gear, but not before Axel landed two more gruesome blows.

In the end it took both Feds, the male attorney and Belmont to contain Axel while the badass cuffed Joffrey. Axel's warning couldn't be stifled. "That's nothin', you loathsome roaster. Ye ever dare lay a fuckin' hand on my woman again, I'll make ye wish you were dead. Ye don't touch her. You don't look at her. You don't bloody *think* about her."

For a little thing, Sylvie was stronger than she looked, because it took a fair amount of wiggling and determination for Lizzy to break free of her hold. She finally managed and splayed a none too steady hand between Axel's shoulder blades. "Axel."

One touch.

One word.

But it was enough.

He turned his wild eyes to her, his breath churning like that of a bull.

Anyone else would have run. Would have at least taken pains to put themselves outside of reaching distance.

But she wasn't just anyone.

She was his.

His Elizabeth.

And he'd never hurt her.

Not so long as he had breath left in him.

She sidled closer. Smoothed her hands along his sternum. Up around the straining muscles at his neck until her forearms circled him and her chest was flush against his. His heartbeat hammered against her. "I'm fine."

Behind Axel, the Feds wisely maximized on the distraction she'd provided and hustled Joffrey out the door.

Axel let out a ragged exhale, buried his face in her neck and gripped her hips almost painfully. "You okay?"

A sharp bark of laughter she couldn't have contained if she'd had to shot past her lips and her torso shook against his. "Okay?"

When he tried to pull her away enough to read her face, she used the dregs of adrenaline still pumping through her to keep him tight against her. "I'm fine." She breathed him in. Let the heady mix of joy, wonder and undiluted love coursing through her flood her system and beamed a smile at the ceiling. "A man I've allowed to rule my life for years, just got his dream job flushed down the toilet, his ass handed to him by a classy woman and an impressive amount of his own manhandling landed on him by my man. Shitty as I should probably feel about that last one, I'm feeling unbelievably gratified."

His low, but strained chuckle rumbled against her. Wrapping his arms more securely around her, he cradled the back of her head in one huge palm and splayed the other low on her back. "Ignore the shitty feelings, lass. He has that and a helluva lot more coming to him."

Olivia's conspiratorial voice sounded beside them. "While I can appreciate the sentiment and wouldn't argue it on a personal level, I'm going to advise against any further retaliation." Lizzy and Axel parted enough to catch her subtle wink. "At least for now."

She snatched her briefcase from Belmont's desk and motioned her partner toward the door. "Mr. Belmont, you've got all of the impacted artists in the file." She strode to the door with the confidence of a woman who'd not only done battle but wiped up the battlefield afterward. "We'll give you and your team a week to huddle and come up with recommended plans for restitution."

Where Olivia had seemed content to take Belmont and his vows of good intent at his word, Axel pinned him with a frightening scowl. "You do anything to side with that bastard or short the people he screwed, I'll take this fucking label apart until the only thing that's left is a memory."

For a man who'd just seen Axel in all his primal glory, Chad Belmont didn't so much as flinch. "While I'm not inclined to buckle to threats, I'd say yours is an unnecessary one. Joffrey won't be receiving any support from Miramar and we'll do right by the people he's harmed with his actions." His unperturbed gaze slid to Sylvie, considering. "I take it he's a relation of yours."

Arms crossed at her chest like she'd single-handedly pulled together the entire outcome, she smirked and cocked her head. "The best son a mother could have and a force ta be reckoned with." Her eyes sparked with what Lizzy had come to recognize as a precursor to all kinds of trouble a second before she uncrossed her arms and dug in the front pocket of her purse. "Ye know, you have the look of a lively lad yerself." She pulled out a card and handed it to him. "That's my daughter-in-law's business card. She's an event planner where we live in Dallas, but if ye ever come that way, give her a call and tell her ta give ye my number. Axel might be prone to punchin' first and askin' questions later, but I'll only take a swing if ye try something I'm not wantin' ye to."

"Holy Christ, Ma. Is there any time ye won't sheath yer claws?" Axel grabbed her gently by the arm, nodded to Belmont and steered them both toward the door.

Sylvie's bold laughter mirrored the joy still buzzing through Lizzy's system. Completely unapologetic and as bright as the sun outside Belmont's window. She waved a flirty farewell at Belmont over one shoulder and leaned in close enough only Axel and Lizzy could hear her. "Ye know what they say—keep yer friends close, and potential lovers closer."

The play on the classic *Godfather* line did what she'd undoubtedly intended for it to do and ripped a throaty laugh from Axel that had all the avid onlookers in the cubicle farm dropping their jaws in surprise. Their usual banter kept up the whole way down to the lobby, the two of them flanking Lizzy on either side. While Sylvie relinquished her hold on Lizzy's arm in the elevator, the way Axel anchored his arm at her waist, she doubted anything short of a nuclear warhead or sheer maneuverability would dislodge it for the foreseeable future.

At the limousine, he opened the door for his mother, but held Lizzy back before she could duck inside behind her.

Stymied by his hesitation, Lizzy studied him. "What?"

He pulled her flush against him, his eyes narrowed in consideration. "I'm just thinkin'. We're in LA."

"Yeah?"

"And you've never been here before."

True. Up until Axel she'd done very little in the way of exploration, but with the tour she'd definitely begun to get her feel, and she had a feeling there was a lot more of it in store for her future. "So?"

"So, we're here. Tell me what you want to do."

Late afternoon sun slanted from between the buildings, casting a golden hue around his wild russet hair. He was everything she'd never known she'd wanted. Honest. Tender even in his ferocity. Loyal to a fault and insanely sexy.

And he was hers. Her champion. Her partner. The other half of her heart. "I think I've seen enough of Los Angeles." She leaned in and whispered against his lips. "Take me home to Haven."

Epilogue

One year, four months and seventeen days. Lizzy had counted it up on the flight to Scotland five days ago and jotted it down in her travel journal. Said out loud, the stretch of time since Axel had first sauntered into her world sounded really freaking long.

It felt more like a blink. A rocket ship ride through some of the most intoxicating, wondrous experiences of her life.

And she wouldn't change a second of it.

Curled up in the corner of the cottage's gray flannel sofa, she tucked her knees tighter to her chest and looked out the picture window to the sloping landscape below. The Highlands were everything she'd hoped they would be and so much more. The people were warm and friendly and seemed to treat everyone they met as if they were their long-time neighbor. The sites were exceptional— craggy cliffs covered in deep green grass with heather and thistle adding dots of lavender here and there, castles to explore, streams and waterfalls she could sit by for hours and simply savor their peaceful sounds and magnificent architecture that ranged from quaint cottages like the one he'd bought for his mother to the jaw-dropping buildings in Edinburgh. Particularly those up and down Royal Mile and Edinburgh Castle.

But mostly, it just felt like things moved at a different pace here. Like the hustle and bustle of Dallas simply couldn't apply and the most important thing for any one person to do was live and honor the life they'd been given. To be. To enjoy.

To live.

She smiled to herself, cradled her coffee mug between both hands and let the steaming brew balance out the soft October chill. Axel had rekindled the fire before he'd gone out for his morning run. Between the gentle crackling of the logs on the grate, her fleece pajama bottoms and fuzzy socks and the soft mist hanging along the tops of the mountains behind, it was a nearly picture-perfect moment. As she rested her mug on the fluffy pillows that lined the back of the sofa, her wedding ring glinted in the morning sunlight—a round center diamond surrounded by smaller ones and a band inlaid with more of the same. The design might have been simple and classy, but—Axel being Axel—the four-karat stone in the center made quite a statement. A Dominant's version of *This one's mine, go get your own.*

Yep. Things had definitely changed in the last year. All for the better.

What Axel didn't know yet was that things were about to change even more.

As if he'd intentionally timed it to coincide with her thoughts, her husband jogged into view, rounding up the steep drive that lead to the cabin's perch at the top of a scenic bluff. Despite the cooler temps outside, he'd headed out in a faded red tee that was now drenched down the center and his loose black track pants clung to his hips. His hair was pulled up in a tight knot and his features pinched in concentration. No doubt puzzling together how best to tackle her next session in the studio and the launch of the next album they'd targeted for early spring. Whatever his plans, she was probably going to throw a sizable monkey wrench right in the middle of them. Not because she needed them to change, but because he was overprotective where she was concerned. Demanding and domineering in the bedroom to be sure, but an unrelenting gladiator when it came to seeing to her needs.

He jogged up the wooden stairs to the porch and spied her through the window. His concentration cleared in an instant, his expression shifting to a manly, pleased with himself grin that showed a healthy amount of teeth. He strode through the front door, the crisp autumn air and wood smoke from the chimney mingling with his manly scent. "I thought you'd still be in bed."

"You mean you hoped I'd still be in bed." She sipped her coffee and studied him over the rim of her mug. "At the rate we're going, we're going to spend our whole holiday fucking like teenagers."

"I'd wager we fuck more than teenagers." He ambled to the sofa, braced an arm on either side of her and kissed her forehead. "And it's not just on holiday, pet. It's all the time with you because it's fantastic." He pushed upright and checked her mug. "You need a top-off?"

She shook her head. "Nope. I'm good. You go shower. I'll start breakfast."

He smirked at that—and with good reason. The last few times she'd tried to cook him breakfast in the quaint yet state-of-the-art kitchen, they'd ended up with burned toast and extra crispy bacon thanks to some highly enjoyable distractions from his mouth and clever fingers. "I'll hurry."

"No. Don't hurry. I'd like to actually make something that's edible this time."

He snatched a hand towel he'd left on the weathered coffee table, ran it along the back of his neck and winked. "Ah, lass. Ye've always got something edible for me. I think we proved that yesterday mornin', but I'm happy tae remind ye again if ye need tae learn the lesson again."

Insatiable man.

Not that she was complaining. She shooed him toward the bathroom. "Go. I'm gonna see if I can come up with something to cook that's distraction proof."

Chuckling, he padded down the hallway. "I'm takin' that as a personal challenge, pet. You'd better be creative."

The bathroom door closed behind him with a muted chunk and the rush of water followed only seconds later.

She pried herself from her cozy nest and bustled to the kitchen. The rustic décor with its exposed weathered beams and whitewashed stone walls was everything you'd expect to find in a Scottish Highland cottage, but with bits of teal and red accents adding a lively personality to the space. Like the rest of the home, the space was small—a veritable postage stamp compared to Haven's kitchen—but comfortable and warm all the same. A place you wanted to linger in for hours and spend time getting to know the people who visited.

From the built-in escritoire in the corner, her phone chimed an incoming text message. She punched in the temp for biscuits on the oven, then meandered to it.

Sylvie: Have you told him yet?

Meddlesome woman. Told him what?

Sylvie: You know bloody hell what!!

Oh, yes. She knew. She was the *only* one who knew. Sylvie, at best, only suspected.

Nope. No idea what you're talking about.

The screen stayed absolutely blank for a moment. Then the little bubbles started up at the bottom.

Sylvie: Don't take that tone with me, missy. A mother knows. Both of them. And when you get around to telling him, Ninnie and I want to know.

Funny. She'd written it perfectly, but Lizzy "heard" every word with her clipped Scottish brogue. No doubt she'd paired it with a hand on her hip, too. She chuckled and typed out a response.

If anything of import should develop while we're here I'll absolutely notify you right away...but I still don't know what you're talking about.

Okay, she was probably pushing it and she'd eat a ton of crow for dodging at some point, but the banter with her family was one of the things about them she enjoyed the most. That and knowing that—no matter what her obligations with the outside world might be—with them she was just Lizzy. A woman they accepted exactly as she was. There was no competition. No backstabbing.

No jealous talk or posturing. Just a safe place to let go, love and be loved.

She set about making the biscuits, using the recipe Sylvie had taught her. By the time she slid the baking sheet in the oven, Axel was humming his way down the hall, his hair wet and loose to his shoulders and only a thick navy blue towel around his waist. She cocked an eyebrow and dipped her head toward the towel. "Did you not hear the part about wanting to have a successful breakfast this morning?"

He moved in behind her at the stove, palmed her hips and nuzzled her neck. "Oh, I assure you. Every breakfast we've had in here has been an off-the-charts success." He nipped the spot where her neck and shoulders met then dragged his beard across it. His hands slid upward, slowly coasting towards her breasts. "How long have I got before the biscuits are ready?"

She covered them with her own before they could get where he wanted. "Not enough time." She turned in his arms and gave him the sternest look she could muster— which wasn't much considering the playful glint in his eyes. "Besides, I need to talk with you about something."

He frowned at that. "Talk?"

She laughed at that, a sharp bark of pure joy that filled the tiny space and made her whole body shake. "You act like that's a bad thing."

"Ye forget, lass. Your brain's got a habit of working overtime and when it does that means I have to work overtime to get you to turn it back off again."

Well, he had a point there. Though, in a minute or two, she wouldn't be the only one overthinking things. The question was which direction his thoughts would take.

She leaned in and pressed a soft kiss to his lips. "You want some coffee?"

He studied her, a lazy predator assessing if he needed to acquiesce for now, or take a more aggressive approach and simply annihilate all hurdles from the get go. Humoring her apparently won the toss up, because he straightened with a grunt and headed for the coffee pot. "How much coffee do I need for this talk?"

Fuck. He'd need a full carafe. God knew, that's how much she'd needed. She shrugged and told the mother of all lies. "It's not a huge deal. I just know you're planning things out for the studio and figure you need to factor in a few things."

He stopped mid-pour and peered at her over one shoulder. "Like what?"

Oh, no. That carafe was glass and was part of a pretty damned expensive brew set. No way was she telling him until he was at the table with a cheap ceramic mug in his hand. She settled at the table, anchored her elbow on the top of it and propped her chin on her hand. "You know…details."

He turned, took a sip and eyeballed her over the rim while he did it. The man was far too cagey for his own good sometimes and, while Sylvie and Ninette might have copped to some clues already, she was pretty sure she'd kept things quiet with him. "You're being sneaky."

"A little." She motioned to the seat next to her.

He sat, turning his chair at an angle as he did so he faced her directly. Needing the contact, she scooted a little closer and rested her sock-covered feet in his lap. "I kind of oopsed that last tour leg to the east coast."

"Oopsed how?"

Ripping the bandage off was probably the wisest

course of action, but getting there was tricky. "Well, we were late getting to the airport and I didn't take everything I should have on the trip."

A wariness crept in to his expression and his body got scary still. "Like what?"

She tightened her hands around her coffee mug.

Everything would be fine.

This was Axel.

He loved her. Proved it every single day.

She forced one deep breath. Then another. "My birth control pills."

No movement.

Not even a hint of what was going on in his head showing in his expression.

"It was just one week," she said to fill the silence. "And it was one of those times the little ovulation thing said I shouldn't have been primed for—you know. But…"

"Elizabeth." It was only one word, but by now she knew exactly what he meant when he paired it with that tone. Translated to anyone else it meant *Get to the fucking point and do it now before I paddle your ass.*

So she did. "I'm pregnant."

His gaze dropped like a stone to her belly and the hand he'd rested on her feet tightened like he expected her to drop to the floor without his steadying grip. He met her stare again. "How long?"

"Ummm…about eleven weeks."

"No. How long have you known?"

Shit. This was the tricky part. Her voice crept upward to more of a mousey squeak. "Maybe a week?"

He let go of his coffee mug altogether and covered her feet with both hands. "Maybe?"

"Okay, I saw the doctor a week ago. I peed on the stick three days before that."

"And you didn't tell me."

"I knew we were coming here. The trip was my birthday present and the doctor said it was perfectly okay for me to fly." She bit her lip and took the Hail Mary she hoped would save her a significantly sore ass. "And I figured if I told you on my actual birthday it'd be like a super special Happy Birthday to me, but for both of us. Assuming it's a good thing?"

One minute she was sitting.

The next she was up, cradled in his arms and headed down the hallway. "Axel, the biscuits are gonna burn."

"Don't give a fucking bloody damn about the biscuits." Where he'd been known to go Neanderthal and get a little wild tossing her to the bed, this time he put a knee to the mattress, laid her down like she was the most fragile thing on the planet and covered her completely. He palmed the side of her face, his lips so close to hers her mouth tingled with the need for contact. "I fucking love you, Elizabeth McKee. Everything about you." His thumb traced the line of her cheek. "You're amazing. Beautiful and smart. Driven. Kind and gracious. And I fucking love you."

"I love you, too." She teased her fingers through his beard along his jawline and soaked in the sincerity behind his eyes. The overpowering love pouring off him. "I take it this means you're not mad?"

His mouth softened to a gentle smile and his fingers tightened against her scalp. "Mad, no. Thrilled, yes. But as soon as that baby's here and the doctor says you're in fighting form, you're getting paddled for not telling me sooner."

Well, so much for the Hail Mary. Then again, she had a little over two more trimesters to make him forget. And with his sweet words still humming through her like champagne bubbles and how good he felt against her, she was inclined to start her campaign as soon as possible. She wrapped her legs around his hips, circled his neck with her arms, smiled and gave him the words she'd learned gave her every bit as much power as him. "Whatever you say, Sir. Whatever you say."

* * * * *

To read more from Rhenna Morgan,
please visit www.rhennamorgan.com.

Acknowledgments

I wrote Axel's book at a time in my life that was both grudgingly painful and exquisitely beautiful. I wish I could say that Axel and Lizzy's story flowed onto the page easily, but the truth is it took an insane amount of discipline and a whole lot of amazing people to help me get across the finish line.

First, a huge thank-you to Cori Deyoe and Angela James. At a time when I wasn't sure how to navigate the new terrain in my writing life, you were both steadfast, comforting voices who helped me find my way. I can't tell you how much your calm, wisdom, experience and understanding helped me settle into my new norm.

I'm not sure there are enough thank-yous in the world to cover the people who listened to my life drama *and* my plot panicking through the course of this book, but I'm sure gonna give 'em a shout-out. To Joe Crivelli, Juliette Cross, Janna MacGregor, Kaleigh Lay, Dena Garson, Lucy Beshara, Jennifer Mathews and Bret Hughes—thank you! Big time! Here's hoping I don't have to activate the plot crisis hotline again anytime soon!

And finally, a thank-you to my daughters—just for being your beautiful unique selves and making me smile every single day.

About the Author

Rhenna Morgan is a happily-ever-after addict—hot men, smart women and scorching chemistry required. A triple-A personality with a thing for lists, Rhenna's a mom to two beautiful daughters who constantly keep her dancing, laughing and simply happy to be alive.

When she's not neck deep in writing, she's probably driving with the windows down and the music up loud, plotting her next hero and heroine's adventure. (Though trolling online for man-candy inspiration on Pinterest comes in a close second.)

She'd love to share her antics and bizarre sense of humor with you and get to know you a little better in the process. You can sign up for her newsletter and gain access to exclusive snippets, upcoming releases, fun giveaways and social media outlets at www.rhennamorgan.com.

If you enjoyed Down & Dirty, *she hopes you'll share the love with a review on your favorite online bookstore.*

When the hunter is your mate, being prey is anything but terrifying.

Coyote shifter Tate Allen has been watching. Learning his mate every possible way before he moves in. Protecting her through the night, always from afar.

He'll be the one to teach her about her gifts. He'll be there when she changes for the first time. With him, she'll fulfill her destiny.

The frantic beat of her heart. That mysterious yet sweet and innocent scent he'd come to crave. Her body well within touching distance and a wealth of unmarked skin on display. The weight of at least half the clan's attention, if not all of it, was firmly locked on Tate and his mate, but those were the only things he could process. That and staking his claim in a way no other man would dare to put his hands on Elise.

Although, given the maneuver Jade and Alek had engineered to trigger his protective instincts in front of everyone, no one gathered here tonight would question what she was to him going forward.

Well, no one except Elise.

Beside her, Priest, Katy and Sara waited and watched. While he knew Priest only lingered to make sure Tate kept his shit in check and Tate appreciated the mix of sympathy and humor in Katy's expression, he could have done without Sara having such a front-row seat. She was a sweet girl. As honest, open and sincere as a woman could be, but talkative, too. Whatever happened in the next few minutes would be grapevine fodder for the whole clan by morning.

Elise twisted, peeling her gaze away from Jade and Alek as they sauntered away and peeking over her shoulder first before she fully faced him. "What was all that about?"

A question that should be simple to answer. One that would've been painfully obvious to her if she'd been raised with knowledge of their clan. Not that her mother hadn't tried to share what it meant to be Volán and the things they could do. Elise just hadn't believed her. And, since Jenny had rejected her gifts, she couldn't prove a word of it. "Alek touched you."

"So?"

This was it. Once he gave in and made physical contact, she'd grow to crave his touch every bit as much as he needed hers. Would feel the pull that started as a subtle tug and grew toward something neither one of them could fight. An inextricable bond that would tie them to one another.

He'd tried to give her time to adjust. To grow accustomed to their clan and the gifts of their race. But he couldn't have stopped himself any longer even if the hounds of hell descended in mass, determined to kill them all. He dragged in a long, slow breath and inched forward, careful not to startle her. "No man touches you." The denim at her hips whispered against his palms a second before he settled his hands more firmly against the luscious curves. "No man but me."

Her breath hitched on a tender gasp and her body jolted at the careful, yet intimate contact. Whether it was the surprise of his words, his touch, or a combination of the two, he couldn't say, but the impact was heady. Her full, parted lips. Each ragged inhalation and exhale.

Those gorgeous and expressive green eyes of hers, wide with surprise and untapped sensual awareness.

Her gaze dipped to his mouth and she pressed her hands to his pecs. She jerked them away almost as quickly and nearly knocked herself off balance in the process.

Tate moved in tighter, bringing her body flush to his and anchoring one hand low on the small of her back and one at the back of her neck. "Easy."

The need to pair the soothing word with the brush of his lips against her neck—across her forehead or cheeks—nearly crippled him. But he held it in check. Barely. Her mother had all but confirmed Elise's past was a difficult one. And while she'd insisted the details were of a personal nature and up to Elise to share, she'd made it painfully clear the scars ran deep. No way was he opening those old wounds when they weren't in a place he could give her the attention she needed to heal them properly.

Instead, he stroked the length of her spine and centered himself in her scent. In the feel of her soft body trembling against his. "Just breathe. I've got you."

Her fingertips skimmed the length of his triceps and up to his shoulders, the touch tentative and uncertain. She shifted just enough to meet his eyes and opened her mouth, more questions than he had a prayer of answering without scaring the hell out of her burning behind her eyes.

"Tate?" Priest's low inquiry saved him before Elise's questions could meet air. "You good?"

In the last two weeks, runs in animal form with Priest in the darkest hours of the night had been one of the few things that had kept him sane. That and the patience

Priest had shown in listening to him ramble about every fear that bubbled up. Tate twisted his head just enough to meet Priest's gaze and gently squeezed the back of Elise's neck before grudgingly releasing her and letting her get her bearings. "We will be."

Priest's tips twitched in that smug way mates who'd already run the gauntlet seemed prone to do and tucked Kateri closer to his side. "Right. You will be."

On the other side of Priest, Sara beamed like she'd just confirmed she was the owner of a grand-prize-winning lottery ticket, and her cheeks were flushed enough to rival Elise's. "Wow. That was *sooo* rom—"

"Intense," Katy cut in before Sara could dig Tate an even deeper hole to climb out of. "When I first got here, all the male posturing weirded me out a little bit," she said to Elise with all the exaggeration of a woman well-versed in clan life. Which was funny as hell considering she'd only shown up at Priest's shop for the first time a month and a half ago and had been in an almost identical situation to Elise, barely having any knowledge of what it was to be Volán.

Still, she was throwing him a bone and giving Sara what he hoped was a solid clue to shut the hell up, so he rolled with it and moved in close to Elise's side, settling his hand low on her spine. "Sorry if the thing with Alek startled you."

Elise twisted as if to confirm his hand really rested where she thought it was, then studied him like she couldn't decide if she'd actually experienced the last ten minutes or conked her head on a hard surface and dreamed it all.

Yet again, Katy moved into damage control. "Hey, Elise. Why don't we plan some time away from the house tomorrow? Maybe see if Tate and Priest could take us along the strip and let you explore some of the shops. They're super touristy, but a fun way to turn your mind off for a while."

"She's got finals on Wednesday," Tate said, startling even himself with the answer.

Elise craned her head to stare up at him. "How do you know that?"

Because he'd stalked her from the day he first saw her. Because he'd been fascinated with the degree she'd chosen and had spent an inordinate amount of time wondering how she'd ended up choosing it. Because he'd just spent an hour and a half prying every detail he could out of her mother so he could arm himself to win her and not hurt her in the process. "Your mother mentioned it when I was painting her bathroom," he said instead.

"Then we'll go after your finals are over that night," Katy said. "Make it a celebration."

Tate scowled.

Katy took one look at his face, apparently realized maybe taking the first open slot on Elise's agenda wasn't the best idea and adjusted plans. "Or Thursday. Maybe Friday." She waved her hand in one of those *no big deal* maneuvers and smiled up at Priest. "You're flexible, right?"

Clearly, Priest thought the whole debacle was hysterical, but he was doing his damndest to rein his laughter in. "We'll work it out, *mihara*." He squeezed her shoulder and lifted his chin toward Tate. "I think we'll let you focus on introducing Elise to everyone." Thankfully, he shifted his attention to Sara and handled the last remaining complication while he was at it. "How about you help my mate make the rounds and make sure everyone's got what they need?"

While she'd apparently gotten the message to keep her revelations to herself, Sara's eyes sparked at the opportunity to cast her front-row experience far and wide. "Absolutely." She grinned at Elise and waved her hand. "It was really good to meet you. My healer magic's not that impressive. Nowhere near what Vanessa has today, or what you'll have after your soul quest, but if you ever need anything…anything at all… I'll help."

With a shake of his head and one last commiserating smile aimed at Tate, Priest steered her away, keeping Katy tight to his side.

"You're a rock star and you didn't even know it," Tate said, hoping to keep conversation on neutral ground.

It worked because Elise frowned and tracked Sara's progress moving from one group to another. "She thinks I'm going to be the healer primo."

"Everyone thinks you're going to be the healer *prima*. Me included."

The frown shifted to something closer to a scowl and her focus seemed to drift, as though her thoughts had turned inward and the activity around her was just extra input. She definitely hadn't picked up on the subtle language distinction between *primo* and *prima*. "I'm not sure how I feel about that." She glanced up and over her shoulder at him and tucked her fingertips into the front pockets of her shorts. "I know almost nothing about our clan. And maybe that Keeper person won't want to have our family keep the whole primo deal after Mom rejected her gifts."

"Prima."

The clarification wiped the frustration from her face long enough to generate some curiosity. "What?"

"It's *prima* for females." He let his gaze travel the length of her, leisurely enjoying every curve and valley along the way. The bra she had on lifted her amazing tits up for an insane amount of cleavage and made him want to kill Alek all over again for being close enough to see the same view. "And you're one-hundred percent female."

For a split second, she responded, her shoulders just barely inching back in a subtle offering he doubted she was even aware of. Just as fast, she spun away and started to leave.

Tate caught her wrist before she could gain any distance. "Please don't."

Beneath his fingers, her pulse raced. While her scent had taken on a hint of the sharpness that came with fear, there was another thread to it now, too. The rich, intoxicating bite of arousal. Faint, but there.

She wanted him.

Had responded to the feel of his lingering perusal. Hadn't broken the loose, yet firm contact at her wrist. She just didn't have a clue how to process what to do with the aftershocks. And fuck if that didn't make him want to howl his triumph for everyone to hear and cart her off no matter who was watching.

He tightened his fingers only enough to gauge her response. To pair the truth of his words with tangible touch. "I want you with me."

She shivered and focused on the single point of contact for too many excruciating heartbeats, then lifted her wide eyes to him. "Why now? You've barely said a word to me since I moved in."

A smile split his face, the fact that she'd inadvertently admitted she'd wanted his presence bringing the response too quickly for him to mask it. He stroked his thumb along her pulse point and moved in close. "Wanting something and being ready for it are two different things."

"And you're ready now?" It came out a little sassy. A delicate dare tangled up with genuine curiosity.

And his beast loved it. "I was ready the day I saw you." Giving in to temptation, he traced her jawline and cupped the back of her neck. Her hair was thick. A silky weight along the back of his hand that made him want to shift his grip, fist it tight and angle her mouth for his kiss. "The wait was for you. To give you time to settle."

God, those eyes. So big and expressive. Loaded with pleasant surprise and a fragility that made him want to wrap her up and keep the whole fucking world at bay. He couldn't wait to see them heavy and dazed with lust. To see what moved behind them the first time he slid inside her.

"What if I'm still not ready?" she nearly whispered.

Inside him, his coyote stilled and let out a short huff. A warning and a keen nudge to keep his derailing thoughts on track. Elise wasn't the coy type. If she'd dared to utter such a statement, it wouldn't be based on flirtation or dressed up as an innocent challenge the way some of the other more aggressive clanswomen would. She'd mean every word of it. And damned if that didn't suck for him because he was absolutely on board with getting her ready in the most tactile way possible.

He filled his lungs with her scent and forced his fingers to uncurl from the back of her neck. "It's always your choice, *mihara*." The second he lost contact and stepped out of her personal space, an empty coldness he'd never felt before settled behind his sternum.

His beast whimpered and paced, fighting the same compulsion to take and claim that burned inside him.

But this was a long hunt. The longest and most important one of his life. To push and try to steal her surrender might be faster and gratifying as hell in the short-term, but it wouldn't build the foundation he wanted. The foundation she'd need to hold her own between them. He held out his hand. "Do you want my company?"

Of all the fights he'd been in—of every harebrained, thrill-seeking stunt he'd pulled in his life—none generated the raw exposure of that moment. The gut-clenching fear as she stared at his hand with open indecision. His lungs burned with the need for more air and his muscles ached to move, the itch and strain no different than if he'd purposefully splayed his hand on a flaming stove. But he kept his hand steady. His breaths slow and even.

Gaze rooted on his palm, she swallowed hard and rubbed her own against her hip.

"Trust me, Elise. It's just a party. Let me introduce you to everyone and get to know you in the process."

She met his stare, such stark uncertainty reflected on her faery face that his whole body seemed to shut down, and he braced for her to walk away. Instead, she slowly placed her hand in his, her fingertips trembling as they skittered across his palm. "I'm not great at social things."

His heart lurched back into motion, the ricochet of its furious rhythm as it tried to catch up a deafening crash in his ears. For the first time in days, he felt balanced. Borderline normal. As if her acceptance had not only latched on and yanked him from the eye of a tornado, but opened up a whole new terrain to explore.

"You don't have to be great at it." He laced his fingers with hers, relief and determination jetting a fresh wave of adrenaline through his bloodstream as he tugged her closer and steered them into the celebration's fray. "I'm a master. Just sit back and enjoy the ride."

He started with a cluster of mated couples who'd been together a while, most of them Priest's age or older. Where the grip she kept on his hand had been painfully tight when they'd joined the group and her input to the lighthearted conversation limited at first, by the time they'd meandered away, she'd unwound enough to comfortably stroll by his side and a small smile lingered on her lips. The next group was even easier, Katy's grandmother, Naomi, and one of the clan's elder warriors, Garrett, each pulling her into warm hugs like a favorite granddaughter and taking over with introducing her to the others around them.

Fortunately for Tate, all the hugs and handshakes had forced Elise to release her hold on him. A fact he took prompt advantage of the second all the hi-how-are-yas were over by moving in tight beside her and sliding his arm around her waist.

She sucked in a quick, indrawn breath. A barely there gasp that would have gone undetected to anyone who'd not yet received their heightened shifter senses, but considering the people around them had all answered their quest years ago and been alive for well over a hundred years each, they all caught it. They may not have turned their heads and openly made note of it, but the quick smiles and chuckles in the wake of her innocent response had obviously triggered fond memories.

Even if they'd turned and pointed, Elise would have likely missed it. She was obviously too flustered, first folding her arms across her chest, then tucking her fingertips inside the front pocket of her shorts.

With a smile he hoped she didn't catch, he leaned to the side and murmured, "It's okay to touch me, *mihara*."

She peeked up at him through her lashes then scanned the people gathered around the gorge as though looking for examples to work from.

Tate smoothed his hand along the ample curve at her hip. A gentle, petting stroke when what he really wanted was to squeeze, pull her in front of him and make it so she could simply lean against him. "Put your arm around my waist. See how that feels."

The hesitation that followed was nowhere near as long or painful as the wait for her to take his hand had been. But the feel of her fingertips tentatively sliding low on his back from one hip to the other? That was a whole different level of torture. Especially, when she dared to snuggle in closer and pressed her free hand lightly on his sternum. "Like this?"

Yes.

No.

Both answers hit him at the same time, part of him insisting the wiser course of action was to let her take her time and explore however she wanted, while the other part fought the temptation to pull her flush, front-to-front, and devour her mouth.

Patience.

His companion might have uttered the message, but even his coyote's confidence was wavering. Patience strained to the point of pain and frustration.

"Perfect," he said, instead. And it wasn't a lie. It might not be as much as he craved, but without the tension of when he'd steadied her against him and calmed her before, now he could savor the contact. Could let the conversation bouncing around them idle as nothing more than background noise and focus on the way her soft body gave way to his and fit so perfectly. The press of her full breasts against his side. The whisper of her hair against his chin, and the heat of her skin even through her tank and jeans.

Pick up your copy of Healer's Need
by Rhenna Morgan.

Available now.